GOLDEN LOVE

J.B. SIMON

ISBN 978-1-959182-47-4 (paperback)
ISBN 978-1-959182-48-1 (digital)

Inspired by real life with Joshua, my golden retriever. Other names, characters, places, and incidents in this story are products of the author's imagination or are used fictitiously.

JB Simon Press

Printed in the United States of America

DEDICATION

This novel is dedicated to my daughter and to our two golden retrievers who gave us such joy and love in our lives.

CONTENTS

CHAPTER 1

Lost

When the phone rang, Kelly barely opened her eyes, turned toward her husband, Deke, and watched him reach for the phone and remove it from the receiver. Putting the phone to his ear, he lowered his head back down onto his pillow as if he intended to go back to sleep with the phone at his ear. As her eyes opened a little more, Kelly saw through the blinds the glow of the streetlight coming from the pole lamp on their property. It was brighter than usual, she noted to herself, because most of the leaves had fallen off their oak tree. In her groggy state, she wondered who would be calling so early in the morning.

As Kelly tried to sit up, she realized how tired she was. She and Deke had stayed well after midnight at the veterinary emergency hospital with Ellie, their golden retriever, who was there overnight under observation for a middle ear problem.

Now sitting up, she overheard just enough of the crucial part of what Deke was hearing on the phone. Before Deke hung up, Kelly gave out a loud, heart-wrenching scream from deep inside her chest and began to cry inconsolably. Her best friend for more than fourteen years had just died suddenly.

The caller had said Ellie had a fever in the night and died in her sleep. Before Deke and Kelly had left the hospital for the night, Dr. Davies had reassured her, "No need to worry, Kelly. Yes, Ellie is an old golden retriever, but she will be fine. Dogs don't die of the ear disease that Ellie has." Something had gone horribly wrong. Ellie was not coming home.

Kelly was engrossed in her own agony. Because she was so consumed by her own loss, she hadn't noticed Deke's departure from the bedroom. He had not said anything to her, nor reached out to comfort her before he left.

As she became more aware of her surroundings and heard the shower going in their in-suite bathroom, she thought to herself, *Perhaps, Deke needs to cry by himself where I can't see him. He always hides his emotions, except his anger.*

Kelly looked at her watch and realized it was time to get her daughter, Darcy, up and ready for school. She put on her bathrobe and slippers, left her bedroom, and went into Darcy's bedroom. Lying down beside Darcy and putting her arm around Darcy's shoulder, she kissed Darcy's cheek. Darcy opened her eyes, turned her head to Kelly, and smiled.

"Darcy, I am so sorry I have very bad news. The veterinary emergency hospital just called. Ellie isn't coming home today." Clenching onto Darcy's blanket, Kelly braced to blurt out the rest, trying not to overwhelm Darcy with her own sadness. She continued with all the strength she could muster. "Ellie got an unexpected fever in the night, and she died in her sleep. I am so sorry. She was such a wonderful dog."

Kelly watched Darcy as she sat up in bed slowly, trying to wake up and process the loss at the same time. Kelly knew she should be strong for Darcy, to focus on Darcy's pain and not hers, to comfort Darcy and help her through this. Darcy was only thirteen years old, and it was only a year after the death of Deke's mom, which was particularly painful to both Deke and Darcy. Kelly swallowed as much of her own pain as she could.

Amidst the tears, Darcy said, "Oh, Mom. I just can't believe it!" Kelly and Darcy hugged for a few minutes, both sobbing until the world interfered.

"Darcy, we need to get a move on. See you downstairs for breakfast."

Kelly gave Darcy another hug and a kiss on her cheek and headed to the in-suite bathroom. When she got there, she was surprised Deke was not there. She had hoped they could at least talk about what had happened to Ellie and perhaps console each other, but he had been too quick for her. She presumed he was retrieving his briefcase and computer from the den on their third floor.

In the shower, Kelly thought about her goodbye to Ellie. She had given Ellie a hug and a kiss, "I love you, Ellie. See you tomorrow."

Kelly was looking forward to bringing Ellie home the next day as she said goodbye to Ellie. For some unknown reason, as she walked away from Ellie, Kelly felt butterflies in her stomach and turned back to scrutinize Ellie to make sure she was okay. Ellie was now sitting up in her crate. The crate door was open so Kelly could see Ellie clearly. Ellie had such a beautiful face, which was now whitish golden around the muzzle, and loving brown eyes. There was a majesty about her in the way she walked and in the way she sat. Ellie lifted her right paw and made a waving motion at Kelly, something Ellie had never done before.

"Deke, I think Ellie wants us to stay. I don't want to leave." "Kelly, it's late. I want to go home. Ellie's fine. Let's go."

Deke gently grabbed Kelly's arm. As they headed to the door, Kelly thought about arguing with Deke but convinced herself she would see Ellie in the morning and bring her home.

As Kelly finished her shampooing, she felt terribly guilty for not having followed her gut, and extremely sad for not staying and being with Ellie when she had died. She wished yet again she had not listened to Deke.

After her shower, Kelly dried herself off and got dressed. She tried to cheer herself up. She remembered how Ellie had helped her raise Darcy from infancy. Whenever Darcy had cried in the middle of the night, Ellie had nudged her arm until she woke up and heard Darcy.

Ellie was always there for Kelly, especially when Deke wasn't. When Kelly was home alone all day looking after infant Darcy, Ellie kept vigil. When Kelly took nature breaks or did chores, Ellie watched over Darcy. If Kelly was in a different room briefly and Darcy was in distress, Ellie fetched her. Ellie kept Kelly company on all those freezing winter walks, walking beside Kelly alertly as Kelly pushed Darcy's baby carriage. During the day, they walked together for miles in Lawrence Park, trying to quiet colicky Darcy. And during those middle of the nights, after a stroll in the freezing cold, Kelly and Ellie napped on the living room couch snuggling together, with Kelly's head on Ellie's back, once Kelly restarted the baby swing to calm Darcy and rock her back to sleep.

As Darcy got older and moved from a crib to a bed, Ellie continued her vigil under Darcy's bed, fetching Kelly as needed, until Ellie's arthritis prevented her from getting in and out from under Darcy's bed.

With those comforting thoughts, Kelly was able to keep her mind on the tasks at hand. Like Deke, she could be very practical. She went downstairs and made some bacon, scrambled eggs and toast, and fresh-squeezed orange juice for everyone. She and Deke also had coffee.

At the breakfast table, Kelly, Deke, and Darcy sat somberly and ate breakfast. Kelly ached as she felt the emptiness in the room. Ellie was not under the table to keep her company and support her. Kelly could tell Darcy was barely holding back her tears. She stretched out her right leg under the table and with her right foot, gently rubbed Darcy's foot reassuringly.

Deke had his poker face on, but trying to be upbeat asked, "Darcy, what's on your agenda for today at school?"

"I have a math test this afternoon, badminton practice after school. And an article I need to finish tonight for the school newspaper."

"Mom, can you help me with my English essay tonight?" "Sure, Darcy, let's get a head start after dinner."

For an instant, Kelly felt that things were unfolding as they should since it would be another typical evening helping Darcy with her homework. Darcy wanted to and was becoming a much better writer, tolerating numerous revisions Kelly had urged her to do as she learned to organize her material more effectively. Kelly was very pleased with Darcy's progress and looked forward to the student surpassing the teacher.

"I'm off. I don't want to be late. Bye, Mom. Bye, Dad. See you after school."

Darcy gave each of her parents a hug and departed. Kelly held onto Darcy a little longer and tighter than usual.

Kelly did a quick cleanup of the dishes and table, while Deke went into the living room and turned off the jazz music on the stereo. He returned to the kitchen, holding his newspapers and briefcase.

"Kelly, we're going to be late. Let's get going. You can finish cleaning up later."

As they put on their coats in the front hall, Deke continued, "I don't like the work you've been bringing in. I want to do more sophisticated change management work with larger companies. I am so bored with the work I do."

"Deke, our staff like the work. They find it challenging. They like the clients, and so do I. I think you'd enjoy it if you'd give it a chance. These middle-sized companies will have to make the transition to more complex IT systems, get rid of some of their manual, paper-based systems, and do some integration. We're on the ground floor."

Kelly paused to see if Deke was taking her words in or just getting angry. With no expression on Deke's face, Kelly continued.

"This should lead to more work once we help with the major transitioning. If we pursue this type of work aggressively, we can corner the local market here in Upstate New York and expand from there. You've always wanted some steady, ongoing work. This could be it! We have an edge by being first and we are very cost-effective. This could be a real money-maker."

Although Deke said nothing, Kelly now observed that his displeasure leaked from his pores. As Kelly felt his negativity, she got butterflies in her stomach. His glaring eyes pierced through her. She did not know how to respond to his anger. She was not quick on retorts like he was.

Debating with Deke had become a fruitless pursuit for Kelly. He would shift the argument with little twists and turns often with exaggerations until she gave up in frustration. Or she would feel his anger mounting, not wanting to see where it would lead and so would stop before he reached a boiling point. She had hoped over time he would open up to the new work she was bringing in. After all, he hadn't brought in any new work to their family-owned, management consulting business in over two years. Kelly was the one who was keeping the business going.

Even though Deke was the president of his own company, the burden of business development and doing the work had fallen fully, over time, onto Kelly's shoulders. He preferred to come up with big ideas, do financial management, and HR hiring and firing. Kelly acknowledged he was good at those things, but she thought he should be doing much more to bring in work, especially since he didn't like what she brought in, although she was beginning to feel he was incapable of bringing in much of any work on his own. She felt the heavy burden of her responsibility. She decided she would redouble her efforts and try to bring in the type of work he wanted, even though she thought there was little chance of that, given the market. She was always trying to please Deke, to quell his anger and earn his praise, but it hadn't happened yet. Keeping food on the table for the family had become more than a full-time occupation for her.

As Deke opened the front door to leave, Kelly's tears welled up. Her leash hand was empty. The ache returned. She picked up her briefcase and went out the door with Deke. They drove silently to the office, only listening to the radio and making small talk about the weather and the traffic.

When Kelly walked into the office, she cried in the reception area. She felt the emptiness of the room without Ellie. Concluding this was unprofessional, she quickly gained her composure, hurried past the boardroom, and up the loft stairs to her office. She did her best to push her pain away and focus on work. Her staff did the same. No one talked about Ellie. It was business as usual.

CHAPTER 2

Getting Help

Despite Kelly's best efforts to engage Darcy and Deke to talk about Ellie, neither would engage. "Mom, I miss Ellie. But I don't want to talk about it. It just makes me feel worse."

"Kelly, stop wallowing," was the usual comment from Deke.

The daily routine of Kelly's workweek continued with a crying bout she tried to submerge each morning as she walked past the office reception and forced herself to gain her composure to get through the day. She saw Deke noticed these indiscretions, but he said nothing, nor did he reach out to comfort her. He harrumphed and snorted at her behavior, but she did not acknowledge the admonishment, although she did absorb it. She swallowed her sadness for the rest of the day until the ache in her heart returned as she looked under their dining table at home and did not see Ellie's reassuring face, keeping her company as she prepared and ate dinner with Darcy and Deke.

The weekends weren't any better for Kelly. Each familiar place brought back the ache of missing Ellie. Kelly avoided going to places she and Ellie had frequented. When she couldn't prevent shopping at their usual spots, she cried before she entered each store, then waited outside until she gained her composure, wiped away the tears, and went in.

When Kelly walked down her street alone to do some shopping, she recalled how neighbors would say, "Ellie is such a beautiful dog and so gentle."

When Kelly drove by Lawrence Park, she cheered herself up as she thought about Ellie at Dog Hill in Lawrence Park. Ellie was the alpha dog. In a typical game of fetch with other dogs there, Ellie would wait until another dog retrieved the ball, and then when Ellie approached the dog with the ball, no matter how large or small the dog was, the dog would drop the ball when Ellie got close. Ellie would gingerly pick up the ball in her mouth and return it to the thrower. Kelly chuckled whenever she recounted this story to herself. These joyful memories lasted only a few seconds until Kelly's grief returned. The tears welled up as she felt the emptiness in her heart. Without Ellie, each day for Kelly brought back the heartache of losing her best friend.

Two months of this routine went by. Kelly noticed she had become increasingly distracted. She stubbed her toe on furniture as she vacuumed or inadvertently dropped a glass as she carried the dirty dishes from the table to the sink. She realized Deke was watching her, but he only mentioned the clumsiness.

"Nice drop, Kelly. That makes two this week. Only four more glasses to go. Then you'll have to buy some new ones."

With Darcy, Kelly was able to climb out of her despair to be present with her in the mornings before school and then help her with homework or have their usual chats about Darcy's day before Darcy went to bed. But once these moments were done, it was back to being with Deke, with no one to talk to about how she was feeling.

There was no Ellie to take for a walk and to keep her company as she took stock of her day, while she and Ellie ambled through the neighborhood. Kelly concluded she needed to do something to help with her grief, so she could move on.

"Deke, I am going to see a psychiatrist, Dr. Sullivan, next Tuesday. She's the same Dr. Sullivan who used to be our family doctor. She sold her practice to Dr. Mahoney. I called Dr. Mahoney and she gave me the referral. I really need to talk about Ellie. I think it will help. Maybe I won't be so distracted and drop things."

"You're serious?" Deke scanned Kelly for any sign of weakening resolve, but Kelly, used to this scrutiny, was careful not to flinch.

"I can see you've made up your mind. Go, if you must," Deke declared.

Kelly could tell Deke felt her need to talk to someone else meant he was deficient in some way, and it was a poor reflection on him. Yes, he was deficient in this regard, she thought. But short of not going to see Dr. Sullivan, she would not be able to make him feel better. Things were always black and white with him. Yes, he was injured.

Kelly knew she would have to figure out some way to make it up to him. But she decided to stand her ground, continue to defy him, swallow his scorn, and get the help she needed.

"Deke, I hope if I see her, Dr. Sullivan can help me. I'd like to give it a try. If it doesn't help, I'll stop."

Deke glared at her. His disapproval swam around in Kelly's stomach, but she said nothing further about her plan to see Dr. Sullivan until the morning of the appointment.

"Deke, my appointment with Dr. Sullivan is this afternoon. I'm going to work at home and then head out to the appointment. I can drop you off at work, work at home in the morning, then take the car there and pick you up after work."

"Fine." He motioned Kelly with his eyes to get moving and take him to work.

Kelly decided to leave home that afternoon with plenty of time to reach Dr. Sullivan's. Dr. Sullivan's office was at the edge of town in a neighborhood Kelly was not very familiar. She wanted to make sure she had enough time to find her way in case she got a little lost.

She had never been to see a psychiatrist before, not even after the death of their first born, Domenic, who had died shortly after the birth of congenital heart failure more than fifteen years ago. Then Deke was a little more supportive. He was so heartbroken when Domenic died. His typical response then was not a negative snort or a sneering harrumph. Kelly considered this change in Deke's behavior to be Deke becoming stodgy in his old age.

She and Deke had cried together holding each other when they learned of the diagnosis the day after Domenic was born and then had repeated that ritual from time to time over a month or so. Kelly did not want to stop that ritual, but Deke was no longer interested, perhaps considering it a sign of weakness.

Even with this physical closeness, Kelly and Deke did not speak about how they were feeling about Domenic, other than to say they missed him. Over time as Kelly continued to express her feelings to Deke about other things and he responded with logic or criticism instead of feelings, she learned these conversations didn't really help. They made her feel worse, so she stopped. But this was leading to Deke's complaints, "Kelly, how are you feeling? Why don't you want to tell me about this?"

Instead of trying to explain another deficiency of his, Kelly preferred to respond, "I'm fine, Deke, really," which just made him more frustrated, but his anger did stay contained.

Kelly still cried to herself on key anniversary days—the day she learned she was pregnant with Domenic, the ultrasound appointments during her pregnancy, the birth, the funeral— but mostly, she buried her sadness and kept her grieving private. With the coming of Darcy, her grieving for Domenic became a dull gnawing, always just at the edge of her consciousness emerging from time to time, often not under her control.

She did her best to conceal her sadness about Domenic from Deke to avoid his contempt. She had always felt Deke blamed her for Domenic's condition and death, even though there was nothing in her family history to suggest her genetics were at fault. It didn't matter. She surmised Deke's anger meant she was culpable.

He had a big ego, which his parents and the rest of the world stroked. There was a long history of congenital heart problems on Deke's dad's side, but Kelly believed Deke blamed her side of the family because her dad had died of a heart attack at a young age. Taking responsibility for bad things was not something Deke did. They were never his fault. He was never to blame. Kelly couldn't recall a single instance where Deke had said he was sorry.

As Kelly approached Dr. Sullivan's street, she was glad to see the right address and parked in the driveway, as she had been instructed by Dr. Sullivan to do. Although Dr. Sullivan's office was in her home,

Kelly did not use the front door but instead entered her office from a separate side door off the driveway. Her office was homey, with a comfortable, three-seat, dark brown leather couch, with big, woolen, brown pillows, one for each of the seats. Small windows with wooden shutters on the back wall opposite the couch allowed some light to enter, but Kelly couldn't see out. As she looked around the room, she concluded it was a comfortable setup. Still, she didn't know what to expect.

"Hello, Kelly. It's good to see you again. I think it has been about six or seven years since I saw you last. I recall my son Jordan and your daughter Darcy are about the same age. Please sit down," Dr. Sullivan said, smiling warmly, as she stretched out her arm, pointing to her brown leather couch, and sat down on the tan leather recliner which faced the couch.

The recliner was strategically located about five feet away from the couch to create an intimate setting, but not too close to be threatening. Kelly sat down on the couch, awkwardly. It was a very wide couch. Despite her five-foot-five athletic frame, she had trouble reaching the floor if she leaned against the back pillows, so she sat up straighter and her feet touched the floor fully.

Dr. Sullivan looked at Kelly. Her warm, dark, brown eyes and slight curve upward of her lips in a not quite full smile helped Kelly to relax as Dr. Sullivan inquired, "Kelly, what has brought you here today?"

"Dr. Sullivan, I'm here because I'm having trouble coping with the death of my dog, Ellie, who was my best friend. She was with me for fourteen-and-a-half years and now she is gone. When she died, I lost my support group. I am extremely sad and very distracted. My husband Deke is not good at dealing with these things or in being supportive. And I don't have friends or family I can talk to about this." As Kelly uttered these words, she sensed a little embarrassment on her face. Did Dr. Sullivan think this was an odd thing to say about a dog? Would she think she was too close to Ellie?

"I understand, Kelly. I just lost one of my dogs. I have a new puppy now, but my other dog is sixteen years old, blind and sick. She is hanging on; she is not in pain. She has been with me through my divorce, my new training, my second marriage, and my new life. I love her dearly."

"Oh, I am so sorry you lost your dog. That's so hard. I'd like to meet your dogs sometime."

Dr. Sullivan smiled and said, "Kelly, you were saying you lost your support group when Ellie died. What did you mean by that?"

"Deke and I got Ellie as a puppy about a year and a half before Darcy was born. You may remember; it was about a year or so after Domenic died."

"Yes, I remember Domenic." Kelly could feel the sincerity of the sympathy in Dr. Sullivan's voice and in her penetrating eyes.

"Ellie was my first dog. I had always wanted one as a child. Deke loves dogs, too. He always had one growing up. At first, Deke and Ellie were best friends. He trained her, and she spent most of her time near him. But the relationship changed after Darcy was born. Ellie spent most of her time with Darcy and me. Remember how Darcy was so colicky. Ellie kept me company on all those sleepless nights and all those walks in the middle of the night. During that period, Ellie and I bonded. She became my best friend.

"Ellie was very maternal toward Darcy, watching over her, like a second mom, Darcy and I would later say. As Darcy got older and more independent, Ellie and I spent even more time together on long walks in the park and shopping. Spending time with Ellie was calming for me. I could think or just enjoy being with her on our adventures together. It was an escape from the constant criticism from Deke and dealing with the intense pace and obligations of my life. I didn't like spending any time apart from Ellie. I depended on her companionship. But Deke began to resent my relationship. I'm not sure exactly when this happened.

"'Ellie used to be my dog,' Deke often complained. 'She is your dog now.' I could tell he was seething inside, but I didn't know what to say to dissipate his anger. It was true. Ellie was my dog, and it had hurt Deke. I think Deke thought Ellie was supposed to be his dog and not mine. I wasn't trying to take her away from him, but it happened. She still loved him very much, of course, but I was number one in her eyes, not Deke.

"In high school when Deke and I first got together, schoolmates had labeled us the perfect couple—you know, that couple in high school that everyone thought belonged together forever. Things came easily to him. He was not used to having to work hard, even on the football field. We were both jocks, both good students and popular, although being this stunning, six-foot-four, captain and quarterback of the football team meant he was much more popular than I was.

"Deke was my first best friend. I lived in such a small town growing up. There were no girls my age for miles. A few years after we finished our MBAs, we married. We were so happy then.

"I discovered early on in our relationship that Deke doesn't support me. He really never has provided emotional support. In our senior year in high school, Deke ran for school president, and I ran for vice president. I managed both our campaigns. Deke's race wasn't close, but I ran against a popular fellow, who later became a famous local media personality. My race was much closer. I sensed Deke didn't have my back.

"After we both had won the elections, I asked Deke why he hadn't supported me. He replied, 'I didn't think you were going to win.'

"That should have been a giant red flag. His not having my back really hurt me, but unfortunately, I was used to that, just not from him. All I thought about was that I had a great boyfriend and a best friend. I was seventeen years old and naïve.

"Unlike my family where I felt like an outsider, Deke's family welcomed me. Deke's dad has a successful real estate business and Deke's mom was a nurse in the local hospital. She was always organizing local charity and other fund-raising events.

"When I went there for dinner or for an evening, it felt familiar and comfortable, but without criticism raining on me which I could count on at home from my mother. At Deke's, we would have a nice dinner, a small chat at the table, and then, often, we all watched TV together. Once we were done with TV, Deke and I headed to his basement where he played his guitar, and then we made out. When I went to Deke's, I felt I belonged. I said to myself, no one in my life supports me. Deke is no different. It probably doesn't matter."

Dr. Sullivan took a deep breath, looked at Kelly with penetrating but sincere eyes. "Kelly, it is time to wrap up the session for today. Is there anything else you want to say today about Ellie and your support group?"

"I think it is hitting me how alone I really am now, without Ellie. I hadn't realized before just how much I depended on her."

After a pregnant pause, Kelly blurted out, "Do you think I will need a lot more sessions?"

Dr. Sullivan replied, "There is a lot of material here."

"This has been helpful. Thank you, Dr. Sullivan. See you next week at the same time?"

"Yes, Kelly." Then she stood up and smiled warmly at Kelly. "We can explore this a little further. You have made good progress, today. You have more clarity on your situation. See you next week."

Kelly stood up, smiled a sincere, half-smile back, and headed to her car. As Kelly got into her car to pick up Deke, she was feeling good about the session. Just being able to talk about things with someone who was listening and not judging was comforting. She turned on the radio to listen to some '60s music and sang along with the tunes she knew as she drove.

As she parked the car in their office parking spot and then walked to the office, she became a little apprehensive. Will I get the third degree from Deke? Will he be angry?

Kelly walked into the office, said hello to the office manager, and walked to Deke's office. "Hi, Deke. How was your day? Are you ready to go?"

Deke did not look up from his computer, but said, "I'll be there in a few minutes."

"Okay, I'll go to the ladies' room and wait for you in the hall by the front door." Kelly concluded he was too preoccupied to be interested in her for the time being.

When she returned from the ladies' room, Deke was standing at the door, waiting for her. He opened the door for her without saying a word, and they walked to the car in silence. Kelly's apprehension grew as the silence continued in the car. She did not want to make small talk with Deke. Instead, she looked out the window and listened to jazz on the radio.

A few minutes into the drive, Deke finally broke the silence and inquired, "How was your session with Dr. Sullivan?"

"It went well. It was very helpful. I feel a bit better. I have another session next week."

"What did you talk about?"

"I talked about Ellie, our time together, and what losing her meant to me. I spoke a little bit about Domenic. She remembered him." "Anything else?"

"It was mostly about Ellie, the relationship I had with her, and how I feel about losing her."

"For a whole hour? Come on. What else did you talk about?"

"Deke, I am uncomfortable recounting every word. It was a good session. I am feeling a little better about Ellie."

Deke turned his head toward Kelly as he drove, just long enough for her to see his scowl. He took a deep breath in frustration and ignored her for the rest of the trip home. Kelly was glad Deke had terminated his interrogation, but she knew Deke was dissatisfied with the explanation and felt she was not being fully forthcoming. She knew this was true but was not comfortable confiding what she had said about him. It would be worse than not telling him. Deke had a short fuse. She was careful not to set it off. She spent the rest of the drive trying to push her unease away by focusing on the music on the radio and looking out the window at the passersby.

CHAPTER 3

Starting to Deal with the Past

The drive to Dr. Sullivan's the following week was much more relaxing for Kelly. She knew where she was going and could time the trip better. As she entered Dr. Sullivan's home, she could hear the two dogs barking, which made her smile. She found their barks comforting. She sat down on the couch. Shortly thereafter, Dr. Sullivan appeared and sat down on her recliner.

Dr. Sullivan gave Kelly a welcoming smile and said, "Hello, Kelly. Let's begin the session. We left off last week talking about Ellie and your support group. You mentioned you don't have family or friends you can share your feelings with about Ellie. Is this something you want to discuss further, or would you like to talk about something else?"

"Okay, let's start there." Kelly paused for a few seconds, waiting for some thoughts to form.

Kelly began, "My family isn't close. My dad died when I was twelve. He was a senior airman during WWII and then stayed for another tour of duty as a master sergeant before starting a new career in commerce as a merchandising manager for Morris Mart, where he stayed until he died. My mom and dad got married after the war. Although she had a college degree in chemistry, Mom didn't like the area and stopped work soon after she got married. I was close to my dad. His loss was devastating. I'm not close to my mom. She lives in Buffington, not far from us.

"I can't recall ever talking to my mother about my feelings. She was never supportive. She criticized me as a child and still does now for just about everything—the way I walk, my clothes, the way I bring up Darcy, that I am not a lawyer like she wanted me to become. I could go on.

"When I was in Grade 1 and then again in Grade 5, both teachers told her that I should skip a grade, but she would have no part of it. How do I know this? The teachers didn't tell me. She did. 'Kelly, Mrs. Ryan wants you to skip Grade 2, but I said, no.' 'Mr. Hayes wants you to skip Grade 6, but I said, no.' When I won academic medals as a child, instead of congratulating me, my mother went to her bottom dresser drawer to retrieve her childhood medals and tell me about each one. 'Oh, Kelly, these are for math and this one is for general proficiency. Aren't these still so shiny after all these years!'

"I am not close to my family on either side. They are so much about money and themselves. My mother's side, in particular, is fond of letting us know they are better than we are. None of them care about me or my brother, Kieran. As children my father's side of the family ignored us; my mother's side teased and belittled us. Being with any of them continues to be unpleasant.

"Deke and I both come from small towns. In my case, St. George was pretty isolated. It was only in high school when I met Deke that I began to fit in more, that I had someone to myself, a best friend who would think of me first.

"Because I am more sociable than Deke, in high school, I made more friends. Deke went along for the ride, but he preferred it to be just him and me. The same was true throughout college and as we began our professional careers. He did not have many friends of his own and he did not see them separately from me. He hung out mostly with my friends. I was okay with that because, before Darcy, we had a good social life. We went to concerts, museums, galleries, and football games. We went on long walks and biked. We dined with friends at restaurants, and we entertained regularly at home. We traveled.

"When Deke was with my friends, he enjoyed himself, but he never suggested getting together with any of them. It was always me. About six of them helped us move into our new house from the apartment, but he was not very gracious. I bought pizza and beer and friends had fun, but Deke was quiet and not that grateful. He was rather cold. He didn't like being with groups of people.

"To accommodate him, I began to organize more one on one activities and dinners. And I became more selective, spending our time with the few friends I was confident Deke liked best. He never explicitly said anything. We had been together so long. I could read his body language, his anger just below the surface, and his strong desire not to be with others, just to be with me. In high school, this was fine. I liked being a twosome. I was not used to that attention and I liked it. But as time went on, I was becoming increasingly isolated and didn't perceive that."

Dr. Sullivan, with no change in facial expression, but with firm resolve asked, "How can you be sure Deke felt that way when you didn't talk about it?"

"Deke is very judgmental. He would criticize and make fun of various friends to me. He would harrumph, sigh, and glare when I asked him if he wanted to get together with so and so, or that we had been invited to this or that. But he would never say, 'No, I don't want to'. It was up to me and so, if he didn't like the event, then it would be my fault. But in the last two or three years, Deke has been daring enough to say 'No, I don't want to see your mother,' when I asked if he wanted to do something with her. Mostly, I insisted anyway. These get-togethers have always been stressful. I try to keep the peace between Deke and my mother; mostly I succeed, but it does not make for a pleasant evening."

Dr. Sullivan tapped her right foot gently on the floor once. "Yes, I can see that your situation can be difficult. Have you ever told Deke you feel isolated?"

"No, I think he would just get angry. He would probably say, 'I never told you not to see so and so. That's on you.'" Kelly paused briefly, feeling a little defensive, and then continued, "I don't see how that would have helped."

When Kelly paused for a moment to rest, Dr. Sullivan interjected, "So in those early years, you and Deke were happy? His lack of emotional support for you was something you accepted?"

"Yes. Losing Domenic was dark, very dark, and still is. But so much changed with Darcy.

"During the first few years of Darcy's childhood, Deke enjoyed Darcy and looking after her. He carried her in snugly and took her on long walks, showing her off to whoever noticed he had a bundle sticking out from his chest under his winter coat. On weekends, when Darcy was between three and five years old, Deke took Darcy on long walks with Ellie in Lawrence Park. But as time went on and Darcy started school, Deke spent less free time with her. He became jealous of the time I spent with Darcy and resented the time I wasn't with him. He complained, 'Why am I always last place in the pecking order?'

"It was true, he was last, after Darcy and Ellie, since they required more immediate care, but I didn't know how to explain that. Before them, he was my number one priority. He wanted it to stay that way regardless."

"Our session is over for today, Kelly. Good work. We are getting into the dynamics of your relationship with Deke. I think it helps to explain why the loss of Ellie has been so traumatic for you. There are strains in your relationship with Deke. We can explore this further in our next session. We are going to have to change our regular time. Please call my office to set up our next appointment." Dr. Sullivan stood up and smiled kindly at Kelly as Kelly stood up and walked toward the door.

On the drive to the office to pick up Deke, Kelly wondered if Dr. Sullivan was being a little judgmental in her questioning. She thought she heard a little frustration in her tone as Dr. Sullivan queried about Deke. Maybe Dr. Sullivan thought Kelly should be stronger with Deke; maybe Kelly was wrong about what Deke wants and what he thinks. "No", she concluded, "I know Deke. Maybe she thinks I put up with too much from him." Kelly let that thought migrate to the back of her mind as she focused on the '60s music, humming or singing as she drove.

This time, Deke was waiting for Kelly at the office front door. As they walked toward the car, Deke inquired, "How'd your session go?"

"It was good. It is helping. I feel a little better." "What did you talk about?"

"I talked about how Ellie provided support to me. I talked about how my mother does not. I told her about how difficult my mother is and we struggle to have a relationship with her."

"Your mother, she is crazy, so irrational, so hard to take."

"Yes, I know."

Based on his remarks, Kelly discerned Deke seemed satisfied to have something to criticize, to feel superior about. With that conclusion, Kelly relaxed a little on the drive home, listening to jazz on the radio.

Three weeks passed unremarkably until Kelly's next appointment with Dr. Sullivan. Dr. Sullivan had been traveling and when she returned, it was hard to find a time that worked for both of them. Kelly had not thought about her last session, but now that it was that afternoon, she was looking forward to it.

"Hello, Kelly," Dr. Sullivan said as she smiled and sat down on her recliner. Kelly was already seated on the couch, looking around the room to see if anything had changed. She had noticed Dr. Sullivan had hung up some crayon drawings.

"I've been admiring the drawings on the wall."

"Jed drew them. He's my youngest son, from my second marriage. I have two boys. Jed is five and loves to draw. He also loves to play with the puppy, but sometimes, he is a little rough. He is learning to be more sensitive."

Kelly wasn't sure if those comments were directed at her in some way or just comments to make her feel more at ease since it was about a puppy.

Dr. Sullivan continued, "At the last session, we talked about your relationship with Deke, his lack of support, your feelings of isolation, and how that may be magnifying the intensity of losing Ellie. Do you want to continue with that or move on to another topic?"

"I'm okay to continue. I want to talk about Deke and Darcy. Deke has turned against Darcy. Last year, she wasn't accepted into the private school, St. Paul's, where he had wanted her to attend middle school and high school. He has professional acquaintances whose sons had graduated from there and went on to have illustrious careers. Deke's ego shattered when Darcy didn't get accepted to St. Paul's. He still isn't past this. He told Darcy, 'The essay you wrote for the entrance exam to St. Paul's was terrible. No surprise you didn't get in. You should have done better on the math portion, too.'

"'Darcy, you are chubby. Look at that land whale over there?' he remarked as we drove by an obese teenage girl soon after Darcy started at Egan. I expressed my displeasure saying, 'Deke, please...' not wanting to criticize him directly.

"Yes, Darcy put on a few pounds when she started Egan, but she has lost them now. When Deke didn't notice, I mentioned it to him, but he just snorted at me, and said nothing to Darcy, as far as I know. She is still smarting from his scorn over her not getting into St. Paul's.

"When Darcy didn't get into St. Paul's, I told Deke, 'Darcy wants to go to Egan. It's an excellent school. The courses are the best fit for her. Darcy can travel to Egan on her own by transit. She didn't like St. Paul's when we visited. It is possible she didn't get in because she didn't want to. She really wants to go to Egan.'

"I reassured Darcy. 'Darcy, I agree. Egan is the best place for you. I am talking to your dad about it.'

"After I pointed out to Deke several times that Egan was the place for Darcy to go, he finally acquiesced, but he never really agreed. He has yet to reconcile with Darcy about it."

Kelly paused to try to swallow her anger at Deke and her sadness over Darcy. She thought she detected a little anger in Dr. Sullivan's eyes. She did not change her posture toward Kelly, so Kelly was unsure whether the anger was directed at her or at Deke. As Kelly continued, the anger in Dr. Sullivan's eyes disappeared and they seemed more sympathetic.

"Deke doesn't believe there is anything wrong with Darcy. He doesn't think her chronic knee and ankle pain is real. He questions whether she needs any special medical attention. She has joint issues. They cause her knees and ankles to give out on occasion when she walks for any length of time. When she was three, she had physical therapy for problems with her knees and ankles. Deke did the therapy with her, moving her legs into the positions the therapist had indicated, and by the time she was five, the therapist said the problem was gone and her gait was normal. I couldn't do the therapy with her. Darcy found the leg movements very painful and I just couldn't bring myself to do it. Deke was able to push through that. All seemed well until Darcy started Egan. She began to experience occasional pain again, but Deke still is skeptical.

"Deke says, 'I don't see anything wrong with Darcy. She can tough it out like I do with my knee.'

"Like his parents, Deke comes from this 'suck it up and get on with it' school of thought. Both our families come from hardworking American stock, but Deke's family is much more stoical. Mine is more open to complaining. Both of his parents were enamored with the space program, so they nicknamed him Deke after the astronaut Deke Slayton, who was also named Donald. I think they liked the hardness and strength of the name, Deke, and the important role Mr. Slayton played in the space program.

"Deke says, 'There is nothing wrong with Darcy. She needs to grow a thicker skin. Life is tough. No hand-outs for her.'

"I ignore Deke's protests about Darcy's knee and ankle pain. I make sure she receives the medical treatment she needs, but I know I do it against Deke's wishes, and likely his dad's. His dad would never say anything about it to me. But maybe he gnaws at Deke about it. That surely would make things worse for Darcy.

"I was shocked when Deke wanted to stop Darcy's violin lessons. She went through a period of not practicing, even though she loved playing the violin. I sorted that out with her violin teacher, who told me her lack of practice was not affecting her performance. The teacher made it clear to Deke that Darcy was progressing well.

"Deke seemed to accept her assessment, but I think he was looking forward to saving the money from not paying for her lessons."

"Kelly, the session is coming to a close. This has been a difficult session for you. You are in pain when you speak about how Deke treats Darcy and how this makes you feel. I can see you are a loving, caring mother. You worked hard today. Good session. Please call my office to make another appointment."

Kelly and Dr. Sullivan stood up at the same time. As Kelly walked past Dr. Sullivan, Dr. Sullivan touched her right arm and smiled reassuringly. Kelly walked out of the office and to the car, feeling a little stronger and encouraged by the touch. She focused on driving while listening to some soothing Chopin on the radio.

When Kelly got to the office, Deke was at the door.

"Kelly, was this your last session? You must be done by now."

"Deke, I am making good progress, but I think I might need a few more."

On the way to the car, they talked about some issue with the bookkeeper and getting out invoices. Once in the car, Deke continued.

"Why do you need more sessions? What did you talk about?"

"I talked about Darcy. You know she felt close to Ellie. Ellie and I spent so much time with Darcy on all those nights when Darcy was an infant."

"Did you discuss me? Did you tell Sullivan Ellie was my dog first?" "Yes, she was sympathetic to you, but she didn't say anything specific."

"You are spending too much time at these sessions. They are expensive. Our insurance is not covering it all."

"I hear you, Deke." And with that, Kelly changed the subject back to the bookkeeper.

It was even harder for Kelly to set up the next appointment with Dr. Sullivan. Kelly left several voice messages over a period of days, but it took over a week for Dr. Sullivan to get back to her. When she did, she did not have anything available for three weeks. Kelly was frustrated and disheartened, but she wanted to continue the sessions.

At the next session, Dr. Sullivan greeted Kelly at the door.

"I have a quick call I need to make. Would you like to go into my living room and meet my dogs?"

"Yes, that would be great. Thanks." Dr. Sullivan showed her to the living room. On each end of the couch was a small dog, lying down, snuggling in a corner.

"The older dog, Daisy, doesn't like to be touched anymore, except by me, but sometimes, she bites me, too. She is very elderly and can't see. She has become a bit disoriented. But Lexi, the miniature poodle puppy, will love the attention."

Kelly sat down on the couch, close to the puppy. She resisted her tears as she patted the pup behind the ears and gave her a tummy rub. "Good girl, Lexi. What a beautiful pup you are!" Kelly continued to pat the puppy until Dr. Sullivan returned.

"Come, Kelly. Let's start the session." They walked together down the stairs to the basement office and each sat in their respective spots.

Once both were seated, Dr. Sullivan continued, "At our last session, we were talking about Deke and Darcy. It was a difficult but revealing session. Do you want to start from there, or move on to something else?"

"After the session, I realized how angry I still am about the way Deke treats Darcy. In fact, I am furious, and I don't know what to do about it. I can't make Deke change his feelings for Darcy. And I feel so sad and helpless about Darcy. I try to be as supportive of her as I can.

"Do you know, Dr. Sullivan, Deke has gotten so lazy? Up until Darcy was eight years old, I ran my own company at home, a strategic planning consulting business, which I started soon after finishing my MBA. Ellie kept me company. Then Deke decided to leave his partnership and start his own change management company. It was not doing well.

"Deke regularly complained to me at the dinner table in front of Darcy about his failing, fledgling company, saying, 'My staff are hiding in their offices and not bringing in new work. Revenues are down. I'm going to lay off more people.' Then he looked at me like it was my responsibility to solve his problem.

"'Come to the office and help me out,' he commanded.

"After a couple of months of this, I couldn't take it any longer. I agreed to go to his company, but only if Ellie could come to the office with me. By then, she was a docile, ten-year-old who loved people. I was convinced she would be well-behaved and not cause Deke any trouble. I wanted her with me. If I had to go to Deke's office, then Ellie had to be with me.

"When I went to Deke's office to help out, I wasn't interested in a career change. I didn't intend to stay long.

"I had planned to help with some cash flow issues, bring in some small contracts to kick start the business, and then return home to run my business. We did some successful business development together and I was able to bring in a large, lucrative, multi-year contract.

"At first, Deke liked working on the project, but then he lost interest, saying 'I don't want to work on this project anymore. The fun stuff is finished. It's a bore. It's all yours.'

"The staff liked the work. I found the project challenging and exhilarating. We were making a big difference in our company profits and in the market. After about a year of working on the project, I realized I would be staying and not going back to my company.

"I said to Deke, 'I'd like to become a partner and director in the company. I'd like to change my title to vice-president. What do you say?'

"He ignored the request, even after I repeated the request over several weeks. I don't even have signing authority. Despite that, after so many years, I feel like the company is the family business. I brought my clients to it. I don't keep my company active anymore.

"Two years ago, Deke's mother died of pancreatic cancer just after Christmas. Deke seemed very shaken by it. Last Christmas, Deke behaved rather strangely. Do you know he sat in front of the television alone in our den morning until night, watching the same sad movie over and over again for four days in a row? I watched the movie with him a couple of times until I couldn't bear any more."

Kelly paused, trying to process what she had just said.

Dr. Sullivan intervened, took a deep breath in exasperation, and asked, "Kelly, why are you still with Deke?"

Kelly was taken aback at the directness of the question. She had not really asked herself that question before.

"There is nothing more important to me than family. I am very loyal. And I love Deke."

Dr. Sullivan took a deep breath and tapped one foot once gently on the floor. Kelly thought Dr. Sullivan was expressing her impatience with Kelly and that Kelly ought to consider taking some action with Deke, even if Dr. Sullivan had not intended to convey that.

"Kelly, the session is over. You have a lot to think about. Good work today. Please call my office to make your next appointment."

They both stood up. Dr. Sullivan walked toward Kelly as she stood up. She reached out for Kelly's hand and held it for a moment while she smiled. Kelly smiled back. When Dr. Sullivan let go, Kelly departed.

On the trip to the office, Kelly listened to calming classical music on the radio and focused on the drive. Deke was at the door when she arrived. He said, "Let's go," so they headed to the car.

Kelly could tell Deke was displeased about something. He was more curt than usual.

On the walk, he said, "You need to bring in more work. Revenues are down again. We didn't have a good quarter."

"We still made a decent profit, Deke, I am guessing."

Once Deke was comfortable with the drive home, he questioned, "Is Sullivan trying to break us up?"

A little surprised by the question, Kelly replied, "No, why would you think that?"

"She's on your side, not mine. It's all psychobabble, mumbo jumbo. If you are making progress, I don't see it."

Kelly sighed, but she did not respond, preferring to listen to the music on the radio and look out the window.

Dr. Sullivan had been out of town. When she was expected to be back, she did not respond to Kelly's voice messages. Kelly was frustrated with her unresponsiveness. Deke's wrath over her sessions with Dr. Sullivan was increasing. He was becoming distrustful of Dr. Sullivan.

Work was becoming more intense with project deliverables. Deke did not help with the work. Kelly was exhausted. Darcy needed some extra help from Kelly with a report she was writing and some soothing related to some girlfriend issues. Coping with her work, looking after Darcy and Deke, and going to the sessions had become overwhelming. Kelly decided she would end the chase to catch up with Dr. Sullivan and instead focus on keeping her family afloat.

Kelly noticed Deke's body relax when she said, "Deke, I can't get in touch with Dr. Sullivan to make another appointment. I am going to stop seeing her." Deke replied, "Good. You've smartened up."

Kelly was thankful some of the stress between her and Deke was now gone, but she was aware she needed another strategy for dealing with Ellie. She just didn't know what. She hoped with time, things would improve. She put dealing with her issues and her needs off to the side. Deke and Darcy were more important. When Kelly didn't dwell on how sad she was and enjoyed the moment, she thought, as she had always thought before, they were a happy family.

CHAPTER 4

Joshua's Choice

About a month after Kelly's visits to Dr. Sullivan had ended, Deke declared emphatically, "I want another dog."

Deke and Kelly were sitting in their den, listening to jazz and reading, waiting for Darcy to come home from her Saturday night party at the next-door neighbor. It had been a quiet evening after a rough week at work for Kelly. She had spent her Saturday doing chores all day—shopping and puttering around the house, doing small jobs that needed to be done. Deke had spent time doing something on his computer after he had tidied up the back yard, piled up the dead leaves that had accumulated over the winter, and bagged them for composting.

His declaration took Kelly by surprise. Deke had not given her any indication he had been thinking about getting another dog. She was startled and a little anxious. She looked Deke in the eye to see if he was teasing her or just trying to provoke a reaction. His face showed no emotion, but he did not take his glance away. She did not sense any anger beneath his surface, so she concluded he was serious and sincere.

"Deke, are you sure? Don't you think it might be too soon? It's only been a few months. I'm not sure I'm ready. I'm still grieving."

"What kind of dog do you want this time, Kelly?"

"Well, I'm not sure I'm ready, but I'm okay to start looking and see how I feel. If I feel it's too soon. I'll let you know. And maybe we can postpone it. But if we are going to get another dog, then I want another golden retriever—a male this time."

"I'll check the newspapers for suitable breeders and schedule some appointments for us the next weekend to see some puppies."

For the next two weekends, Deke and Kelly went to visit two kennels a day. They asked the breeders questions about the operation of the kennel, the health of the dogs, and the availability of puppies. While Kelly liked the owners and appreciated their descriptions of how well the dogs were cared for and the dogs did seem healthy to her, she was not keen on the kennel environments.

Driving back in the car from the last kennel visit, Kelly told Deke, "The kennels we saw are good, some much better than others. In all of them, the dogs are well treated and happy, but it is so factory-like. I just don't feel good about it."

Deke didn't snort or harrumph, so Kelly concluded he had agreed. "Next Saturday, we're going to see two more breeders," he replied. "Both keep their dogs in their home and not in kennels. Their homes are not that far from each other."

"That sounds great," Kelly responded.

The next Saturday morning, Deke and Kelly headed out for the hour-long drive out of town into farm country. Dale Perry the breeder had a big farm with acres of corn and a swimming pool in her large, fenced-in backyard. When Deke and Kelly arrived, Dale was outside on her front lawn to greet them.

After the pleasantries, she informed them, "I've been breeding golden retrievers for more than 10 years. These four females beside me are all related. Maggie is the great grandmother, Sophie, the grandmother, Jamey, the mother, and our two-and-a-half--year-old, Jesse, her daughter, who is pregnant and due in two months."

As she said that, the dogs surrounded Kelly. In sorrow and in joy, Kelly cried, as she patted each of them. The eldest ones had white muzzles, but they were all very robust and very beautiful. After another minute or two of Kelly engaging with the dogs, they all went inside Dale's home.

Once inside, Dale showed Kelly and Deke how even the great grandmother could still jump up on the grooming table to be brushed. Dale said, "Up," and the great-granny effortlessly hopped up, got a treat, sat down on the table, and waited. With a "Down, Maggie," gentle command from Dale, Maggie jumped down off the table and lay down by the couch next to a young golden. Kelly was very impressed.

Dale continued, "Did you see the swimming pool when you arrived? That's for us and the dogs. Every year, I have a pool party with the owners of my dogs. Sometimes, there are 30 or 40 goldens here for the day. It is great fun."

"Oh, that sounds fantastic," Kelly replied. "Your dogs are so wonderful." Kelly was struggling to hold back her tears and failing. "I lost my fourteen-year-old golden a few months ago. My feelings are still very raw. Your dogs are so friendly and so gentle. If we want a pup, what is the procedure?"

"Jesse's pups are spoken for, but I can put you on the waiting list. In the fall, I plan to breed Susie, over there—the young dog by the couch next to Maggie—so the next litter would be the following spring."

Kelly was disappointed and relieved at the same time. She was not sure she was ready for a new puppy.

"I guess we could put ourselves on the waiting list and see what happens. What do you think, Deke?"

"Fine."

Dale gave Deke the papers and he signed them. While he was doing that, Kelly patted Maggie and Susie. She felt the warmth of their bodies and found it reassuring. She was smiling, but there were tears trickling down her face.

After Deke signed the papers, Dale said, "I'll keep you posted on Jesse. Thanks for coming by." They all shook hands and then Deke and Kelly departed.

In the car, Deke said, "Kelly, let's get lunch. I saw a burger place just off the highway, about five minutes from here. It is on the way to the next breeder."

"Sounds good."

At lunch, Kelly told Deke, "Being with the goldens felt good. I'm still very sad, but a pool party, that really sounds wonderful. What do you think?"

"Dale has a nice place. There's not much chance of getting a dog soon from her. We need to keep looking."

After lunch on the drive to the next breeder, Kelly was excited and a little anxious. She was still not sure she was ready for a new dog, but she tried to keep an open mind.

Deke declared, "We are going to Kate Munsey's. She is a writer for a magazine about dogs and she breeds golden retrievers."

"Oh," Kelly said. That sounded good to her. She thought Kate was probably a sucker for goldens like she was.

When Deke and Kelly arrived at Kate Munsey's front yard, they were greeted by an army of female golden retrievers, many with some whitish faces and others who were much younger. They were all wagging their tails and giving them a joyous greeting. Kelly was delighted. She became a little teary-eyed as she patted the dogs, but the sadness was soon dampened by the joy in being with such exuberant, but well behaved gentle dogs.

Kate advised, "One of my dams, Julie, who is two-and-a-half-years-old, is pregnant. She will give birth toward the end of May. If you sign up now, you will get a puppy if all goes well. I'll introduce you to the other dogs when we go into the house. My husband and two kids have gone shopping. They may be home in time for you to meet them."

As Kelly walked toward Kate's front door, she met the pregnant Julie, sitting on the front porch. She looked around and saw that Julie and her family lived in a large ranch house flanked by a grassy yard, bordering cornfields on three sides and the road at the edge of the front yard. "What a great place for a family and their dogs!" Kelly thought. As Kelly approached Julie, she could tell Julie was tired; it was a hot day. Julie moved away before Kelly could pat her with her outstretched hand. Kelly had hoped Julie would be more amiable toward her after her pups were born.

Kelly found Kate's house very homey. As they walked past the living room, Kelly saw two older females on the couch, snoozing, one at each end of the couch. Kate took Kelly and Deke to one of the bedrooms. She explained, "This is Lincoln. He is Julie's sire. He has won many awards."

"He is very handsome," Kelly noted. "And he is so calm and gentle."

After the tour, Kelly and Deke sat on the couch in the living room. Kate sat down in a comfy wing chair opposite them.

Once seated, Kelly spied an alcove adjacent to the living room where there was a large wooden bed filled with fleece blankets.

"Kelly, that is where Julie will have her pups and they all will stay there until the pups are weaned," Kate explained.

"Kelly and Deke, would you like to sign up for one of Julie's pups?"

Deke looked at Kelly but didn't say anything, nor did his body language suggest in what direction he was leaning. He waited for Kelly's decision.

Kelly looked around the room at the dogs. There was joy in her heart being with them. There were still pangs of sadness about Ellie but, overall, she was feeling new positive energy from the dogs.

"Let's sign up, Deke," Kelly exclaimed. "These dogs are so gentle and friendly. May is not far away. We are on a waitlist with another breeder. I'll call her tomorrow and ask her to take us off the list."

"That's wonderful!" Kate declared. "Here are the papers." As Kelly read over and signed the papers, Kate continued, "I do personality tests on the pups. I match up the pup to the family based on the pup's personality traits and the family requirements. Typically, my pups screen for traits of a hunting dog, a seeing-eye dog, a farm dog, a young family dog, and a calm dog for a more mature family. What kind of dog would you like?"

Kelly replied, "I would like a gentle, quiet male who will be well-suited to office life and socializing with people. I want to bring him with me to the office every day."

Deke was quiet, but not displeased, Kelly thought, noting his body language, which had not changed since they had sat down. He was not revealing any anger. Kate smiled at Deke. Kelly took Deke's non-reaction to mean he was happy with the selection. On the drive home, Kelly smiled to herself as she thought about the dogs she had met and looked forward to her new pup.

Kelly began doing some research on puppy food and bought a puppy leash to bring home the new pup. While waiting for news about Julie, Kelly focused on work and family, pushing away as best she could her heightening anticipation to hear from Kate. Finally, the big day arrived. On that breezy, sunny day in May, close to dinner time, Kate telephoned Kelly to let her know Julie had given birth in the alcove to the Delmonico's new puppy.

Kelly announced to Deke and Darcy at dinner, "Kate telephoned. Julie gave birth this morning to a litter of eight pups—four females and four males, four-light golden and four dark brown ones. The pups are a good size and healthy. This is so exciting!"

When the pups were four weeks old, Kate called Kelly again. "It's time to socialize the pups. Please come by on Saturday afternoon to meet them. The pups are still too young for their personality tests. They won't have names, only color designations.

"It's too early to assign the pups to their owners. The weather is going to be good on Saturday, so it should be great fun. See you then."

When Deke, Darcy, and Kelly arrived at Kate's to play with the pups, there were several couples and children on the front lawn, engaging with the dogs. Darcy scampered over to greet one of the pups.

"Mom, is this cute, little, dark brown pup going to be ours?" Darcy asked as she gently patted the pup that was now in her lap as she sat on the grass.

"He is a cute little pup," Kelly agreed. "They are all so adorable. We don't know yet who will be our pup."

Although Deke, Darcy, and Kelly were mostly visited by dark brown golden retriever pups, a light golden pup came by and stood in front of Kelly. Kelly reached out and gave the pup a gentle pat on the head and a light scratch behind the ears and then the pup left.

Kelly thought they all had enjoyed the visits with the pups. On the drive home, as they listened to the radio, she couldn't help wondering which pup she would be bringing home.

When the pups were eight weeks old, Kate called Kelly again. "I have great news. You can come to pick up your new pup on Saturday afternoon. According to the results of the personality tests I did, there are two pups—a male and a female—that are a best fit for your family. You will get a chance to meet both pups when you come by and you can choose which one you prefer."

After Kelly hung up the phone, she mused, "Personality tests, I think they are bogus, but who knows?"

For Kelly, Saturday came quickly. Work was hectic and Darcy needed help with preparing for two tests she had that week. Deke and Kelly arrived at Kate's and sat down on Kate's front lawn, waiting for the two pups to trot out. The male went straight for Kelly, sat on her lap, and didn't move.

While Kelly patted the pup sitting on her lap, she called out to the female, who was sniffing some twigs and grass about eight feet away. "Here, girl, come. Here, girl, come," but the female did not venture close to Kelly or Deke.

About fifteen minutes passed. Kelly continued to tenderly pat the docile pup warming her legs, but she still had not made a decision on the puppies.

Kate joined Deke and Kelly and asked, "Which pup have you picked?"

Kelly paused briefly then replied, beaming at the pup as he contently sat facing her, "We picked him. Hello, Joshua." Kelly wondered to herself, *How could I not choose this perfect pup on my lap?*

"What a lovely name!" Kate exclaimed. "No one has ever picked that name for one of my pups before. Here's a book about Joshua, his heritage, and advice on puppyhood. Kelly, you won't be sorry about your choice. Joshua will be the love of your life."

Kelly reflected to herself, *How peculiar. How could a dog be the love of my life? What did she mean by that?* Kelly didn't have an answer, but the question niggled at the back of her mind.

CHAPTER 5

Joshua's First Cottage Vacation

Kelly was ready this time for the trip home from the breeders with her new puppy. "Deke, isn't this great? Joshua has been quiet and content in my lap since we got into the car. What a difference from Ellie!"

"Ellie cried the whole time. It was a distracting drive."

Gazing at her eight-week-old pup on her lap, Kelly remarked, "What a handsome fellow you are, Joshua!"

She noted his whitish-yellow, furry golden fur on his back, his long furry paws, and his straight, flowing tail that fit perfectly over his hind end. He was a big pup, weighing in at twelve pounds is what Kate had told her. Because his perfectly formed ears were darker than the slightly curly fur on his body, Kelly knew when Joshua was full-grown, he would have a medium-golden color with a light wave in his fur. After she scanned his body, Kelly stared into Joshua's soulful eyes and her heart melted even more.

Smiling at Joshua, Kelly said, "Deke, Joshua's red collar is a good match with his coloring, don't you think?" Deke harrumphed and drove on. Kelly gave Joshua a little kiss on his forehead.

Kelly had timed perfectly the annual two-week family holiday vacation at the cottage in the Adirondacks she routinely rented. The day after she and Deke brought Joshua home from Kate's, they all went to the cottage.

Kelly knew that for the first half-hour or so at the cottage, Deke would be grumpy until he settled in enough to unwind. To spare herself this unpleasantness, she avoided confrontation and small talk and spent the time in their bedroom on the second floor of the cottage unpacking and organizing the room.

Kelly liked the privacy of their cottage. The neighboring cottages were about 100 feet away on either side. With the wooded area between the cottages, Kelly couldn't really see what the neighbors were up to, except when they were on their docks.

She also enjoyed the privacy inside the cottage, especially when they had guests, which was almost every year. Guests could use a three-piece bathroom on the main floor near the front door, but the bathrooms upstairs, a four-piece bathroom off the main second-floor hall was for Darcy, while she and Deke had their own in-suite four-piece bathroom off the master bedroom. She relished the aloneness of her bedroom sanctuary as she unpacked.

Kelly found their cottage roomy. It was a two-story pine cottage built by the owner. On the main floor was the kitchen, fully equipped, which delighted Kelly because she enjoyed cooking. The kitchen had plenty of naturally stained pine cupboards, a laminate countertop, and a built-in dishwasher. Kelly really liked the spacious storage space. It was ideal for storing stuff from home, in particular her mother's Italian spices for the vegetables and her secret seasonings for her father's Irish stews she used for marinating the meat for the barbecues. The dishwasher made her stay even more relaxing—she didn't have to wash all those dirty dishes and Darcy was spared the drying, except for the largest pots that didn't fit into the dishwasher.

After unpacking, Kelly prepared their dinner, while Deke, Darcy, and Joshua relaxed on the back deck. The back deck was off the kitchen sliding doors and overlooked the grassy plateau just below it and Loon Lake, about thirty feet away and down the hill from the plateau. From the deck, there was a good view of the dock and the Adirondack chairs that were strategically scattered by the water. Kelly liked that the deck housed the propane barbecue as well as a picnic table and chairs. It made it easy to transport things to and from the kitchen to the deck.

Kelly could see Deke, Darcy, and Joshua from the kitchen window as she washed the fresh vegetables at the sink. She appreciated the time alone with no one watching her or demanding her attention. When she had worked at home in her own business, she had spent more time away from Deke, so the time spent with him was more precious. But since they had been working together, she felt a little claustrophobic, spending so much time with him. The time with him plus looking after Darcy and the household, and volunteering as chair of a not-for-profit hospital board of directors, meant she had almost no time to herself, so whenever she had a few moments alone, she cherished them.

Kelly was pleased the family dining experience that evening was typical. She appreciated the calm of the routine. Deke and Darcy talked about computer things and the latest in stereo technology. Kelly made sure they had enough to eat and listened to their conversation. She was content to eat, not to think, and to just enjoy the moment.

They all sat at the dining room table. Although Kelly liked having the large maple dining room table as it made entertaining cottage guests easier to accommodate, she did not approve of the eight clunky maple chairs or the wooden wheel converted into a chandelier that hung over the dining table. Over the years, she warmed up to the wheel and considered it to be quaint. But she wondered whether she was just getting used to it.

After dinner, Kelly and Darcy each liked to stretch out on one of the three living room couches and read. Deke napped on the third. The board games and books Kelly had unpacked she had placed in an organized fashion on the coffee table in front of Darcy's couch, which faced the large living room television and video player.

Kelly always felt a certain relief when Deke napped. It was an opportune time to watch something that only she and Darcy enjoyed together. That evening while Deke was snoozing, Kelly asked, "Darcy, would you like to watch some 'Pride and Prejudice'?"

"Sure, Mom, but only two episodes—no binging. We can space it out over the next couple of days."

Laughing, Kelly replied, "Alright, if you insist."

After the two episodes, Deke woke up. It was time for bed.

"Joshua, come. Let's go out," Kelly called. She picked him up and they went out the sliding doors in the living room into the backyard. Once outside, she put Joshua down onto the ground to saunter a few feet and relieve himself. She brought a flashlight so she could see where Joshua was, while she waved away the bugs flying around her.

When he was done, she called, "Joshua, come. Time to go in."

Joshua looked up at her intently and then walked toward her. She picked him up and smiled at him, and they entered the cottage. Then he had a drink of water he slurped from his ceramic water bowl that Kelly had placed next to his food bowl in a corner of the kitchen.

When he finished his drink, Kelly gave Joshua a loving hug and said, "Good night, Joshua."

Then Kelly watched a little sadly as Deke put Joshua in his crate, and they all went to bed.

Right after breakfast the next day, they all started Joshua's training to teach him to come when called. Deke, Darcy, and Kelly formed a big, equilateral triangle on the grassy plateau with Joshua in the middle.

"Joshua, come," Darcy called. When he scurried to her feet, Darcy rewarded him with a tiny morsel of toast.

Deke called out, "Joshua, come." And off he went to get his toast bit from Deke, which he gulped down.

"Joshua, come," Kelly called out. She was so taken with his exuberance that she gave him many bits instead of one at a time when he arrived on command.

"This game is cool," Darcy exclaimed, "Joshua knows his name. What a fast learner!"

After the toast game, it was time to go for a late morning swim. *Going to the lake with Joshua is so stressful,* Kelly thought to herself. *He is so tiny in the water. All I can see is the top of his light golden body, his short tail sticking up, and his little head and ears right beside his head, with the ear tips soaked in the water. Deke is not stressed at all. I am probably more concerned than even Joshua is. I need to relax about it.*

After watching Deke with Joshua in the water, Kelly gained some confidence and copied Deke's training approach. As she entered the water, she held Joshua in her arms. Then she released him a few inches in front of her, primed to catch him, and pulled him out of the water. As he swam, Joshua stared at her with piercing intensity, those dark brown eyes and black nose darting toward her. She could tell he was a natural swimmer and not frightened.

Once soaked, Kelly saw that Joshua's fur stuck close to his body. He looked much smaller except for his paws, which now stood out to her as being quite long. With less fluffy fur, his face looked much more in proportion to the rest of his body.

After the morning swim and before lunch, Joshua and Kelly went on a short stroll around the cottage, leaving Deke and Darcy to rest together on the deck, reading and listening to jazz.

"Come, Joshua, let's go for a walk," Kelly called out.

When off-leash on the walk with Kelly, Joshua did not try to run away. Despite this, she did not let him off leash for the entire walk. He explored a rock garden at the front of the cottage, climbing up the hill until he reached the top of the garden, about three feet from the ground, but they walked around for the descent.

"Come, Joshua, let's go around. The hill is too steep."

After the walk, he found a shady spot by a large rock, laid down, and chewed a small stick he held with great dexterity between his paws.

"Good boy, Joshua." Kelly gave him a cuddling hug before resting in one of the Adirondack chairs in the shade of the front garden.

After a few minutes of resting, Kelly said, "Come Joshua. Time for lunch." He stared at Kelly, got up, and followed her into the kitchen.

While Kelly prepared lunch for all of them comprised of ham and provolone sandwiches on Italian bread, a mixed green and radicchio salad with balsamic vinegar and olive oil, and watermelon slices, Darcy set the table on the deck. Joshua lay down close to Kelly in the kitchen and enjoyed any little crumbs of bread that happened to fall his way.

"Lunch is ready," Kelly called out.

The cottage had foam swimming noodles they could use. There was one noodle on the deck, a blue one that attracted Joshua's attention.

"Look, Mom. Joshua has latched onto that blue noodle again. He had it in his mouth when we sat out here for breakfast. So cute!"

"Yes, he does seem to love that noodle," Kelly replied. "He keeps it secure between his teeth, just lying there and watching us."

I think this is endearing, Kelly said to herself. Darcy does, too, but Deke thinks it is just a curiosity.

After they ate lunch and Darcy brought the lunch dishes into the kitchen, Kelly watched from the kitchen window as Darcy joined Deke by the water. Darcy sat on an Adirondack chair in the shade beside Deke near the dock and read. After Kelly cleaned up, she gave Joshua some scraps of bread crusts and a tiny bit of ham.

Once Joshua was finished with his snack, Kelly noticed he needed to relieve himself. Whenever Kelly observed that Joshua got restless or started to walk in a circle, Kelly quickly called out, "Joshua, let's go out. Time to whiz."

She picked him up and they exited out the sliding doors off the kitchen and onto the deck, down the stairs, and to the grassy plateau. Kelly marveled at the woods adjacent to the cottage as she waited for

Joshua to complete his business. Then they joined Deke and Darcy by the water.

That afternoon, Deke, Darcy, Kelly, and Joshua went on another swim together. After the swim, Deke, Darcy, and Kelly dried off on the chairs by the dock, while Joshua snoozed in the shade next to Kelly's chair. When it was time to get ready for dinner, they all went back to the cottage. For dinner, Deke was going to make a barbecue.

Kelly was delighted Deke was skilled at the barbecue, typically grilling pork chops, ribs, or steak, steaming sweet corn, and baking potatoes and assorted sweet peppers. Being a gourmet cook, she appreciated a good meal and she enjoyed a barbecue.

Much to her chagrin, Deke and Darcy had less refined tastes than she did. Over the years, Kelly had scaled back her cooking to suit her family's more traditional taste buds. To the barbecue steak meal that night, Kelly added a Caesar salad and antipasto, some steamed rapini, and a crusty Italian bread with butter. Before their afternoon swim, she had baked a fresh apple pie which she served with fresh berries, vanilla ice cream, and a cheese plate for dessert.

Instead of asking Darcy to help her with the dishes, Kelly decided to let Deke and Darcy continue their conversation. Kelly often did this. There was tension between Darcy and Deke ever since Darcy had not gotten accepted to St. Paul's. Kelly hoped if the two spent more time together, the rift between them would gradually disappear.

Whenever Kelly left them alone, she did perceive a reluctance on Darcy's part. Darcy did not say anything, Kelly had noticed, but her departure to do the dishes was met with a big sigh from Darcy and a masked distress in her posture Darcy concealed from Deke, but not from her. Kelly hoped that distress would dissipate over time. Kelly's departure to do the dishes also gave Kelly some alone time. As Kelly did the dishes, Joshua ate some leftovers Kelly had just put in his bowl on top of the remaining dried dog food.

That evening, Deke, Darcy, and Kelly read while resting on their respective couches but took breaks from their reading to watch some TV, while Joshua chewed on a rawhide and then snoozed by Kelly's couch. Before bed, Joshua took his constitutional with Kelly, and then Deke put him in his crate for the night.

For Kelly, the remainder of their cottage stay passed smoothly, primarily with small talk, swimming, reading, TV, videos, and eating. They only had two days of bad weather. On those days, they all stayed indoors. Joshua chewed on bones, retrieved some spongy balls Kelly threw in their front hallway, or he snoozed, only going out when necessary. Kelly and Darcy played some board games. Deke joined in occasionally or did something on his computer. They all watched videos and bad TV. Deke was not big on playing cards, so he read or watched TV, while Darcy and Kelly played hearts, gin rummy, or crazy eights.

Over the course of the cottage stay, under Kelly and Deke's supervision, Joshua swam longer and longer distances until he swam six or seven feet before Kelly grabbed him. Kelly noticed that Deke did, on occasion, let Joshua swim a little further than that before Deke caught him. It did make her a little nervous. When Deke noted her anxiety, he glared at her for a second or two and then resumed his focus on Joshua.

Joshua's gentleness and tranquility rubbed off on Kelly. She began to relax more and more as their stay went on. Deke was content with the daily routine, Kelly thought, as he did not complain, get angry, or pick on Darcy. Instead, he seemed to enjoy being in the water and teaching his pup to swim. Darcy and Kelly enjoyed their time together as usual. It was a restful time for Kelly and her love for Joshua grew as quickly as he did.

CHAPTER 6

Adjusting to Life at Home

After the return home to Buffington from the cottage, Kelly spent time with Joshua on house training and crate training.

Housetraining involved Kelly carrying Joshua in her arms out the sunroom, sliding glass doors at the back of their kitchen and onto their wooden deck which was the width of the house, then down the railway tie stairs which descended into their ravine and to the earthy plateau to play and for Joshua to relieve himself. Because of the incline and the distance, Kelly found repeating this trip multiple times a day quite fatiguing.

In the early days of this ritual, there was no time for Kelly to pause at the landing, which had been her custom before Joshua. The landing was almost ten feet down into the ravine and from there, Kelly could soak in the beautiful surroundings of their backyard. She could admire the mature maples and oaks scattered about and in the late spring take in the aroma of the lilacs from the large hedge that formed a wall along the back fence. When she was focused on the yard, she did notice the change in microclimate as she descended from the landing to the plateau, from cool and windy at the landing to damp and hotter at the bottom. Other than the trees and some weeds, there was little natural vegetation in the yard because of the lack of sunlight and the steepness of the ravine slope. Although she had tried repeatedly for a number of years to grow local species on the slope and Deke had tried many watering strategies, the ground was largely devoid of greenery.

When Kelly and Joshua would arrive at the plateau, she would lightly place Joshua on the ground. "Joshua, here we are. Go whiz."

Sometimes immediately or after a minute or two, he relieved himself. Each time he did, Kelly rewarded him with a pat and a "Good boy, Joshua." Then Kelly would say, "Joshua, let's play. Go get the ball, go get it."

Joshua quickly retrieved the ball and when it was in his mouth, Kelly called out, "Joshua, come. Bring me the ball."

Joshua brought her the ball, gazing at her intently, eager for another throw. Kelly gave him another, "Good boy, Joshua," and threw the ball for him to fetch.

Kelly was joyous in the play and in the present with Joshua. They would play three or four iterations of retrieving the small rubber ball. After playing, he would sniff a few trees or weeds. Kelly would peer over the back fence through an opening of the lilac bushes to see what birds might be by the bank of the stream at the bottom of the ravine. When the trees were in full bloom, she couldn't see the stream flow into the lake, but in the fall when the leaves were off the deciduous trees, she did get a glimpse of the small lake beyond the stream.

"Isn't it beautiful?" Kelly would say to Joshua. He would turn toward her. She felt he had agreed, and so she smiled at him.

After Joshua did his business, Kelly and he played again for a few minutes. When he was done, Kelly said, "Come Joshua," and he did. Then she would pick him up and carry him up the stairs and back into the house. Door to door, this routine took about fifteen minutes. They repeated this ritual every couple of hours.

Kelly was surprised when after several days of repetition, Joshua took charge. Kelly carried Joshua out. He did his business and they played. But before Kelly was finished playing, he decided he was done, bolted up the stairs, and waited for her patiently at the sliding door.

Joshua wasn't even three months old. He was this little ball of fur flying up the big railway ties with great gusto and steely-eyed intensity. Although Kelly was a little dismayed he didn't want to play any longer, she was impressed he knew when he wanted to stop and go back inside.

Until Joshua was house trained, he spent his nights in the crate as he did at the cottage. Also, if he was to be home alone, Deke or Kelly would put him in the crate so he would feel secure. Before putting him in, Kelly would place a soft cotton blanket on the metal floor, arrange some small pillows on the blanket, and add some soft toys. Then she would call him, "Joshua come, crate time." He would come, pause, gaze into her eyes, and then begin to unpack the crate.

Kelly watched in astonishment as Joshua carefully fished out each item, one at a time, until only the bare metal inside the crate remained. Then he willingly entered his metal sanctuary. Kelly experimented with different ways to organize things in Joshua's crate, and chose different items to include, but Joshua followed the same protocol each time, emptying his crate and lying on the cold metal.

Exasperated, Kelly asked Deke, "Why is Joshua emptying his crate like that? Is he okay? Any suggestions?"

Deke shrugged and left the kitchen.

After a few more occurrences of Joshua emptying his crate, Kelly decided to call Kate for advice.

Kate chuckled. "No need to be concerned. All my dogs do that. They find it too hot to lie on a blanket. They prefer to have their entire body on the cold metal to keep cool."

"Thanks, Kate. I am so relieved. I will stop being an interior designer."

After she hung up from speaking to Kate, Kelly emptied out Joshua's crate. Joshua looked on with great interest. When she was done, he willingly entered, laid down, and gazed at Kelly. Kelly did not want to leave his crate totally empty before her departure. She had read that dogs love peanut butter and extracting it from the inside of a hollow toy. She decided she would try this out and put the new flavorful toy in Joshua's crate for him to enjoy.

"I love you, Joshua. Back soon," Kelly said and left the room to join Deke and Darcy before they went out to go to the mall.

When she returned from the mall and let Joshua out of his crate, she was disheartened to learn that extracting the peanut butter was too much work for him, even though she had put peanut butter on the outside of the toy to entice him to do the search. He had licked the easy stuff off and ignored the rest.

Kelly called out, "Joshua, you are such a lazy fellow. Love you!" He looked back at her as if to say, "Who me? More peanut butter, please."

It didn't take long for Joshua to be trusted outside his crate when he was alone. For the most part, Kelly observed that he learned quickly what he could chew and what he shouldn't and how to behave in the house. He did have a passion for grabbing at her sleeves near her wrists.

"Look, Joshua. See this little hole? It is from your sharp tooth. Have you noticed that it is a little bigger than the last time I showed it to you? It grows each time I wash my shirt." Then she smiled at Joshua, laughed, and gave him a big hug.

Kelly worked to change this behavior by steering Joshua away from nipping at her clothing to biting his softer toys, then to old dish towels, and then to large towels which he loved to shred, but not before he and Kelly had a good game of tug-of-war.

"Joshua, let's play tug." When Kelly called Joshua, he was attentive and listened. He came over to her, sat down opposite her, and was ready to play. With tug-of-war, Kelly twisted the towel to the left and then the right, trying to dislodge it from his teeth. His grip was strong. He just stood patiently as she twisted and pulled.

Eventually, he yanked the towel away from her. Sometimes, she pried it loose from his teeth. Typically, Kelly did most of the work until she capitulated. He reigned victoriously, laid down, and tore the towel apart until he was satisfied with the number of pieces he had cut. Kelly watched him somewhat amused, in awe at his enthusiasm and reveling in his joy.

After he was house trained, Joshua spent time in his crate by choice. He chose where he wanted to sleep for the night, which was on the red oak floor by the bank of windows in the master bedroom. Although Kelly had purchased a large, comfortable dog bed for him and placed it by the windows, he never slept in it.

"Joshua, bedtime." Kelly would repeat the refrain a few times, but Joshua would just look at her and watch her get into bed where Deke was waiting for her. When she was in bed, Joshua leaped up and lay across the foot of the bed, rested for a few minutes, and then went to lie down on the floor by the windows.

Kelly and Joshua were happy with this arrangement, although Kelly would have been happier if he had stayed on the bed. Deke was not happy about it. He didn't approve of a dog on the bed, but Kelly hoped he would acclimatize this time with Joshua.

Kelly did not make eye contact with Deke until Joshua was on the floor. Once Joshua was settled there, she could focus on Deke. She was keenly aware Deke wanted to have sex most nights. When they first lived together, this was great fun, but over time with her long hours of work, looking after Darcy and feeling Deke's displeasure which was there most of the time, her sex drive and interest in Deke had waned somewhat. She knew this was just another source of anger for Deke. Many nights, she wished Joshua would just stay on the bed beside her.

CHAPTER 7

Joshua Adapts to Office Life

Deke and Kelly worked together in Deke's company in an office space in Buffington Deke leased that was a ten-minute drive from their home. The office neighborhood, once home to factories and warehouses along Grand Lake, had gentrified gradually over a ten-year period and was now a bustling, mixed-use, popular, downtown area. Since Joshua was now thirteen weeks old and fully housetrained, Kelly had decided she would tell Deke that morning after breakfast that Joshua was ready for office life.

"Deke, Joshua is housetrained, so I think we can bring him to the office with us this morning. I don't want to leave him home alone, and I need to get back to working in the office, instead of at home with Joshua. I can bring Ellie's old food and water bowls with me, some chews, and some dog food."

When Deke just stared at her and snorted but did not reply, she concluded she could override his objections. After packing Joshua's things into a cloth bag with handles she had previously used to carry Ellie's things, Kelly called out, "Joshua, let's go for a drive." Joshua came quickly and Kelly put on his leash.

Deke harrumphed. "I'll get my briefcase and meet you and Joshua in the car."

The car ride was calm. Joshua lay outstretched in the backseat with his doggy seatbelt on, occasionally sitting up to look out the window. Deke and Kelly listened to jazz on the radio, with Deke focusing on the morning traffic and Kelly checking on Joshua in the back seat from time to time and smiling at him, saying, "Good boy, Joshua."

Once they had arrived at the office and Deke had parked the car in the outdoor parking spot beside their office building, Kelly opened the passenger door, removed Joshua's seat belt, and said, "Joshua, come," and he jumped out onto the pavement. Then Kelly grabbed his leash and closed the car door. The three of them walked to the office building, went up the stairs, into the building, and walked along the hallway and into the elevator.

Joshua was not used to being in an elevator. Although he was a little distressed at first, panting and pacing a little when the elevator moved from floor to floor, he was content, sitting by Kelly patiently by the time they reached the highest floor, which was the fifth floor, where their office was.

As Kelly watched Joshua sniff along the corridor carpet and baseboards from the elevator to the office door, she wondered if Joshua could smell the old odors from when this restored colonial was part of a furniture factory. It was so long ago, but smells can get embedded in the wood. Kelly's mother's cigarette smells were embedded in her jewelry.

When the threesome walked into their office, the office manager smiled at them and greeted Joshua. "Hello, Joshua! How are doing, buddy?" After a few pats, he said, "Come here, boy. I have a treat for you." Joshua followed him to his desk, sat down, and waited for the treat, which he ate, while the office manager gave him a little scratch behind the ears and on his butt.

Joshua was soon entertaining some other staff who had come by to meet him. "Oh, he is so cute! So adorable! Good boy!" was a common refrain as Kelly looked on, delighted by the attention Joshua was receiving and the joy it brought him.

After a few minutes of this, the staff headed back to their desks. Joshua escorted Kelly to her office. They walked past the kitchen on the right and the boardroom on the left and then past some staff offices until they reached the steep staircase.

"Joshua, come. Let's go up," Kelly said. Joshua followed Kelly up the stairs to the loft. As he and Kelly walked along the loft corridor toward her office, Kelly noticed that the light from the skylights along the length of the corridor enhanced the golden color of Joshua's fur. As he walked beside her, he investigated the pots of palm trees that dotted the length of the south side of the corridor.

Once he and Kelly reached Kelly's office at the end of the corridor they walked in, Kelly removed his leash. Then Kelly sat down at her desk, but Joshua sniffed around and then sat under her desk for a few minutes. Shortly thereafter, he decided to go back to the top of the stairs and poke his head through the black metal railing. Kelly had determined that although Joshua could probably see Deke in his office below at the other end of the office because the office was an open concept, Joshua stayed at the top of the stairs and monitored office life from his perch. From this vantage point, he could see everyone below and the front entrance in case anyone visited.

During the course of the day, if Kelly went to a meeting in someone else's office, a breakout room, or the boardroom, Joshua followed her.

He was always under a table or in a corner of the room, watching her or sleeping.

On the drive home, Kelly remarked to Deke, "I think the day went well. Joshua was well-behaved. Our staff really like him."

Deke replied, "He'd better not be a big distraction. We have work to do."

With each successive day at the office, the staff further acclimatized to the new puppy, but an issue did arise. Joshua continued to solicit good greetings when he arrived and pats and small treats throughout the day. As he moved about the office with Kelly, he did leave his mark. He shed tiny fur tumbleweeds, which scattered about the office. After only a week or so, these tumbleweeds were strewn along the length of the office beside the windows as well as the back wall of the boardroom. Kelly loved those tumbleweeds but considered she might be the only one.

"Kelly, please do something about this dog hair everywhere. This dandelion-like fluff is unsightly. And it is all over my clothing," one staff person remarked.

"We'll figure something out," Kelly replied.

Deke overheard the complaint as he walked by and glared at Kelly. She absorbed his anger in her gut.

Unbeknownst to Kelly, Deke had decided to deal with this matter on his own. She discovered this when two days later at the staff meeting, he announced, "Here are some rollers and sticky tape to remove the dog hair. I'll leave them in the kitchen supply cupboard for your use."

With the rollers now available, Chloe, a senior manager, developed her own routine for dealing with the dog hair. "I see you have the dog hair problem all sorted," Kelly remarked to Chloe one evening a couple of weeks later just before Chloe was leaving for the day.

"Yes, and I am determined to wear black. But I love it when Joshua comes over to nuzzle, so I have mastered the art of the roller at the end of the day."

Most workdays, Joshua went with Kelly to the family business office, although some days, she still worked at home with him. If she had an all-day meeting at a client's premises or had to travel, Deke and Joshua went to the office together. When Deke or she couldn't take Joshua to the office, Joshua spent his time with Lydia, his dog-walker, and her dog pack, mostly playing in Lawrence Park. Kelly and Joshua had met Lydia and her dog pack there. Kelly had observed that Joshua liked being with her dogs when they walked and played together in the park, so she made arrangements with Lydia for Joshua to have a bi-weekly vacation day with them in the park.

Initially, when Joshua started going to the office, Kelly, Deke, and Joshua left home about half an hour after Darcy departed each morning for school. Darcy was just starting her freshman year of high school.

About twice a week, as Darcy headed to school, she telephoned to say, "Hi, Mom. I'm almost at the transit stop, but my knees gave out. I'm in a lot of pain, having trouble walking, can't put weight on my feet to walk. I can't make it the rest of the way."

"Darcy, I'm on the way. I'll bring the car down the street to pick you up and take you to school. Hopefully, you'll be able to manage for the rest of the day."

If the issue happened at the other end of the transit trip, Darcy needed another strategy.

"Hi, Mom. I know I'm only a few blocks from school, but I can't make it there. My knees gave out. What should I do?"

"You are too far for me to pick you up. Use your allowance to take a cab, and I will reimburse you."

Deke didn't support Kelly's driving Darcy to school.

"I don't see why your daughter can't take transit to school like every other kid."

"Deke, her knees give out, and then she can't walk. But if I take her, she is fine for the rest of the day."

"You spoil her. If you are going to continue to drive her, you're going to have to do that on your own. I don't want anything to do with it."

Dr. Capaldi, Darcy's sports medicine physician who had been treating Darcy for her mobility issues since she had started Egan for middle school, had advised Kelly, "There does not seem to be a significant deterioration in Darcy's condition from the walking she does to and from school. Driving her in the mornings warms up her muscles and then she manages for the rest of the day. What you are doing is working."

Deke thought Darcy's treatments for her knees and ankles were "hooey," as he repeatedly told Kelly. As a result, Kelly did not inform him about Dr. Capaldi's latest conclusions. Her experience told her Deke would be dismissive and just get angry. She tried to avoid introducing any new opportunities for his anger as much as she could.

Kelly didn't know for sure why Deke was always seething below the surface. She had presumed the root of his anger related to her not having agreed to get married right away as Deke had wanted so many years before. She always had guilt over that. She thought it had been a big injury to him, so she had excused his anger. Most recently, she had concluded his anger from the past might still be there. But there were all the recent things regarding Darcy. Their views on parenting had diverged. Deke was clearly angry about it.

By the end of September of Darcy's freshman year of senior high, Kelly was driving Darcy to school every morning. After breakfast, Joshua and Kelly would get ready for the drive. Putting on Joshua's leash, Kelly would say, "Let's go, Joshua."

Darcy, Joshua, and Kelly would go out the front door and walk to their white oak tree by the driveway. Then Kelly would say, "Joshua, go whiz." And she was delighted as he did each time.

When Joshua was done, Kelly would open the back door of the car, and Joshua would hop up, sit up, and look out the window, leaning with his right paw on the armrest. Kelly would put on Joshua's seat belt, and before closing the back door, would kiss his forehead and say, "Good boy, Joshua." Darcy would sit in the front seat and buckle up.

When they arrived at the school, Kelly would find a place for the drop-off and wake Darcy with a tenderhearted nudge.

"Darcy, we're here. Time to get up."

Giving her mom a hug, Darcy would say, "Thanks, Mom. See you later."

"I love you, Darcy. Have a great day!"

After leaving the school, Joshua and Kelly would go to Lawrence Park for a walk. Lawrence Park, the largest park in Buffington, was a magnificent, several-hundred-acre park less than a five-minute walk from their home. It had both manicured and naturally wooded areas and a large off-leash area with trails through the woods.

Kelly was always excited when they met a playmate for Joshua along the trails. A typical encounter went something like this.

"Oh, look, Joshua—a nice yellow lab. Let's go play."

As Joshua and the young lab wrestled and ran about, Kelly marveled at the play and chatted with his owner.

"Murphy has so much energy. I am so glad he is getting a good workout with Joshua."

"Yes, they do play so well together."

As Joshua got engrossed in his play, Kelly lost track of time. When she realized that Deke was at home waiting impatiently, she was under pressure to leave.

"I'm sorry I need to cut the play short," Kelly said. "I've got to pick up my husband and go to work. Hope we see you and Murphy again soon."

"We'll be here most mornings. See you again."

When Joshua and Kelly arrived home after their play in the park, Deke would be standing inside the house near the front door, holding his briefcase.

"Let's go, Kelly. Come, Joshua."

Kelly wouldn't say anything. She just picked up her briefcase that was waiting for her in the front hall and walked out the front door with Joshua and Deke. The trip to the office would be quiet. They listened to music on the radio and didn't chat.

At lunchtime at the office, Joshua and Kelly would go for a short walk to the park across the street from the office, before Deke and Kelly would go together to their local favorite spot for lunch. Kelly and Joshua walked on the grass the length of the green space, past the mature maples, oaks, and spruce, and to the back edge of the park. Joshua sniffed at the picnic tables and benches as they walked. Kelly would find a good-sized stick and throw it a short distance so that Joshua could retrieve it on a leash.

At the back edge of the park, except through the winter, the hot dog guy sold hot dogs from his stand. He was a friendly, elderly fellow with a thick eastern European accent. Joshua and he became instant friends. As Kelly and Joshua walked, Joshua could smell the hot dogs cooking on the grill.

"Hi, Jake, how are you today?" Kelly would ask.

"Fine, Kelly. What a beautiful day!"

As Joshua explored around the shelf under the grill, Jake continued, "Joshua, you have found my special stash for you. Here, have some tasty bits of a Michigan I saved for you." After Joshua swallowed the stash easily with one gulp, Jake offered him more hot dog leftovers from the general stash.

"Please, Jake, that's enough. Joshua is going to get fat. There are lots of hungry dogs in the neighborhood," Kelly urged.

After work, Deke and Kelly would take Joshua to relieve himself in this park. Joshua investigated some choice trees and located a good spot to perform. Kelly knew Deke was not keen to allow Joshua to play during these short trips, unless it was unavoidable, usually because she and Joshua were already interacting with the dog and his owner. Kelly would feel a little discomfort in her gut as she watched Deke make varying attempts to be sociable with the owner until the dogs finished playing and they headed for the car. When it was only the three of them in the park, their stay would be short. They would quickly head back to the car to go home.

During puppyhood, Kelly and Joshua's daily office experiences followed the routine of taking Darcy to school, going to Lawrence Park, picking up Deke, going to the office, taking two walks to the park near the office, and then going home. However, there was one unusual incident that occurred one afternoon when Joshua was a little over five months old.

Deke, Joshua, and Kelly were in the boardroom in a meeting with Michael McGee, the CEO of McGee Tool and Die. Michael had come to their office to discuss some work he wanted done and was looking forward to meeting Joshua. Kelly had done the marketing and had set up the meeting.

They were mostly finished with the meeting when Michael decided to play a little with Joshua. In their play, Michael's finger and a few of Joshua's baby teeth met, drawing some blood.

"We are so sorry, Michael. Joshua was not trying to hurt you," Kelly said.

Laughing, Michael replied, "Of course. We were just playing. My finger is fine. I'm experienced with puppies. I've had dogs most of my life."

"Let's have some wine, Deke. I'll get some snacks," Kelly announced.

Deke uncorked the company bottle of good California wine saved for special occasions while Kelly spread out some cheese and crackers.

"Let's toast to Joshua and to our new working relationship!" Michael declared. Kelly thought Deke seemed happy with the meeting. She did not notice any new anger. He wasn't displeased when Joshua played with a pug in the park across the street before they went home. Deke even chatted briefly with the dog's owner. On the drive home, Deke discussed the new project they had just won. Deke was excited about the new opportunity. Kelly hoped he would actually work on this new project with her.

CHAPTER 8

Puppyhood After Hours

Twice a week after school, Kelly, Joshua, and Darcy journeyed to Darcy's physiotherapy appointment at Dr. Capaldi's sports medicine clinic. After Darcy got settled in her session to deal with her knee and ankle pain, Kelly retrieved Joshua from the back seat of the car.

"Joshua, come. Let's go for a walk."

Kelly would remove Joshua's seat belt and then Joshua would jump out of the car. Kelly would clutch his leash and off they would go to the grassy, open field adjacent to the elementary school grounds across the street from the clinic.

"Joshua, go get the ball. Go get it," Kelly would cry out as she threw the tennis ball. Joshua trotted to retrieve it and brought it back to Kelly at a pace slower than the original trot.

"Good boy, Joshua," Kelly would say, giving Joshua a scratch behind the ears. Then she would throw the ball again, a little further each time.

After about ten retrieves, Joshua would stare at Kelly briefly and either walk to the ball or not retrieve it at all.

"Oh, Joshua, you can be such a lazy fellow," Kelly would say in frustration, but she really didn't mind that much.

After the retrieving, she was content to stroll with Joshua along the perimeter of the field before going back to the car and the clinic. She enjoyed this time with Joshua—the walk, the play, and being in the moment with him. It was an adventure they both savored.

When Joshua was almost six months old, after returning home from one of Darcy's physiotherapy appointments, Kelly walked from the kitchen into the dining room to set the table and found Joshua sitting on a dining room chair at the dinner table next to Darcy's seat, which was opposite Kelly's. As Joshua sat on his chair, he was quiet and patient, waiting for his dinner with the family.

"Deke, Darcy, come see Joshua," Kelly called. You won't believe it!" When they arrived, she continued, "Joshua is just the right size for the seat. He is sitting up so straight. His manners are impeccable."

Deke went to get his camera while Kelly and Darcy finished setting the table. When Deke returned, he took a photo of Joshua on his seat. Kelly was delighted. Then they all sat down at the table and had dinner.

Joshua sat in his chair for a few more dinners. Kelly was elated by each occurrence. Looking at Deke and Darcy, Kelly realized that her pleasure for Joshua at the table was not equally shared. She did not let their lack of enthusiasm spoil the occasion. Unfortunately for Kelly, Joshua grew too big for the chair.

Most school nights after dinner, Kelly helped Darcy with homework or studying, or they just chatted until it was time for Kelly to take Joshua out for his final evening constitutional. During those evenings, Joshua kept Kelly and Darcy company. The focal point for these activities was Darcy's room. After Joshua's after-dinner constitutional, Joshua and Kelly would go to Darcy's room. Joshua would dive onto Darcy's bed and rest his head on her pillow.

Failing to get comfortable on her bed, Darcy would nudge Joshua off the bed and onto the floor saying, "Joshua, you're too big. You take up too much space."

Once on the floor, Joshua hopped up at the end of the bed and lay beside Kelly who was seated beside Darcy. He stayed for a few minutes, then jumped off the bed and spent the rest of the time quietly watching.

Darcy had decided to take her geography course in Spanish in the first term of her freshman year of senior high. Egan had a special program that offered that. This meant each geography class was taught entirely in Spanish, so she had to speak Spanish in the class and write her assignments, tests, and exams in Spanish. Other students in the class had been taking geography in Spanish for a few years. Darcy had started with a limited Spanish skill set and was well behind her new classmates. Kelly had been nearly fluent in Spanish many years back, but now her Spanish was rusty. Darcy and Kelly spent almost every night together that fall learning geography in Spanish together.

"Mom, you look up the words on these pages. I'll do those," Darcy would say, as she organized the tasks. "This is exhausting, Mom. We have to look up almost every word."

"Yes, it certainly is. But it will get better. It's going to take some time. Hang in there. You can do it." Then Kelly would smile at Darcy and look up a few more words.

One fall evening after completing the geography tasks Darcy had given her, Kelly paused while Darcy continued working. Kelly harkened back to when she and Darcy were doing Stamp Club together. When Darcy was in Grade 3, Darcy went to an after-school stamp club, which she loved.

When the teacher who ran it no longer wanted to do it, Darcy asked her, "Mr. Anderson is quitting Stamp Club and no other teacher will take it over. My friends don't think their parents will do it, either. Would you do it, Mom, please?"

Kelly knew how devastated Darcy was at the prospect of the club folding, so Kelly agreed to keep the club going even though she was not particularly interested in stamps.

After three weekly Stamp Club meetings Kelly had led, Darcy exclaimed, "Thanks, Mom, for doing Stamp Club! It is so fun. All my friends like it, too."

Smiling to herself about Stamp Club, Kelly was nudged back to the present by Darcy's declaration.

"Mom, those verb sheets you prepared for me last week take so long to finish. Each set takes at least an hour to fill out. But I did notice they are getting easier. My Spanish is a lot better now. Thanks for all your help, Mom."

Joshua must have learned some Spanish that fall because he kept them company with each lesson. But Kelly never tested his vocabulary. She appreciated his companionship, although she didn't directly acknowledge it. She did notice she could feel his presence when he was in a room with her. It gave her confidence and inner peace.

After helping with Darcy's homework, Kelly and Joshua would go for a late-night constitutional up and down their street or for a few blocks around the corner. Being a teenager, Joshua pulled a little on the leash. A halter eliminated this problem, but he didn't like wearing it and eventually figured out how to remove it. Kelly was not pleased the halter was no longer an option but was very impressed Joshua had figured out how to remove it. Joshua soon heeled well without it. It was as if he understood what he needed to do and did it on his own.

On one of their evening walks in late October, Kelly and Joshua met Griffin and his owner, Gregg.

"What a stunning, gentle soul Griffin is!" Kelly remarked as she patted his head and gave his butt a little rub. "He is the biggest golden I have ever seen. How old is he?"

"He's a year and a half," Gregg replied. "Yes, he is taller than Joshua. But look at those paws! Joshua could be bigger than Griffin."

Kelly thought this was nonsense. Kate had told her all her dogs grow to be average size. "Kelly, you don't need to worry. Deke will be able to carry Joshua up the stairs like he did for Ellie," Kate had confirmed.

"Have you been in the neighborhood long?" Kelly asked.

"Griffin and I moved in down the street only a couple of months ago, but we like it here. Don't we, Griff?" Gregg gave Griffin a rub behind his ears.

Kelly was very pleased about these new acquaintances and looked forward to meeting them again. She enjoyed the company. Joshua enjoyed Gregg's attention but seemed indifferent to Griffin. While she looked forward to the solitude away from Deke, she did relish the social interaction with Gregg to talk about their dogs and the opportunity to be with another golden. It turned out that Joshua and Kelly met Griffin and Gregg about twice a week on their evening constitutionals. They walked together around the block and then went home.

Kelly often said to Gregg, "What a handsome fellow Griffin is! He is the biggest golden of my acquaintance."

Gregg did not reply but grinned as he stared at Joshua's big paws.

When just Kelly and Joshua were out for their evening stroll, they went to the pocket park at the end of their street on the south side, which they often did on strolls on their own. The pocket park had a few scattered, young trees and bushes and private tennis courts.

A few weeks after their first meeting with Griffin and Gregg, when Kelly tried to take their usual route through the pocket park with Joshua, he refused to enter. He planted his paws firmly on the sidewalk and resisted her pulling on his leash.

Kelly repeated, "Joshua, let's go. Joshua, let's go." But he didn't budge.

After another round of pulling on his leash and trying to get Joshua to enter the park, Kelly gave up, deciding there was probably a good reason for Joshua's hesitation, and said, "Okay, Joshua. Let's cross." They crossed the street to take a different route.

On the way back home, Kelly saw a drunk, thirty-something man sitting under a tree in the pocket park, nursing his liquor bottle, and making rude noises.

"Thank you, Joshua," Kelly declared, "Good boy!" Then she gave him a rub behind both of his ears, and they walked home.

Across the street from the pocket park on the north side, a steel fence and a wall of prickly bushes protected a gated retirement community. Some public property extended from the fence to the public sidewalk.

The public property featured a steep but small grassy hill with one mature maple on it. Joshua and Kelly often climbed the hill on their evening walks together after walking through the pocket park, before going home. Joshua enjoyed a sniff around the tree trunk for messages from his friends or strangers.

One late November evening, not long after the incident with the drunk in the pocket park, Joshua and Kelly were standing together at the bottom of this hill, taking in the fresh, calm, night air. Joshua saw something that caught his attention and pulled Kelly in that direction with force. Kelly was not expecting his charge and fell face forward into the snow. Joshua stopped abruptly and looked at Kelly. As Kelly stood up and wiped the snow off her face, she patted Joshua, who had now come back to her side.

Kelly looked into his eyes and said, "Joshua, I'm okay. Let's go." Although Kelly was not harmed by her fall, she sensed Joshua's discomfort about the event. He seemed startled and unnerved by her fall. She concluded Joshua would never pull her like that again.

Now that Joshua was a little older, Kelly and Joshua went on longer weekend walks in Lawrence Park. Kelly basked in Joshua's joy as he played and jostled with other young dogs. Joshua was particular about whom he engaged. He preferred Airedale terriers, Labrador and golden retrievers, German shepherds, and Great Danes.

However, he was happy to play with the smaller dogs as well. For them, Joshua was so gentle. He lay on his side and let the little dog jump on him, climb along his back, and walk on his face. Some of these dogs were so small they could easily fit into Joshua's mouth! But he was never aggressive. If the little dog misbehaved, Joshua stood up slowly and walked away, careful not to hurt his little pal. Kelly was so taken with Joshua's gentleness and his instinct for how to play with the other dogs.

"Joshua is so calm and gentle. Is he a therapy dog?" one dog owner asked Kelly on one visit to the park. Her friend agreed, saying, "Both of our dogs are therapy dogs. We take them to the long-term care hospital nearby once a month. Joshua is a natural."

"Joshua isn't a therapy dog." Kelly smiled and patted the two therapy dogs. She was flattered these ladies thought Joshua could be a therapy dog. But she realized she was just too busy to make it happen. The time to get him certified and then to take him on the therapy outings was free time she just didn't have. She was so busy with the family business and looking after Deke, Darcy, and Joshua. While she was sure she would really enjoy the therapy sessions, she was disappointed it would not work out and felt bad about Joshua's missed opportunity.

Initially, Deke had accompanied Kelly and Joshua on walks to Lawrence Park on the weekends. But Deke soon tired of these trips, joining Kelly and Joshua rarely. Deke's left knee in middle age had become slightly arthritic from a torn ACL he had suffered on the football field in his sophomore year in senior high, requiring surgery at the time to repair it. This lingering pain encouraged him to be a little lazy. Kelly was saddened by Deke's discomfort but did enjoy the solitude without Deke.

Without Deke, the trips to Lawrence Park were more relaxed. Without the watchful criticism of Deke, Kelly gave Joshua more freedom to run and play and delighted in watching him run up and down the hills. She was captivated as he wrestled, watching the back and forth of young dogs at play.

Joshua played somewhat to entertain Kelly as well as himself. He often looked back at Kelly to gauge her reaction and then resumed his play.

Joshua had to be neutered. It was part of the standard agreement with the breeder. Kelly had arranged to get the job done before the start of Darcy's winter school term. But an adventure one weekend in early December in Lawrence Park brought matters to a swifter resolution.

Joshua and Kelly were on one of their long weekend walks. Not far from the Lawrence Park entrance, they frequented an off-leash area. It contained a large expanse of grass, now snow-covered, with some trees and picnic tables with benches. The off-leash area continued from the grassy expanse down a steep hill— Dog Hill—and onto the main trail branching into other trails up and down smaller hills through the woods and to the edge of the park not far from the entrance. The dog and human traffic cleared paths of compressed snow on the snow-covered trails, making the paths easy for Joshua and Kelly to walk along.

After walking from the park entrance to the top of Dog Hill, Kelly and Joshua paused to take in the view. "Joshua, no. Don't eat the snow."

After a swallow or two of snow, Joshua changed his focus. Lying on his back in the snow, he twisted and turned in delight making what Kelly referred to as snow angels. When Joshua was finished with his artistic endeavors, Kelly looked away and spied a pretty golden retriever nearby. Kelly approached her and as she did, the docile female lay on her back, ready for a tummy rub, which Kelly enthusiastically obliged.

"What a sweet, beautiful golden you have! How old is she?" Kelly inquired to her owner.

"Jennie is a year and a half. How old is your dog? He is gentle and handsome." "Joshua is almost seven months old."

After the small talk, Joshua and Kelly walked down Dog Hill and onto the main trail. As they continued their walk, Kelly looked on keenly as Joshua wrestled and ran with the other dogs. She chatted with the owners of Joshua's playmates. About twenty minutes later, she and Joshua reached the end of the off-leash area, and Kelly put on Joshua's leash.

One of his pup buddies, a German shepherd, approached to play. Removing Joshua's leash, Kelly said, "Joshua, Rex is here. Go play." To her total surprise, Joshua dashed in the other direction at top speed and disappeared. He had never done this before, so Kelly was alarmed. Why did he take off and in such a hurry? Where did he go?

Kelly ran as quickly as she could, racing up and down the hills in the direction Joshua had escaped, but there was no sign of him. She kept going. As she approached the bottom of Dog Hill, she caught a glimpse of Joshua. He was standing at the top of the hill about six feet from Jennie. Jennie's owner, who was standing near Jennie, didn't say anything when Kelly arrived, puffing and a little uneasy. Kelly put on Joshua's leash and started walking along the off-leash trail with him, homeward.

When they approached the spot where Joshua had bolted, they encountered another friend of his ready to frolic.

Kelly concluded that after having walked another twenty minutes, Joshua had probably forgotten about Jennie. Maybe Jennie had gone home.

Not wanting to deprive Joshua or herself of an opportunity for sport, she took off his leash, ready to watch the pups play. Before she had a chance to reexamine her decision, Joshua was gone.

By now, Kelly was tired and not in good enough shape to do that marathon run again, so she walked quickly. When she approached the top of Dog Hill, Joshua was standing about four feet from Jennie but ignoring her.

"Joshua is smitten with Jennie," Kelly remarked, catching her breath, but the owner barely smiled.

"Jennie is spayed," she stated.

"Oh. Joshua hasn't been neutered yet."

Kelly was dismayed Jennie's owner did not appreciate the compliment Joshua was paying to Jennie. Kelly put on Joshua's leash again, and this time, she kept it on until they reached their front door.

A few days later, Kelly and Deke took Joshua to the vet to be neutered.

CHAPTER 9

Joshua, Cara, and Kelly

One January evening just before dinner time close to Joshua's eight-month birthday, Kelly's mother, Cara, telephoned.

"Kelly, I have an appointment with Dr. Cameron again. He did some tests last week. I'd like you to come with me when he tells me the results. Can you come with me on Thursday morning at eleven?"

"Sure, Mom. I'll pick you up at ten. Is everything okay?"

"Yes, Kelly, I'm fine."

Cara had overcome one bout of lung cancer and suffered from a chronic obstructive pulmonary disease from smoking, but otherwise, Kelly thought her mom was in good health. Kelly could feel some butterflies returning from the thought of seeing Dr. Cameron again, but she pushed those thoughts away.

After Kelly hung up the phone with Cara, as she sat at her sunroom table with Joshua snoozing by her feet under the table, Kelly recalled that as a child, she always had trouble breathing around her parents when they smoked. They were both such heavy smokers. She was convinced her dad's smoking had killed him when she was twelve. Being so overweight didn't help him either, she thought. She remembered the smoke was so thick her eyes teared. She recalled her final confrontation with her parents about their smoking in the car.

"I can't breathe back here! Please open some windows," Kelly would call out and then try to catch her breath.

"Kelly, don't be ridiculous. Don't you dare open a window!" Cara would retort. No one opened a window for Kelly. This situation repeated itself for a long time, until finally, when she was about seven years old, Kelly screwed up her courage.

Despite her mom saying, "Kelly, don't be ridiculous. Don't you dare open a window!" this time, Kelly ignored her.

Kelly recalled the clicking of the crank of the back window next to her as she turned it to open the window. She quickly stuck her head out, took a deep breath, and felt the air fill her lungs. She turned her head slightly and got a glimpse of her dad as he turned to her mom, but she couldn't see what had transpired between them. She recollected how she kept her window open until her parents finished their cigarettes. From then on, she opened her window whenever her parents smoked in the car. No one made any further remarks about it.

With the timer on the oven going off at that moment, Kelly was startled back to the present, realizing it was time to finish getting dinner ready.

Until the time came to go to Dr. Cameron's, Kelly did her best not to worry about Cara and the impending appointment. On the morning of Cara's appointment, Kelly telephoned, "Mom, I am on my way. I should be there in about 20 minutes. Is there anything you need? I can pick it up on my way."

"No dear. I would like to go to the library on the way back to return some junk books and get some new ones."

The drive to Dr. Cameron's and the short walk from the parking lot to his office was filled with small talk about shopping. After Kelly and Cara sat down in his waiting area, Kelly looked around the room anxiously and started to daydream. Her thoughts took her back five years to the unfortunate turn of events that had occurred the first time she went with her mom to see Dr. Cameron.

She painfully remembered Cara had asked her to go with her to a doctor's appointment. But Cara had neglected to tell her they were going to an oncologist's office. Kelly only discovered that disturbing fact when she read Dr. Cameron's credentials on his office door as they entered.

When she and Cara sat down in Dr. Cameron's office that first time, he said, "Cara, it is just as we discussed. You have lung cancer. You have a sizable tumor on your left lung."

Kelly was shocked by Dr. Cameron's revelation but retained her composure. She stood up and moved toward Cara to comfort her. At that moment, at the back of her mind, she was aware that being affectionate was not something her parents were toward her, especially her mom, but nevertheless, she went with the normal affectionate behavior she had displayed toward Darcy since Darcy's birth and reached out to hug Cara.

By this time, Cara was standing in front of Kelly. With all her might, Cara pushed Kelly's shoulders away with both her hands. In those days, Cara was still quite strong. Cara shoved Kelly back a few feet. Kelly was hurt and astonished by Cara's behavior but didn't say anything about it. Dr. Cameron continued as if nothing extraordinary had happened.

"Cara, I suggest you meet with Dr. Franklin. He is an excellent surgeon. I think he will be able to help you."

When Cara shook her head no, Kelly weighed in, "I'll go with you." But her pleading fell on deaf ears.

After the appointment with Dr. Cameron, Kelly continued to encourage Cara to see Dr. Franklin until she finally agreed to go with Kelly to see him.

About a week passed and then it was time for the appointment. Kelly picked up Cara and they went to Dr. Franklin's office, which was in the community hospital. He was head of surgery there.

After reviewing Cara's x-rays, Dr. Franklin explained to her, "You have a tumor on your left lung I think I can remove and leave just enough tissue for you. You could have another five years. Five years!"

When Cara looked skeptical, Dr. Franklin persisted, "Cara, not everyone gets this chance. Take it. You could have another five years."

"Mom, Dr. Franklin says he can help. It's worth a try. Please."

After a few more of Kelly's pleadings, Cara finally agreed to the surgery. Kelly remembered how she spent every day of Cara's hospitalization with her, keeping her company, brightening the room with flowers, and bringing her the foods she wanted and was allowed to eat.

Kelly was very grateful Cara's surgery had been a success and had given Cara the gift of more time, which Cara had enjoyed, mostly by shopping from the television shopping network, playing cards with friends, going to the theater and art galleries, and having weekly dinners with Kelly, Deke, and Darcy.

Now Kelly and her mom were back to see Dr. Cameron, but Cara had reassured her she was fine. Cara had not said anything to Kelly to indicate there was a problem, so Kelly was hopeful.

Kelly turned her thoughts to Joshua and the fun she hoped he was having with Deke at the office. She wondered whether Deke would take him to see the hot dog guy for a snack at lunch.

After a few more minutes in the waiting room of Kelly looking out the window and occasionally glancing at Cara to see her investigating the contents of her purse, Dr. Cameron opened the door. With his arm outstretched and motioning with his hand for them to come in, Cara and Kelly walked into his office.

"Cara, this time surgery is out of the question," he said. "You know you have been living on borrowed time. You may have six to eighteen months."

Kelly was shattered by the news. Cara was not surprised, nor particularly moved by the prognosis. Cara's expression remained flat, but this time, Kelly knew not to try to approach Cara to comfort her.

The next day was Friday and their usual Friday night dinner with Cara. Since Joshua had joined the family, Kelly, Deke, Darcy, and Joshua had not been to Cara's place, nor had she gone to theirs. They had visited with Cara only at restaurants once a week, usually on Friday nights, for fish. Joshua stayed in the back seat of the car while they dined. During those trips to the restaurant, Kelly would be sad her mom would ignore Joshua. Cara didn't even acknowledge Joshua was in the car.

As Deke drove them all to the restaurant that Friday night, Kelly got lost in her thoughts. She recalled she used to walk other people's dogs. Her parents didn't approve but they tolerated it. One afternoon after school, Kelly had brought her favorite dog home for a visit—this tiny half German shepherd, half dachshund. When the dog saw her mom, the dog was keen for a pat and approached her bed to say hello. Cara was sitting up in bed and reading one of her junk-book romances.

Instead of obliging, Cara said, "What is that dog doing in here? Take it home immediately."

Anger and sadness gripped Kelly as she ruminated on that event. She became present long enough to look out the window and conclude they were about halfway to the restaurant. She continued to think about her mom and dogs.

She recollected a story about her mom that had happened one Saturday morning a few months after her dad had died. Kieran and she loved dogs. She had always wanted one. Of course, her mother knew this but had always refused to get them a dog, blaming Kelly's allergies and saying to Kelly, "We can't have a dog. You are allergic. I don't like dogs. They are dirty and hard work."

For some reason—and Kelly never knew why—Cara had changed her mind and found an opportunity to get a dog.

Cara said to Kelly and Kieran, "I found out about some free Dalmatian puppies, a new litter of six pups. I am going to call and get us one."

"Fantastic, Mom!" Kelly and Kieran shouted in unison.

Kelly and Kieran waited and waited, but Cara didn't make the call. By late afternoon, Kelly and Kieran were sitting at the kitchen table in anxious anticipation.

"Mom, when are you going to call?" Kelly asked.

About ten minutes later, Kieran repeated, "Mom, when are you going to call?"

Thinking about this as they drove, Kelly could feel the angst of that wait in her body. She pictured her and Kieran at the kitchen table fidgeting impatiently, glancing at each other and then at Cara until it was close to five o'clock that afternoon. Kelly remembered watching Cara as she rose slowly from her chair, walked over to the turquoise-colored phone, carefully removed it from the stand high on the wall beside her kitchen chair, and dialed the number.

"Hello, I'd like one of your puppies, please." Then Cara listened briefly to the person on the other end and hung up.

"No puppies left, children," she announced.

Now about five blocks from the restaurant, Kelly tried to cheer herself up with happier thoughts. Unlike Cara, Kelly's dad loved dogs. He had told her, "Growing up, I always had dogs and cats."

Kelly painfully recalled Cara telling her often, "Your father wants a dog, but he can't have one because of you and your allergies."

Kelly scoured her brain, but she couldn't think of a single time when her dad had complained to her that he couldn't have a dog because of her.

She did recall a pleasant experience that had occurred when she was seven or eight years old. One of the neighbor's dogs, a beagle, regularly jumped the six-foot metal fence that surrounded his property and went off on a several-mile journey involving a trip to a butcher shop and a return with a large steak bone. One summer evening, the beagle leaped over the fence, ran across the street and up their front porch steps to join Kelly and her dad, who were both sitting on the top step, enjoying the breezy, cool, summer night air.

"Here, Skippy, have a grape," her dad said as he lovingly fed green grapes to Skippy and patted his head.

"Dad, may I give Skippy some grapes, too?"

"Sure, Kelly, but give him them one at a time." Her dad smiled at her as she patted Skippy and fed him the grapes. Kelly wondered if Skippy reminded him of any of his childhood dogs.

Kelly was jolted back to the present when they arrived at the restaurant and Deke called out, "Here we are. Let's go."

Before leaving the car to go to the restaurant, Kelly gave Joshua a hug and said, "I love you. Back soon." Darcy gave Joshua a little pat on the head. Kelly watched as her mother ignored Joshua and got out of the car. After dinner, they drove Cara home. Kelly was discomfited that Cara ignored Joshua the entire time.

That weekend, Cara called Kelly. "I want to die at home. Not in a hospital. Promise me, Kelly, you'll take care of that."

"Yes, Mom. Of course."

This promise put a burden on Kelly, but she accepted it after having mulled over the situation as she and Joshua sat in the sunroom after the call.

Kieran lived several hundred miles away but could make the trip a few times. He was not adept at dealing with severe illness. And he had difficulty getting time off from work. Aunt Celeste, Cara's sister, lived nearby. She would come to visit Cara often and bring food, but she was not a caregiver. Darcy would not be eager to spend any time with Nonna. Deke liked Cara even less.

While Kelly understood their reluctance, she found it was just as difficult as they did to tolerate Cara's critical nature, her constant complaining, and her belief in her own victimhood. What really upset Kelly the most was that Deke and Darcy would not even want to try to be with Cara, even for Kelly's sake.

Kelly concluded she had no alternative. She would have to be the primary caregiver. Joshua would keep her company. He would be a great comfort and a wonderful companion.

The first time Joshua and Cara spent any quality time together was after Cara's radiation therapy in February. When Kelly and Joshua arrived at Cara's that first time together, Cara was lying in her bed. Joshua sensed Cara's discomfort. He spontaneously jumped up onto her bed and quietly laid down parallel to her, with his head near her feet.

"Get your dog off my bed this instant," Cara commanded.

"Mom, Joshua won't hurt you. He just wants to rest beside you and comfort you."

"I don't want him here."

"Mom, you're fine, really."

By this time, Joshua weighed around seventy pounds. He was lean, long, and tall and still had puppy awkwardness. He stayed on the bed in the same position and didn't move until he and Kelly departed an hour or so later.

Kelly continued to bring Joshua with her on their subsequent twice-weekly caregiving visits to Cara's. Twice a week was sufficient for the time being, Kelly felt, as Kelly had arranged for a community worker to come by every other day to do housekeeping, cook meals, and a general check on Cara. When Cara was comfortable and occupied, Kelly took Joshua to the park nearby, which was mostly an open field, with some bushes and mature trees along the perimeter. They walked the perimeter and played with other dogs if any came by. Kelly was happy to be outdoors and focused on fun.

Cara sighed and rolled her eyes when she saw Kelly and Joshua coming into her bedroom after their walk. As she glared at the two of them, Cara said nothing.

After two weeks of the same routine at the caregiving visits, Cara exclaimed, "Kelly, I don't want Joshua here. Don't bring him with you again."

"Why not? I don't understand. He is so well-behaved. He's not bothering you. He's keeping me company. What's the problem?" "Kelly, enough. I don't want him here."

Quickly, Kelly quelled her objections to Cara's disapproval of Joshua since her mother was so ill. Instead of being with Kelly, Joshua went to the office with Deke, and Kelly visited Cara alone.

As Cara's morphine doses and other medications increased and her ability to manage on her own worsened, Kelly sought nursing care. This started as daily care, nine to five. At first, Kelly was at Cara's part of the day most days to make sure all was well. She conducted matters related to the family business from her mother's dining room table, making business calls and reviewing or writing reports. In part, working was a distraction for Kelly, allowing her to focus on something she could control, and, in part, she needed to continue to manage the company projects.

With Cara's condition continuing to deteriorate, Kelly soon found herself at Cara's every evening with a list of her medications and a timetable to follow to administer them. Cara took some medications every four hours, some every eight, and some every twelve. Kelly supervised while Cara took these medications every night before bed.

It became apparent to Kelly that more care was needed, but Cara was defiant.

"Kelly, I can manage. I don't need more nursing care. No."

"But, Mom, I am here every night. Your meds are complicated. I think we need more help."

"Kelly, I don't want more help. No."

After a couple of weeks of this fruitless dialogue, Kelly no longer sought Cara's approval. She secured the nursing help she needed but didn't reduce the amount of time she spent at her mother's. She continued to look after Cara, Darcy, Deke, and the family business.

One day faded into the next. Winter ended. Spring had come and gone. Summer was here and Kelly had barely noticed.

One early July afternoon just before Kelly was about to head home from Cara's, Cara vomited. She was in terrible pain. Kelly rushed her by car to the hospital, not knowing what was specifically wrong.

Upon arrival at the hospital, Kelly and Cara had to stand in line to enter. "As you know, we have a community flu epidemic," the young nurse at the entrance said to Kelly and Cara, speaking through her gray surgical mask. "Do you have a cold or the flu? Have you had a cold or flu in the last forty-eight hours?"

"No," Kelly replied to both questions and took the forms the nurse handed to them.

"Please wash your hands with the antibacterial liquid before you enter the emergency room waiting area. Please note only one visitor is allowed with each patient."

Kelly telephoned Deke to notify him of the situation.

After a couple of hours of sitting in the waiting area, Kelly asked one of the triage nurses, "Do you know when my mother might be seen? She is very tired."

"Please be advised that you will still have to wait a while. Kindly remember she is not allowed to eat or drink."

Kelly joined Cara in the waiting room and resumed sitting. They didn't speak. They both just looked around the room. From time to time, Kelly escorted her mom to the washroom as needed. Eventually, Cara's vomiting stopped. Both Cara and Kelly were worn out from the ordeal.

Just after midnight, a night nurse brought Cara into the main emergency room and gave Cara a bed to sleep in. Kelly followed them.

When Cara was settled in bed, Kelly sought some assistance. "Please tell me where I can find extra blankets and water," Kelly inquired to a nurse at the nursing station. "My mother is cold. And I am thirsty."

After finding blankets for both of them, buying and drinking bottled water, Kelly closed the gray cloth curtains to surround Cara's bed and curled up in an uncomfortable, large, green, vinyl armchair beside the bed.

An emergency doctor examined Cara the next morning. The doctor admitted Cara to the palliative care unit soon after.

In the hospital, Cara got a semiprivate room. Her bed was near large windows that overlooked the downtown street. That night, as Kelly sat in her chair beside Cara's bed, she saw that a small crowd had gathered around Cara's roommate's bed. At least ten people huddled around the bed, speaking Italian in low voices. Kelly stayed until her mother was asleep for the night and then walked quietly past the crowd, who were now speaking in very low voices.

When Kelly arrived the next morning to see Cara, the woman next door was gone. Her bed was made. She overheard one of the nurses just outside the door remark to one of the other nurses, "Mrs. Francatelli died during the night of a brain tumor."

The butterflies flew in circles in Kelly's stomach.

Over the course of Cara's three-day hospital stay, Kelly was there every day to make sure Cara was okay and well looked after.

"Mrs. Delmonico, we have adjusted your mother's medications. She should feel a lot better. You can take her home tomorrow," her palliative oncologist counseled. "Please bring your mom back if you notice any further changes."

CHAPTER 10

Kelly and Cara

Once Cara had stabilized at home from her hospital stay and the evening caregiver Kelly had hired to look after Cara was working out well, Kelly was determined that Deke, Darcy, Joshua, and she would go to the cottage for their usual two weeks for some respite. At this juncture, Cara was still able to take care of herself at home overnight. Kelly reasoned that with the care she had arranged and Aunt Celeste being in town, with two of her children nearby, there was a family who could help out if necessary.

Kelly informed Cara about the upcoming trip to the cottage. Cara did not seem to mind. Cara was expressionless and had said nothing in reply when Kelly had told her. Kelly knew Deke and Darcy were keen to go to the cottage. She also knew Joshua would be delighted to swim and go on their walks together. With the plans in place, Kelly got organized for the trip.

Kelly was relieved when the drive to the cottage went smoothly. While Kelly experienced Deke's usual grumpiness until an hour or so after arriving at the cottage, she was happy that he was eager to cook a steak barbecue.

Before dinner, Kelly telephoned Cara.

"How are you doing, Mom?"

"Doing fine, Kelly. I am just about to have dinner. I just finished reading one of my junk books. After dinner, I am going to watch tennis on TV."

Cara told Kelly what she was going to have for dinner, what she had eaten during the day and other details that were even less interesting to Kelly. These were things Cara routinely reported to Kelly, long before Cara had taken ill. While Kelly was not terribly thrilled with listening to what was in Cara's fridge, she took comfort in Cara's display of her typical behavior. Kelly was reassured that Cara seemed to be managing on her own, and she was engrossed in her usual routine. With that knowledge, Kelly was able to unwind a little and enjoy cottage life.

The next day was a beautiful, sunny, warm day. They decided to spend most of it by the lake. After lunch and before their afternoon swim, Deke, Darcy, and Kelly lazed on the dock in their Adirondack chairs, while Joshua snoozed up the hill in the shade.

Deke called out, "Joshua, come. I'm going to teach you how to dive off the dock." Kelly stopped reading her book and focused on Deke and Joshua. Joshua ran down the hill and along the twelve-foot wooden dock until he stopped beside Deke and stood in earnest.

"Joshua, jump," Deke said, but Joshua just stood still beside him.

"Joshua, jump," Deke repeated, this time giving Joshua's butt a little nudge, pushing him into the water.

Joshua was a little surprised at first, but then he swam to shore and trotted back to stand close to Deke.

"Joshua, jump."

Joshua raised his right paw above the water and moved it in a circle but did not jump in.

"Joshua, jump." This time, Deke gave the command as he put his hands around Joshua's chest and gently tossed him into the lake. Joshua kept his head above the water, swam back to shore, and scampered back onto the dock to where Deke was standing.

"Deke, I am a bit uneasy," Kelly said. "Do you think Joshua minds the toss?" "No, he's fine."

About ten tosses later, Kelly was less disturbed by the activity. She surmised Joshua was adjusting to the toss. After another day of Deke's repeating the dock tossing, Kelly was delighted Joshua was jumping off the dock on his own and loving it.

Joshua and Kelly now had a new ritual they practiced each morning. As Kelly threw the ball into the lake for him, she called, "Joshua, jump." He ran the length of the dock and made a flying, running leap into the water. He landed about eight feet from the dock, swam out to retrieve the ball, and then swam to shore, returning to the dock for more. After about ten leaps, he tired. He sunned himself on the dock or climbed up the hill for some shade and a snooze. Kelly rested in her chair as she read a book in the shade of the birch tree by the water's edge.

Sometimes, instead of going for a dive off the dock right away, Kelly watched as Joshua would explore the shoreline first. He would access the lake by going down the woodsy hill, which was covered in leaves, oak saplings, and tall birches intermixed with some large conifers, mostly white pine and white spruce. After his explorations, Joshua would wade into the shallow water a short distance and swim. Then he would drink some lake water. His big tongue flicked the cool water into his mouth in even, rhythmic gulps. After his drink, he was ready to resume his diving adventures with Kelly.

Joshua joined Deke, Darcy, and Kelly in the water when they were all swimming together in the afternoons. They played "Joshua in the middle," a variant of "monkey in the middle" with a tennis ball.

"Joshua, go get the ball!" Darcy yelled as she threw the ball to Deke.

"Deke, look out," Kelly warned. "If we aren't careful, we'll get flayed by those nails."

While Kelly loved the game, she could tolerate only so much of Joshua not capturing the ball.

"Okay, it's time to throw the ball so that Joshua can retrieve it. It isn't fair he doesn't get a chance with the ball. We have been swimming for a time. I am concerned Joshua may be tiring."

"Joshua, go get it!" Darcy exclaimed as she threw the ball as far as she could away from her.

Kelly was enthralled by Joshua's play in the water. She looked on as Joshua, seeing the tennis ball, would swim to retrieve it, and grab it in his mouth, making a little air-out-of-the-tire noise with the slight crush of the ball. Then he would swim in a semicircle and to shore. Once on shore, he carried the ball up the hill and hid it. On occasion, Joshua lost interest in the ball as he went up the hill, dropped the ball, and forgot where he had dropped it. He never quite grasped gravity. If they were lucky, the ball came rolling down into the water or landed at the bottom of the hill, becoming an easier retrieve for another round of "Joshua in the middle."

After a few rounds of "Joshua in the middle," Deke, Darcy, and Kelly would swim with their swimming noodles. In a town near the cottage, Kelly had purchased foam swimming noodles, one for each of them in a different color. Kelly had forgotten about how much Joshua had become attached to the blue swimming noodle that had been at the cottage the previous year. If Deke didn't restrain Joshua onshore when Darcy and Kelly were getting used to the water near the dock, Joshua dove in as soon as he could, landing on or near the top of Kelly's head and making her go underwater. Kelly rapidly learned to move away from the dock after descending the ladder into the water and then completely dunking. Joshua never jumped that close to anyone else's head, only Kelly's.

Once in the water, Joshua tried to steal Kelly's noodle and shepherd her to shore. Kelly was locked on to avoiding his paws. She released the noodle into his custody, and he sunk his teeth into it. As soon as he had a good grip on the noodle, Kelly watched him as he circled her and swam to shore. The noodle was his prize and he wanted to make sure it was not easy for them to retrieve. He took the noodle up the hill, raced back down and along the length of the dock, and dove off the dock into the water to trap the next noodle. He was relentless until he had all three. When Kelly looked up toward the cottage, she saw a rainbow of colored noodles in a zigzag up the hill. Once Joshua had all three noodles, Kelly realized she was next. His urge to bring her back to shore was overwhelming.

"Time for me to get the noodles," Kelly declared and raced out of the water to retrieve the noodles, throwing a tennis ball into the lake as quickly as she could to distract Joshua and to give her some time to retrieve the noodles and take them back into the lake. Since Deke did not stay in the water as long as Darcy and Kelly did, he took over retrieving the noodles once he was onshore.

The four of them swam in the lake most days. They only stayed out of the water when the weather was inclement. As long as there wasn't a thunderstorm, Joshua swam on his own in the lake for short swims on bad weather days, while Deke or Kelly watched him. After Joshua's swim, he napped or chewed on a bone or a treat.

Other than the evening call to Cara each night, the cottage time for Kelly was not stressful. She was enjoying her stay. Deke, Darcy, and Joshua were all having fun as well. Kelly found the time distracting, with lots of swimming, reading, movies, good food, and resting by the water.

Toward the end of their second week at the cottage, an event did disturb the peace. A major power failure caused a blackout across most of the state, but they were lucky. The cottage got its electricity from the local town's small hydroelectric dam, so they had power the entire time. However, Cara being in Buffington did not fare as well. That evening when Kelly learned about the power failure in Buffington, she called Cara right away.

"Mom, we just heard about the power failure. Are you okay?" "My nurse never came. I am alone."

"I'll try to reach her and call you back."

Kelly spoke to the night nurse. She stated, "I can't get to your mother's place tonight. There is no transit. Taxis are scarce. I'll be there tomorrow."

This was a disaster. With the power outage, Kelly would not be able to drive to Cara's safely or in time for her overnight meds. Kelly made another call.

"Hello, Aunt Celeste. It's Kelly. I am in the Adirondacks at the cottage. Mom is at home, alone in the dark. Can one of the twins get to her and make sure she is okay for the night and help her with her meds?"

"Yes, Kelly. Carlo is not far away and has a flashlight with him. Don't worry. It'll be fine."

Relieved, Kelly hung up and called her mom. "Mom, Carlo is on his way. He will help you out tonight. I'll stay on the phone with you until he arrives."

Once Carlo arrived and Kelly had explained the meds regimen to him, Kelly said goodnight to Cara. Kelly was exhausted. When she joined Deke and Darcy as they watched TV, they did not say anything to her about Cara. Soon, Kelly got immersed in the movie they were enjoying and suppressed her worry.

Kelly called Cara first thing the next morning. There was another problem.

"Kelly, the nurse is not here yet."

"Okay, Mom. Not to worry. I will help you through your meds and stay with you on the phone until the nurse arrives."

By the time the nurse came, Kelly was wiped. Her shoulders relaxed a little when Kelly spoke to Cara later in the day and learned Cara's power had been restored. The rest of the day followed the normal routine for Kelly of an afternoon swim, a walk with Joshua, dinner, a movie, and then Joshua's late-night constitutional before bed.

The next day was their last at the cottage. They packed and cleaned up, had their last barbecue, and retired for the night. Joshua watched Kelly and stayed by her side as he had done every day on this trip to the cottage.

Kelly enjoyed the uneventful trip in the car back home to Buffington. Darcy and Joshua slept, while she and Deke listened to jazz on the radio and made small talk about the cottage trip.

About two weeks after the return to Buffington from the cottage, Cara took a turn for the worse. Kelly drove Cara to the hospital to recalibrate her medications since she was now experiencing some mild pain.

"We are taking your mother into intensive care. You can stay with her," the emergency nurse told Kelly soon after they had checked in with the triage nurse. After half a day in intensive care, Cara went to the palliative care ward.

Kelly had hoped Cara would receive more radiation therapy for pain once in the palliative care ward. After a day of making inquiries to try to speak with the appropriate doctor, Cara's radiation oncologist informed Kelly, "Your mother cannot have any more radiation therapy. She has received the maximum dose. Her bones are too brittle. Her spine is collapsing. Medication adjustment is the only option. I'm so sorry."

"Thank you," Kelly replied, noticing the butterflies were back in full flight. She did not process everything the doctor had said. The part about the spine collapsing did not completely penetrate. She let it have one horrific moment and swept it aside.

Cara's doctors neglected to tell Kelly that after this pain adjustment, Cara would not be very lucid. Kelly soon realized she had missed her opportunity to say goodbye. But given their last tender moment together—that push—perhaps this was for the best, she thought. When Cara had been lucid with Kelly, Cara's prime interest had been in sorting out her belongings, designating what was for Kieran and what was for Kelly. Cara never asked Kelly about Kieran, Darcy, Joshua, or anyone. Neither Kieran nor she wanted Cara's stuff, but Kelly made the list as Cara dictated it. She would ensure she and Kieran respected the list, even though they didn't really want to.

After the medication adjustment at the hospital, Cara required twenty-four-hour nursing care at home.

"Mom, I need to get you overnight care. I'll try to arrange something this week. Your evening nurse says she will stay over until I can find a more permanent solution. I am going to order a hospital bed for you. It will be much more comfortable. It comes tomorrow."

This time, Cara did not resist or complain. Kelly was a little alarmed by that.

Finding an overnight nurse was not easy. Some disasters occurred. One nurse had trouble turning Cara over and caused her great pain. As soon as Cara notified Kelly about the problem, Kelly found another overnight nurse. A few days into this nurse's tenure, Kelly got a call from Cara.

"Kelly, my nurse is asleep. I'm all alone in the bathroom. What should I do?" "Mom, please call out to Louise loudly. She will wake up and come to you."

With the help of one of Cara's excellent day nurses and changing agencies, Kelly was able to establish a suitable regimen of twenty-four-hour nursing care and ongoing biweekly and then weekly oncologist home care for Cara. This was incredibly expensive. Kelly did the math and wondered how she was going to manage.

"I don't think there will be any money left," Cara advised Kelly one evening after the overnight care was routine. Rather than issuing a caution or offering a solution, Cara was just making an observation. Cara was oblivious to the impact of the situation on Kelly and Kieran and their families. Kelly was using up their inheritance at an accelerating rate to pay for Cara's care, but Kelly remained faithful to the promise she had made to her mom.

Although Cara now had care around the clock, Kelly continued her routine of daily visits to Cara. She worked a full day and looked after her family.

After Kelly had returned home from Cara's one early November night, Deke gave Kelly a stunning surprise. He was sitting on his reclining chair in their third-floor den and spoke to Kelly after she walked in and before she sat down.

"Kelly, you are never home. You don't spend time with me. Things are not getting done. I want a divorce."

"What? Deke, I can't believe you are saying this now, out of nowhere. I am exhausted from dealing with Mom, the family business, and trying to maintain some kind of home life with you, Darcy, and Joshua. We have breakfast and dinner together. I've been driving Darcy to school each morning before I go to Mom's. I've been helping Darcy with her homework when I can and working on office stuff. I am doing the best I can."

He stared at Kelly with a flat facial expression. Grasping at anything, Kelly continued, "I'm sure we can work this out. This is a really stressful time."

With no response from Deke, Kelly did her best to keep her composure and left the den as quickly as she could. Joshua followed her down the stairs and the two went out for Joshua's late-night constitutional. On the walk, Kelly pushed Deke's remarks away and focused on how beautiful the pristine snow that had just fallen looked on the tree branches. She held Joshua's leash tightly as they walked, occasionally saying to Joshua, "I love you, Joshua. Good boy."

When they stopped to take in the night, Kelly smiled at Joshua and he looked into her soul. She felt better. After the walk, Kelly went to bed. Joshua joined Kelly on the bed and then hopped off to keep cool by the windows. Kelly tried desperately to get to sleep before Deke joined her in the bedroom.

Kelly waited for Deke to mention the divorce again, but days went by and it seemed forgotten. Kelly let the matter drift into her unconscious. She continued with her regular routine.

One afternoon at Cara's a week or later, Cara's day nurse suggested, "Kelly, why don't you take a little break and spend some time at the office? We can manage."

With that encouragement, Kelly was now spending most workdays at the office and after-dinner time with Cara. When she arrived home late in the evening from Cara's, Joshua was at the front door to greet her. Sometimes, she and Joshua went out for a late evening walk to unwind before going to bed. Other times, Kelly was just too weary and went straight to bed.

One night in mid-December after dinner with Deke, Darcy, and Joshua, Kelly went to Cara's as usual.

"How is my mom doing?" Kelly asked the night nurse, who was seated on the living room couch, as she walked past the kitchen and toward Cara's bedroom.

"She is waiting for you. She has been waiting for you all day."

Kelly thought this was an odd statement. She had no idea what it meant. Kelly proceeded into the bedroom to be with Cara and stood beside the bed. Cara looked at her in earnest, with her eyes fully open. Kelly picked up Cara's hand nearest to her and held it gently between her two hands.

"Hi, Mom. How are you doing?" When Cara didn't say anything, Kelly continued, "I had a good day. Work went well. Darcy is fine.

She is enjoying her violin and badminton. Her exams are coming up, so she is studying tonight." When Kelly couldn't think of what else to say, she added, "I guess that's it then."

Cara stopped breathing. Alarmed, Kelly gently nudged Cara's arm with her elbow as she held her hand. When there was no response, Kelly nudged a little harder. Cara took another breath, and then she was gone. Still holding Cara's hand, Kelly broke down and cried.

CHAPTER 11

Joshua Meets Bailey

In the spring following Cara's death, Joshua and Kelly got a marvelous surprise. A black Labrador retriever, Bailey, moved into the neighborhood down the street into Griffin's old digs. Kelly had been dejected that Griffin and Gregg had moved away in early March, but was thrilled that Joshua and Bailey, a handsome, muscular dog who was a little over a year older than Joshua, had become instant friends.

Joshua and Bailey played so well together that Kelly and his owner, Liz, made playdates to go to Lawrence Park together on weekends. Kelly and Liz and the two dogs would walk over to the dog park and meander along the trails. Kelly enjoyed the serenity of the walks and the light banter with Liz.

Often when they reached Dog Hill, dogs would hump Joshua, even other golden retrievers. Joshua tolerated the humping, regardless of Kelly's best efforts to train him to insist the other dog dismount.

"Joshua, move," Kelly would say. "Get him off you! Get him off you!"

Joshua looked at her as if to say, "It's okay. I don't mind. Be patient."

Kelly would pull the dogs off Joshua and hope Joshua would not let them mount again, but they always returned. If Joshua got tired of standing around as he was being humped, Kelly looked on as he just walked away. Kelly appreciated that Bailey was protective of Joshua in the park. If other dogs humped Joshua, Bailey would stop his explorations and run over to Joshua and the humping dog would stop the humping. Joshua didn't care about the humping, but Kelly was glad Bailey came to the rescue.

After Dog Hill, the boys, as Kelly and Liz referred to Bailey and Joshua, would continue their adventure along the trails, wrestling with each other, running, and sniffing. From time to time, Kelly and Liz would toss the red, white, and blue-striped, hand-sized, rubber ball for the dogs to retrieve.

"Liz, Joshua is slow and lazy. He won't go for the ball if he thinks Bailey is going to get it. I'll throw the ball in the opposite direction away from Bailey so it will be a sure thing for Joshua."

After a few tosses for Joshua, Kelly would throw the ball for Bailey. Then after Liz threw the ball for Bailey a few times, Liz cheated for Joshua as well.

"Here, Joshua. Go get it! Good boy!" Liz called out.

"Bailey, good boy!" Kelly cried out as Bailey galloped and retrieved the ball. Bailey was not as sociable as Joshua was with other dogs in the park. Liz revealed to Kelly, "Bailey used to be aggressive with other dogs in the park. Since he has been carrying the rubber ball and stick in his mouth, he is calm and happy."

Despite Joshua's friendliness with dogs in the park or on the street, he was not a cordial host at home. When Bailey sojourned with Joshua for a day visit or a few days when Liz and Ben were away on holidays, Joshua hoarded his toys and bones. Kelly had to intervene.

"Joshua, no. That's Bailey's bone. Stop growling at Bailey. You have a bone. Be a good host."

"Bailey, come. Here's your bone. Good boy."

When Joshua stayed at Bailey's house, Bailey was the perfect host.

"Hi, Bailey. What a beautiful cloth gorilla you have!" Kelly would exclaim.

After prancing around the living room showing off his cloth gorilla, his favorite toy, Bailey would drop it in front of Joshua.

After a play or a walk when the boys were together with Kelly, each dog enjoyed a chew on a meat bone or a rawhide. Kelly loved to watch the boys curl up and snuggle beside each other for a snooze. The tranquility of their snooze brought her some inner peace as well.

Kelly told Liz, "The boys behave like brothers, with Bailey, the older brother, looking out for Joshua."

Kelly and Liz exchanged house keys so that the boys could be together even if the adults in one of the houses were away. Kelly found herself taking Joshua over to Bailey's often, but Liz was seldom able to come over with Bailey to see Joshua when Joshua was home alone as there was little opportunity. If Deke, Darcy, and Kelly went out for dinner or shopping, Kelly insisted on bringing Joshua in the car with her. When the hosts permitted it, Kelly brought Joshua with her to friend or family gatherings. The infrequent times Joshua was home alone usually occurred if he wasn't permitted to attend the event like a football game, a school event for Darcy, a concert, or a movie in a theater.

That summer, Kelly invited Liz, Ben, and Bailey to spend a day with them at the cottage. They drove up separately, with Kelly, Deke, Darcy, and Joshua arriving in the morning and Liz, Ben, and Bailey arriving after lunch.

Drives to the cottage for Kelly were often stressful.

"Hurry up," Deke would demand. "We are going to hit the traffic. You and Darcy are taking too much stuff. The SUV is packed to the gills. I won't be able to fit all of this in. Where am I supposed to put it all? Can't your daughter take less stuff?"

Kelly had learned to ignore these protests, as an oral response was fruitless. Deke would shift his argument with each of Kelly's responses and grow angrier or would lose his self-control.

"It's okay, Deke. We'll fit it all in," Kelly replied innocently one time.

As he threw the suitcases out of the trunk, Deke retorted, "You must be joking, Kelly. Get out of my way! Now I have to start again and repack the entire car. We are never going to get to the cottage on time for a check-in!"

Instead of challenging or disputing, Kelly knew the best strategy was a workaround. This time, she waited until Deke went back into the house to bring out more belongings. She used the time to reorganize and pack to make room for more. When Deke returned and saw what Kelly had done, he was furious. Kelly felt his scorn in her body, but she and Deke both said nothing.

By the time they were ready to depart for the cottage to spend the day with Bailey, Ben, and Liz, the SUV was jammed to the roof with swim noodles, pillows, towels, food, clothing, and other items. In the back seat was just enough space for Darcy to sit upright and for

Joshua to stretch out as long as Darcy allowed him to lie on her upper legs and cuddle with her.

In previous trips to the cottage, after complaining about Joshua's lying on her legs and how heavy he was, Darcy settled down and eventually fell asleep with her head on Joshua's head or on his back. This time, Darcy could not adapt.

"Mom, Joshua is so heavy. I don't want him on me. There's no space. I'm so uncomfortable. I won't make it the entire way with him on my legs. Joshua, move, move."

When he didn't move, Darcy grew frustrated and tried to push him off as Kelly looked on from the front seat. Darcy's efforts made no difference, so she repeated, "Joshua, move, move."

Before replying to Darcy, Kelly looked over at Deke in the driver's seat and felt the steam pouring from his ears. She took a deep breath and replied, "Okay, Darcy. Let's change places. You'll be more comfortable in the front seat with Dad."

After Kelly and Darcy exchanged places, Kelly settled into her new spot. She was happy to sit in the back seat, away from the displeasure of Deke and into the solemnity of Joshua, with his head and upper body in her lap. She enjoyed the quietude in patting his head and the warmth of his body on hers. Joshua soon fell asleep, resting on her.

The remainder of the drive went smoothly. Kelly and Deke listened to music on the radio and commented on the country landscape as they drove. Darcy slept in the front seat. After arriving and unpacking in the solitude of their cottage bedroom, Kelly prepared some ham and swiss sandwiches with a green salad and watermelon slices which they enjoyed on the cottage deck. Shortly after Kelly and Darcy cleaned up from lunch, Bailey, Liz, and Ben arrived.

Bailey, Liz, and Ben visited the cottage on a cool, sunny day. Only the dogs dared to enter the lake and spent the afternoon swimming together. Liz, Ben, Deke, and Kelly took turns throwing the tennis balls into the lake for the dogs. While the adults threw the balls for the dogs, Darcy recorded the action on her new video equipment.

Initially, when one of the adults threw a ball into the lake, both Joshua and Bailey jumped off the dock and raced to fetch it. Bailey was a much faster swimmer, so the adults took turns throwing in two balls so each dog could retrieve one.

Eventually, Bailey preferred to enter by wading into the lake. This gave Joshua an advantage, diving off the dock. The boys ended up sharing the balls, so each retrieved a ball. When Joshua could keep up, the boys swam beside each other. Kelly reveled in all the action and in the play of the dogs.

The boys swam most of the afternoon, taking short breaks to sun themselves on the dock or to go up the hill toward the cottage to snooze in the shade. After the dogs swam and dried off a little, Kelly asked everyone to go to the cottage for a drink. The adults each had a cold beer and Darcy had a glass of cold milk, while Deke and Kelly began to prepare dinner.

For dinner, the adults and Darcy ate pork chops, sweet corn, and sweet potatoes Deke had cooked on the barbecue, with some apple sauce, mixed green salad, and Italian olive bread Kelly had prepared. For dessert, they all sat on the deck. Kelly served a peach pie she had baked that morning after she had unpacked. The adults enjoyed coffee with the pie, while Darcy reviewed her video footage as she drank her pop.

After their dog food dinner, each dog enjoyed a beef bone Kelly gave them. When the dogs had tired of chewing, it was time for Liz, Ben, and Bailey to depart. Soon after they left, Joshua lay down and slept until Kelly took him out for his late-evening constitutional before bed.

Before bed, Darcy announced, "Mom, Dad, I'm going to do some editing of the footage I took of the dogs. Then I think I'll add some music and credits, too. I'll show you the video as soon as I'm finished."

"That's wonderful, Darcy. I'm looking forward to it!" Kelly replied.

Deke looked up at Darcy and didn't say anything. Kelly was disappointed with his lack of support, but she knew there was nothing she could do about it.

With the departure of Bailey, Liz, and Ben, the family returned to their normal cottage life routine. From time to time during the remainder of her stay, Kelly daydreamed as she did chores or cooked, thinking about Bailey and Joshua swimming in the lake together, and broke out into a big smile.

A few weeks after returning home from the cottage, Darcy was very proud to show on the TV screen in the den the video she had made. Kelly loved the video, the '60s rock music Darcy had added, and the amusing credits, especially, "No humans or canines were harmed making this movie. But many mosquitoes were."

"Darcy, this is fantastic! I love it," Kelly exclaimed, while Darcy beamed at Kelly. Deke snorted, but Kelly concluded he liked it. Joshua snoozed through it.

Like a good movie classic, the video stood the test of time. Every so often, Kelly retrieved the treasure and watched it over and over again.

CHAPTER 12

Joshua's First Annual Wellness Checkup

Kelly had planned Joshua's first wellness checkup for right after the return from the cottage that summer. This was separate from the annual checkup which included flea and heartworm medications Joshua had received before the cottage trip. Kelly was concerned about him having thyroid issues like Ellie had suffered and wanted him to have a more comprehensive annual exam.

Ellie was a salubrious dog for most of her life. Except for stitches she required after stepping into a muddy puddle with broken glass and some bouts with hot spots from cottage swimming, Ellie was in excellent shape until she was eleven. Kelly hoped Joshua's health would be at least as good.

Ellie's hypothyroidism went undiagnosed. At age eleven, when she experienced difficulty walking, she and Kelly frequented her vet for some answers and treatment.

"Dr. Seymour, something is wrong with Ellie," Kelly told the vet. "The arthritis medications you gave her don't work. She moves slowly and drags herself around."

"Ellie is eleven years old. She's an old dog. What you are seeing is just old age."

Dr. Seymour changed Ellie's arthritis medications a few times, but Kelly did not perceive any improvement. Ellie was lethargic and walked really slowly behind Kelly, often as far as the leash permitted. In one Saturday, Kelly witnessed Ellie experiencing a more pernicious problem.

Deke, Kelly, and Ellie had just gotten into the car to go shopping when Kelly heard some labored breathing from Ellie.

"Deke, I think Ellie is having trouble breathing. Can you hear that wheezing?"

"No, she's fine," and he started the car.

"Deke, I am going to sit in the back seat with Ellie." Kelly was dismayed by Deke's response. He rolled his eyes at her, but she persevered.

After a minute or so in the back seat, Kelly cried out, "Deke, Ellie's lips are bluish. Let's go to the emergency hospital."

"Kelly, really."

"Deke, please."

Deke parked the car, got out to take a look at Ellie, got back into the car, and said, "What do you want to do?"

"Let's go to the hospital now."

On the drive to the emergency hospital, Kelly telephoned the hospital, "Hello, this is Kelly Delmonico. We are on our way with our golden retriever, Ellie, who seems to be having trouble breathing. We will be there very soon."

When they arrived, an internist at the hospital was outside near the hospital entrance. He looked at Ellie and said, "Hello, I'm Dr. Davies. Let's take a short walk."

After Ellie took a few steps, Dr. Davies advised, "Ellie has severe hypothyroidism. I'll need to give her a more thorough exam and decide on the next steps." He took her leash, and they all headed into the hospital. Dr. Davies escorted Ellie into the treatment room beyond the push doors.

A few minutes later, Dr. Davies returned and sat down beside Kelly. "I have some bad news. Ellie needs emergency surgery. The lining in her throat is collapsing. It has thinned due to her untreated thyroid condition. She might die."

"Yes, please go ahead with the surgery right away," Kelly said.

In the waiting room, Kelly concealed from Deke her intense anxiety. She knew he would tell her there was nothing to be done except wait, and her anxiety would do nothing constructive. This was his typical response. Kelly considered it a reasoned response, but a dissatisfactory one. In such situations, she was seeking compassion and support. Instead, she made small talk about other things. Darcy was with a friend at a movie theater, so Kelly decided to wait to call her until the movie was over. Deke did not bring up the subject of telephoning Darcy.

Ellie had the surgery within the hour, stayed a few days in the hospital, with Kelly and Deke visiting her every day, and then started taking thyroid pills twice a day upon her return home. At first, Deke gave her the pills, with Kelly observing and learning from his technique. As time went on, Kelly took over that duty and became quite skilled at throwing the tiny pills down Ellie's throat. Once the pills were down the hatch, Kelly always rewarded Ellie with a loving pat and a "Good girl, Ellie, well done." Ellie required ongoing regular monitoring of her thyroid situation, which Kelly was happy to do to note any changes in her weight or energy so Dr. Davies could adjust Ellie's dose.

Because of the thyroid issue with Ellie, Kelly was hyper-vigilant with Joshua. At Joshua's first wellness exam, she explained to Dr. Samuels, "I think Joshua may be hypothyroid. I know he is only two years old, but he is dragging himself around in a similar manner as my first dog, Ellie, had done, and she was hypothyroid. Please test Joshua."

When Dr. Samuels telephoned Kelly with the results of Joshua's thyroid blood test, she stated, "The test came back inconclusive."

"Please see what you can do. Joshua's lethargy is like Ellie's. Can you do another test?"

Kelly and Deke took Joshua back to see Dr. Samuels a week later. She did another more conclusive test and called Kelly with the results a few days later.

"Hello, Kelly. I have the results of Joshua's bloodwork. Joshua is mildly hypothyroid. I will get his meds ready for you to pick up. He will need to take pills twice a day and get tested regularly for his hypothyroidism."

"Okay, Dr. Samuels. Joshua and I will be there later today to pick up his meds. Thank you."

Although Kelly was somewhat relieved Joshua's condition was now being treated, she was upset to learn he faced the same problem Ellie had. While hypothyroidism was not uncommon among golden retrievers, at the time of Ellie, Kelly had discovered the hard way the disease was not well known among vets.

"Joshua, come. Time for your thyroid meds," Kelly called out, hoping Joshua's first dose would go down smoothly. Joshua came at once, curious about why she was calling.

"Joshua, sit." And he sat calmly and gazed at Kelly, waiting patiently to find out the reason for the summons.

"Joshua, open." Kelly gingerly opened Joshua's mouth with both hands, one above and one below his mouth, and then threw the two tiny pills down his throat.

Joshua looked at Kelly as if to say, "I understand. This is for my own good. Thank you."

Kelly rewarded Joshua with a big smile and a gentle hug. "Good boy, Joshua. Well done."

CHAPTER 13

Joshua Swallows a Chew

Joshua enjoyed a good chew, especially in the evening after dinner. In addition to beef bones, Kelly bought him tasty dental treats that required a lot of chewing. One cool evening that October, about a month after Joshua was diagnosed with hypothyroidism, Kelly gave him one of those dental chews.

Joshua and Kelly had just left Darcy's room. Kelly was doing some work at her computer in her home office, which was next to the den on the third floor. Joshua kept her company, lying down about three feet away from Kelly's desk and facing her as he chewed, with one eye on Kelly as she looked up at him from time to time and smiled, and the rest of the time focusing on his chew.

Suddenly, Kelly heard Joshua make a noise. Startled, she looked at him. "Joshua, what's wrong?" He was vomiting, but only a tiny amount of liquid was coming up.

At first, Kelly was not alarmed and continued to work, but she paid more attention to Joshua. When he continued to vomit intermittently for fifteen minutes or so with little fluid coming up, she became much more concerned. Perhaps, the vomiting was due to a trapped chew.

She walked over to Joshua. "Joshua, open." She opened his mouth with her hands and then stuck her right hand down his throat to see what she could feel, but she didn't find an obstruction. She called the animal emergency hospital and told the nurse what had happened.

"Kelly, please bring Joshua in right away. I'll tell the desk to expect him."

This time, Kelly just told Deke, "It's an emergency. Joshua may have swallowed his chew and it may be stuck. Let's go to the emergency animal hospital right away. They are expecting us."

Deke snorted at Kelly. She deduced this meant Deke was a little annoyed at having to get up from his chair and leave what he was doing in the den on his computer. She watched him with Joshua by her side as he got ready and they departed together.

When Deke, Joshua, and Kelly arrived at the animal emergency hospital, Kelly checked in at the front desk where two staff members were seated in front of their computers. Then she sat down beside Deke in a waiting area chair, with Joshua seated in front of her on the floor. After a minute or two of Kelly patting Joshua's head and chest and giving him little hugs, a technician emerged from the push doors, came over to Kelly, took Joshua's leash from her, and walked with Joshua into the treatment area at the end of the hallway through the push doors. Deke and Kelly made small talk about the hospital and work, while they waited for the news about Joshua.

After about twenty minutes, Dr. Davies, the internist who had saved Ellie's life, came through the push doors and sat down beside Kelly. He explained, "The x-rays don't show an obstruction. But since

Joshua is still vomiting, I recommend we keep him overnight for observation and see how he is in the morning."

"Okay, Dr. Davies. May we please see Joshua to say good night?" "Certainly."

Dr. Davies led Deke and Kelly to Joshua's crate. The door to the crate was still open.

Looking directly into Joshua's eyes, Kelly said, "Joshua, you are going to be okay. I love you. Back soon." She reached into his crate and gave him a giant hug and two soft kisses on his cheek. Then Deke and Kelly departed, with Kelly holding back quite a few tears until she and Deke were well beyond the push doors.

After work the next day, Deke and Kelly went to the hospital to take Joshua home. "Joshua is still vomiting intermittently," Dr. Davies advised them, "I would like to keep him here another night."

"Okay, Dr. Davies. May we please say good night to Joshua?" Kelly replied.

"Come this way."

Kelly looked into his crate again. "Joshua, Dr. Davies wants to keep you here again tonight. I hope you feel better tomorrow. I love you. Back soon." She gave Joshua a long, lingering hug, two soft kisses on his cheek, and another shorter hug. Then Deke and she departed. Kelly did her best to be strong and not upset Joshua.

On the third night, Kelly went alone to bring Joshua home as Deke had stayed home with Darcy. After Kelly's arrival, Dr. Davies emerged through the push doors, sat down beside Kelly in the waiting area, and advised, "Joshua is not getting better. He is getting weaker. He is not eating well. I recommend he have surgery in the morning so we can see what is going on."

"Okay, Dr. Davies," Kelly replied. Kelly said goodnight to Joshua, giving him two longer hugs and a few extra kisses before departing for the night, and said, "I love you, Joshua. Back soon." Kelly noticed the butterflies were back.

The next morning, Joshua had the surgery. After the surgery, the surgeon called, "Kelly, I have good news. The surgery went well. Joshua is recovering nicely. We opened up Joshua's entire gut and sewed it back up, but he should heal well. I found scarring in his intestine that suggested something had passed through and roughed Joshua up a bit. But if there was an obstruction, it is gone now. You can visit him tonight."

"Thank you. We'll be there tonight."

For the next two nights, Deke and Kelly visited Joshua. He was not allowed out of his crate, so Kelly just patted him reassuringly, and occasionally repeated, "Good boy. I love you, Joshua."

On the third night, Dr. Davies discussed Joshua's progress with Kelly and Deke. "Joshua's surgeon is concerned Joshua is not eating well. He is lethargic and not thriving. The surgeon feels Joshua may have an underlying physical issue, but I think Joshua is depressed and needs to go home, where he will recover better. What do you think?"

"Yes, I agree," Kelly quickly replied. "When can we bring Joshua home?"

Dr. Davies released Joshua the following afternoon. Deke and Kelly went to pick him up.

When the technician brought Joshua to the waiting area, Kelly exclaimed, "Joshua, let's go home." Then she gave Joshua a hug, took his leash, and they left the hospital. She was so delighted to be taking Joshua home. She noticed there was a little extra spring in Joshua's step as he walked alongside her on the way to the car.

At home with Kelly who had stayed home to nurse him for three days, Joshua recovered rapidly. Kelly gave him his meds, took him on short walks, and gave him reassuring hugs and pats, repeating, "Good boy, Joshua. You are getting stronger. Love you."

Kelly thought Joshua knew he was getting better, as he had more energy, no sign of depression, and a bigger appetite although he had lost ten pounds during his hospital stay. Even with this weight loss, Dr. Samuels was not satisfied with Joshua's weight.

At Joshua's check-up a week after his surgery, Dr. Samuels reported to Kelly, "Joshua is almost at the right weight—another three pounds should do it. Because he is such a big golden retriever, we need to keep weight off his joints. He should be skin and bones, with all his skeleton sticking out. To stay in top shape, he needs to be very lean."

"I'll try harder, Dr. Samuels, but I really don't see how he can be thinner than he is now."

After the hospital stay, Kelly monitored Joshua's eating habits more closely. Some of his favorite treats—dental chews she had bought at Dr. Samuels'—were not ideal for him. He was too lazy to chew them, so he gulped them down instead. After performing two separate extractions of a chunk of this type of chew from the back of Joshua's throat, Kelly didn't buy those treats anymore. Instead, she found small, vegetable-based, low-calorie biscuits he chewed fully and relished.

Joshua liked compressed beef chews, especially the ones that were twisted in a braid—the bigger, the better. Because they were high-calorie, Kelly gave him these chews less frequently. The smaller compressed beef chews disappeared in a couple of minutes. Joshua didn't take more than twenty minutes to eat the entire large braided chew, while other dogs his size like Bailey spent longer chewing them.

Either Joshua was too lazy to chew and swallowed instead or he chewed constantly, but not quickly until the chew was finished.

Watching Joshua chew was now a new source of joy for Kelly. Deke and Darcy were not particularly interested in availing themselves of this opportunity. However, Kelly was fascinated as she watched Joshua manipulate the chew between his two front paws. As the chew got shorter, Joshua turned the chew over at particular moments and chewed the other side. He looked up at Kelly from time to time as he chewed. Kelly, awed by his skill and focus, felt a calm come over her as she watched him chew.

CHAPTER 14

Darcy's Senior Year in High School

The two years between Joshua's surgery for the removal of the chew and the beginning of Darcy's senior year of high school had passed rapidly and without major incident. Kelly had gotten into a routine of taking Darcy to school, going to Lawrence Park with Joshua before work and on weekends, taking Darcy to therapy twice a week after school, going to the school grounds across the street from the sports medicine clinic to go for a play with Joshua, helping Darcy with homework or with life most evenings, looking after the household, dealing with her hospital monthly board of directors' meetings, and keeping the family business afloat. Kelly dumped her needs in a box and secured them at the back of her mind. She focused on those of Darcy, Joshua, and Deke.

When Darcy started her senior year in high school, Joshua was three and half years old, a young adult. At ninety pounds, with his long, golden, furry body and large handsome head, Joshua was an imposing figure. With his six-foot, four-inch, football jock frame, wavy black hair, and bright blue eyes, coupled with his sharp wit and intellect, most considered Deke to be quite a catch. Darcy, now almost eighteen years old and with her lean, five-foot-seven frame, blue eyes, and wavy black hair, looked just like Deke. Kelly looked more Irish than Italian despite her fifty-fifty heritage. She was very attractive—slim, five-foot-five, and with slightly wavy chestnut brown hair and green eyes. On the rare occasions when Deke, Darcy, Joshua, and Kelly all went on a family walk together, they all looked like they belonged together.

Kelly relied on her escapes with Joshua during their morning walks and evening constitutionals, but especially the long weekend walks with him for relaxation and socializing. On the walks in the neighborhood or in Lawrence Park, Kelly and Joshua met old friends and made new ones. Joshua's old friends were always delighted to greet him, and passersby also wanted to make his acquaintance.

In a typical meeting with Kelly and Joshua and an owner and her dog, Joshua greeted the person and then the dog, while Kelly did the reverse. Kelly was always pleased to chat with owners about their dogs. In this way, Kelly and Joshua had an extended social circle, which was intertwined, joyous, and always growing. Kelly admired how Joshua greeted people with such sincere affection. He looked at each person he met intently and swished his tail from side to side, generating a little breeze behind him.

If the person stopped patting him and he believed he might get more pats, his paw gently touched the person on the leg once or twice, nudging the individual to resume their affections.

Joshua adored making new friends. People remembered him and Kelly even after only one meeting and asked Kelly about him when she wasn't with him. When a passerby was a willing candidate to make Joshua's acquaintance, the meeting made Joshua's tail wag profuscly. Seeing him revel in his new friendship brought Kelly much pleasure. She was elated to see him so jubilant. In such encounters, he glanced at Kelly, looking for her approval. When she beamed back at him, she saw his tail swish a little faster.

If the passerby wanted to approach Joshua but was a little reticent, either because the person was not accustomed to being in the company of dogs or was not familiar with the friendly disposition characteristic of golden retrievers, Kelly would say, "Joshua won't hurt you. He loves people."

After a moment or two, the passerby would start to relax, quelled by Joshua's welcoming eyes, breezy bushy tail, and kind heart.

When the meeting was over, Kelly would say, "Good boy, Joshua. Let's go," and they would continue on their journey. Kelly and Joshua were both energized and pleased by the encounter. On a family walk with Joshua, Deke was more interested in how impressed people were by Joshua, or he was just impatient to move on. Kelly was not sure what Darcy thought as she did not really ever seem that interested in Joshua.

If someone new did not want to be his friend, Joshua was offended. Kelly would console him, "Good boy. I love you, Joshua." In response, Joshua would blink once at her, which Kelly interpreted as indicating he had understood, and all was well. Reassured that Joshua was alright, with a gentle tug of Joshua's leash, Kelly would say, "Come, Joshua, let's go," and they would continue on their trip.

Joshua had a soft spot for children and longed to kiss babies across the cheek with his tongue. "Joshua, no!" Kelly would state firmly, pulling Joshua away from the baby. She knew the baby-kissing was not all that appreciated.

Despite Kelly's best efforts, Joshua was able to steal a baby kiss or two. The last time Joshua followed his baby-kissing routine upset

Kelly. After Joshua stole the little kiss on the baby's cheek, Kelly quickly pulled him away from the stroller but not before glancing at the baby snoozing. Kelly noticed a small doll beside the baby in poor condition, with a tattered dress and some hair on her head missing. Kelly found this disconcerting but didn't know why. After that, Kelly redoubled her efforts and made sure she and Joshua avoided baby carriages.

Often when Kelly walked alone down her street, a neighbor gardening in his front yard would call out to her, "Where is Joshua? I didn't recognize you without him." She would laugh, toss her head slightly, and continue on her way. When she wasn't walking with Joshua, she always missed him.

That fall on walks with just Kelly and Joshua in Lawrence Park, Kelly allowed Joshua to explore off-leash further into the Lawrence Park woods now that he was older and reliably returned, usually quickly, when Kelly called him. She basked in the quiet and the scenery, while Joshua sniffed his surroundings and chased a squirrel or two up a tree. They walked for an hour and sometimes longer. If they met some dogs, Joshua wrestled and chased for a few minutes and then he and Kelly were on their way. Their explorations into the woods were not without drawbacks, but the lighthearted bliss they shared in the exploration was worth it.

On an adventure with Kelly in Lawrence Park, Joshua often got dirty, either because the ground was wet from the rain and the mud got caught in his fur or he rolled in something stinky. Police on horseback ambled along the park trails Kelly and Joshua frequented. The police did not pick up the horse droppings. If Joshua found those, Kelly could count on Joshua to roll in a pile, whatever the size. He rolled where Kelly couldn't see him and then returned triumphantly and smelly. This triggered Kelly's hosing routine. She stayed upwind from Joshua on the trip to the hose.

When the water hose in the dog park was working, Kelly hosed Joshua down. The hose was surrounded by a sandy area they had to cross before reaching the main trail to the rest of the off-leash area. Kelly held onto Joshua's leash and turned on the hose.

"Joshua, I love you. You need a bath. You are smelly. Stay."

As the cold water poured down his back and onto the sand, Kelly interpreted Joshua's look in his eyes to mean, "Are we done yet? Please hurry."

Kelly persisted, even though her hands were freezing from the cold water. "Joshua, I need to get enough off for the walk home. You'll need a bath at home."

Even on days without a smelly adventure, no matter how clean Joshua was after the hosing, and even if Kelly wiped his paws and belly with a towel, if she had been organized enough to have brought one with her, his paws and belly would still be wet. Once wet, he gathered loads of sand in his paws and thin belly fur. By the time they got home, some of the sand would have dried off, but typically, Kelly would clean up the small sand hills he deposited in the kitchen, hallways, or living room, depending on where he rested and dried off. If Kelly hosed him down in their front garden before entering the house, the sand mostly came off, but she only hosed him down at home when absolutely necessary.

At the start of the hosing at home, Kelly would tie Joshua to the balcony railing at the bottom of the stairs to the house. Then she would say, "Joshua, I'm going to get the doggy shampoo and beach towels. Back soon." Joshua would blink once back at Kelly, indicating to her he would be fine while she was gone. Kelly, reassured, went to get the shampoo stuff.

When she returned about two minutes later, she pulled the hose off the rack, turned the water on, took a deep breath, held Joshua across his shoulders, and wet him thoroughly with the cold water from the hose. When he was soaked, she soaped him down, saying, "Joshua, stay."

She interpreted his gaze at her to mean, "I love you, but I hate this. Hurry up."

Joshua did not like the hose, but Kelly had no choice and cleaned him up as quickly as she could. After round one of soap and rinse, Kelly performed the smell test. Did she smell anything but shampoo, or did she smell faint remnants of their adventure in the park?

If she smelled something other than lavender, she repeated the process, but usually, he didn't require more than one repeat. When all was pleasantly aromatic, she turned off the water and set the hose back on the rack.

"Joshua, you smell great. Shake." This was a skill Kelly was proud to have taught him to do on command. Before he shook, she rushed to move out of the way, otherwise, she got drenched.

After the shampoo and rinse, she toweled him off until the towels were soaking wet, which only took about two minutes. Then, much to her amazement, Joshua shook again and removed more water than the towels had absorbed.

When the washing was done, she announced, "Joshua, good boy. We're done. Let's go home." Then she untied his leash, and they went up the stairs and into the house.

Although the washing was a tiring process for Kelly, the process energized Joshua. Once in the house, Kelly would watch in amazement as he raced randomly about the first floor around the kitchen, through the living and dining rooms, and back to the kitchen, dispelling all his water energy.

When Joshua sneaked in a swim in Lawrence Park when he and Kelly were on one of their fall walks, he also needed a hose bath. A good stretch of the main off-leash trail in the park was fenced on either side by a metal fence, five feet high. On the south side of the fence was a steep hill and a shallow creek at the bottom, with flowing water over rocks. Along the other side of the creek just beyond the bank of the creek was a walking trail Kelly and Joshua occasionally frequented.

Kelly didn't like Joshua's going through the holes in the fence people or their dogs or both had cut to go for a swim. Even though the town repaired the holes often, the repairs didn't last. Ominously, they reappeared. Kelly was concerned Joshua might hurt himself, get trapped in the creek, or both. Somehow, he had figured out where all the holes in the fence were where he could escape. Kelly was always amazed when he squirmed through such small holes with lightning speed before she could stop him.

As he raced away, Kelly would scream, "Joshua, come! Joshua, come! Joshua, come!" until she got hoarse. Once through the fence, he went for a swim. Kelly waited for him to finish and climb back up the slope. She couldn't see what he was doing. The fence was too high for her to climb without injury from the metal. It did not have a top she could grasp on to. Walking along the trail and then down the hill to one of the bridges that spanned the creek would take her too long, so she marked time and hoped for the best.

After two or three minutes, Kelly was relieved to see Joshua galloping up the hill in ecstasy. The water had invigorated him. He was soaking wet and savoring it. Kelly loved seeing him so delighted but couldn't really enjoy it fully until she had guided him through a hole back to the other side of the fence where she was standing. Kelly was always surprised when he squished himself through whatever hole he had chosen so quickly to go for a swim and yet struggled to get back through the same or bigger hole to the other side upon his return. As long as the dog hose was still working, Kelly took Joshua to the hose for initial cleaning to get the creek off him. If that cleanse wasn't enough, she hosed him down in the front yard.

After a swim, there was an explaining to do. "Joshua is soaked," Deke would say. "Can't you keep him clean and out of the creek? He stinks like a wet dog. He makes such a mess."

"Deke, I gave Joshua a hosing. He'll stay off the furniture. Nothing to worry about."

Kelly wondered why Deke was concerned. Joshua didn't get him or the furniture wet. Deke never had to clean up anything in the house.

When Kelly and Joshua were off on their fall weekend walks, Deke and Darcy were left behind. Neither seemed to mind when Kelly and Joshua departed on one of their walks and they were not interested in joining them. Kelly often speculated whether Deke and Darcy used this time together to bond closer, or whether they continued doing whatever activity each had started. If by some chance they were watching TV together, they were still engaged in that when Kelly and Joshua returned. Kelly felt as if she and Joshua had never left. Neither Deke nor Darcy ever inquired about the walk.

Darcy's bedroom continued to be the gathering place for Joshua and Kelly in the evenings to help Darcy with homework or just to chat about what was on her mind. This was where those heart-to-heart talks about the boys or girls in Darcy's classes or her teachers took place, where her angst was exposed, and where her emotions felt like riding a roller coaster.

Kelly was able to help Darcy with most of her subjects. But with the higher calculus she had started that fall, Darcy needed Deke's help. "Darcy, I don't remember this calculus," Kelly told her. "I haven't really used it since college. Your dad uses it. Please go ask him for help."

Kelly and Joshua followed Darcy into the den, where Deke was using his computer and watching TV.

"Dad, I need your help with these two problems. I can't figure them out." "Why can't you figure this out for yourself?"

"Dad, these are the last two problems. I figured out the rest."

"Alright. Let's see." He looked at her paper and then said, "Darcy, this is so obvious." Then he tersely and angrily explained how to solve the problem.

"Thanks, Dad. I get it now."

After Darcy experienced a couple of these help sessions, Darcy told Kelly, "I think my calculus teacher has after-school office hours. I want to check that out after school tomorrow."

"Sure, Darcy, please let me know how that goes. If it isn't helpful, we will figure something out," Kelly counseled.

As Darcy became more active and engaged at school, Darcy's body lost the ability to physically cope with all of her schoolwork, extracurricular sports and clubs, newspaper running, and classical band practice. In the previous year, Darcy had begun to experience some upper body pain, but it was intermittent and tolerable. With the physiotherapy Darcy was doing, Kelly had thought things were under control, but with Darcy's increase in activity that fall, it was taking its toll. Darcy complained to Kelly that she was in more pain.

"Mom, I made the badminton team!" she announced on a good day. "Martha and I won our doubles match. I won one of two of my singles matches. Softball practice is tomorrow morning at seven-thirty. Is that okay for a drive?"

"Yes, that's fine, Darcy. How is the school newspaper going?"

"Just great! We are putting out the next edition on Friday. I'm training some writers to become school newspaper editors. One is particularly promising to take over from me as editor-in-chief.

"That Ms. Jenkins is such a hoot. She is so funny, but not everyone thinks so. She has an odd sense of humor I appreciate. I think some of the jokes she tells are for my benefit.

"Bonnie and I are going to a movie on Saturday. Joe and I are doing our science project at his house on Sunday. Do you think Liam will ask me to the dance?"

On a bad day, Kelly noticed differences.

"Mom, my wrists are so sore. I'm having trouble holding a pen. I don't think I can type on my computer, either. Do you think you could rub my back and neck? They are so sore."

"I'll get some ice packs for your wrists and the heating pad for your back after I give you a massage," Kelly replied.

As Christmas approached, Darcy's pain worsened. Kelly called Dr. Capaldi to make an appointment for Darcy. During her winter Christmas break, Darcy was able to rest from her sports and computer, but her pain persisted. After the Christmas break, Darcy, Joshua, and Kelly drove to see Dr. Capaldi.

Dr. Capaldi explained, "Darcy is doing too much physical activity. She should stop doing her sports teams, take a respite from the violin, and get some rest. Her upper body issues are different from the lower body ones, but I am not exactly sure what is causing all her pain. Her response time may be too long. She does not recover fast enough from her physical activity. Let's try some more aggressive and longer physiotherapy sessions as well. Here's a prescription for some painkillers. Kelly, you need to think outside the box to help Darcy with her pain."

When the cutbacks in activity and rest helped but did not eliminate the pain, Kelly took Darcy to see Dr. Capaldi again.

Kelly asked, "Dr. Capaldi, Darcy needs some special dispensation at Egan to minimize her pain. Would you please write a letter to the school asking for the provisions you think will help?"

"Of course."

Kelly met with Egan's principal to discuss Dr. Capaldi's letter.

"Mrs. Delmonico, we can provide a quiet room and a place to stretch when Darcy writes an exam. She can also have extra time to complete the exam and more time to rest between her exams."

"Thanks so much," Kelly replied. "Would it also be possible for Darcy's locker to be on the first floor closer to her classes? You know, when she sits out at her gym classes, she sits on the floor or on a hard gym bench. This is causing pain in her lower back and neck. Do you think she can sit out those classes in the library instead?"

"I will look into securing both of those provisions. We should be able to accommodate them."

"Darcy and I really appreciate all this help. Thank you again."

Even with the cutbacks in movement, the extra rest, the special provisions, the pain medications, and the therapy, Kelly was disheartened as Darcy was still in chronic pain that winter. Kelly suffered along with her. Darcy's pain became Kelly's mental anguish. Kelly told herself she would do everything she could to make Darcy's pain go away.

Kelly watched over Darcy more diligently to make sure Darcy didn't overdo it, so she could maintain her social life and successfully complete her schoolwork.

Kelly advised Darcy, "You are very bright. You can accomplish whatever you want to, except perhaps being an Olympic athlete." Darcy and Kelly both chuckled over that.

"But you need to be careful not to overdo it. Remember to take breaks and rest, otherwise your wrists, neck, and back will get so sore you won't be able to do anything. I heard you playing the violin a little. It was beautiful, but Dr. Capaldi said you need to rest. I know this is so hard. You are used to doing so much more. But if you take it easy and with proper management, you'll get stronger and be able to do more."

Almost every other week, Darcy would say, "Mom, I am so sore. I won't be able to do my homework or write the test tomorrow. I am so upset."

After hugging Darcy, Kelly typically responded, "I'll write you a note with an explanation and ask for an extension. I know this is so difficult for you. Please try to remember to take breaks from your work. Try not to do so much at once. Chronic pain is awful. I want it to go away. I know you don't want to accept this limitation, but you will be so much better off if you focus on managing your pain properly."

Dr. Capaldi had informed Kelly, "Darcy is likely to experience this kind of chronic pain for some time. The more she learns to manage it more effectively, the less distress it will cause. Please do continue to look for innovative treatments to help her. I have exhausted what I can recommend."

Deke never said anything to Kelly about Dr. Capaldi's note or the extra provisions. She was glad that except for his snorting disapproval when she told him about the provisions, he remained silent on the subject.

During that unusually cold winter, Darcy's pain heightened with the coldest temperatures. Her joints stiffened, causing the pain to become more acute. Kelly arranged for a therapeutic massage for Darcy on those weekends and got her a heating pad with moist air to loosen the tightened areas, which also helped. Kelly sought escape and solace from Darcy's pain in her long walks with Joshua in Lawrence Park. In the park, she was in the present, savoring their walks in the woods and Joshua's romps with other dogs.

That winter Lawrence Park seemed different to Kelly. She gained a greater appreciation of the beauty of the park and the quietude she experienced in the cold, alone with Joshua. Kelly was struck by the starkness of the greys and browns of the trees against the snowy backdrop of the walking trails and the grey sky. She found the view of the park from her vantage point enchanting, especially if snow had just fallen and covered the tree branches. The air was crisp and often quite cold, even colder with a strong wind.

Kelly dressed in layers for their walks. On the coldest days, she bundled in snow pants over her jeans and long underwear, with a balaclava, a hat over it, and a hood. Joshua, in his thick double fur coat, was not chilled by the cold. Except on the coldest days, they walked for an hour through the woods along the off-leash trails.

Occasionally, Kelly brought a green or orange tennis ball for Joshua to retrieve.

"Joshua, go get it," Kelly called out each time she threw the ball for him. Off he ran to dig the ball out of the snow with verve, but he trotted back more slowly with the ball in his mouth. After six or seven fetches, he either kept the ball in his mouth or hid it in the woods and then forgot where it was. After losing more than thirty balls that winter, Kelly threw sticks she found, but they were often scarce. She became quite skilled at finding sticks in the snowy woods for Joshua to retrieve.

With the winter and early spring freeze-thaw cycle, the snow melted on the walking trails in Lawrence Park and then froze. This made the walking trails a skating rink and impassable for a human without footwear to grip the ice. With this footwear over her boots, Kelly walked safely. Joshua maneuvered well on the ice. They avoided walks in Lawrence Park on the iciest days. Instead, they kept to snowy green spaces near local schools or in the pocket park near where they lived, or they promenaded in the shopping village near their home.

In the spring, the snowmelt in the park often flowed as a stream of mud. Kelly wore high boots, but Joshua got filthy. The park hose was not yet connected, which meant a hose down in the front yard and the darkness of Deke. Kelly braced for these occasions, but only after she had returned home. On each walk, she was grounded, and not thinking about Deke or what was waiting for her at home. She just enjoyed nature, the tranquility of the walk, and the joy of being with Joshua.

With Kelly's help and a lot of determination and hard work, Darcy pushed through her pain that winter and spring and completed her school year. Kelly took Darcy shopping for a beautiful, graduation dress and a matching purse and shoes to wear at her graduation ceremony coming up in mid-June. Kelly tried not to be tearful during those shopping events as she realized her little girl would soon leave home and start college.

On the day of Darcy's graduation, Kelly busied herself with getting her and Darcy dressed and ready for the event. As she put on her new dress, Kelly's mind wandered back to Darcy's first assertion of independence. Darcy was almost three years old and ready to spend her first full day, instead of a half-day, at the local Montessori school. The principal of the school had come to interview Darcy as well as Deke and Kelly and had concluded, "Darcy is ready to be a full day at the school. She can start in January."

Kelly replied, "She seems awfully young to be a full day. Are you sure? Deke, what do you think?" But Deke stayed out of it and did not reply. "Yes, Mrs. Delmonico, Darcy is ready," the principal affirmed.

Kelly asked Darcy, "Darcy, do you want to be a full day?" Darcy nodded firmly.

"Okay, then!" Kelly exclaimed. "Congratulations, Darcy, you are a full day!" Kelly gave Darcy a big hug, and as she did, Darcy grinned and beamed.

When the big day came to drop off Darcy at Montessori, Darcy and Kelly walked up the school steps together. The school building was in a converted turn of the century, renovated ranch house. Kelly opened the big wooden door and Darcy walked in. The door closed in front of Kelly. While Kelly was very impressed with Darcy's independence, she cried at the door. Her little girl was growing up.

With her makeup now complete, Kelly was back to the reality of the day and realized with mixed emotions she would soon have an empty nest.

After they were all dressed and ready to go to the graduation ceremony, Deke, Darcy, Kelly, and Deke's dad, who had stayed with them overnight to go to the celebration, got into the car and went to the church where the festivities were being held. They all sat together in seats which afforded them a good view of the stage, where the teachers and principal were sitting. The teachers took turns announcing the academic awards. Deke was very busy taking photos and videos with his new fancy cameras. Kelly was a little teary-eyed throughout as Darcy walked onto the stage and accepted an academic award for every subject she had taken in her senior year.

With the announcement of the award to Darcy for geography in Spanish, Kelly's tears of joy streamed down her face. Kelly heard Deke harrumph beside her as he snapped a picture of Darcy. After the subject awards, Darcy won the prize for coming first in her graduating class as well as a recognition award for being the editor of the school newspaper and for leading the robotics club and film club.

At the buffet lunch after the graduation, Kelly went for a stroll with Darcy to get some food. Students, teachers, and even strangers came up to Darcy and congratulated her on her accomplishments.

"Congratulations, Darcy. I am so glad to meet you," said the boyfriend of one of the graduating girls.

"Darcy, go girl. You're so awesome!" cheered Bonnie, one of Darcy's closest friends.

When Darcy and Kelly joined Deke and his dad at their table to eat, Deke's dad said, "My goodness, Darcy, you have won so many awards!"

Despite all the accolades Darcy received, Deke offered no congratulations. Instead, he said, "Darcy, guess you'll need a wheelbarrow to carry all your awards. So many books and they are big and heavy."

Darcy must be very hurt with such faint praise from Deke, Kelly thought. She is maintaining that "tough it out" stance of Deke's side of the family. She is hiding her feelings. This is heartbreaking.

That evening, when Deke still had not praised Darcy for her accomplishments, Kelly mulled over the situation. How could Deke be so cruel? Why was he making this about him? Why can't he get over St. Paul's? His anger below the surface is so disconcerting.

Kelly tried to picture her life without Deke, but she couldn't. They'd been together for so long. Both her professional and personal life were so tied up with his. She could not visualize anything different. Her mind went blank as she tried to concoct an exit strategy. She looked at Joshua as if expecting some guidance from him. He gazed at her lovingly and blinked, which she took to mean, "I will stand by you. I love you."

With no exit strategy, Kelly concluded Darcy would be better off if she kept things together. Perhaps, on this upcoming trip to the cottage, Darcy and Deke would sort things out. If not, she'd wait to do something drastic until after Darcy finished college in town.

When it came time to go to the cottage, Kelly was looking forward to the rest and relaxation. She was quite exhausted from work and fulfilling all her responsibilities. Kelly was pleased the ordeal of the packing of the car and drive to the cottage on this trip was rather mundane. There were Deke's usual complaints, but he seemed less ornery.

Once at the cottage, everyone began to unwind. Kelly was delighted Deke cooked all the dinners on the barbecue. Darcy spent more time reading. Kelly and Joshua were able to go on long walks. Daily, she and Joshua played fetch up and down the gravel-sandy road that led to the cottage, which rarely had any vehicles traveling on it. Kelly had bought some red, dense rubber balls, which she could throw really far. Joshua watched the ball bouncing up and down high off the road, trotted to retrieve it for a few iterations, and then tired, became bored, or both. Then they walked on leash about a half-mile in one direction or the other along this road and returned to the cottage.

Joshua had developed his own signaling system to let Kelly know when he wanted to go for a walk at the cottage. He stood in front of her, stared at her, and then moved his hips slightly in the direction he wanted to pursue, which Kelly interpreted as meaning, "Kelly, come. Let's go for a walk. Let's have some fun."

If Kelly didn't pick up on this signal, he went away briefly and then returned and repeated the signal, looking at her more eagerly. Eventually, she apprehended these cues, and off they went.

By this time, Joshua was an excellent swimmer, although he was still not fast. He was a four-year-old, big, burly, muscular, one-hundred-pound golden retriever and perhaps a free ticket to shore. One afternoon during the first week of their cottage stay when Joshua was paddling back to shore with Kelly's orange swim noodle between his teeth, Kelly swam behind him and gently put her left hand between his left front and back thighs and the right hand in the same location on the right. Being concerned she might be too heavy for him to pull without any help, she flutter-kicked lightly. Initially, she hung on for short pulls. As she gained more confidence in the ride not causing Joshua any discomfort, she hitched a ride to shore or to the dock.

"Darcy, why don't you go for a ride with Joshua? It's great fun." "Are you sure?" she asked. "Do you think he will let me?"

"Try it out. I'm sure he will."

With some continued malaise, Darcy watched as Kelly showed her where to put her hands. She gently held Joshua and stretched out her legs, kicking behind him. As he pulled her into shore, Darcy smiled at Kelly and Joshua. "This is awesome!" she cried out.

After the first try, Darcy and Joshua enjoyed many rides together, while Kelly looked on with joy. Deke looked on as Darcy and Kelly took rides with Joshua, never saying anything about it and not trying it himself. Kelly noted his behavior, didn't understand it, and decided not to dwell on it.

There was a small motorboat that belonged to the cottage that was part of the cottage rental. Kelly looked forward to the trips in the boat with Deke, Darcy, and Joshua.

Kelly would say, "Deke, let's go for a boat ride."

Deke would reply, "Alright, let's get the life jackets and go."

Deke enjoyed the boat rides and so was not displeased to accommodate the adventure. He got in first to stabilize the boat, followed by Darcy, Joshua, and Kelly.

Deke ran the motor and steered the boat, while Darcy sat near the stern or in the bow. Kelly sat in the middle and watched the cottages, rocks, and trees go by. During the rides, Joshua stood upright, sometimes with his four paws on the bottom of the boat near Kelly and other times with his two front paws on the bow seat and his back paws on the boat bottom in front of Kelly, with the wind blowing briskly through his fur. He moved around in the bow and in front of Kelly. Kelly discouraged these movements because his weight affected the balance of the boat.

The boat rides lasted about an hour. As they passed by the cottages, Kelly returned any smiles and waves from swimmers nearby. When they passed by other dogs either in the water, in another boat, or on a dock, Joshua did not return their barks. Joshua just stared at them, mirroring Kelly's calmness. Sometimes, the boat ride was so sedating Darcy dozed off. Deke steered the boat and rarely said anything.

Kelly had hoped Deke might invite Darcy to go on a boat ride with just the two of them, so they might have some heart-to-heart talks and sort things out between them. But as far as she knew, Deke did not ask.

Toward the end of the cottage stay, when Darcy and Kelly were sitting on their chairs by the dock, with Joshua snoozing in the shade beside Kelly, and Deke napping in the cottage, Kelly inquired, "How are you and dad doing? I am still picking up some tension between you."

"Yup, it's there. I think it's best to just let it be. I don't want a confrontation with Dad. This cottage stay has been very fun, Mom. I've read a lot and rested."

Kelly gave Darcy's hand a gentle squeeze, smiled lovingly, and went back to her book. At the end of this cottage trip, Kelly concluded everyone had enjoyed themselves.

Deke and Darcy seemed to get along despite no clear reconciliation. She and Joshua had gone on lots of walks and swims. There was good food, good books, and relaxing by the lake. She was hopeful things were turning around for the better in their lives.

CHAPTER 15

The Empty Nest Begins

Adjusting to life without Darcy at home now that Darcy had started her first semester in college was a challenge for Kelly. She missed the closeness with Darcy, although Darcy's living in residence in downtown Buffington freed up time in Kelly's schedule to do other things. Deke was excited by Darcy's departure.

With the loss of her daily routines with Darcy, Kelly created new ones. She and Deke took Darcy out for dinner on Friday nights after her classes. Often, Darcy chose to spend the weekend at home, which afforded Kelly and Darcy the opportunity to catch up on Darcy's courses and personal life. On a Saturday, they might all go to a matinee, and then on Sunday, as usual, they had Sunday dinner at home and watched a football game together, before returning Darcy to her dorm.

Since Kelly no longer needed to drive Darcy to school, she used her extra time to get more sleep. Joshua got the short end of the stick. Kelly no longer took him for their morning walks in Lawrence Park. Instead, most mornings, Deke, Joshua, and Kelly went for a quick trip to Lawrence Park, spending about ten minutes walking with

Joshua until he relieved himself. Then they returned to the car and drove to work.

Occasionally, on a nice day that fall, the three of them walked from the car down the steep, grassy slope to the gravel-sandy trail along the big pond to catch a glimpse of some turtles, swans, and Canada geese, or if they were really lucky, the great blue heron.

Deke often spied the great blue heron first. "Kelly, look in the weeds by the willow tree. Do you see the great blue heron hiding there?"

Kelly strained and eventually saw the heron, which she found very exciting.

In addition to watching birds and turtles in the water, Deke, Kelly, and Joshua might meet another dog or two and some folks on bicycles or fishing by the side of the pond. While Joshua was interested in the people and the dogs, he was most eager to plunge into the pond.

Kelly declared, "Deke, those geese are menacing. Joshua wants to chase them. They look like they are ready to attack him."

In response, Deke pulled on Joshua's leash and they continued their walk along the shore. Kelly dodged as best she could the myriad of goose droppings on the walking path and on the grass.

Kelly compensated on the weekends for her weekday morning laziness with Joshua. She and Joshua went on ninety-minute afternoon walks to Lawrence Park on Saturdays and Sundays.

"Deke, Joshua and I are going to the park. Would you like to come?"
"No, you go."

By early October, Kelly had stopped asking Deke to come along. Instead, she just disclosed when she and Joshua were going for a walk.

Kelly was not displeased by Deke's lack of interest. She preferred the time alone with Joshua to enjoy nature and their friends in Lawrence Park. On these weekend walks, Kelly and Joshua promenaded along the off-leash trails in the woods. Joshua cavorted with other dogs while Kelly watched and conversed with dog owners. Kelly did her best to stay away from the holes in the fence and mostly prevented Joshua from escaping through one and down the steep slope to the creek.

Occasionally, on these weekend journeys to Lawrence Park, Kelly and Joshua met Jennie at the entrance to the dog park. Joshua and Jennie never got close enough to sniff each other and never played together. Kelly was always delighted to see Jennie, give her a tummy rub, and say hello to her owner. Joshua always approached Jennie but never got closer than four feet. He stood nearby until Kelly was done with the small talk. By this point, Joshua resembled a big teddy bear, but Jennie was still a petite, pretty, demure golden. Kelly thought Joshua and Jennie made such a nice couple.

One fresh Saturday mid-October morning that fall, Kelly let Joshua out into the backyard from the sunroom sliding doors, as usual, to do his business. Kelly watched him for a few moments, as she often did. He did his reconnaissance around the entire backyard, starting at the top of their deck, where he reviewed his domain for a few minutes. Then he climbed down the railway ties to the landing, and to the plateau, where he investigated the terrain around it, including along the fence and retaining wall at the back edge of the plateau, which separated the yard from the woods below. From there, he climbed up the steep slope, and ended up on the Butlers' property but near the closest part of the Butlers' deck. While the Delmonico yard was also fenced on the right facing the back and had a gate into the lane between their house and the house on the right, only about eighteen inches separated their house and the Butlers' house on the left.

Kelly heard the phone ring in the front hall and went to answer it. Joshua continued his reconnaissance.

Without a fence between their yard and the Butlers', Joshua often went into the Butlers' yard. Kelly no longer tried to stop Joshua from this exploration. "It's fine, Kelly, if Joshua goes into our yard and explores. We don't use that part of the yard. We stick to our large deck," Brian Butler had told her.

That morning after Joshua had completed his morning reconnaissance, he returned home as usual. That afternoon when Kelly and Joshua went for the usual walk in Lawrence Park, they had a surprise visit in Lawrence Park from old friends.

"Hi, Gregg. I almost didn't recognize you. Is this Griffin? He looks fantastic," Kelly remarked, patting Griffin's head and giving him a massage on his hind. "Are you back in the neighborhood?"

"Great to see you, Kelly. Griffin and I moved back about six months ago. We live on Fuller Drive, not far from the park. Hey, Joshua, how are you doing?"

Then Gregg and Kelly silently compared their two dogs.

"Kelly, Joshua grew into his paws! Griffin is taller, but Joshua is longer, furrier, and more massive. Griffin is eighty-five pounds. How much does Joshua weigh?"

"Oh my! Joshua is ninety-five pounds." Kelly said to herself, *Joshua is huge. Oh, well . . . more to love!*

Later that afternoon after Kelly and Joshua had returned from Lawrence Park, they went into the backyard to admire the woods from the landing just above the plateau.

"Hello, Kelly!" Brian Butler called out. "Did you know Joshua is a hero? He scared off a burglar this morning."

"What? I don't know what you're talking about."

"I was in the basement rummaging around when I heard Joshua in the backyard by the basement window below the kitchen. When I went outside to see what was going on, Joshua was already at home. I found crowbar marks on the window frame where the burglar had tried to get in. Joshua must have scared him off."

"That's amazing! Dear Lord, I'm really glad the burglar is gone, and everyone is okay."

A few minutes later, Kelly and Joshua went back inside. Kelly gave Joshua a big hug, and said, "My hero, good boy." Carrying a cup of espresso she had just made, Kelly sat at the sunroom table sipping her coffee, with Joshua keeping her company under the table.

She went over Brian's story in her mind. She surmised Joshua must have approached the burglar because he had been curious about the noise. She was pretty sure Joshua had approached with his tail wagging, but the burglar was probably startled and scared by the confrontation with such a large dog. Then the burglar probably took off in a hurry.

Although Kelly was proud of Joshua's heroism, she suspected his stoutheartedness was largely inadvertent. Upon further reflection, as she took her last sip of coffee, she changed her mind. Her initial assessment had been wrong. Joshua knew what he was doing. He smelled a problem and took care of it.

When Kelly told Deke about Joshua's act of heroism, he replied, "Hmm. Kelly, the hall carpets are dirty again from Joshua's trips to the park."

Later that afternoon as Kelly was preparing dinner, Deke came into the kitchen and announced, "Kelly, now I am number one. No more excuses! I want to fix up the house to give us more adult space."

Kelly interpreted Deke's remarks to mean more sex, more doting on him. She was not feeling equally amorous. Deke's treatment of Darcy over the years culminating in Darcy's graduation fiasco had created a greater gulf between them. In addition to his treatment of Darcy, the widening gulf was due to Deke's constant criticism and inexplicable seething anger toward her and his lack of support for her at work. Now that Darcy was gone, Kelly knew Deke was expecting a rebirth in their relationship, but she did not feel the same way. She did not know how she was going to deal with his expectations, so she shoved the matter aside.

"Deke, Darcy just moved out. Let's keep her room and the basement as is. Darcy will be coming home on weekends. She'll want her room to stay in and her basement space to hang out. We can do other renovations."

Deke said, "Kelly, come into the dining room. I have some things to show you."

Deke handed Kelly his pencil drawings and continued, "I have done some research. I want to renovate our bathrooms. The bathroom beside Darcy's room is really outdated. The fixtures and design are over thirty years old. I want new fixtures in the powder room on the first floor, too. And the third-floor bathroom beside the den looks dated. Take a look at my drawings. I arranged for us to have an appointment tomorrow at the bathroom fixture store I picked out."

"The drawings look great, Deke." Kelly reviewed the designs more carefully and said, "The designs are extensive. Does the store have any designers or contractors to help us?"

"We'll find out when we get there."

Kelly thought the renovations looked expensive and did not think they had that kind of money to spend. But she did not want to spoil Deke's excitement or efforts, so she concealed her concerns. It turned out there was a designer at the fixture store who was able to preserve Deke's designs for the most part and helped them find fixtures that were somewhat affordable. The store designer also recommended a contractor, Norman Natas, whom the designer used for renovations.

In the past, Kelly was stuck being responsible for renovations and watching over the contractors. This time, she asked, "Deke, I am super busy at work. Do you think you have time to oversee the bathroom renovations?"

Although Kelly felt his displeasure creep into her bones, she was consoled when Deke replied, "Fine, Kelly."

The renovations started in mid-November. Kelly was not happy about the disruptions or the construction mess. Darcy would be spending her first Christmas as a college student back home, meaning there was a lot of cooking, cleaning, and preparations for Kelly to make for a Christmas at home and also contribute to one later in the day at Deke's sister's home with the extended family. Christmas eve they would all go, as usual, to the family church for a carol service. Kelly lamented that she had not been to a midnight mass since Darcy was little.

As Christmas approached, Kelly was also busy organizing things for staff at the family business. Each year, Deke hosted a holiday celebration dinner just for their staff and spouses at a trendy restaurant downtown and a lunch for their clients. Feeling bored with the usual client holiday lunch, Kelly considered doing something different.

She decided she was going to make this client lunch a party for clients and their dogs. She knew several of their clients who have dogs. They might really enjoy this. She would e-mail some of the most likely ones and see. A buffet lunch would work. She could pick up some of Joshua's favorite dog treats for the dogs. Deke likes food from Tomaso's so she would order from there.

Excited, Kelly told Deke about her idea for the client party. She knew he would probably not like the idea. She had noticed over the years he had become rather stuffy and stodgy about trying new things.

"Deke, I am going to organize a dog party this year. Janice Peters and some of her other colleagues have dogs. And I can also invite Bailey, Liz, and Ben."

Deke harrumphed but said nothing. Kelly could feel his discontent, but she shoved it aside. After Kelly sent out the invitations to the five most likely people who would want to attend, she received very positive responses, so she sent out the remaining five.

"Kelly, how wonderful! I would like to bring both my golden retrievers. Would that be okay? Do you know Carl, our marketing manager? He also has a golden retriever. May I invite him?" telephoned Janice Peters.

"Of course! They are all invited."

The next day, Kelly received two more positive calls. "May I bring my new pug? He is just trained," inquired another client.

"Sure, I'm looking forward to meeting him," Kelly responded. "The puppy pictures you e-mailed me of him are so cute."

"I'd like to bring my black lab, Daisy. She is eight years old but acts like a pup," said one of the senior labor lawyers Deke and Kelly worked with.

When Kelly notified their office building property manager about the dog party and the likely number of dogs, the property manager asked, "Would you mind if I sent out a general invitation to the dog owners in the building?"

"Sure, but please ask the owners to contact me to let me know they are attending and with how many dogs. Please give them my e-mail address to respond."

On the day of the dog party, staff helped Kelly organize the office space, while Joshua looked on from a corner of the boardroom. They moved the boardroom table to one side of the boardroom and put chairs along the other walls. Kelly, Chloe, Christian, Karen, and Fatima arranged the food on the boardroom table and the side table beside it. The buffet consisted of cheeses and crackers; Caesar, green, and pasta salads; assorted sandwiches; and fruit and cake squares for dessert. Wine and beer were prominent to help digest the food. Kelly prepared some non-spiked as well as rum eggnog for the more adventurous. Deke surveilled the room with a flat expression, but when guests arrived, he was gracious.

At first, the staff considered the dog party a crazy idea and just humored Kelly. But once the dogs arrived, they got into it. Whatever lingering reservations they had were gone.

Everyone sat in chairs in the boardroom, chatted, enjoyed the good food, wine, and beer, and cheerily watched the dogs. The dogs jostled and wrestled in the boardroom and in the office reception area. Kelly was impressed the dogs were good about not jumping up at the buffet table or begging for food. Some dogs were inquisitive. She looked on as they climbed the loft stairs and then ran back down again, repeatedly until something else caught their attention. The dogs played with the toys disbursed around the common areas of the office and with one another, garnering plenty of human affection. Kelly was delighted as Joshua played with the dogs, ran up and down the loft stairs, and was showered with attention and presents from their guests. Although Joshua was reticent at first when his space was invaded by the other dogs, he soon overcame his misgivings. He had a wonderful time.

After the partiers had dessert and engaged in a livelier conversation about the holiday season, the guests got ready to go home. With a big smile and a pat on the head, Kelly gave each parting dog a holiday loot bag she had filled, containing dog treats and a small dog toy.

"Thanks, Kelly. What a great idea! Please do this next year," was a common comment to Kelly from a departing guest.

After all the guests had gone, the organizing team cleaned up, reorganized the boardroom, and went back to work. Joshua went up the loft stairs with Kelly, stuck his head through the railing, and took a snooze. The rest of Kelly's day was routine.

Back at home that evening, Kelly continued her Christmas preparations and did so most evenings until just before Christmas. When Christmas finally came, Kelly, Deke, Darcy, and Joshua spent an uneventful Christmas morning and early dinner at home and then a later Christmas dinner and evening at Deke's sister's home. Kelly delighted in having Darcy home over Christmas, their private talks, and their occasional walks with Joshua in the neighborhood.

The first Thursday morning in January, Kelly's first day back at work from the Christmas break, Kelly and Joshua were in the boardroom in a conference call. Kelly and Joshua were with Fatima, Karen, and Chloe, while Janice Peters and some of her staff were in their boardroom at their regional office in Ithaca. Kelly was making a presentation with a slide deck she had previously sent to the meeting participants the day before.

"As you can see from the chart," Kelly said, "the change management plan is divided into three phases. We expect each to take about four months. Joshua, get out from under the table! After the first phase, we will have a meeting with your senior operations staff in Ithaca."

Kelly finished the presentation without missing a beat. She didn't think twice about what she had said until about two weeks later when Janice called her to discuss the next steps in the change management process.

"Kelly, do you realize what happened at the teleconference?" "No. Is there a problem?"

"Edward, Lewis, Daniella, and Davante were stunned. After the call, they wanted to know, 'Who is this fellow Joshua and what is he doing under Kelly's table?' Their imaginations were running wild until I explained Joshua is your golden retriever. Then we all roared!"

Kelly didn't share this story with Deke. She knew he would consider her behavior unprofessional. It would just be fodder for him to criticize her for bringing Joshua to the office. But she did share the story with Darcy that weekend.

"Oh, Mom, that's so funny!" Darcy responded as she and Kelly sat at the dining room table, enjoying some coffee and a snack. Then after she finished her snack, Darcy got up to leave but gave Joshua a big pat and a smile before she left.

The next evening, Kelly spent her time with Deke, Darcy, and Joshua watching movies together in the den. After the first movie,

Kelly decided to go into the kitchen to make more popcorn and refill the coffee mugs for her and Darcy and get Deke another lager. As Kelly walked to the fridge, she felt a downpour on her head. She was soaked. She surmised this was caused by a giant leak from the second-floor bathroom.

She called out to Deke, "Deke, come quick. I'm in the kitchen. We have a big problem."

Deke arrived, scowling at having been disturbed from his activities in the den. He scanned Kelly and saw she was drenched.

"What happened?"

"On my way to the fridge, I got a shower through the kitchen ceiling. Should I call a plumber?"

Deke paused for a few moments, then said, "Go ahead."

A week later, Kelly was putting away some laundry in her bedroom. Where she was standing by her closet was just below the bathroom shower on the third floor. She got soaked again.

On this second visit, the plumber repeated his advice, "I can't tell what the problem is unless I take down the shower tiles and see behind the shower wall. Once I do that, I can give you an estimate to fix the problem."

After the plumber left, Kelly suggested to Deke, "I have been talking to Wright Engineering about partnering on some change management projects. Their office is on the floor right below ours. They have architects and engineers who do forensic work. How about I connect with them on Monday and ask them to investigate the bathrooms?"

"Fine," Deke replied, "Better not be expensive."

The Wright Engineering investigations revealed that the bathroom showers had to be completely gutted and redone due to shoddy workmanship. After relaying the results of the investigations to Deke, Kelly asserted, "Deke, I would like the repairs done by Wright Engineering. I can call them this weekend to come by and give us an estimate."

"I want to interview Norman Natas as well. He called yesterday and said the bathroom fixture store had told him about the problems we were having. He said he wants to put in a bid."

"I don't want to see Norman ever again. He did awful work. Why would we hire him to fix his own mess?"

"Let's see what he has to say."

When Norman arrived at their home a few days later, Norman revealed, "Deke and Kelly, I am offering to do the work to repair the bathrooms for the same price as I did the original work. There is a lot of work to be done. The plumbing wasn't installed properly. That's why the bathroom showers leak."

Kelly asked, "Norman, why didn't you do the installation properly in the first place?"

"I really like you, Kelly. When I did the installation, I didn't know you. Now since I know you, I will do a good job."

"I don't understand why how well you know us should matter. Why should we pay you to fix your mess? Why shouldn't we just sue you instead?"

"Stand in line, Kelly. If you sue me, you'll get nothing. I have no money. My house is in my wife's name. I have no other assets."

"Thanks for coming by, Norman. We'll let you know," Kelly replied. Then she showed him to the door."

After Norman departed, Kelly declared, "Can you believe him? He doesn't care that he intentionally did a poor job. Now he wants us to pay him to fix his mistakes. He purposely did a bad job, and he is fine with that. How disgusting."

"What do you want to do, Kelly?" inquired Deke.

"Norman took advantage of us. How could we possibly hire him?" "Do you want to hire him or not?"

"No, Deke, I don't want to hire him. I want to sue him."

Kelly was astounded by Deke's response. She wondered what was wrong with Deke. Where was his outrage? Didn't he think Norman treated them terribly and had no remorse? Kelly didn't understand why Deke wasn't upset by this.

In a staff meeting in the office boardroom a couple of weeks later, Kelly was equally shocked by Deke's offensive behavior. Deke turned to Fatima, one of their best staffers, and yelled at her, "I can't believe you just said that. You are so incompetent. What a stupid conclusion!"

Kelly had never witnessed such an inappropriate outburst from Deke before. Being so taken aback, she said nothing. After the meeting, Kelly approached Deke and said, "Deke, you hurt Fatima's feelings. Do you think you might apologize to her?"

Deke just glared at her and changed the subject. Kelly later apologized to all the staff and indicated she did not know what had triggered Deke's eruption.

"Fatima, I am so sorry Deke spoke to you in such a derogatory manner," Kelly said.

"You do excellent work. I am really happy you are part of our team."
"Thank you, Kelly. Deke was harsh."

The next day, Deke and Kelly were having an evening meeting with their insurance agent at their home to review their coverage, something they hadn't done since Darcy was three years old.

"Deke, I recommend you take out life insurance on Kelly for the family business," the agent stated. "Kelly is so valuable to the business. This will protect you and Darcy should anything happen."

"No, I don't think so," Deke replied. "No one is irreplaceable. Everyone can be replaced."

The insurance agent was astonished by Deke's declaration. Kelly tried not to show how upset she was at Deke's remarks. It was like being told by your husband in public that you don't matter enough to be insured and are replaceable like toilet paper. She was stunned and hurt.

Instead of apologizing to Kelly, Deke continued the meeting as if nothing out of the ordinary had happened. Kelly did not participate in the rest. The end result was Deke and Kelly did not make any changes to their insurance coverage.

A few weeks later, Kelly and Deke were at a client meeting together with one of their excellent junior staff members, and Deke introduced her to their clients. "This is Karen. She has been with us for four years. She does an excellent job. She is irreplaceable."

Then that evening, Deke mentioned Karen's irreplaceability to Kelly twice, saying, "Sweetie, we are lucky to have Karen. She is irreplaceable." Sweetie was a pet name Deke rarely used. These two uses were doused with fake affection, which burned a hole in Kelly's heart.

Karen was someone Kelly had trained over the years. Deke was not a big fan of Karen's during her early days at the family business. During Karen's first two years, Kelly had spent a lot of time training her. Deke would say repeatedly to Kelly, "Karen is a low performer. I want to fire her."

And Kelly would respond, "Deke, she is making great progress. She is on a steep learning curve, just being out of school and in a different field. She is very smart. Give her a chance."

Now in a stunning turn of events, according to Deke, it was Karen, and not Kelly, who was irreplaceable.

Kelly mulled over Deke's recent behavior—the Norman Natas incident, the outburst at Fatima, and now this. What's gotten into Deke? His behavior had regressed since Darcy had left home. The worst part is he knew he had stuck a knife in Kelly's chest. And he seemed to have enjoyed it.

CHAPTER 16

Adjusting to the Empty Nest

Kelly continued to cope with life as an empty nester. She spent more time developing the company. She had grown the family business by 10% each year since Darcy had left home. There were more projects to look after and more staff to manage. There were government cutbacks to address regarding her hospital's annual budget and 3-year plan. She rarely relaxed except on her walks with Joshua which provided her an escape from Deke's seductions and criticisms and her hectic life.

One cool, breezy Saturday afternoon in November in Darcy's senior year at college, Darcy, Joshua, and Kelly were out together for a stroll in the neighborhood.

Darcy revealed, "Mom, I've outgrown res. It's too noisy, too many late-night parties. I need quiet to study and sleep. I don't go to the res parties anymore. And I really want to be able to cook in my own kitchen, instead of reheating prepared food in a communal microwave. I want to live on my own. I think I need my own space.

For the past few weeks, I've been searching for a place near my classes. Will you come with me to look at my top three picks?"

"Sure. I'd be happy to. Moving into an apartment instead of back home is a good idea. I would like you to be able to live on your own, manage your pain, and be independent. After you finish your master's next year, I know you want to pursue Ph.D. in neuroscience out of town."

"Can you come with me on Thursday afternoon?"

"Yes, I think so. I'll need to make sure I can get away from the office without drawing any attention."

"Dad's not going to be happy about this. He wants me to move back home if I can't afford to pay all my expenses."

"I'll continue to help cover your shortfall. I want you to be able to manage your physical limitations in your own space. Your financial independence will come."

On the late-night constitutional that evening with just her and Joshua, Kelly reviewed her situation. She recognized that her subsidizing Darcy more was going to further strain her finances. She looked at Joshua as if to ask his opinion on what she had been thinking. He stopped sniffing for a moment, and with his eyes, told Kelly she was on the right track.

With that confirmation, Kelly decided her financial strain would be worth it. Darcy needed to learn how to fend for herself while managing her pain, which would not be easy.

When Darcy starts to cook her own meals, it will be some getting used to for her. All that standing or figuring out how to prepare her vegetables and her ingredients for baking while sitting, and for how long, before she has to move around. Then the cleaning up afterward. It will be a challenge for her to figure it out, but a good one. All the more reason for her to have her own place and develop her own strategies. Deke won't be supportive at all, Kelly concluded, but since he won't be paying, he would grumble at Kelly, his seething would grow, but Kelly would cope for Darcy's sake.

Kelly said to Joshua, "Together, we'll be able to manage with Deke, don't you think?"

Joshua blinked back with reassurance.

At the dinner table the next night, Deke fidgeted in his chair and scowled as Kelly served each course. Darcy glanced at Kelly but said nothing. Kelly looked at Joshua and felt his strength engulf her.

When Kelly brought the fresh apple pie she had baked for dessert, Deke declared, "Your daughter tells me she wants to live on her own and not on campus and you think this is a good idea. Since her scholarship and lab work won't cover all her expenses, she'd be better off coming back home. But you are paying the difference, she says, so that's that."

Deke quickly changed the subject and began a discussion with Darcy about the latest in mobile phone technology. Kelly was mildly interested but did not participate in the conversation, preferring instead to focus on eating her apple pie slice, and smiling at Joshua intermittently under the table.

Both Deke and Darcy enjoyed their technology talk. And they also talked about music. But there was underlying tension Kelly picked up on, especially now that Darcy was moving to an apartment against Deke's wishes to save money and have her live at home.

Darcy moved into her new digs just before the start of her winter term. Her boyfriend James and some of his friends helped her with the move. After Darcy moved to her new place, Kelly bemoaned that Darcy spent fewer weekends at home. Darcy still went out to dinner with them on Friday nights, but she usually went back to her apartment after the meal, instead of going home over the weekend. With the opportunity to cook, Darcy e-mailed Kelly about her cooking adventures.

In her first e-mail about her cooking, she wrote, "Mom, I am so excited! I understand now why you really love cooking. Here are some photos of the ginger beef I made last night. I marinated the beef overnight and then did a stir fry. Do you like the arugula garnish? I also made some garlic broccoli with porcini mushrooms and steamed rice on the side."

"Looks delicious!" Kelly wrote back. "Please send me the recipe."

When Kelly went shopping for groceries, she picked up some for Darcy as well. Delivering food to Darcy was a practice Kelly had initiated when Darcy was in residence. During that time, Kelly brought fresh fruit and vegetables as well as easy to microwave prepared food to Darcy's dorm to fill her tiny dorm refrigerator. Now that Darcy had her own place with a kitchen and table, Darcy invited Kelly to join her for a coffee and a snack whenever Kelly made the food deliveries. Joshua couldn't join them. He stayed in the car, as he did on the deliveries to Darcy's res. Dogs were not permitted in Darcy's res or apartment building.

Kelly relished these chats with Darcy but knew she could not stay that long, as she did not want to attract Deke's attention to her time away. When she was ready to go shopping, Kelly would say, "Deke, I'm going shopping for food and taking Joshua with me. Anything special you want me to pick up for you?"

And Deke would reply, "No."

Deke had not complained to Kelly about the food deliveries to Darcy when she lived in residence. But Kelly knew he would not approve of her buying food for Darcy now, since he wanted her living at home. She also thought he would be jealous about the extra time she was spending with Darcy and not with him. Kelly decided not to tell Deke about the stopover between the store and home.

Although Kelly had one eye on the clock while she was at Darcy's, she occasionally stayed too long, getting engaged in the conversation. In those instances, Deke grilled her when she got home. The first time Kelly got the third degree, she was unprepared.

"What took you so long, Kelly? You've been gone an hour-and-a-half."

"I got carried away with testing some of the free antipastos at the food displays and then there was more traffic than usual."

After returning the following week from another delivery to Darcy's, Deke asked, "Kelly, why are you late? Everything okay?"

"Everything's fine. I met Wendy at the grocery store. We had a good chat. Since Antonio's was out of chestnut honey, I went to the Specialty Shop on Deacon Road to buy some."

After that second interrogation, Kelly hurried through her shopping list at the grocery store and then to the parking lot to get her car. Once at Darcy's, she watched the time more carefully and tried harder not to be late. She prepared a plausible story for each subsequent delivery, just in case. It turned out she needed one as Deke interrogated her about each prolonged shopping trip.

With the growing strain on her finances from covering Darcy's shortfall on rent and food, Kelly asked Deke to make a larger contribution to their household expenses. When Darcy was attending Egan, Deke had paid for her tuition and Kelly had covered household expenses. At the time, Kelly had thought this was reasonably equitable. With Darcy in college, Deke did not pay tuition since it was covered by Darcy's scholarship, but Kelly still paid for all the household expenses, both Darcy's and theirs. When Kelly was forced to use her personal line of credit to cover Darcy's shortfall from the apartment expenses, she no longer considered the financial arrangement with Deke equitable.

"Deke, I need more money from you to cover household expenses, Joshua's bills, and all of our other expenses. Please give me a raise or just some extra money each month."

Deke looked up from his computer and harrumphed but said nothing. Then he resumed whatever he was doing on the computer.

After a few more tries yielding a similar response from Deke, Kelly became more frustrated and a little angry. But she did her best, she thought, to hide it. She knew the family business could afford to pay her a raise. She didn't understand why Deke was being so difficult about it. After all, it was their living expenses, too. She knew she was bringing in lots of new work and the family business was thriving.

She considered using their joint line of credit but realized Deke would object since he used that for the business. Kelly did not believe using their joint line of credit for that purpose was appropriate, but it was one less thing not to argue with Deke about and incur his ire. She was afraid to move the money from their joint line of credit and she was not sure why.

As Kelly's financial situation worsened over the winter, she became more inquisitive about the company's finances. She asked Deke, "Where did that large profit go from last year from the Robotics

International project that I brought in? I'm sure the project netted a profit of a half-million dollars or so. What happened to it?"

Deke snorted and ignored her each time despite several repetitions of the question.

"Deke, I'd like to see the company books," Kelly insisted to Deke, but he continued to ignore her financial queries and changed the subject.

Despite Kelly's frequent repetition of each question at different intervals over a period of weeks, Deke continued to ignore her questions. He was trying to wear her down, hoping she would forget. She didn't forget, but she did give up. She grew to believe he would never share the specifics of the company's financial situation nor show her the books.

Not only was Deke thwarting her efforts to assess the company finances, but he also was preventing her advancement in the corporate world. Kelly was becoming increasingly discouraged and resentful.

Kelly had met an old colleague at Darcy's high school graduation, whose job was to find women to serve on boards of directors.

"Kelly, are you interested in serving on a private board of directors? I know you have chaired a few not-for-profit boards, so you are an ideal candidate."

"Yes, Shirley, that would be great, maybe in a couple of years. Please keep me on the list."

Shirley must have kept Kelly on the list, as she had just called to ask her about being on two boards.

Shirley advised, "Kelly, in order to serve on these boards, it would be easier to get you elected if you had the title of 'President' or 'CEO' instead of 'Vice President'. Could you make that change?"

Kelly replied, "Well, I am the de facto president. I'll ask Deke and get back to you."

"Deke, Shirley called me today out of the blue, haven't spoken to her since Darcy's high school graduation. She said there is an opportunity for me to serve on the board of directors of Cantor's Cement and Regional Brewers. But there is one caveat. I need to change my title to 'president'. How about I be president and you be CEO? You always told me that our titles in the company didn't matter, so what do you say?"

"We'll see," he replied.

Based on her experience with Deke, she knew "we'll see" meant "no." She would lose those opportunities.

With more time to focus on her relationship with Deke now that Darcy spent less time at home, Kelly's resentment grew. She noticed more keenly Deke was routinely criticizing her, and this was starting to get under her skin. For years, she had reasoned his criticism was helpful, thinking Deke's criticisms made her a better person. Since she was always trying to improve herself, she had considered this feedback helpful. Rather than finding his comments helpful now, she considered them a little mean.

On a long walk in Lawrence Park with Joshua in mid-March, Kelly recalled some noteworthy conversations with Deke as she and Joshua enjoyed the brisk winter breeze and the powder snow on the walking trail as the light snowfall continued.

"Kelly, the house is a mess," Deke had said.

Instead of replying to Deke, Kelly put the lasagna in the oven, tidied up the house, dusted, and vacuumed. Deke did nothing.

She recalled that before Darcy was born, she used to do a lot of entertaining with family and guests, cooking gourmet meals. She thought Deke had enjoyed those occasions. But as Darcy got older, she noticed Deke's palette seemed to change. Feeling Deke's displeasure, she entertained less and less until it was a rare event.

Now if she cooked something that was a little different from a typical Italian or Irish meal, Deke would say, "Kelly, I don't like this dinner. Stop experimenting on me."

When she would ask Deke for help, he always made her feel incompetent, like she should know what to do and not bother him. This was especially an issue with technology or software, where she was the least interested and the most in need.

"Kelly, c'mon. Of course, you can figure out this computer program. You didn't even try," Deke would chide her.

"Deke, I have been struggling with it for a few hours now. It would be great if you could help me. It won't take you long and it will save me time and frustration."

If Deke chose to help her, he sneered and harrumphed before he did. Kelly would take some deep breaths, bear the scorn, and swallow his derision because she needed the help.

Over the years, Kelly had tried to avoid thinking about how little work Deke did at the office. Instead, she had focused on making the company a success. At some point, Kelly did notice Deke lost interest in the business. He did not seek out new opportunities and relied on Kelly to bring in the new work. Instead of challenging Deke, Kelly worked harder and did her best to accomplish Deke's goals. Kelly worked evenings while Deke watched TV or read. It was the family business, after all, she thought. She wanted Deke to be happy and to make sure there was enough food on the table.

Now as she and Joshua walked along the powdered trails, she began to reconsider. She asked Joshua, "Why is Deke always criticizing me? Why is he never satisfied with how hard I work or the work I bring in?"

Joshua turned his head to the side as if he were deep in thought, trying to understand Kelly's situation and how he could help.

Kelly felt she was being listened to and this felt good. She continued, "I don't understand why Deke bellyaches when I spend less time with him and complains about revenues in the next breath. He can't have it both ways. Does he expect the work will magically get done?"

Kelly looked at Joshua again. He blinked at her and then began to sniff a pile of snow mixed with leaves and small tree branches. At that moment, Kelly realized her thoughts were making her angry and overwhelming her. So instead, she concentrated on the snow pile, being present and enjoying the rest of the walk with Joshua.

Her mood soon improved as she watched Joshua make a snow angel. Then they did a little run together through the woods before returning home. Kelly wanted to make the walk as fun as possible for Joshua and her as she knew she had to leave town the next day to go on a business trip to Cleveland for two days with Tony, a prodigy of Deke's, to make a presentation to an important client.

Once Kelly and Tony arrived in Cleveland and got settled in their hotel, they went out to dinner at a nearby popular Italian restaurant to prepare for the full day meeting with the client the next day.

Just before dessert, Tony, who had worked hard with Kelly on the Robotics International project, asked Kelly, "What does Deke do at the office? He doesn't seem to do anything."

Kelly paused, struggling to determine how to answer the question. "Well, he sets company direction and manages the business finances and personnel issues."

At that moment, Kelly grasped what Tony had meant. In such a small company with an outside accountant, full-time bookkeeper, and office manager-human resources person, Deke's tasks didn't even fill a full-time executive position.

To herself, she wondered, *I can see that a lot of what Deke does is not apparent. He is very strategic and does a very good job finding talent.* Then she stopped, realizing Tony was right. What Deke did to contribute was hard to discern.

For the most part, Kelly thought she had hidden her growing malaise about her life from Tony, her other work colleagues, as well as Deke and Darcy. But it did surface a little that spring on a walk together with her, Darcy, and Joshua in the neighborhood.

Kelly revealed, "I don't know what's going on with the business books. Your dad won't let me see them. We made a lot of money from that big project with Robotics International last year, but I don't know what happened to it. I had a chance to be on some company boards of directors, but your dad was not supportive. I work so hard and he doesn't appreciate it. He just complains about my efforts, but he doesn't do much work himself."

"Mom, why don't you see a therapist and talk about it? It will help, just like talking to Dr. Farina helps me through my relationship with James."

"Yes, good idea, Darcy. But your dad will not like it at all. He will be very angry."

A week later, when Darcy was back at home, Kelly and she went on an afternoon stroll in the neighborhood with Joshua. On the return home from the walk, Darcy declared, "Mom, I want you to be happy. Don't worry about me. I'll be fine. Do what is best for you."

Within the context of the conversation, it meant, "Leave Dad, if that is going to make you happy."

Kelly found Darcy's remarks reassuring. She was glad Darcy was so supportive, but she also got the message Darcy did not want to hear about whatever was going on between her parents. In any event, Kelly wanted Darcy to focus on college life and not her life. She did not mention to Darcy again her situation with Deke.

Kelly continued to spend as much time as she could alone with Joshua, walking and playing, mostly in Lawrence Park. Being with Joshua was her sanctuary in the neighborhood and in the woods.

CHAPTER 17

Trip to Italy

Deke was looking forward to resuming their regular family trip to Italy, which was coming up in early June. When Deke and Kelly were in their thirties and early forties, they traveled extensively with Darcy, and occasionally went on romantic adventures with just the two of them. Kelly was hoping to have a good time on this trip, but the pressure would be on to have great sex with Deke or he would be disappointed, annoyed, and likely angry.

Kelly and Deke had been unable to go to Italy since Darcy had started college due to inconvenient work deadlines. Now, three years later, the trip to Italy was finally happening. Darcy, having just completed her junior year in college, was working at the college doing neuroscience lab work for the summer, so it would be just Deke and Kelly traveling that June. Joshua, now six years old, had by this time spent several weeks of his life with Bailey, when Deke and Kelly went on holiday without him. Kelly never liked to leave Joshua but felt he was in good hands with Liz and Ben.

"Kelly, is everything organized at home for Italy? My cousins are expecting us. I booked our flight, trains, and hotel."

"Yes, Deke, we're all set. Joshua will stay with Liz, Ben, and Bailey. I've alerted our clients. Staff will be ready to take over before we leave. I'm looking forward to spending time in Sorrento and Naples and then relaxing on Rabbit Beach for a few days."

Kelly and Deke liked to stay at a luxury hotel in Sorrento, overlooking the Mediterranean. Kelly had fond memories of watching the sunset over the water from their balcony, sipping a fine, red Italian wine. The hotel was a five-minute walk from the city center, so they could walk to most places of interest. Kelly knew she would be a bit jet-lagged, as she did not sleep much on plane trips, but that it would pass quickly.

Deke slept on the plane on this trip for a good part of the time when he wasn't reading or watching a movie, while Kelly read, watched some lame movies, and listened to Mozart between her short-lived dozing. After deplaning, they went through customs expeditiously, picked up their baggage, and took a cab to their hotel. Deke fell asleep as soon as his head hit the hotel pillow. Once he was asleep, Kelly fell asleep shortly thereafter.

During their first full day in Sorrento, Kelly and Deke visited their favorite museums in town, one that specialized in ceramics and another in fine inlaid furniture. They had breakfast at their hotel, took sandwiches the hotel had packed for them for lunch, and headed to the museums.

Kelly loved to visit the street market. Shopping there was an adventure she savored on each trip to Sorrento. After strolling through the museums, they went to the market and spent over an hour investigating the foods and wonderful smells. Kelly noticed Deke smirking at her as she inspected jam jars for the brand of jam she preferred. She grinned back at him as she walked over to the cashier to pay for 6 large jars of lemon jam spiked with limoncello.

After the promenade through the market, Kelly and Deke dined at a restaurant on the Corso Italia. Kelly had fresh lobster, while Deke had gnocchi alla Sorrentina, his favorite. They chatted about the food and how delicious it was. Deke had limoncello sorbet for dessert with his coffee, but Kelly was too full for dessert. They both were quite satiated and relaxed by the time dinner was done.

Back at the hotel after dinner, they had a long romantic night, which Kelly enjoyed and thought Deke was pleased as well since he had said so verbally and in other typical ways for him.

For their second day, Deke had planned that he and Kelly would take the train to Naples to visit his eldest cousin and his family, stay at his cousin's overnight, and return to Sorrento the following day. Once they were on the train, Kelly daydreamed as she sat in her seat, thinking about her upcoming stay at Rabbit Beach. She loved to swim, but she was also looking forward to resting and reading on the beach. Her mind wandered to Joshua and holding onto his haunches back to shore, which brought a smile to her face.

She overheard some children talking about their upcoming week-long venture at their usual summer camp. For a moment, she felt very uneasy but didn't know why. She pushed that out of her mind and thought about swimming with Darcy and Joshua. This made her forget about the anxious thought. Every so often, she brought herself back to the present away from swimming with Joshua and Darcy, opening her eyes to glance at Deke, and saw he was spending his time doing something on his computer.

Kelly delighted in the visit with Deke's family, catching up on family gossip and getting to know some of her nieces and nephews again. She especially enjoyed eating the fresh, homecooked, Italian seafood Deke's cousin had perfectly steamed. Deke and Kelly left Deke's cousin late the next day and ended up arriving at the train station during the afternoon rush hour. The train was overcrowded. They were packed in like sardines. Kelly had nothing to grip for stability, so she hung onto Deke's arm to avoid falling.

When they got off at their stop in Sorrento, Kelly reached for her purse. "Oh, my Lord! Deke, my purse is gone."

Deke said, "I'll find the nearest police station and report it."

Outside the train station, Deke spotted a police officer. In his best Italian, he recounted the story. Kelly listened as the officer gave Deke directions to the police station, a few blocks away.

"Deke, I had about two hundred dollars in my wallet, all my credit cards, my driver's license. I need to call to cancel the cards right away."

"Report the theft first. Then sort out the rest."

When they arrived at the police station, they entered through the big glass doors and stood in line. When their turn came, the officer asked what the matter was. Still in his best Italian, Deke explained what had happened.

The officer told him, "This happens on occasion. Your wife may get her purse back, but she will not get her money or credit cards returned. You may have to wait a few days."

Kelly and Deke filled out the paperwork together and departed for dinner. At dinner, to Kelly's surprise, Deke did not reprimand her for losing her purse, for not hanging onto it securely enough. Instead, he sat patiently and ate his dinner calmly as Kelly reported her stolen cards.

"Do you think my purse will be returned?" Kelly asked Deke.

"I don't know. The officer said it was possible. How is your dinner?"

"It's delicious—the fish is perfectly prepared, and the vegetables are al dente the way I like them. How is your ravioli?"

"Very good. I'm going to have some dessert, too."

Dinner conversation was light and focused on the family gossip Deke's cousins had shared. On the walk back to the hotel, Deke and Kelly talked about what they wanted to do the next day, which was to be their last before going to Sicily to relax on Rabbit Beach for a few days before going home. By the time they were in the elevator on their way to their room, Kelly thought they were content but tired.

Kelly had only bits and pieces of memories of what happened next. She didn't have any recollection about entering their hotel room or how she ended up on their bed. Once on the bed, she noticed the orange-red bedspread, which was mottled and felt rough to her skin. Deke had somehow pinned her on the bed. He was on top of her, but she couldn't see his face. He pressed his full weight against her chest and abdomen so she couldn't move. His right hand wrapped around the front of her throat. No one had ever forcibly pinned her down like that before. No hand had ever wrapped around her throat. No one had ever made her so helpless.

She was laser-focused on the hand on her throat. She stayed as still as she possibly could. Her whole body stiffened. She dared not move a muscle in case the movement led to a tightening of Deke's grip. She had no idea how long Deke's hand was around her throat, but she did remember the great relief she felt when he removed his hand after he was done. She could feel herself starting to breathe again as her terror began to subside.

She said nothing about the incident to Deke, and he said nothing about it to her. They both behaved as if nothing out of the ordinary had happened.

Kelly woke up the next morning beside Deke, as usual. The phone rang soon after. Deke picked up the phone from his bedside table and answered it. Kelly overheard what the police officer told Deke, "Mr. Delmonico, we think your wife's purse has been returned, but it is empty. Please come today to pick it up."

After an ordinary breakfast at the hotel with a conversation regarding the plans for the day, Deke and Kelly walked to the police station. After standing for a few minutes in the short line, Kelly retrieved her purse from the police officer at the desk and signed the release form. Then Kelly and Deke left the station, went back to the hotel, and packed up to go to Sicily a little earlier than originally planned.

Kelly didn't remember much else about this Italy trip, except fragments of dinners and short walks alone on Rabbit Beach, as she watched the waves crash against the shore. She didn't tell a soul about the hand on her throat or what had happened while it was there. It was buried in a lockbox in her mind. She had tossed the key in a dark corner of her purse.

Once back in Buffington, Kelly resumed her busy routine, looking after the family business and her family. When asked by staff and friends about her holiday, she recounted what a lovely time she and Deke had enjoyed in Italy.

CHAPTER 18

Last Family Cottage Trip

The last time Kelly, Deke, Darcy, and Joshua all went to the cottage together was the following summer. Joshua was then eight years old. Darcy had just completed her undergraduate studies and was starting her master's classes in the fall at the same college. Deke had taken the initiative to invite some friends and their children to spend the two-week cottage time with them. They had been their cottage guests before.

Saturday mid-afternoon, one week before this cottage trip, Deke and Kelly were sitting at their dining room table together in their usual seats, having a snack. Kelly was drinking some sparkling water with lemon and Deke was nursing a cola. Joshua was under the table near Kelly, dozing.

Deke had spent the morning and a good part of the early afternoon criticizing Kelly. He began with, "Kelly, the house is a disaster. Did you see the hall carpet? It's filthy."

Kelly cleaned the carpet with carpet cleaner and vacuumed, while Joshua looked on from a corner of the hall. Deke rested on the living room couch, listened to music, and read the newspaper.

After lunch, he went on, "Make sure your daughter doesn't pack too much stuff for the cottage. Can't you deal with that? I don't want any stress."

During their mid-afternoon snack, Deke continued his criticism. "We need more contracts. Revenues are down. I don't want to do the work you bring in. It's boring."

Kelly was rattled by these remarks. She reviewed the situation as she sipped her water. Deke had not brought in any new work in over two years. Staff found the work exciting. Deke would enjoy this work if he only would give it a chance. Kelly said to herself, *I am fed up. He is so lazy, especially since he criticizes me for the work I do and the time I spend.*

"Deke, I can't take it anymore," Kelly confided while dipping her left hand into her mostly full glass of water and scooping some water from her left hand at her face. She had never done anything like that before and was stunned by her own actions.

Before she had a chance to analyze them, Deke got up from his chair, smoldering. Kelly was alarmed by the rage creeping across his face and puffing out his chest. Silently, he stood up, grabbed her right arm firmly, pulled her out of her chair, and dragged her through the dining room doorway and into the middle of the kitchen, a distance of about ten feet. To avoid being hurt, Kelly moved her feet along with him. She was shocked by this new and aggressive behavior of Deke. She was frightened. Still holding her arm tightly, Deke yelled at her, "You are behaving like a two-year-old. I don't want to see you. I'm going out."

As Deke released her arm, Kelly noticed Joshua was standing alertly beside her. Joshua stared at Deke until he left the kitchen. Kelly and Joshua stood together and didn't move until they heard the front door slam shut. Once Deke had departed, Joshua followed Kelly upstairs to her home office. Kelly sat at her desk and logged into her computer. Joshua lay down under her desk.

After a time, Kelly decided to check her e-mail. She opened one from Deke at the same time as she realized Darcy was standing beside her. They both read the e-mail.

"I want a divorce. I am going to leave town. You will be much better off without me."

Unprepared for the e-mail, Kelly was horrified by the contents and that Darcy was reading it as well. After seeing the e-mail, Darcy abruptly left and went downstairs.

Kelly needed to talk to Darcy right away about the e-mail. She could not let it fester, so Kelly went downstairs to join her. When she and Joshua arrived near where Darcy was standing in the basement, Darcy was in her boyfriend James' arms with her head on his shoulder. Kelly could tell from the flood of tears pouring down Darcy's face that Darcy was devastated after having read the e-mail.

Over the years, Darcy had often remarked to Kelly and Deke, "Unlike my friends, I like spending time with my parents. We are a threesome."

"Darcy, I am so sorry you read the e-mail," Kelly said. "I should not have opened it when you were there."

Kelly recognized her timing was off. It was clear Darcy did not want to speak to her about what had happened, at least not at that moment.

Kelly left and went back to her computer, with Joshua following her back upstairs.

Kelly was so concerned about Darcy that the dragging incident with Deke had slipped her mind. She did not tell Darcy about the incident or seek her and James' assistance.

After working at her desk for a while, Kelly heard music coming from the living room. She went downstairs with Joshua to speak to Deke, who was sitting in the black leather wing chair adjusting the stereo controls. The wing chair faced the black leather couch and was adjacent to the stereo bench. She quietly walked into the living room and approached the wing chair, standing about three feet away from it. Joshua was standing beside her.

"Deke, I think we should try to work things out. Let's go to couples' therapy."

"I'll think about it."

She left Deke in the living room. Joshua and she went back upstairs to her home office where Joshua lay on the floor beside her as she sat at her desk and did some work.

Before dinner that night, Darcy and James departed to go off on their own. Kelly and Deke had dinner but barely spoke except for small talk.

"Deke, please pass the butter." Then later, Kelly added, "Let's have dessert on the deck."

After dinner, Kelly spent the evening at her computer, avoiding Deke. Joshua lay on the floor beside her. They went out for their usual evening constitutional, walking through the pocket park and then around the block. It was a calm, warm night and the sky was clear, so Kelly marveled at the stars.

"Joshua, isn't it a beautiful night? Not a cloud in the sky. Look at all those sparkling lights."

Joshua looked at her as if to say, "Yes, enjoy the tranquility of the night. You deserve it. I love you. I will stand by you."

After their walk, Joshua and Kelly returned to Kelly's office. When Deke fell asleep in front of the television in the den, Joshua and she joined him. Kelly changed the channel and watched one of her favorite dramas. When she rose from her chair to get ready for bed, Deke woke up, and they got ready for bed. Joshua jumped onto the bed and lay parallel between Deke and Kelly, with his head at their feet, facing the open door. Kelly patted Joshua's head, relaxed, and went to sleep.

The next day, Kelly, Joshua, and Deke went to work at the family business office as usual, but Deke and Kelly hardly spoke. Kelly was too numb to say anything, still feeling Deke's anger. She didn't know whether their marriage was over, or they were going to couples' therapy.

Darcy telephoned Kelly every night. "Mom, did Dad say anything? Are we going to the cottage on Saturday?"

"I don't know, Darcy. Your dad hasn't said a word about it."

"I'll sleepover on Friday night just in case. That way, we can all leave for the cottage together on Saturday morning."

On Saturday morning, when Darcy woke up, she asked, "Mom, are we going to the cottage?"

"I'm not sure. Your dad still hasn't said anything about it. Let's finish packing and take our stuff downstairs anyway."

Close to the typical cottage departure time, Deke picked up two suitcases Kelly and Darcy had brought to the front hall and took them out the door. Kelly and Darcy glanced at each other. Then they each picked up some stuff to carry out to the car.

The trip to the cottage in the car was quiet. Kelly and Deke listened to music on the radio, while Darcy listened to her own music with her headphones. Joshua slept stretched out in the back seat with Darcy, with his head on her lap. Kelly hoped there wouldn't be any traffic, so Deke would be less grumpy upon arrival at the cottage.

They arrived at the cottage in good time. By the time Kelly had unpacked, Meg and Morgan and their two children, Lamar and Livia, had arrived. Deke, Darcy, and Kelly greeted them and then Deke showed them to their rooms to unpack.

On this trip to the cottage, Kelly did not want to sleep beside Deke. She did not want to have sex with him. She did not even want to be in the same room as he was. But after reviewing her predicament, she concluded there was no place for her to go. All the bedrooms were taken. She didn't want to embarrass Deke by sleeping in Darcy's room on the spare bed. Feeling trapped, she did not know how she was going to survive the two weeks. She decided she would put all their strife aside and make the best of the bad situation.

During the day, they all swam, rested in the shade or sun, and went boating. Deke and Morgan took turns barbecuing the meals, while Kelly, Meg, Darcy, and the two children helped with food preparation, set the table, and cleaned up. Most days, Kelly baked an apple crumble or berry pie from berries the children had picked around the cottage grounds. Joshua stayed close to Kelly throughout the day, being especially alert beside Kelly for any food scraps that might fall his way.

In the evenings, they all relaxed. Lamar and Livia played their guitars, while Darcy joined in with her violin. Darcy, Lamar, and Livia also played board games and cards. Deke enjoyed late-night chats with Morgan, sipping lager, munching on corn chips and salsa, and discussing world affairs, which Kelly avoided, trying not to overhear. She was not interested in getting into any debates with Deke. Instead, she and Meg chatted over coffee about their children and families, while Joshua lay close to Kelly, chewing on a braided chew or a beef bone before snoozing, going out with Kelly for his constitutional and then bed.

The first few evenings, Kelly and Deke were exhausted and speedily went to sleep. When Kelly's attempts at avoiding sex failed after that, she took a few deep breaths before each encounter and tried to be in the present, worried she would anger Deke if she displayed any angst. For the first time, she realized she was very afraid of Deke.

One afternoon at the end of the first week of their stay, Darcy joined Kelly and Joshua on the back lawn overlooking Loon Lake.

"Mom, Dad is being mean to me. He is insulting me. I don't want to stay. I want to go back to Buffington."

"I understand, Darcy. If you want to go, I will make the arrangements for transportation so you can go back tomorrow. But before you go, I think you should try to make peace with your dad. If you tell him firmly but with no negative emotion that he has hurt your feelings, you and he may be able to reconcile. Be careful not to criticize him. Focus on how you feel. Why don't you give it a try?"

"Okay, Mom. I'll try." Darcy went back into the cottage.

Instead of accompanying Darcy, Kelly chose to go for a walk with Joshua along the road. She did not want to absorb any ire from Deke, preferring instead to walk and play with Joshua. After five retrieves, Joshua tired of the play and so they went on their usual walk along the road. Kelly could tell Joshua knew she was upset by the conversation with Darcy, so he was on his best behavior as they walked. When Kelly and Joshua returned from their walk, Darcy joined them outside by the rock garden.

"Dad and I are okay. I'll stay. Thanks, Mom." Darcy and Kelly hugged.

"I'm glad you're going to stay," Kelly said as she gently caressed Darcy's right shoulder. Then the three of them went back into the cottage.

The rest of the cottage stay passed uneventfully for Kelly with the daily routines she had created. She and Deke barely spoke to each other. Kelly had no idea what to say. Deke was not interested in speaking with her, which to her was a great relief.

Kelly spent her time with the group as much as possible and on walks with Joshua, engulfing herself in the solitude and distraction of their time together.

Before leaving, Meg and Morgan thanked Deke and Kelly sincerely for a terrific time. After their guests left, Deke, Darcy, and Kelly packed up the car. On the way home, Joshua lay on Darcy's lap in the back seat and slept, while Darcy listened to her own music with her headphones and napped. Kelly and Deke listened to jazz on the radio in the front seat. They were all quiet in the car. Deke dropped Darcy off at her apartment and he, Kelly, and Joshua went home.

CHAPTER 19

Emotional Bonds

After Deke, Kelly, and Joshua arrived home from the cottage, Kelly unpacked and took Joshua for a leisurely afternoon walk in Lawrence Park. They took a turn through the woods and returned by the main trail. Kelly made some short stops along the way to admire the scenery, while Joshua explored the smells of the oak trunks and retrieved some sticks Kelly threw for him.

Kelly remarked, "Joshua, are you glad to be home? Me, too, but things are so unsettled. I love this park."

Joshua looked lovingly into her eyes with a tacit understanding. Kelly felt better, and they continued with their walk.

When she and Joshua returned home and joined Deke in the living room, he was seated on the couch listening to jazz and playing with his computer. Before Kelly had a chance to sit down, Deke announced, "I have done some research on couples' therapy and therapists. Here's a book on a therapy technique that's a good fit for us. Dr. Lenore Grayson practices this technique and lives nearby."

Kelly read the front and back cover of the book about the therapy technique and flagged to herself a phrase on the back cover, "This technique is based on developing more secure emotional bonds between couples in a safe environment." She thought this sounded good and committed to herself she would read the entire book later.

"Let's try it out, Deke," she responded.

"I'll call Dr. Grayson and make an appointment to start the sessions."

Kelly read the entire book over the next two evenings. Joshua kept her company under her desk and dozed. As she read, she noted that the only contraindication to the couples' therapy technique the author pointed out was if one partner was threatening the other in some way with no safety between them. Kelly concluded the technique was a good fit and it should work out well.

Once a week, Kelly, Deke, and Joshua drove to Dr. Grayson's. During the session, Joshua stayed in the back seat of the car. Once in Dr. Grayson's office, Deke sat on one end of the tan corduroy couch and Kelly sat on the other. Dr. Grayson sat opposite them on an upholstered, light brown armchair.

At the beginning of the first session, Kelly scanned the room and noticed the natural-stained oak side tables on each side of the couch and the square, off-white, linen ceiling fixture between the couch and Dr. Grayson's chair, which illuminated the discussion space. Kelly mused to herself, taking a deep breath, "It will be in this room where we will discuss the heart-wrenching details of our marriage."

The first two sessions with Dr. Grayson were mostly about getting to know her and her process, as well as Kelly trying to be upbeat. Dr. Grayson gave Deke and Kelly homework to write down five positive things that happened during the following week and five positive things about each other. They shared them in the next session.

Once these preliminaries were over, the session intensified.

Dr. Grayson stated, "We are now going to discuss arguments you have had with each other that loop around with no resolution. We'll start with Deke and then Kelly. The purpose of doing this is to help you identify your patterns when you argue, and then how to make a more constructive pattern based on understanding."

Deke began, "Every time Kelly and I get into a heated discussion, Kelly withdraws. She doesn't respond. I ask her over and over again to talk to me. She doesn't answer. This just makes things worse."

Kelly responded, "Deke, arguing with you is difficult. You are so fast on your feet. The details of the debate shift as you challenge me. I can't keep up. As you know, I've learned a pattern of withdrawal, trying to avoid my mother. When I feel threatened, I withdraw."

"You don't want to talk to me. You just don't care."

"Deke, remember all those long conversations we had when we were dating and before Darcy? We talked for hours about sports, especially football, and how we would right the wrongs of the world. We talked about the ACLU and what it meant that we were members. We discussed Lincoln, our favorite president. But after Darcy was born, it became harder and harder to talk to you, especially about the family business and things we disagreed on. I can see this really upsets you. I will try harder. Perhaps, you can be softer toward me when I try."

Deke glared at Kelly and said nothing. Kelly felt some pressure in her gut from his glare, but she did her best to ignore it.

"Kelly, your turn," Dr. Grayson said.

"I am upset I have to work so hard in our family business. Deke doesn't work as hard. He criticizes me for the time I spend on work and doesn't appreciate the work I do. I don't know how to discuss this with him."

Deke replied, "Kelly, you are to blame. I overheard you say you do all the business development and bring in all the work. I decided if that's the way you feel, then go ahead, do all the work!"

Kelly was flabbergasted by Deke's response.

Instead of saying something about Deke's remarks, Dr. Grayson reviewed the principles behind breaking the patterns. Then Dr. Grayson said, "This is a good beginning. See you next week."

In the car on the way to the office listening to jazz on the radio in silence, Kelly had a gnawing in her gut. She felt worse off now than before the session.

For the rest of the day at the office, Kelly avoided Deke. She stayed close to Joshua and took him on their usual walk at lunch and after work before they went home with Deke.

In the next session with Dr. Grayson, Deke cited more examples of Kelly's withdrawal and complained about them. Kelly monopolized the session time by talking about Deke's issues and skirting hers. Her responses to the examples typically went,

"Deke, good point. Yes, you are right. I did withdraw there. I dislike confrontation. Withdrawing was not the right thing to do. It has a negative impact on you and our relationship. I should have responded. I have more clarity now on the problem, so I can address it better. I will work harder on this."

Dr. Grayson did not say anything about Deke's examples or Kelly's responses. Perhaps, she thought there seemed to be more communication between Deke and Kelly. But that's not what was happening. Kelly just withdrew more strategically to minimize her pain.

At the next couples' therapy session, Kelly reported on an exchange between her and Deke that had taken place the day before.

"I went to see Dr. Mahoney in the morning for my annual routine exam. She said my high blood pressure was like a ticking time bomb. I needed to take more steps to make sure it stays under control. All I focused on was the 'ticking time bomb.' My father died suddenly when he was fifty from a heart attack. Deke knows I have issues with my father and my father's death. When I got back from the doctor's, I was so distraught. I went to Deke's office to talk to him about what the doctor had said. I told him how disturbed I was. I was holding back tears. Deke said nothing. I repeated how upset I was. He said nothing. I left his office."

Dr. Grayson queried, "Deke, try to imagine the doctor has said this to you. How do you feel?"

"This is silly. Kelly doesn't have a ticking time bomb. This is an exaggeration. I don't see the point."

"Deke, this is a sensitive issue for Kelly. She is scared. She is thinking about what happened to her dad. Try to comfort her."

"Kelly, you know you are fine. Your doctor didn't mean it."

Dr. Grayson prodded, "Deke, imagine you are Kelly and your doctor has said this to you."

"I did. Don't pay any attention to what your doctor said, Kelly. She exaggerates. What else is there to say? What?"

"Oh my God. Oh my God," Kelly said quietly as she hung her head almost into her lap and covered her eyes with her hands.

Dr. Grayson took out a pencil and a blank sheet of white paper and drew a long, straight, horizontal line across the page, dotting some points along the line. "This is an autism continuum, showing mild to extreme. Deke, you have a blind spot. You are lacking in empathy. You can't see it, but it is there. You might be on the very mild end of the autism continuum. Consider seeking a medical determination. I can provide a referral."

Deke just listened, but his body language said, "You are joking, right? What hooey!"

In the car on the way back to the office, Kelly asked Deke, "What do you think about her drawing?"

"What do you think?"

"I don't know. I'm skeptical."

Deke said nothing. Kelly changed the subject.

Kelly was disturbed by the possibility of Deke's being on this continuum. When she took Joshua out for his lunch break that afternoon at the office, they went to the green space for a walk. Kelly stopped to make a phone call by one of the wooden picnic tables. She couldn't stay still. She and Joshua paced as she pressed the phone keys. During the call, she and Joshua continued to pace back and forth in front of the picnic bench and then beyond it for three or four feet in each direction.

"Hello, Dr. Farina. This is Kelly Delmonico. I am calling to ask for your advice. Deke and I just had a couples' therapy session. Dr. Grayson says Deke lacks empathy. She referred to it as a blind spot.

He may be on the autism continuum. This is upsetting. Do you think Deke is autistic?"

"I don't know. He could be on the autism continuum or he could be on the narcissism personality disorder continuum. In order to make a determination, Deke will have to undergo some medical testing."

"Thank you, Dr. Farina. I appreciate your insight."

What is narcissism personality disorder? Never heard of it. It sounded awful. Kelly had heard of Asperger syndrome. It's on the high-functioning end of the autism continuum. Friends of theirs have an autistic child, but Deke was not like Salvatore at all. Thanks to Dr. Grayson, Kelly could now see Deke has difficulty with empathy. She was determined to see what she could learn about autism online.

Each evening for the next three evenings after Deke and Joshua went to sleep, Kelly got out of bed. When she looked at Joshua, he opened one eye sleepily, and then the other, and watched her leave. Kelly crept up the stairs to her desk and spent the next hour or so on her computer reading about autism. The more she read, the less of a fit she determined Deke to be.

At dinner on the third night, Kelly asked Deke, "Would you be willing to get tested to understand the blind spot better?" He harrumphed and rolled his eyes.

The next couples' therapy session was about sharing injuries from the past the other partner had caused. Kelly decided to bring up the injury regarding Deke's saying she could be replaced.

After Kelly recounted the story, Dr. Grayson said, "Deke, this is an injury to Kelly. Put yourself in her shoes and experience how she is feeling. What would you do differently if you could have a do-over?"

"I don't see why this is a concern. From a business perspective, no one is irreplaceable. This is a practical matter."

Dr. Grayson reiterated, "Deke, consider how your remarks made Kelly feel. Is there anything you would do differently?"

"Again, I don't see the personal issue here. This is a business matter."

Kelly tried not to look shocked and disappointed, so she did not look at Deke, but instead focused on Dr. Grayson.

At the end of the session, Dr. Grayson stated, "Deke, you have a blind spot regarding empathy. I can give you a referral to get it checked out so you will have a better understanding of how to deal with it."

"Deke, it would be helpful if you got tested. I would also like to begin my own psychotherapy to help me deal with your blind spot," Kelly added. "Dr. Grayson, I would like to read some books on the subject. Please recommend some books or a bookstore where I might be able to purchase them."

Kelly's eyes still avoided Deke's. She knew he would be angry, and she did not want to experience the anger directly.

Dr. Grayson wrote down the name of a bookstore where Kelly could buy some technical books. Then Kelly and Deke left Dr. Grayson's office, went back to the car, and drove to the office with Joshua. Kelly made her best efforts to make small talk in the car on the way to the office, avoiding touchy subjects. Neither Deke nor Kelly discussed any part of the therapy with each other until the next session the following week.

At the next session, Kelly raised an injury that had rankled her for most of her life with Deke.

"When I was nineteen, Deke proposed. We had just sat down beside each other at a table at our favorite café near our college campus and ordered espressos. When the waiter left, Deke held both my hands, gazed into my eyes with a little tear in his left eye, and asked, 'Kelly, will you marry me?'"

"Surprised but delighted, I replied, 'Yes, of course, I will marry you.' We kissed and then I continued, with Deke's hands still in mine, 'But not now. We can't afford it.

"Our parents won't agree to us getting married now. They won't help out. How will we live? Let's wait until we can live on our own together.'"

"Deke nodded in agreement. I took this as our pact for the future. We were engaged, but we didn't tell our parents.

"After graduate school and when we both had our first jobs, I said, 'Deke, let's get married. We can afford it. It will be wonderful.'"

"'I don't want to,' Deke said. 'I love you. That should be enough. I don't believe in the marriage institution. We have been living together since graduate school. What is the point of being married? There is no difference.'"

"After Deke's refusal, I asked him again each year for about two years. I got the same response, 'I love you. I don't believe in marriage.' I resigned myself to the prospect of living together indefinitely. I wanted a child, Deke agreed, and I got pregnant about a year later. After the death of our infant son soon after he was born, Deke and I were both devastated. Although I was still grieving, my biological clock was ticking. I would have preferred to have been married before becoming pregnant with Darcy, but my desire for a child was greater than my desire for a church wedding. I got pregnant quickly after

I decided I was ready, and we agreed to try. We were both ecstatic about the pregnancy, I thought.

"Then one evening, soon after while we were watching television in the den, Deke said, 'Let's get married.' I agreed. While I was relieved, the joy in the event was gone. Since then, I haven't really enjoyed celebrating our anniversary. Deke played hard to get to punish me for not marrying him right away when he had asked me. Deke's not wanting to get married is a major injury to me."

"Kelly, I don't remember the café or my asking you to marry me then," Deke responded. "Each time when you did ask me to marry you and I asked you to explain why, I pointed out the weaknesses in your arguments. Your arguments were not convincing. Under the law, it makes no difference. We knew we loved each other. What else really matters? I regret not getting married earlier hurt you. My saying I love you and am staying with you should have been enough."

"Deke, your saying 'I love you and am staying with you' was not enough," Kelly retorted.

Deke became agitated. Kelly could see this was going nowhere. She was just getting reinjured in raising the matter.

In subsequent couples' therapy sessions, they continued to explore Kelly's injuries.

"Deke, I was so hurt when you asked me for a divorce one night just before my mother died. I had just gotten home from a late-night with her. I was so spent. I walked into the den to join you. Before I sat down, you asked for a divorce."

"I don't remember asking you for a divorce."

How could Deke not remember asking me for a divorce? Kelly questioned to herself. *This can't be happening.*

Once at home that night after Deke and Joshua had gone to sleep, Kelly crept upstairs to her office with a renewed zeal to pinpoint Deke's affliction. Based on all the reading on the internet she had done, she was confident Deke was not autistic. She speculated to herself in a half-joking manner—*Was all this caused by one too many concussions on the football field?*

After an off-site business meeting the next day, Kelly went to the bookstore Dr. Grayson had recommended. It was crammed to the ceiling with books stacked on pine shelves. A small walkway separated the rows of shelves. Books on the pine counter near the cash register were piled five high, ready to be filed.

She asked the fellow at the cash register, the only salesperson in the store, "Please tell me where I can find books on personality disorders."

He motioned for her to follow him. "On these three shelves are the most technical books. Across from the cash register, you can find the wider audience books."

After scouring the shelves, Kelly picked out a few books to purchase and went to the cash to pay.

"You have picked excellent texts on personality disorders," the salesperson at the cash register told Kelly.

"See you again." Kelly smiled and exited the store.

That night, once Deke was asleep after they had all gone to bed, she resumed the ritual of sneaking upstairs to read. Joshua watched her get out of bed, but he stayed put. She smiled at him as she left the room. Quietly, she slinked up the stairs to her office, sat in her chair at the computer, and covered her legs with a fleece blanket to keep warm. By three in the morning, she returned to bed. She was exhausted but exhilarated by the quest.

She repeated this journey for three nights in a row. Based on her reading, Deke either suffered from borderline personality disorder or narcissism personality disorder. She was locked onto the intellectual challenge of discovery but did not have enough information to draw a conclusion. She needed more material.

The next week, she returned to the bookstore after a follow-up client meeting. This time, she bought two technical books on each of the two disorders she was still investigating and a broader audience book on each. As she spent late nights in her home office reading these books, she was invigorated by the pursuit. She was not getting much sleep, but it was worth it. She needed to know.

One night, a week later after she had gone to sleep after a long night of reading, Deke woke her up. He was crying loudly, sitting up in bed beside her. As she opened her eyes, she heard Deke say, "I had a nightmare. I am not myself. I am upset and depressed."

When she sat up to comfort him, he turned his back to her and said angrily, "Go to sleep. Go back to sleep." Then he lay down with his back to Kelly. Kelly continued to sit up until she was certain Deke was snoring. She was shaken up by the incident. It took her longer than usual to fall back to sleep.

The next night, Kelly took a break from her reading ritual. Deke and she both fell asleep rapidly, with him falling asleep first. In the middle of the night, Kelly awoke.

Deke was sitting up in bed, sobbing, and saying, "I am a broken man. What I thought was secure isn't. I will do whatever you want."

This time, Deke let Kelly comfort him. She put her arms around him and told him, "We will get through this together." This was one of the rare times in many years she felt close to him, that they had made a real connection.

In the next couples' therapy session, Kelly described the two middle-of-the-night events with Deke.

Deke responded, "I don't remember waking up for the two nights. I remember only one night. I recall being awake but not crying. I remember your touch. It was gentle and loving. This is the first time in a long time I felt that way about it, but I don't remember what you or I said."

Kelly was dumbfounded. She was shocked Deke could not remember what had happened. How was that possible? Was she the only one who has memories of their life together?

Dr. Grayson did not react to Deke's remarks. Kelly did not know what to make of that, either. She felt even worse.

The next night Kelly continued her late-night reading. Deke was not a great match with borderline personality disorder. Refreshed from having taken a few deep breaths, she focused her reading on narcissism personality disorder.

After a few more late nights of reading the books she had bought on narcissism personality disorder, Kelly began to reach some conclusions. Deke was manipulative. He does think highly of himself and poorly of others. And he is critical of her and others. He has a big problem with empathy. If Deke were at the low end of the continuum, his empathy could just be impaired. It could emerge with some coaxing. But despite Dr. Grayson's efforts to do that, there was no success as yet.

Kelly continued her reading. "People suffering from this disorder feel entitled," the author stated, "and exploit others in order to feel special. They can be vindictive." That sounds like Deke, she thought.

"'At the higher end of the continuum," the author continued, "empathy is absent. When a narcissist is not admired enough, he may sculpt his reality to bolster his ego. Facts about the situation are ignored. If a person with narcissism personality disorder morphs along the continuum, the narcissist can become sadistic and engage in gaslighting, meaning the narcissist tries to make a person believe he or she is losing his or her grip on reality or becoming insane. The most deviant narcissists can become killers."

"Oh my!" Kelly said aloud in a barely audible voice, then paused and said to herself, *Based on all of this, Deke is likely on the lower end of the continuum.*

Kelly was pleased her analysis was complete, and she had come to a conclusion on Deke's affliction. She did not consider the implications of what it meant in her life to be married to someone with this affliction. She went back to bed, more relaxed with the success of her quest, and slept well.

Kelly had inadvertently timed her completed assessment of Deke's disorder to the night before Dr. Grayson was to hold a private check-in meeting with Deke and one with her. Dr. Grayson had explained to Kelly that the purpose of each meeting was to discuss how the sessions were going and to find out if she and Deke were still committed to working out their relationship. The individual meetings were scheduled to take place the day before the couples' therapy session. Deke's check-in meeting with Dr. Grayson was in the morning and Kelly's was in the afternoon.

In Kelly's private session, Dr. Grayson stated, "Kelly, I have given this matter some scrutiny. I do not think Deke is on the autism continuum. He likely suffers from narcissism personality disorder. Medical testing is necessary to do a proper diagnosis."

"Dr. Grayson, I have been doing my own reading, and I have come to the same conclusion. I don't know what I am going to do. I don't think I will be able to go on with the marriage."

After her check-in session was over, Kelly greeted Joshua in the back seat with a hug and a smile. "Hello, Joshua. Let's go to the office."

At the office, Kelly behaved like she usually did—it was just another ordinary day—even though she told herself Deke may be a sociopath. When her mind was blank from that thought, she moved on. She wondered what she should cook for dinner and decided on a barbecue.

At couples' therapy the next day, Kelly raised financial issues. Christmas was about a month away, and she was feeling the financial pinch. She wanted Deke to take more responsibility for Darcy's expenses and for their household expenses. Her personal line of credit was maxed out. She wanted to move this debt to their joint line of credit.

Dr. Grayson helped with these matters. At the end of the session, Dr. Grayson summarized the agreement they had reached.

"Deke and Kelly, you have both agreed to consolidate liabilities in a fifty-fifty sharing of expenses. Kelly will consolidate her line of credit debt with your joint line of credit. Deke will reimburse Darcy for medical expenses she pays out and for which the insurance reimburses Deke. Deke, you have agreed to Kelly's going to her own psychotherapy. Good job, both of you. See you next week."

For the first time, Kelly was buoyed by a session. She thought she and Deke had actually made real progress.

CHAPTER 20

The Challenge

That evening after the session with Dr. Grayson, Deke and Kelly went to their favorite burger joint, while Joshua stayed in the back seat of the car. Deke ordered the burgers and fries, while Kelly secured a both and waited for Deke to join her.

After he sat down with the tray of food, and he and Kelly had enjoyed some small talk about the meal, Kelly began a more serious discussion.

"Deke, we are making great strides. I would be so happy if we both worked on the blind spot. We could each go to therapy just for that. We would still continue with Dr. Grayson."

"I'll think about it."

As usual, after a burger outing, Kelly brought Joshua beef, tomato, and bun bits to enjoy. Before leaving for home, she opened the door to the back seat and fed Joshua the food in small bites. She relished watching him eat as much as he enjoyed eating. When he was done, she closed the door and went into the front seat, content with the burger outing. The drive home was routine as was the rest of the evening. There was no more talk about therapy.

Kelly didn't deal with the consolidation of the financial liabilities until the next day. She had a business meeting that took her away from the office, arrived home early, and decided to walk to the bank ATM to make the transfers for the consolidation. Joshua was at the office with Deke.

Kelly was enjoying the leisurely stroll down her street on her way to the bank when her phone rang.

Deke asked, "How did things go at your meeting? What are you up to now?"

"I'm going to the bank to consolidate the lines of credit like we discussed at couples' therapy yesterday."

"We have not discussed this fully. We need to discuss this more."

"I'm just doing what we agreed to in couples' therapy. We have already discussed this in detail."

"No, we have not. We need to talk about this. There is more to discuss."

"We did discuss this for almost the entire session. I'm going to the bank. There is nothing more to discuss. You already agreed." Then Kelly hung up.

As she walked, she recognized she had experienced this tactic of Deke's before: step one—insist on a discussion to delay and obfuscate; step two—wear her down with the twisting and turning of the truth so she would yield in total frustration. This had happened countless times before. Kelly was determined it would not happen this time.

Kelly arrived at the bank about fifteen minutes later and stood in line to use the ATM. While she waited, she became weak and her hands shook. When her turn came, she could hardly hold the bank card. She held her left hand with her right hand as she pressed the keys. She had to go to two different banks and then return to the first bank because she had made an error in the initial transfer. By the time she had finished the transactions, she was still trembling but proud of herself for not backing down.

On the walk back home, she was thinking about what to make for dinner, not the bank transaction or Deke and Joshua waiting for her at home. Joshua and Deke were in the den when she got there. Deke was sitting in his usual chair, which was the middle of three comfortable, upholstered, reclining chairs, located side by side, almost touching each other and facing the TV and surrounding sound system.

Instead of going to sit in her chair, which was the one to Deke's right closest to the bank of windows, Kelly sat down at the edge of Darcy's chair, which was the recliner to Deke's left, closest to the door and Kelly's office. Joshua was in his usual spot, lying down next to the bank of windows, where it was coolest.

After Kelly sat down, she asked Deke, "What are you watching on TV?"

Instead of replying to her question, he transformed. Deke's blue eyes bulged out. His face morphed. The being in the chair no longer resembled Deke. His face was deformed, having grown a few inches in length with a stretched-out chin. He got up slightly from his chair and leaned next to Kelly, less than an inch away. He screamed at her with such rage in his voice and in his body. Kelly had no idea what he said. She froze, petrified by the monster with bulging eyes so close to her.

A few moments passed. Her mind was blank. Then she heard Joshua barking loudly. This started to wake her from her freeze.

Joshua was now sitting directly in front of the being's chair about two and a half feet away and was staring at him. He was barking in the strongest and most threatening manner, with short, loud, deep barks. A few more seconds passed before Kelly became fully aware of the situation. She concluded there was no way Joshua would tolerate the monster moving a muscle. She rose from her chair and backed slowly out of the room. Joshua did not permit the monster to stand up until after Kelly had exited.

When she had backed away to near the windows in the adjacent room about fifteen feet from Deke's recliner, Joshua joined her and stood beside her, still staring at the monster. By this time, the monster had left the den and was standing five feet away from Kelly.

The monster glowered at Kelly and stated, "I'm going out." It went downstairs and slammed the front door on the way out.

Kelly and Joshua did not move until they heard the front door close. Then Kelly hugged Joshua. They were both shaking.

Inexplicably, Kelly and Joshua walked down the stairs to the living room, and Kelly sat down on the living room couch. She couldn't stop shaking. Joshua sat in front of her, facing her with his right paw on her left knee and gazed at her. He didn't move.

Kelly, trying to calm herself, called Dr. Grayson, looking for advice on what to do, but Dr. Grayson didn't answer. Kelly left a voice mail in a shaky voice, "Dr. Grayson, this is Kelly Delmonico. Please call me back. This is urgent. I need your help. Thanks."

Becoming more unsettled, Kelly telephoned a good friend, Bea, who lived alone nearby.

"Bea, I've had a terrible fright. Deke scared me. I don't want to be alone with him. Can you come over?"

"Of course. I'll be there in about a half-an-hour. See you soon."

Kelly telephoned her brother Kieran, but his wife Camille answered. Although she did her best to placate Kelly, Kelly remained trembling and terrified. During the conversation with her sister-in-law, Joshua sat in front of Kelly the whole time. Kelly stroked his neck and behind his ears with her left hand and held the phone in the other hand. Being so upset, she was unable to explain to Camille what had happened beyond indicating she had been frightened by Deke. Eventually, the doorbell rang.

Kelly let Bea in. They sat on the living room couch together. Kelly got off the phone with Camille.

A minute or two after Bea's arrival, Kelly's phone rang. She was hysterical as she spoke with Dr. Grayson, trying to explain what had happened. Before she got far, the front door opened, and in walked the monster. It entered the front hall, poked its head into the living room, didn't say a word, and headed upstairs.

Now that Deke was back, Kelly panicked and whispered to the therapist, "Deke is home. I have to go," fearful he might overhear the conversation. Kelly did not want to anger Deke any further. She remembered they weren't supposed to have conversations with the therapist the other didn't know about.

After she hung up the phone with Dr. Grayson, Kelly said to Bea, "Let's go for walk. Joshua hasn't been out all evening. He needs to go out."

"Sure, let's go."

Kelly felt safer once Bea had arrived. She was a tall, strong woman, a triathlete, and also an important person in their professional community. Kelly thought the monster would be on his best behavior as long as Bea was there with her.

Kelly found the walk a welcome distraction. Walking enabled her to quiet herself and focus on the matters at hand. When they arrived back home from the walk, Kelly divulged to Bea, "I haven't prepared my presentation for tomorrow's conference. Will you help me?"

Kelly led Bea and Joshua upstairs to her home office. Kelly sat down at her office computer. Bea pulled up a chair and sat beside her. Joshua lay under Kelly's desk at her feet. From her chair, Kelly could see the monster sitting in his recliner in the den across the hall. It took about an hour and a half for Kelly to finish her presentation. When it was done, she asked Bea, "Will you stay overnight? I am afraid to be alone with Deke."

"No problem. Glad to help," Bea replied.

Bea slept in Darcy's old room. Kelly and Joshua were still trembling as they huddled together in the bedroom until Joshua made his move off the bed to lie beside the windows.

About three in the morning, Kelly awoke to hear Deke crying in the den, where he was spending the night. She waited a few minutes, hoping he would stop, but he didn't, so she went upstairs to comfort him.

When she got upstairs and crouched down beside his chair, Deke continued to cry, saying, "I want to die."

"Deke, we are going through a rough spot. You don't really want to die. But we need help."

"We don't need help. I need you. Why do you hurt me so much over such a trivial thing? Why do you push me away and not want to discuss what happened?"

"You hurt me. I am just too upset to talk about it now." "I don't know I hurt you."

"I love you, Deke. Please be patient."

Although she repeated, "I love you, Deke" a few times, Deke was not assuaged by her reassurances. Since she felt she was not making a difference, Kelly said goodnight and went back to her bedroom. She wrote down what had happened for posterity. This was something she had never done before, but she felt driven to do it. "Even after what he did to me, Deke made his actions all about him, his pain, and what it did to him. But when I was comforting him, his manipulation was working. I actually believed I was responsible."

The next morning, the chatter at the breakfast table with Deke, Kelly, and Bea was benign and full of small talk. No one even alluded to the events of the night before. After breakfast, Joshua went to the office with Deke.

Kelly and Bea went to the conference together. Kelly gave her presentation, and it went well. At the last minute, one speaker was unable to attend, and the organizers asked if Kelly would speak on that topic as well. The audience laughed at her witty remarks as she spoke extemporaneously.

At the end of the conference that afternoon, Kelly reflected that her unprepared speech went better than the one she had prepared. She didn't remember what she had said. No one could tell she had been traumatized by the events of the evening before. Kelly looked at her hands and saw she was still shaking.

Despite the shaking, Kelly was impressed with herself. She was pleased she had pushed the night before out of her mind, did her speeches, networked, as well as did some effective business development. She went home alone with only the positive experience of the conference in her consciousness.

When she got home and greeted Joshua with a hug, she wondered what kind of day Joshua had with Deke at the office. Was Joshua okay? Did Deke give him a hard time? Kelly could feel Joshua trembling and she was trembling, too.

After dinner, Kelly caught up on her e-mails. She read an e-mail exchange between Deke and Bea. First thing in the morning of the conference, Deke had sent an e-mail to Bea to thank her and had copied Kelly on it. "Thanks for coming over last night to help Kelly. We both really appreciate it."

Bea replied and copied her. "Of course. Hopefully, you both can work things out."

How civilized, Kelly thought. You'd think I had spilled some red wine on a cloth napkin. Good thing, my friend was with me to put seltzer water on it when my husband wasn't. Let's hope the stain comes out.

As usual, Kelly and Joshua went out for their evening constitutionals that night. With each one, Kelly and Joshua were still shaking. At bedtime, they were both still trembling. She didn't know exactly when Deke had stopped looking like a monster, but it must have been after he had returned home when Bea was there.

Kelly was relieved when Deke agreed to spend another night in the den. With Deke upstairs and Joshua by her side, Kelly felt safer and was able to get to sleep.

Over the next two days, Kelly behaved as if nothing unusual had happened. She went about the business of living. She and Deke had dinner with Darcy at a trendy Thai restaurant on Saturday and watched the football game on Sunday.

Kelly experienced some back problems from coughing. Her allergies were bad and the drip down her throat was making her cough. She was feeling nauseated and having nightmares. She stayed close to Joshua. They went on long walks together in Lawrence Park during the day and in the neighborhood in the evenings.

On Monday, she and Joshua stayed home to work. They went on a lunchtime walk in Lawrence Park and a quick jaunt there before Deke got home for dinner.

On Tuesday, Kelly, Deke, and Joshua went to the office to spend the day. At some point in the afternoon, Kelly opened up an e-mail from Deke. It contained the balance sheet from their joint checking account. He pointed out that the account was overdrawn by a large amount of money. When Kelly read his e-mail, she became lightheaded and had trouble breathing.

With Joshua by her side, she went to the small meeting room where Deke was meeting with one of their staff, poked her head into the doorway, and said, "I'm going home early."

Fatima responded, "Kelly, is there anything wrong? Are you ill? You are as white as a ghost."

"I am unwell. It's best if Joshua and I leave now."

"Fine, Kelly. Take the car. I'll take transit home later," Deke replied.

Kelly and Joshua exited the office right away. As Kelly drove home, her stomach settled. When she arrived and they got out of the car, she hugged Joshua and said, "Good boy, Joshua, love you." Even though she noticed she wasn't shaking any longer, as she hugged Joshua, she could feel him still shaking a little.

That evening, Kelly got another e-mail from Deke while he was sitting in the den and she was at her desk, only a few feet away from him. "The joint account is no longer overdrawn. I moved some money into the account from the business."

Kelly felt some relief and went back to her work.

The next day was couples' therapy. Kelly and Deke drove together, and as always, Joshua was spread out in the back seat. Kelly and Deke got out of the car, leaving Joshua behind, and climbed up the therapist's front stairs. Deke knocked on the door and put in the security code. They entered Dr. Grayson's office and sat down. When they began the session, Kelly described the events leading up to the emergence of the frightening face. As she spoke, she became hysterical, first sitting up straight and then hanging her head down low, trying to narrate what had happened.

Dr. Grayson took control of the situation. "Deke, you need to leave the family home and give Kelly some space to recover. Kelly, here is a list of shelters in case Deke does not want to leave and you have no place to go."

Kelly said, "Dr. Grayson, I am going to Hartford on business next week to deliver a two-day training course on change management at a tool and die plant. I am reluctant to go. Do you think I should go?"

"A change of scenery will be good for you," she answered.

Deke offered, "I will leave tonight and go back into the house to look after Joshua until Kelly returns. Once Kelly is back home, I'll leave again."

Dr. Grayson handed Deke a piece of paper, "Here is a referral for a psychologist I recommend you see, and Kelly, here is a referral for you for a psychotherapist. Let's cut this session short. See you after Kelly's trip."

After the session, Kelly, Deke, and Joshua went to the office. Everyone was quiet in the car. Deke and Kelly did not discuss the session at work or at home. After dinner, Deke packed some things to take with him. Kelly was in a daze and just watched Deke pack. Deke was silent as he packed. When he was done, he did not pat Joshua to say goodbye nor did he say anything to Kelly as he walked out the door.

Kelly took Joshua out for his evening constitutionals that night and enjoyed them. She behaved as if it was just another ordinary night in her life. She did see that Joshua stayed closer to her than usual as they walked, and he seemed less interested in the surroundings as they ambled through the pocket park and around the block before going home.

That night before bed, Deke sent Kelly an e-mail from his hotel room. "Kelly, we want the same things in life. Please take me back. I want to be by your side through these difficult times you are experiencing. I love you."

The next day, Kelly went into the office with Joshua and stayed away from Deke. In the evening, she received another e-mail from him. He waxed poetic about how wonderful Kelly was and promised to remind her of that more often. Then he said, "You are not replaceable."

That angered Kelly. She wondered why he bothered to say nice things to her and then the 'not replaceable.' Did he think she was actually going to believe he meant it?

She tried to recall the last time Deke had offered her faint praise before the frightful-face incident and concluded it was so long ago, she couldn't even remember.

What she did recall were the encyclopedias he filled about her full of scorn and derision. He makes me feel so small I have trouble seeing myself. Yet, look at him now! Deke the poet has emerged again. Faced with losing me, he cares. Or maybe he is just desperate, fearful of losing me, or maybe he thinks this is a clever manipulation that worked once, and maybe it will work again. I haven't seen this poet since our high school days. This time, it is not working. I still need a magnifying glass to find my ego.

Kelly continued to go into the office each day with Joshua until her trip to Hartford. Deke also went to the office, but they did not arrive at the same time. She evaded Deke and concentrated on her work and staff. Kelly was scattered except when she was working, looking after Joshua, or going on their walks together.

The day before her trip to Hartford, she had her first session with Ella Wiser, the psychotherapist Dr. Grayson had referred her to. When Kelly walked into Ella's office, she noticed the big windows on two sides and the original watercolors on the walls. As she sat on the two-seater couch facing what she assumed was Ella's armchair, she glanced at Ella's desk and ergonomic chair. Waiting for Ella to start, Kelly strained to read the titles of the books that filled Ella's three bookshelves on the wall opposite her desk. She noted the bookshelves were also tastefully filled with lovely knickknacks.

Ella introduced herself, and said, "Welcome, Kelly, let's begin."

Kelly assumed Dr. Grayson had briefed Ella on her file, so she went right into the frightful-face encounter and the immediate dilemma of the trip to Hartford. Ella helped her to stay grounded and think more clearly about the trip.

"Ella, I think I need to come twice a week. There is so much stress in my life. I really need the support."

"Certainly, Kelly. Let's try two sessions and see how that goes. We can alter the schedule, as needed. My assistant will get in touch with you to set the appointments."

"Thank you, Ella, see you next week after my Hartford trip."

That night, Kelly spent all her time with Joshua. She wanted to make sure Joshua and she had a good time before she left for Hartford in the morning. They went for a long walk in the neighborhood that evening and a long morning stroll in Lawrence Park through a wooded trail before going to the office together. She told Joshua, "I'm going to miss you, but I will be back soon. Deke will be staying with you. I hope that goes well. Love you!"

Joshua blinked once at Kelly, which indicated he had understood. While that made Kelly feel a little better about leaving him, she still hated to do so, especially now, when she was leaving him with Deke. She hoped she had concealed her discontent and distress about it from Joshua. After their morning walk, Kelly and Joshua went to the office.

Before Kelly left for the airport, she hugged Joshua, gave him a kiss on his left cheek, and said, "Good boy. I love you, Joshua. Back soon." He blinked at her again, and feeling somewhat reassured, Kelly gave him another hug and kiss and then departed.

When Kelly arrived at her hotel room in Hartford, she found a beautiful bouquet of long-stemmed red roses on her desk. Deke had sent a nice note with the roses which read, "You are amazing. Have a great trip. I love you."

"How lovely!" Kelly said aloud. As she smelled the roses, she tried to recollect the last time he had bought her roses. Perhaps, it was years before on a Mother's Day or an anniversary. She was touched and riled at the same time. When Deke and Kelly spoke that night on the phone, she thanked him for the flowers and kept the chat about work.

Kelly's time in Hartford passed quickly. Her days were long with the training and her evening was filled with a working dinner with the senior staff of the tool and die plant. Kelly had packed her home troubles in a box before the training began. This was a successful strategy. Kelly concentrated on work and the client was delighted with the training.

When she arrived home from Hartford that evening, Deke came to the door and hastily left as soon as she entered. They did not speak. A little teary-eyed, she hugged and kissed Joshua, saying, "I love you, Joshua. I missed you. Good boy."

The next morning was couples' therapy. With everything that had taken place, couples' therapy was the only place where Kelly felt safe enough to talk to Deke.

That morning, she and Joshua drove to couples' therapy. After hugging Joshua and telling him, "Love you, Joshua, back soon," Kelly walked toward Dr. Grayson's office. Shortly thereafter, Deke arrived by cab. He acknowledged her with a nod, but neither of them said anything as they climbed up the stairs and entered Dr. Grayson's office together.

Dr. Grayson started the session, saying, "I am terminating your sessions. I recommend you both take a few months apart from each other and see where the relationship is after that."

Kelly was shocked, not knowing what to say.

Deke questioned, "Why are you terminating the sessions? We want to continue them."

"My therapy approach is based on both partners wanting to keep the relationship going in a trusting and safe atmosphere. There has been a breach in the relationship. Take some time to see where it goes. Then if you both want to continue the relationship, please contact me. Goodbye and good luck."

Dr. Grayson approached Kelly and gave her a hug. "I am proud of you, Kelly. You are very brave."

"Thank you for all your help, Dr. Grayson. Goodbye," Kelly replied.

Kelly and Deke left Dr. Grayson's office, got into the car, and headed to the office with Joshua.

In the car, Deke made light of the situation. "We just got fired by our therapist. That's a first."

Kelly did her best to smile sincerely at Deke. Then she looked out the window, admiring the Christmas decorations on the trees and front lawns as they drove while listening to jazz on the radio. She tried not to pay attention to the butterflies swarming in her stomach.

CHAPTER 21

Christmas Messages

As usual, once she and Deke arrived at the office after the firing, Kelly behaved as if it was an ordinary day. When it was time to go home, she departed with Joshua efficiently and quietly down the loft stairs, smiling at staff as she and Joshua left, without saying a specific goodbye to Deke.

Once home, she unwound a little while making dinner, with Joshua by her side. She sipped a glass of sauvignon blanc as she stir-fried her shrimp and vegetables and gave Joshua some raw carrots and celery to chew on, while he watched her cook, as he sat by the pantry door. The joy of cooking filled her thoughts. It was one of her favorite meals, and having prepared vegetables for two, shared them with Joshua.

After dinner, she and Joshua went on their evening constitutionals and enjoyed the night air and the solitude of the evening. Joshua wagged his tail in big side-to-side swishes as he walked beside Kelly, occasionally checking out the smells of a tree trunk or bush.

After the last evening walk, they went upstairs to the den together to relax. Kelly read the newspapers while listening to some Chopin and Liszt, as Joshua snoozed by the windows. When it was bedtime, Kelly and Joshua went downstairs. She stopped to enter the second-floor washroom to retrieve some toilet paper from the cabinet under the sink. As she opened the cabinet door to remove a six-pack of toilet paper rolls, she noticed that the steel garbage can, which was supposed to be on the floor next to the cabinet, was gone. It had been replaced by a cheap, lidless, white, plastic basket they used in the basement for storing items to be recycled.

Some months back, Kelly had bought two small, identical, stainless steel garbage cans, one for the bathroom on the second floor and one for the bathroom on the third floor. She really liked those cans because they opened by pressing down on a foot pedal. They were compact and looked sleek for garbage cans.

When she realized the steel garbage can was not where it should be, she was upset and perplexed. She exclaimed to Joshua, "Oh my goodness! How strange? Where did the steel can go? Let's go to the basement to see if there was a switch."

Joshua turned his head to the side as if he were trying to figure out the problem. He accompanied Kelly to the basement and stayed beside her as she did a search for the missing can.

"Joshua, it's not here. I don't understand. What is happening?" Joshua gazed back at Kelly, which Kelly interpreted him saying, "I don't know. I'm sorry you are stressed."

Kelly calmed down enough to smile at Joshua. He blinked back at her, which meant he had understood her dismay, but she should not worry about him, as he was fine. It was late so she decided to ask Deke about the missing can in the morning.

After breakfast the next day, Kelly called Deke to ask him about the steel can, but he said, "I didn't know it was missing," and offered no guidance on where it could be.

With that response, Kelly called Darcy to ask her about it. "Mom, I didn't know it was missing. I don't know where it could be. Did you ask Dad?"

Kelly was surprised that neither Deke nor Darcy knew about the missing can, nor found it strange it was missing. How very perplexing! Kelly thought.

After calling Deke and Darcy about the garbage can, Kelly decided to wrap the Christmas gifts she had purchased. Kelly thought it would be good to get the wrapping done so she and Joshua could spend the afternoon in Lawrence Park. It was such a sunny day so she anticipated there would be lots of dogs in the park.

Before, the trip to Hartford Kelly had made a large dent in her Christmas shopping. She had completed the shopping for Kieran and his family and had stored their presents in an open, green, garbage bag untied on the sunroom floor, near the plants and shelving. She had also picked up some purchases for Darcy that Darcy had requested—a big glass water pitcher and some green cloth napkins, which she also put in the bag. For Deke's sister Allegra, Kelly had bought a beautiful large ceramic tea mug; for Allegra's husband Stan, a dress shirt, and for Allegra's twin daughters, some bath things, all of which she had stored in the bag. The only exceptions were the presents for Deke's dad—six wine bottles and a cloth carrying bag for the wine—which Kelly had placed beside the green garbage bag, now stuffed with presents.

When Kelly got home from each shopping trip, she showed Deke what she had purchased and told him where she was going to store the gifts.

Kelly went to the sunroom to retrieve the presents for wrapping. When she emptied the garbage bag, she exclaimed to Joshua, who was standing beside her, "Oh my goodness! The garbage bag is here where I left it. But some presents are missing. Where did they go?"

Accompanied by Joshua, Kelly surveilled the sunroom and the kitchen but did not find the missing presents. They hunted around the living room and dining room and the bedrooms upstairs. Joshua was at her side as she moved from room to room, searching for the presents.

When she went back to the kitchen to get a cup of coffee to regroup and think, she noticed one wine bottle was missing from the cloth bag. "How is this possible? What is going on?" she asked Joshua. He had a puzzled look on his face.

After doing her laundry and having lunch, Kelly and Joshua went on their long walk to Lawrence Park. They played some ball. Then Joshua wrestled and ran with some of his buddies. In the park, Kelly was awed by the starkness of the woods against the snowy backdrop of the trails and the frolicking of the dogs. The walk allowed her to be present and embrace the serenity of the park.

Once back home again, she sidelined her thoughts of the missing presents. She spent the rest of the day, evening, and next day with Joshua as if nothing unusual had occurred.

The next morning, Kelly and Joshua went off to work. Deke was not there when they arrived, which suited Kelly. She and Joshua spent the workday with Joshua keeping watch at the top of the loft stairs and following Kelly as she went to meetings with staff in meeting rooms or in the boardroom. Kelly felt less anxious and more relaxed because Deke was not there. At the end of the day, she and Joshua left the office, saying goodbye to staff before leaving, behaving as if it had been a routine day.

Once at home, Kelly began to prepare dinner. When she went into the dining room to set the table, she saw one of the missing green napkins on the dining room table, but there was no sign of the second green napkin. This was very suspicious. She said to Joshua who was beside her at the table, "Where did this napkin come from? There is nothing else on the table. Am I going crazy? Or is this Deke messing with me?" Joshua blinked at her to reassure her she and he were both fine.

In psychotherapy two days later, Kelly discussed the details of the disappearances.

"Ella, I just told you the story about the steel garbage can. There's more. Two days ago, I discovered one of Darcy's missing green napkins on the dining room table. This is so odd because there wasn't anything else on the table except for the napkin when it did appear.

"Yesterday, an even more unnerving thing happened. Joshua and I had just arrived home from the office. We climbed the steps to the porch and front door. I put my briefcase down and unlocked the door. I went in and turned on the outdoor light. Joshua went in, too. When I went back out to the porch to retrieve my briefcase, I saw the missing wine bottle standing on the porch near the side railing.

"I think Deke is sneaking into the house, taking things, and moving things around. Do you believe me? Do you think I'm imagining it?"

"Yes, I believe you, Kelly."

"Why is Deke doing this? It is very unnerving."

"I don't know Kelly, but I understand why it is so disturbing."

"Are you sure you believe me, Ella? You aren't just saying that?"

"Yes, Kelly. I believe you. You are not imagining this."

On the drive home, Kelly reviewed her situation. *Even though I know Deke is messing with me, it still makes me think I might be losing it. I know I'm not crazy. It's Deke who is going crazy, but I just can't believe this is happening to me!* "I love you, Joshua. I don't know what I would do without you."

When Kelly returned home after the session, she was still upset. Even Joshua beside her did not quell her anxiety. It affected her sleep that night. She stayed awake for a long time before she drifted off to sleep.

This sleep problem persisted. With increasing sleep deprivation and the stress of all that had happened to her, Kelly was becoming foggy in her thinking, only being firmly in the present and centered on her walks with Joshua and when she was looking after him. She was overwhelmed.

At the next session with Ella, Kelly had more strange incidents to report.

"I had borrowed a set of office keys from our office manager. I kept them in my purse. The next day at the office when I went to return them, the keys weren't in my purse. I emptied my purse and couldn't find them. Later that afternoon, I mentioned to Deke I had misplaced the office keys and couldn't figure it out. The next evening, Deke and I went for dinner with Darcy. I went to the ladies' room and left my purse on my seat. When I went to the office the next day to report the missing keys to the office manager, I discovered the keys were back in my purse.

"Also, I have an envelope with my cleaning lady's name on it I use to enclose a cash payment for her. I have kept this envelope in the same kitchen drawer for years.

"When I went to find the envelope for the cleaning lady to leave her some money, it was gone. After checking all my kitchen drawers, I found the misplaced envelope in the cutlery drawer, where it didn't belong.

"I asked Deke and the cleaning lady if they knew where the missing presents were. I asked the cleaning lady to have a look around and see if she could find them, but she didn't find any. Deke said the presents may have gone out with the garbage by mistake.

"Do you think I'm losing it? Am I going crazy? I am pretty sure Deke is doing this, but it is still so disturbing. I feel like I'm walking on shaky ground. I am not sleeping well. I am having trouble seeing clearly."

"Kelly, you need to stay grounded. You are not going crazy. You are not losing it. Let's do some trancework to help you relax and be more centered."

Between sessions with Ella, Kelly's fog thickened. Except for her walks with Joshua, she remembered little about the time she spent either at the office or at home.

At the monthly managers' meeting just before Christmas, Kelly and Joshua entered the boardroom to find Deke sitting at the head of the boardroom table. Kelly chose to sit on the side closest to the door, at the other end of the table. Joshua stayed close by her under the table.

After the meeting, Chloe went up to Kelly's office in the loft. "Are you and Deke okay? Did something happen to Darcy?" she asked.

"No, we're all fine. Why?"

"Neither you nor Deke seemed present at the meeting. The way you were both behaving, I figured something horrible must have happened, like Darcy had died. I am so glad everything is okay."

"Thanks, Chloe. I appreciate your concern."

Then they discussed the planning for the dog party. The following day, Kelly hosted another successful dog party.

On her way home from the office dog party, Kelly knocked on her neighbor's door with Joshua in tow. Brian came to the door and agreed to check out the house with Kelly.

After the wine bottle incident, she had decided to get help from her neighbors. Because of all the things moving about in the house, Kelly no longer wanted to enter her house without another adult. She looked at everything in the house with wariness. She would knock on Amy and Brian's door and ask one of them to go into her house with her. Then she and Amy or Brian would walk around to make sure that Deke was not there. Once all was well, Kelly thanked Amy or Brian, each of whom was happy to oblige her and help to allay her fear.

After Brian and Kelly checked the ground floor of the house, Kelly asked him, "I know this sounds weird, but please check out a mark I saw on the shower floor tiles."

After lightly rubbing the tile with his hands, Brian advised, "It is just a shadow cast by the light coming through the bathroom blinds. Nothing to worry about."

Kelly felt stupid but mollified. With so much moving about, Kelly had wondered if Deke was taking things to the next level, but she was relieved to learn he had confined his unconscionable behavior to gaslighting, not causing physical damage to their home.

That evening, Kelly received a detailed e-mail from Deke telling her where he had put various presents she was supposed to wrap. Near the end of the e-mail, after he had finished doling out directions on what she was supposed to do regarding his presents for Darcy and her, neighbors, and others, he wrote, referring to Christmas presents, "I have a plan for the hidden ones. I will take care of them. You don't need to be concerned about them."

He added, "I went to the psychologist after work. I went because I know you want me to go. Dr. Grossman wants me to take some tests or he won't continue to see me. I'll take them if I have to, even though I think they are bogus."

Although Kelly found the reference to the hidden ones curious, she let it go. She did not confront Deke about it. Instead, she focused on the positive.

"I'm so happy you are going to take the tests."

Kelly wanted Deke in therapy to get help and perhaps get better, even though everything she had read suggested his being cured was next to impossible. Still, she did not want to give up.

On the weekend, Kelly complied with Deke's Christmas present directions, which involved some shopping, wrapping, and delivering gifts. Once she had fulfilled these directions, she barely noticed the passage of time. One day blurred into the next until Christmas finally arrived.

On Christmas Day, Deke picked up Kelly and Joshua at home to go to his sister Allegra's for Christmas dinner, while Darcy spent Christmas with her boyfriend James' family. At Allegra's, they would open presents, enjoy the afternoon with the extended family, and have Christmas dinner.

Normally, on Christmas, Kelly would mingle and chat extensively with everyone, but on this Christmas day, Kelly tried to sidestep everyone, in particular, Deke, not saying anything to anyone about the situation. Over the course of the day, Kelly chatted briefly with her sister-in-law, her in-laws, her nieces, and father-in-law but spent as much time alone with Joshua as possible. Kelly and Joshua played a little ball in Allegra's house, and then Kelly took him for a walk to a nearby park. She had brought him and Allegra's two dogs some beef chews they enjoyed. Kelly and Joshua went out to toss around the tennis ball a few times in Allegra's fenced-in backyard. As always, Kelly gave Joshua turkey, ham, some lasagna, bread bun, sweet potato, broccoli, and turnip scraps, as well as food she scraped off people's plates as she helped with the dishes.

As Kelly helped with the dishes, she thought about Deke. She knew he was unhappy and unstable at Christmas time. His mother had died a few years back not long after Christmas, so the day had become a bittersweet time for everyone. No one said anything, but the grief was palpable. This year, Deke had more reasons than usual to be distressed.

Kelly dreaded the drive home from Allegra's. When she, Joshua, and Deke got into the car for the return home, she couldn't help but think about a play she and Deke had seen together some years back. It involved a depressed fellow who fantasized about speeding his car into oncoming traffic, crashing into the approaching cars, and becoming ecstatic by the noise and the breaking glass. Deke admired this scene, as he often had recounted it to Kelly over the years. Kelly clung to her seat, trying not to look nervous, and spoke in pacifying tones. Deke drove through the freeway traffic without incident. With great relief, after Kelly dropped off Deke at his hotel, she and Joshua returned home and parked the car in the driveway.

After Joshua jumped out of the back seat of the car, Kelly gave him a huge hug and a little scratch behind the ears, and said, "Good boy, Joshua, love you." Then Kelly removed the presents from the trunk, went into the house to put them under the tastefully decorated Christmas tree in the living room, before going out for Joshua's late-evening constitutional.

Kelly was exhausted from the stress of the day. She was glad to be home with just her and Joshua. After the walk, she got ready for bed. When she entered the bedroom, she found Joshua lazing on the bed. Kelly gave him a tummy rub, saying, "Good night, Joshua, love you." Then Joshua hopped off the bed and lay down beside the window. Kelly watched Joshua for a while, tossed and turned, and eventually, at some point, hours later, dozed off.

On Boxing Day after breakfast, as Kelly was putting away her Christmas gifts from under the tree, she realized how on edge she was. She needed to get out of the house for a period of time. She didn't feel safe. She was not sleeping much. Ever since the frightful face, when she lay down in bed to go to sleep for the night, her eyes didn't shut. She was on high alert. The hammer she took to bed those two nights before Christmas didn't help. In fact, it had made things worse. It felt like a crazy thing to do. Even with Joshua by her side, she couldn't relax.

Kelly checked the weekend papers for some short-term rentals downtown where she and Joshua could live for a short time but long enough for her to get her bearings back and feel safe. She found a fully furnished condo to rent downtown by the lake for a month that allowed dogs. She called the owner to discuss the rental opportunity, explained her predicament, and secured the rental for the month of January.

The next few days were a foggy blur for Kelly. She did not go to work, nor did she see Deke or Darcy. She could not remember what she had done the day before. She and Joshua spent New Years' eve alone, with Joshua snoozing beside her, while she listened to music and read. She did not want to see Deke. Darcy had not gotten in touch with her. Normally, that would have been upsetting for Kelly, but being so unsettled, she was okay to be just with Joshua and away from family pressures.

On New Year's day, she packed up a few things for the month and got Joshua's dog food ready in a large bag, placing it on an empty shelf in the sunroom. She made sure the bag was clearly visible so she would remember to put it in the car with the rest of their belongings for the temporary move. She spoke with Brian and Amy about her impending short-term move. By this time, these next-door neighbors were becoming closer friends.

Amy, a real estate agent, advised, "I don't think it's a good idea to move out of your house, even for a short period of time. To keep possession of the house, it is best if you stay in it. You will be better off if you stay."

Kelly was convinced. She felt lucky she was able to cancel the rental without losing her deposit.

That evening after speaking with Brian and Amy, Kelly got an e-mail from Deke, reminding her to go to the broom closet to fetch the recycling and put it out for pick-up the next day. Kelly thought this was odd. Deke had never reminded her about putting out the recycling before.

She soon understood what had transpired when she went to the broom closet. There she found Joshua's food bag she had packed and stored on the sunroom shelf.

Deke had been here and moved Joshua's food. Kelly didn't know when. Maybe when Joshua and she were in Lawrence Park. Even though she knew he did this, a little part of her was wondering if she was imagining this and going crazy. Why was Deke doing this?

The next day, Deke e-mailed Kelly, asking, "Did you see Joshua's food bag in the broom closet? Have you noticed we have mice living in the pantry?"

Kelly thought Deke was joking and played along. "Yes, Deke. The mice are happy there." She soon forgot about the mouse reference.

In therapy, Kelly described these events to Ella. She asked again, "Do you believe me? Do you think I'm crazy? I thought I had a normal life. This is so disquieting. I don't understand. I feel like I am walking on shaky ground. I can't believe these things are happening to me."

"Yes, Kelly, I believe you. Let's focus the rest of the session on grounding you and calming you down. Let's do some trancework."

For Kelly, this helped to reinforce she was not losing her mind. But it did not mollify her distress with her life and her feeling unsafe.

The walk with Joshua to Lawrence Park after each session with Ella became more important to Kelly to maintain her stability. She and Joshua enjoyed longer walks along the off-leash trail in Lawrence Park. After the session that afternoon, she and Joshua walked along the trail beside the creek bank and played in the snow. Kelly threw sticks in the creek for Joshua to retrieve. After they had walked from one end of the trail along the creek to the other, they crossed one of the walking bridges that spanned the creek, went up the hill, and followed the dog trail on the other side of the fence before going home.

That evening after dinner and a short constitutional with Joshua, Kelly decided to do some laundry. Joshua accompanied her to the basement laundry room, which didn't have much more in it than a laundry sink, some kitchen-type cupboards, the washer and dryer, and a furnace. After loading the laundry into the front-loader and closing the door, Kelly picked up the empty laundry basket and screamed. She ran up the flight of stairs to the main floor of the house, with Joshua right behind her. Her heart was racing. A tiny gray mouse was lying dead on the top of the washing machine!

After settling from the initial shock, Kelly deduced the mouse didn't look like any mouse she had seen in her house. To her, it looked more like a mouse she had dissected in first-year biology.

She said to Joshua, "Oh my, it's a lab mouse. How I hated those dissections! Hmmm, I smell a rat."

She decided not to call Deke this time. "I need to grow up and face this phobia myself," she told Joshua.

Accompanied by Joshua, Kelly went to her bedroom closet, took out her light summer jacket with the hood, put on the jacket and hood and tied it securely, went downstairs to the kitchen, retrieved some rubber gloves from under the kitchen sink and put them on, got a broom and a dustpan from the broom closet, and grabbed the garbage can with a bag in it from the powder room. Then she and Joshua went downstairs into the basement.

Her heart was pounding. She paused and took a few deep breaths. With Joshua beside her, giving her confidence and courage, she entered the laundry room with her gear, stared briefly at the mouse, confirmed it was dead, swept it into the garbage can, and tied the bag. She took the garbage can upstairs, and then deposited the bag into the outdoor garbage can on the back deck and closed the lid securely.

After removing her protective clothing from her bedroom and placing the clothing in a laundry bag in the hall for dry cleaning, she gave Joshua a huge hug.

"Thank you, Joshua. That was quite the procedure we just did together."

Kelly never mentioned the mouse to Deke.

At her next therapy session, Kelly talked about the mouse incident.

"Deke knows I am irrationally terrified of mice. One Saturday night when we were in college after Deke had brought me home from his parents' house, I went into the living room to keep Kieran company. He was watching TV. Suddenly, we both saw something dark scurry across the floor. I screamed and ran into my mother's room. She opened her eyes for a second or two, enough to see me, and then turned her back to me with a gentle sigh and went back to sleep. Then I telephoned Deke. He was amused, but he did reduce my disquiet. I was able to go to sleep.

"Years later, I was cleaning the basement of our house and saw a mouse scamper by. In a panic, I called Deke. He helped to pacify me. He suggested I go out and buy some mouse traps. And I did.

"About two years ago, Deke and I discovered a mouse infestation in our pantry. With Joshua's help, we trapped about twenty mice, with Deke doing the bulk of the trapping and disposing of the remains. Joshua lay beside the gas stove adjacent to the pantry and watched, but he did catch one or two mice we had missed as they ran by.

This was impressive since Joshua had hardly moved to carry out the capture.

"After this, I called an exterminator to deal with the infestation.

"And now this—a dead lab mouse on top of my washing machine. I didn't call Deke this time. I took care of it myself. But can you believe it, why would Deke do this?"

The story left Ella speechless. All she could muster was, "Kelly, this is a stunning story."

"Even though I know Deke is sneaking into the house and doing these things, I am becoming unglued. I want to change the locks to keep him out, but I've been informed it is illegal. What am I going to do?"

Ella spent the rest of the session helping Kelly to stay present, whenever Kelly froze, saying, "Kelly? Kelly? Where are you? Let's focus. Take a couple of deep breaths. What are you feeling?"

The session ended with some trancework that helped to calm Kelly down and be a little less foggy.

The following day, Deke got the results of his psychological testing and telephoned Kelly to discuss them.

"I sent you details of the results. It says I have narcissism personality disorder. I think this is bull. I found a book on the internet about it. Do you think I have magical thinking?"

Deke read out loud some excerpts from the book and stated, "I don't think I fit any of these descriptions. What do you think?"

"I don't know. I need some time to think about it," Kelly replied. He pressed Kelly again, "Kelly, c'mon, you must have an opinion."

"Deke, I really don't know." Kelly could feel his anger over her unwillingness to confirm he was not a narcissist.

Deke continued, "Dr. Grossman wants me to do more testing. I won't. These tests are pseudo-science. But he says he'll only continue my treatment if I agree to sign up for a two-year program. If I miss a session without a good reason, according to him, he'll terminate the treatment. Two years is a long time to put up with this."

"Deke, I think you should give this a try. If it doesn't work out, you can always stop the sessions."

"Fine. But I think it's a waste of time."

Kelly absorbed Deke's hostility and anger as he spoke. She felt so uncomfortable talking to Deke that when the call ended, she decided, this would be the last time she would speak to Deke on the phone. It was just too hard.

After the call, Kelly opened the e-mail file with the results from Deke's psychological testing. Deke scored as being on the mild to medium end of the disorder, but the notes said, "Mr. Delmonico may have some hidden pathologies. Further testing is necessary to make a fuller determination."

This statement unnerved Kelly, but instead of dwelling on it, she pushed it aside. However, in her next session with Ella a day later, she did inform Ella about the results of Deke's testing. She and Ella did not discuss the implications. Instead, this session and the next two sessions were about calming Kelly down and helping her to be grounded. In each session, Kelly did some stretching and moving about to feel her feet firmly on the ground. Then there was trancework to help her relax and reduce the fog.

Kelly knew she was becoming increasingly fearful of Deke, but even in session, she could not concentrate on what to do about her relationship with him. She did not discuss Darcy, either. Although Darcy was not contacting her, Kelly was too overwhelmed to consider what to do and take action.

Kelly relied on Joshua's comfort more and more. On their walks during the day and during their evening constitutionals, Kelly was focused on play and the delight in being with him. At home, with his paw on her knee, as he looked into her eyes, Kelly gazed into his and smiled. She hugged him and his warmth energized and quieted her. "I love you, Joshua. Good boy," she told him.

CHAPTER 22

Treading Water

Kelly had hoped her time off work during the holiday season would bring her clarity on her path forward. But instead, she was a mass of symptoms and pathology which fogged her thinking even more. Her allergies were on overdrive. She was sneezing and coughing and suffering from sinus congestion, which led to bouts of intermittent laryngitis. Her back ached from all the coughing. She wasn't sleeping much and when she did, she had nightmares. She experienced intense vaginal itching from stress. Only ice packs relieved the itch.

Joshua helped her to stay centered. He was her constant companion, observing her, gazing into her eyes, providing a comforting paw on her knee, and barking when she cried, which was usually daily. He dammed her outpouring with distraction and love.

Kelly waited until she was back at work and Darcy was back in classes before she tried to broach with Darcy the subject of her separation from Deke. Kelly had not wanted to upset Darcy needlessly in case there was a quick resolution. When Kelly telephoned Darcy to have the discussion, Darcy was not open to it.

"Hello Darcy, it's Mom. I guess your dad has told you he has been out of the house since Christmas. I was hoping we could chat about it."

"Yes, he told me, but I don't want to hear any more about it. It is between you and Dad."

"I understand, Darcy, but clearly, you know something."

"Mom, please . . . change the subject. It is too upsetting for me."

Kelly was dispirited Darcy did not want to hear her side of what had happened. While she understood Darcy did not want to be in the middle of things, Deke had already put Darcy there. For some reason, Darcy had allowed Deke to tell his story and was not willing to hear what Kelly had to say. Kelly, feeling helpless, hoped the situation with Darcy would change with time.

While Kelly was trying to figure out her relationship with Deke, she worked very hard to keep the family together. During January, Kelly continued to arrange their weekly, family Friday night dinners. On Fridays after Darcy's last class, Kelly, Deke, and Joshua went from work to pick up Darcy and take her out for dinner. Joshua stayed in the back seat of the car and enjoyed the food scraps Kelly brought back for him.

At these dinners, Deke would intermittently sob and say, "I am so sad. My life is terrible. I am so unhappy."

Watching Deke's behavior, Kelly perceived he was seeking sympathy from Darcy and Darcy was just being supportive. Look how Darcy responds, Kelly thought, she loves him, she puts her arm around him, and comforts him.

Over the course of a couple more dinners and watching similar behavior from Deke, Kelly drew a different conclusion. Deke may be sad, but he is manipulating Darcy, and it is working. She doesn't even make eye contact with me. What can I do about this? She does not want to talk to me about it.

These family dinners with Deke did not resolve Kelly's dilemma about her relationship with him. Her brain was telling her, your marriage is over. How can you consider staying with Deke? But her heart was resisting with, I love Deke. I have spent almost forty years with him. I don't want to give up. I don't want to lose my family.

In addition to the Friday night dinners, Kelly met with Deke regularly outside of work. They went to dinner together once a week at a favorite restaurant, usually on Saturday night. When they kept to small talk, Kelly had a pleasant evening. But if Deke wandered into relationship territory, she became uncomfortable.

In those encounters, Deke went from, "Kelly, I love you. Please take me back," one moment, to "I don't understand why I can't come home. I can help you better than your therapist can. Why are you doing this to me?" the next.

Each January night, an e-mail from Deke with similar sentiments greeted Kelly. She explained at their private dinner outings and in e-mails to him with variants of, "I am torn between my love for you and the terrifying scare I had. I am just not ready yet."

She found the alone time she spent with Deke awkward, especially the time between leaving the restaurant and the goodbye at his hotel front entrance. What could she say? She was not ready to take him back, but she did not want to anger him either.

She couldn't bring herself to hug or kiss him. She just could not get that close. Instead, she smiled and said, "Good night, Deke," and hoped he would not press the matter, which he didn't.

Deke had bought tickets to a jazz concert for Kelly, Darcy, and him which was to take place the first Saturday in February. He had bought the tickets several months before the frightful-face incident. It was a family Christmas present from Deke.

Deke had invited Kelly to dinner at his hotel suite before they were to go together to the concert that evening and meet Darcy at the concert hall. Kelly was a little uneasy on her transit trip to Deke's hotel, wondering what was in store for her. This would be the first time she and Deke would be alone together in a private space since the separation. Deke welcomed her at the front door of his suite, saying, "C'mon in. Do you like the place?"

Kelly looked around and thought it was very modern and nicely decorated. She caught a glimpse of Deke's bedroom which was off the living room. She could tell photos were in frames on the bedside table but of what she couldn't determine.

"Deke, this place is great. Very well designed and looks very comfortable."

Deke outstretched his arm to her, motioning her to sit down on the couch. Relieved, she quickly sat down and waited. Deke poured her and himself a glass of good California red wine from the bottle on the kitchen counter, brought Kelly her glass, raised his glass, and toasted to, "Better times."

They clicked glasses and as they did, Kelly echoed, "To better times." As she made the toast, she recalled Deke used to make her special dinners, cooking some of her favorite foods, when they first moved to Buffington after graduate school. He stopped soon after he started working. She really didn't know why but never pressed the matter. This was the first time he had made her a special dinner since then.

Deke had decorated the dining table with lit candles and had dimmed the light over the table. He had set the table perfectly.

"Deke, the table looks lovely."

Expressionless, Deke looked at Kelly, removed the food casserole from the oven, and placed it on the cream-colored, ceramic square on the dining table. He motioned Kelly to join him at the table. At dinner, they chatted about the upcoming concert.

With the focus on small talk, Kelly began to relax. She was feeling a little lightheaded from the wine.

After dinner, when she stood up to get ready to leave for the concert, Deke stood up, too, moved very close to her, put his arms around her waist, and gently lowered his head to kiss her. Kelly felt strong temptation, but, looking him in the eye with all the kindness she could muster, pulled away. She became keenly aware of how easy it would be for her to fall into old patterns without thinking.

"Let's clean up and get going, Deke. We don't want to be late." "I'll clean up later. I'll get your coat."

Deke did not appear angry she had resisted his advances, but she was not sure. He was not displaying any emotion. She decided to be optimistic about the encounter.

The concert became another awkward family moment. Darcy sat in the middle between Deke and Kelly. During the concert, Kelly could hear Deke sobbing, but not what he was saying. Darcy was leaning in his direction in her seat, trying to comfort him. Kelly thought to herself, *This is another manipulation. Darcy is focused on Deke. She doesn't seem angry at me, but she isn't interested in me, either. I don't know what to do.*

The last time Kelly and Deke went somewhere alone together was the following Saturday when they went to their local jazz bar together. They had supper at the bar and listened to two sets of live jazz. The club was small and noisy, making conversation difficult. What conversation they had was about the food and the music. When they both were in the car for the drive home, Deke handed Kelly his house keys and car keys without saying a word.

Kelly took the keys without saying anything about them as if she were expecting them. Why is Deke doing this? Why now? Why didn't he mention he would be giving me his keys? With only jazz music on the radio interrupting the silence in the car, Kelly drove Deke back to his suite and went home.

Once at home, she was eager to see Joshua. "Joshua, good boy. Love you. Let's go for a walk."

Kelly found Joshua's gaze and blink at her comforting, as she put on his leash to go for a short evening stroll before bed. During the walk, Kelly focused on the journey and the coolness of the brisk, night air against her cheeks, while Joshua sniffed for messages. By the time they were home again, Kelly had calmed down enough to go to sleep.

After a relaxing Sunday of more walks with Joshua and keeping to herself, except for some routine shopping for groceries and doing some laundry, Kelly was ready to resume her work routine on Monday at the office with Joshua. She managed to avoid any unpleasantness with Deke, by staying away from him, which turned out to be relatively easy to accomplish since Deke was away at a conference most of the day.

The next day, Kelly and Joshua spent the workday at home. After lunch, Kelly got a disquieting e-mail from Deke, asking her, "What work did you do this morning? Did you stay in? Did you and Joshua go out at lunch? Where did you go? Who did you see?"

Deke had never been so interested in what she had been doing before. Why now? Why was he being so aggressive?

It was time to take a positive step forward. She would seek legal advice for a divorce. It was something she had been thinking about but had been too busy with family and work to initiate. She had obtained some referrals from lawyers she knew and was determined that afternoon to make a connection. She had planned to interview a few lawyers to find a good match—a lawyer who understood Deke's disorder and could protect her. When she reached her first choice, she set up an in-person interview for the next day.

After making the call to the lawyer, she continued her work routine. At the end of the day, Deke's interrogation continued with a follow-up e-mail, "What work did you do this afternoon? Whom did you speak to today? What is your plan for tomorrow?"

She replied, "I am staying home tomorrow with Joshua and working."

The next morning, as planned, Kelly stayed home with Joshua to work. Her appointment with the divorce lawyer was in the afternoon. When she got home from the appointment, she opened an e-mail from Deke with the subject line "truthiness."

Deke asked, "Where were you at three-thirty this afternoon?"

What a coincidence! Deke had sent her an e-mail just when her appointment had begun.

When she didn't respond, Deke sent her another e-mail about it, saying, "I know you were downtown at three-thirty. What were you doing there? Why didn't you tell me you were going?"

How could Deke know where she was? He was sitting in his office in a different part of town when Kelly was in the meeting.

Deke did not mention the meeting to Kelly again. Kelly pushed it out of her mind and went to work at the office with Joshua the next day. Nothing consequential happened at work. After returning from the office, Kelly made dinner for her and Joshua. Then they went out for a quick constitutional around the block and returned soon after so that Kelly could finish up some work on her computer. When she finished earlier than she had expected, she decided to take Joshua on a longer than usual late-evening constitutional before bed.

It was a clear night, but not cold. Kelly and Joshua walked down their front porch stairs together side by side. As they promenaded along their walkway toward the town sidewalk, Kelly looked up at the sky and briefly admired the stars. Then she and Joshua continued walking to the town sidewalk.

When Kelly and Joshua approached the edge of the town sidewalk to cross the street, she spied a car parked across the street with the motor running and the lights on in the car. She saw two women seated in the car, the driver in her late forties or early fifties, and a younger woman, in her thirties, sitting beside her. The two women looked lost. They were peering at a large map.

Kelly and Joshua walked toward the two women. When she and Joshua reached the middle of the road, Kelly was close enough to the car to see the two women had GPS—all those red and blue lights flashing from the monitor. Were the two women waiting for someone? All the lights were out in front of the house where the women were parked. In fact, the lights were out at all the houses across the street.

Slightly disquieted, Kelly returned to their side of the road. As she and Joshua continued on their walk in the neighborhood, Kelly forgot about the two women and their GPS. She and Joshua walked about a quarter of a mile to the nearby high school, where they played some ball on the snow-covered grass at the side of the building. On the way back home, they went around a block before going home. This detour was on a sedate street like theirs—a crescent, with mature oak trees on both sides and lovely manicured gardens. Lydia lived on this street. Sometimes, when Kelly and Joshua made this journey, Lydia was in her front yard and they visited with her. But as Kelly surveilled the street, she noted only she and Joshua were out on the street that night.

Kelly decided to go on one side of the street to the end of the crescent and then return home via the other side of the street. Joshua enjoyed sniffing along this route. As they walked along the curve of the first side of the street, Kelly fixed on a disturbing site.

She whispered to Joshua, "Joshua, look. There is that car with the two women parked on the opposite side of this street. Their motor is running. I can see the flashing GPS lights from here."

Kelly and Joshua crossed the street to the side where the women were parked, for their last leg of the trip home. Still whispering, she asked Joshua, "Are they following me? No, that is preposterous." She tucked that thought away and walked homeward with Joshua, enjoying the night air and the solemnity of the evening.

The next morning, as usual, Kelly let Joshua out into the backyard to relieve himself before they headed off to work. Ever since he was a young pup, Joshua had taken a backyard constitutional in the morning before breakfast, completed a search of the surroundings, relieved himself, and returned to the house. But, when Kelly opened the sliding door that morning for Joshua, he just stared at her and didn't move.

"Joshua, time to go out. Go for a whiz." But he stayed still.

Kelly repeated the command, but Joshua looked her in the eyes and did not budge. After a third try, with a gentle nudge to Joshua's butt that did not produce results, Kelly gave up and decided to let Joshua relieve himself on the way to the car. Kelly thought it was very peculiar Joshua did not want to go into the backyard to relieve himself, but she shrugged it off.

In psychotherapy after work that day, Kelly told Ella about the truthiness e-mail and the late-night walk with Joshua where they had encountered the car with the flashing GPS lights.

"Ella, how did Deke know that I was downtown that afternoon? He was in his office, a couple of miles from there.

"Were those women following me? I feel like I am living in the 'twilight zone'."

Ella replied, "I don't know, Kelly. It does seem unusual."

"In just about every e-mail Deke sends me, even when he criticizes me like in the truthiness e-mail, he still presses me to let him come back home.

"Deke's e-mail would say, 'Kelly, I love you. I miss you. I want to come back home. I want to be with you. When can I come back?'

"Then I would respond, saying, 'I'm not ready for you to come home yet. I am doing the best I can.' But Ella, I know my answer is wearing thin. It is how I feel, but Deke doesn't want to accept it."

"Kelly, do you want Deke to come home?"

"No, I don't think so, but the constant pressure is wearing me down."

"Let's continue with some trancework to help you clear the fog and relax. This will help you stay strong."

Kelly was relieved that night when Deke did not invite her out for Valentine's Day, which was the next day. After his returning the keys, the gulf between them had grown. She did not expect him to invite her out to celebrate the occasion and she had no intention of inviting him. He knew she would refuse and so had decided not to ask her.

The next morning, Joshua declined again to go into the backyard for his morning constitutional. After a few tries, Kelly got her coat and went out with him. Why won't Joshua go into the backyard by himself? She decided not to force the issue.

Kelly was pleased to accept an invitation from Chloe to spend Valentine's evening over dinner. They dined at a local Thai restaurant they often frequented together. The restaurant had modern décor and large floor-to-ceiling windows on two sides. They sat at a glass table near the windows. The table had a bouquet of cut flowers in a small glass vase in the middle.

During dinner, Chloe leaned over and whispered into Kelly's ear, "Do you see that couple at the table next to us? They have been watching us and eavesdropping.

"Look, that woman is taking notes. If I didn't know better, I'd think they were spying on us."

Kelly looked them over, but as she did, they glanced away. She and Chloe got engrossed in work topics and ignored the couple. The remainder of the dinner passed pleasantly. Neither thought about the couple.

The rest of the weekend, Kelly spent with Joshua following their normal routines. There was almost no interruption from Deke except for the usual daily e-mails flagging her faults and ending with, "I want to come home. I can help you. I miss you."

On Monday morning, Kelly went to the dentist, while Joshua stayed at home. She had been experiencing some gum pain for a little over two weeks and wanted the pain investigated more fully.

Her dentist advised, "Kelly, you have contracted a disease common to our soldiers during the First World War. I don't see it often today. It happens with a weakened immune system. If you rinse with a bacterial oxygen wash three times daily for the next few weeks, the condition will clear up quickly. Come see me again in three weeks."

"Wow, this is disturbing. Yes, I will do that. Thank you. See you in three weeks."

That evening, Chloe telephoned. "Kelly, I was right. That couple was spying on us.

"When Deke came into the office this morning, he glared at me, marched by my office, and didn't say hello. Before I left for the day, I learned Deke had given everyone a 5 percent raise except me. Remember we discussed how Deke was not treating staff well. I said everyone deserved a raise and a 5 percent raise would be appropriate. To get even, Deke did that for everyone but me!"

"Oh, my Lord! I am so sorry, Chloe. That is not fair. You certainly deserve the raise."

The next day was work as usual at the office and Kelly's appointment with Ella. Kelly had noticed strange sensations on the left side of her face from her eye to her chin, from her left elbow to her left wrist, and from her left knee to her left ankle.

Ella asked, "Do you feel numb, or is it a tingling sensation?"

"Neither. It feels more like a heightened sensation in those areas. I checked to see if I had any muscular heaviness, but my coordination was fine. The only heaviness I felt was around my left eye. This can be so intense it's hard for me to keep my eye open.

"When I go on walks with Joshua, the distraction and movement help dissipate the response. I talk to him, saying things like, 'Look, Joshua, there is a cat on the porch. Did you see that baby raccoon running in the yard across the street? Let's go around the corner. Do you think Lydia will be out? Let's walk faster, almost home.'

"Sometimes these sensations come back again after the walk. Joshua stays close beside me. I usually pace back and forth from one end of the kitchen to the other. Joshua watches me."

Ella replied, "These sensations, or somatic responses, are being triggered by something. In future sessions, we can work to identify the triggers and uncover any patterns."

Although Kelly found Ella's counsel helpful, after the session, Kelly decided to take more action. To redress her worry over what these somatic symptoms actually were, Kelly obtained a referral from Dr. Mahoney to a neurologist and had an MRI done a few weeks later.

Kelly was not prescribed any medication to calm her before the MRI. She discovered she was quite claustrophobic and started to panic in the chamber. Realizing she had to calm herself down, she focused on Joshua, daydreaming about throwing sticks for him in the cold water of the Lawrence Park creek, and the joy in watching him return with the sticks. The more she concentrated on their play, the more she relaxed. After a few minutes, she dozed off despite the banging in her head from the machine.

The timing of the MRI coincided with the last of Darcy's midterms that semester. During her midterms, Kelly had paused the weekly Friday night dinners with Darcy, Deke, and her. But when the midterms were over, Kelly did not reinstate the dinners. Neither Deke nor Darcy stepped in to take over the task.

After the MRI results were in, Kelly went to see her neurologist, who advised, "Your MRI is normal. You do show an abnormality for migraines. The somatic responses you are experiencing are body migraines. I can give you some medication for that. Also, you have a very old injury, a broken facial bone on the left side of your face, which has healed nicely."

When did this injury happen? How is it that my parents didn't notice and didn't get me any treatment?

That evening, Allegra telephoned. "Deke told me you and he have been living apart since before Christmas. Why didn't you tell me? I hope you and Deke can work things out." She paused and then continued, "Stan and I haven't seen you since Christmas. It's been about two months. We would love to have dinner with you."

"Allegra, I haven't told anyone about Deke and me. I am not really up to having dinner with you and Stan right now. Perhaps in a month or two."

"Kelly, you really need to get out and enjoy yourself more. We are family. How is next Friday?"

With Allegra's continued pressing, Kelly weakened and agreed. This was a big step for her. She had steered clear of socializing with any extended family. She did not want to be triggered with even more intense somatic responses. After she hung up the phone with Allegra, Kelly pondered whether she would be able to maintain a relationship with members of Deke's family. Did she even want one?

Kelly had chosen to meet Allegra and Stan for dinner at one of her favorite local French restaurants. At dinner, Allegra recounted:

"I have an amusing story to tell about Deke and me. We were at odds as children. He was extremely mean to me. When he wasn't making fun of me or criticizing me directly, he was mocking me to my parents. One day, when I was about ten, I decided I'd had enough. I went into the kitchen, opened the fridge door, and took out a bottle of wine. I went outside to where Deke was sitting on the front porch steps. I casually and without warning broke the bottle over Deke's head. After that, he didn't bully or berate me again."

"Oh my," Kelly replied. "That is quite shocking. I'm glad Deke has been kinder to you."

"Kelly, I really miss you," Allegra confided. "Let's get together more often. Is there anything we can do to help you?"

"Please help Deke to control his emotions."

CHAPTER 23

The Lowlife Brigade

Working at the family business office with Deke was becoming insufferable for Kelly.

Chloe revealed, "There is real tension between you and Deke. He scowls at you every time you enter the room. He criticizes you at every turn. I told staff to just keep their head down. You can cut the negative with a knife. Joshua does not leave your side. Anything I can do to help?"

"Thanks, Chloe. I don't think so, but I really appreciate the offer."

That evening, Kelly began to look for a job, something she hadn't done since before Domenic was born. She spent the evening searching the internet for positions and writing letters to headhunters. "Joshua, do you think I will find a job? There are such slim pickings out there. Do you think I will get a positive response from some headhunters?" Joshua looked up at Kelly, opened his mouth slightly, and turned his head, trying to understand her plight, then he blinked, and Kelly felt better.

More than a dozen headhunters got in touch with Kelly in response to her e-mails. She met with a few, most of whom were at the vice president level and above. They all pretty much said the same thing.

"Mrs. Delmonico, you have a very impressive and very diverse resume. And after having met you, I can see you are very intelligent and engaging. The problem is that you don't fit into any job position slots. I wish I could help you."

As time went on and Kelly wasn't finding anything, her doubts increased. She told Joshua, "I haven't been an employee since I was in my twenties. I am an entrepreneur, not an employee. How am I ever going to be an employee again? Yes, Joshua. I'm over fifty. Who is going to want to hire me?"

Joshua could feel her angst and looked at her as if to say, "I will stand by you. I love you."

Kelly concentrated her subsequent job search on positions that built on her expertise but were outside the change-management and strategic-planning industries. She focused on positions where her life and Deke's would not intersect. With almost nothing that met those criteria, she also applied for positions in both change management and strategic planning, but with minimal likely competition with the family business. When this strategy failed, she applied for just about everything she saw, regardless of how ill-suited it was or how little she wanted the job.

Kelly found a job ad for a relatively senior position. It was a long commute from her home. She didn't really want to work at the company, but she was desperate. As she prepared her application, she buried her misgivings.

She was invited to an interview for the position and drove there with Joshua. After the interview and back in the car, she chided herself, *My interview was terrible. I am so embarrassed. I didn't get any questions that should have been a surprise, but I wasn't prepared. I guess I should just be thankful I was able to make an appearance and not fall apart.* "Glad to be going home with you, Joshua! Love you."

Toward the end of March, with nothing happening on the job front, Kelly got more assertive about finding an alternative work situation. She decided to resurrect her company and bring in some contract work. While she would still work full-time at the family business to keep it afloat, if all went well, she would subcontract some of her company work to the family business.

She set up some meetings with past clients—in particular, individuals with whom she had done work and had developed a good rapport. Her walks with Joshua were now a little longer and more active. She often told Joshua, "I need to keep the faith. With you by my side, things are looking up."

She arranged a meeting for the first week of April with a previous client, a biotechnology company. From home, the firm was about an hour's drive away, if traffic was light. She sang along to some '60s music on the drive there. On the drive back home with Joshua, she told him, "It was a good meeting, Joshua. No work though, but glad we came. It was good to connect with that firm again. It built my confidence. Let's go home. Love you."

The next day, Kelly and Joshua went to the office. She and Deke had lunch at their usual place near the office. Ever since they had begun working together in the family business, they regularly lunched together when they were both in the office. The lunches were mostly working lunches, but like everything else with Deke, Kelly was finding they were becoming more onerous to countenance. She did her best to steer their conversation away from their relationship and locked on work.

During lunch, Deke uttered, "Were you at Buffington Biotech yesterday?"

Kelly was surprised by the question. The meeting was not on her computer calendar. No one she met with knew Deke or would have contacted him about the meeting.

She responded, "How do you know? Were you following me?"

Kelly was startled to see that Deke's face had elongated. He looked more tearful than like a monster.

He proclaimed, "Yes, I hired a private investigator."

"Is that why you have no money?" "Yes."

Kelly did not process the conversation. Her mind was blank as she watched Deke pay the bill. They left the restaurant together. As they walked back to the office together, Kelly struggled to breathe.

"I need to go for a walk," Kelly told Deke.

"May I go with you?"

"No. I really need to be alone." Kelly turned away from Deke and walked swiftly down the street.

She went for a short walk, but it didn't soothe her nerves. She returned to the office to get Joshua and go home. When she arrived back at the office, she and Deke crossed paths as he went out. When she saw and absorbed his hostility, she fell apart and cried, collapsing onto a chair near the front door. As she began to calm herself and stood up with Joshua to leave, Chloe approached her.

"Kelly, I am concerned about you. You shouldn't go home alone. Let Fatima accompany you."

"I'm okay. I just need to leave now."

"Are you sure, Kelly? It will be no trouble." "Yes, I'll be fine when I'm home with Joshua."

At home with just Joshua, Kelly's stress level became more manageable. She sat at the sunroom table sipping her sparkling water with lemon with Joshua nearby.

"Oh my God, Joshua! Deke is having me followed. I can't believe this. This can't be happening. This is not my life!"

Joshua got up and came over to her, sat down in front of her, and put his right paw on her left knee. Kelly gave him a hug. "I love you, Joshua." Then he lay down again under the table.

That evening, Kelly had plans to dine with Bea. Kelly took transit to their chosen dinner spot. She got off at the correct stop, but inadvertently exited out the wrong door of the transit station and ended up in a sprawling cement courtyard. Kelly had been in that courtyard during the day when it was bustling with office workers eating their lunches or traveling from the street into the office building. But in the evening, no one had a good reason to take that route.

Just at that moment, she got a sense that someone was following her. If someone is following me, then whoever it is will have to whisk by me if I sit down here on one of the cement benches and wait.

Sure enough, a man in his mid-forties—a lowlife with a black baseball cap and graying hair at the side of the cap, a short jacket, and a backpack—walked toward her. At first, he kept his head down, but then he made eye contact with Kelly for a few seconds. She didn't retreat. She stared right back at him. He laughed, tilting his head to the side slightly away from her as he paraded by.

At dinner with Bea, Kelly explained, "Deke told me today he hired a private investigator to follow me. On the way here, I think I spotted one. As he walked by me and I stared at him, he laughed."

"Wow, Kelly, that is stunning, really unbelievable."

Does Bea believe me, or does she think I made the whole thing up?

After dinner, Kelly went home to Joshua. Going to the high school to amble around and play was now part of their routine evening constitutional. On their way to the school, Kelly saw again whom she now began to refer to as "Lowlife," marching by on the opposite side of the street, away from her. This sighting was not happenstance. This Lowlife had probably been following her all evening.

The next afternoon, Kelly had a psychotherapy appointment. She and Joshua drove to therapy. While driving down the street to park near Ella's office, Kelly saw Lowlife again—baseball cap, short jacket, knapsack, and all. He was walking toward Ella's office. Kelly wanted to be sure it was the original lowlife, so she slowed down to confirm, and it was. Then she parked the car in front of Darcy's apartment, which was just up the street from Ella's office. Kelly had parked many times on the street where Ella's office was. For some reason, parking in front of Darcy's building bestowed some inner tranquility to her, even though Darcy did not know Kelly was there.

Before leaving Joshua in the car to go to Ella's, Kelly followed her routine departure ritual with Joshua, "I love you, Joshua. Back soon." She gave him a hug, closed the car door, and went to her appointment.

Kelly recounted the lunch with Deke, meeting the Lowlife, and dinner with Bea. Kelly asked Ella repeatedly, "Do you believe me? Am I crazy?"

And Ella responded in turn, "I believe you, Kelly."

That evening, Kelly went to dinner at the home of Lorraine and her family. Lorraine was a labor lawyer who had worked with Kelly many years before. Now she was a successful partner in a prestigious law firm. Over the years, they had kept in touch through lunches they had together from time to time. Lorraine lived in the north end of Buffington.

On the way to Lorraine's, Kelly decided to smoke out the followers. When she and Joshua were driving on a busy street with a town bus on it, she switched into the right lane and drove behind the bus. They stopped at every bus stop with her and waited behind her and the bus. Since she had never driven to Lorraine's home before, any followers would not know her route. They would have to stay close by unless they had some other way to track her. Eventually, only four cars drove behind her, then three, and then only one. The last car stayed behind her for about a mile, crawling with her car and the bus. She watched as the car behind her switched to the middle lane and stayed in tandem with her car. Kelly lost interest in the followers as she had to determine where to turn right to go to Lorraine's.

After parking her car across the street from Lorraine's home, Kelly went into the back seat of the car to chat with Joshua and give him a goodbye hug. "I love you, Joshua. Back soon."

Kelly enjoyed seeing Lorraine again, as well as meeting her husband Sam and her two lovely preteen girls. Dinner was delicious and the companion red wine was excellent. Kelly delighted in the evening banter.

As the end of the evening approached, Kelly began to think about the trip home.

"Lorraine, I know this sounds crazy, but Deke is having me followed. They followed me here and will likely follow me home. This all started after Deke really scared me just before Christmas. I really don't know what to do."

"I know a criminal lawyer who is a friend of mine," Lorraine replied. "I can arrange for you to have a meeting to get some advice. I'll phone him first thing in the morning and let him know you are going to call."

"Kelly, before you go, I'm going to go outside and see if I can ferret out any cars parked that look suspicious and might be following you," advised Sam. But when he came back inside, he said, "All's clear, Kelly. Everything looks fine."

"Thanks, Sam. And thanks so much to both of you for a wonderful dinner. See you again soon."

On the way home, Kelly identified a car that was following her and Joshua. To avoid the tail, she drove through her old neighborhood of many years back, where Deke and she had lived before Domenic was born. In her old neighborhood, she was able to relax a little as she drove. She did not see any cars following them on these side streets. Eventually, she had to revert back onto the main streets to go home.

She exclaimed to Joshua, "There they are again, and only a mile from home. Nothing I can do about it now."

That night, Kelly saw Lowlife again. She and Joshua were on their way to the high school to make their usual late-night trip. While they were walking toward the school, Kelly saw Lowlife across the street, walking in the opposite direction.

Was he in one of those cars that had followed them from Lorraine's? What does he do during the day that he has to do this at night?

The next morning, Joshua stayed home while Kelly went to the office. She had called the criminal lawyer before she had departed for the office and had scheduled an appointment with him in the afternoon. Liz was going to pick up Joshua to spend the day with her and Bailey.

Just after Joshua had turned three, Liz decided to change careers and set up her own dog-walking business. Joshua was her first and longest-standing client. Kelly thought being with Liz and Bailey was a great opportunity for Joshua and Bailey to spend more time together. Kelly made sure Joshua spent one day every two weeks with Bailey.

When Kelly arrived at the office that morning, she was astonished to see a person posted at each end of the hallway outside their office. To see someone at both ends of this hallway was bizarre. When there was someone lingering, the individual was on the phone in a personal conversation. What was going on?

When Kelly headed to the ladies' room later that morning, she needed to approach the young woman who was stationed closest to the door that opened into the stairwell next to the ladies' room. As Kelly got closer, the woman turned away from her, went into the stairwell, bowed her head, and talked into her mobile phone.

Another lowlife! They all behave the same way. No matter where I go, I see them. How can I shake them off?

Kelly left the office after lunch to go for a stroll before her meeting with the lawyer. She covered a few blocks in the direction of downtown. She saw lowlifes ahead of her, anticipating her direction, and waiting at corners. Whenever she looked at one directly, the lowlife turned away and talked into his mobile phone.

When it was time to go to her meeting, Kelly hailed a cab. She slumped down into the back seat, trying not to be spotted. When she got out of the cab, she quickly ducked into the building of the lawyer's office. Alone in the building elevator, she pressed every elevator button, hoping to fool the followers.

Slumping in the cab and pressing the elevator buttons were stupid. These are acts by a fearful person not thinking clearly. What am I going to do?

At the meeting with the criminal lawyer, Kelly recounted the frightful-face incident with Deke, the dragging from the dining table a few years back, and being followed.

The lawyer advised, "I usually defend people like your husband. I don't deal with nice people like you. The law is strict on such offenses now because of what happened to some women before the law was amended." Then he read Kelly the clause that defined assault.

"Kelly, based on what you have described, you were assaulted by Deke recently when he scared you and earlier when he dragged you from the table."

"Oh my God! I hadn't thought about the possible criminality of what had happened to me, until now."

"You can go to the police. If the police believe you, they will arrest Deke, keep him from you, and may keep him away from the family business."

"What if they don't believe me?" I'm too fragile to risk another Deke-like experience of being dismissed.

"If they do believe you, it would be like a nuclear bomb going off in Deke's life."

What would Deke do to me? Would Darcy ever forgive me for going to the police?

"Here is the name of a private investigator to sweep your car, house, and phone for bugs. Please buy a new mobile phone. And here is some wording I have written down you can use in e-mails to Deke to make him stop following you."

Why didn't I think of that? Just declare to Deke decisively to stop.

That evening, Kelly and Joshua went out for their usual constitutional to the high school. On the way to the school, Kelly identified more than one lowlife and in different places as they strolled. Each lowlife wore the lowlife uniform—a baseball cap, a knapsack, and a jacket and carried a mobile phone. As they passed by one lowlife, he put his head down and talked on his phone for a second or two and continued onward.

Kelly boldly went up to the next lowlife ahead, "Sir, do you have the time?"

"Yes, it is ten-thirty."

Kelly stared at him, saying, "Thank you."

When Kelly was out of earshot, she told Joshua, "I know this lowlife is part of the crew. These fellows aren't doing anything of note in the neighborhood. They don't have a dog or a direction. Since it is so late, no neighbors are around. These lowlifes are here just to follow me. Joshua, stay close. I love you."

On the return home from the high school about fifteen minutes later, Kelly noted a couple walking just ahead of her and Joshua. She took a better look. She recalled they had passed this same couple on the way to the high school. The couple certainly had not made much progress in their walk. This twenty-something couple has the right look, each with a cap, knapsack, and short jacket.

When the couple caught onto Kelly's following them, they separated, with the fellow walking several paces ahead of the young woman, acting like he didn't know her. In spite of Kelly and Joshua being so close behind them, they didn't speed up or slow down to let Joshua and Kelly pass. This continued for a block until the couple crossed the street. The female entered one of the houses, and he walked on.

That night, Kelly did her best to get some sleep, but she struggled to close her eyes and relax. As she patted Joshua beside her on the bed, it made her feel better, but she awoke a couple of times in the night in a sweat.

The next day was a big one for Kelly. She had a psychotherapy appointment in the morning and oral surgery in the afternoon. Since she was advised not to drive after the oral surgery, Joshua stayed home for the day.

All winter long, Kelly had been wearing a full-length, dark brown, goose-down winter coat. That morning, she had decided to wear a more appropriate coat—her shorter, navy blue, wool, three-quarter coat—in honor of the balmy April morning. As she walked down her street toward the transit station to go to psychotherapy, a white SUV approached her from the transit station on the wrong side of the road. As the car came closer, it slowed down near the sidewalk where she was walking to steal a good look at her. After the once-over, the driver drove away.

There was no apparent reason for this behavior. There was no one else on the street, walking or outside. Kelly exclaimed aloud, "Of, course! This behavior is directed at me." I'm dressed differently. The team of lowlifes has to make sure it's me.

When Kelly arrived at the access to the transit station, the usual twenty-something male was standing around, waiting for her to arrive. She entered the station, walked down the steps to the platform, and stood with her back almost against the back wall to wait for her train.

All of a sudden, another male with a knapsack, short jacket, and thick, wire-rim glasses came too close to her, sticking his face about two inches from hers, and peered into her eyes. After a few moments of staring at her, he walked away and stood with his back against the wall, about three feet from where Kelly was standing. He only moved away from her after he was sure it was her.

When the train arrived, Kelly stood behind him. He waited there and did not enter the train. Then after five seconds, Kelly bowed and pointed with her right arm and hand palm up like a maître d' toward the opened train door. "This way, sir."

He said, "Excuse me," entered the train, and sat down not far from where Kelly had sat down.

In psychotherapy, Kelly told Ella about the SUV and her too close for comfort encounter with the young man with the glasses.

"It was scary. I was so startled. I froze as he stared into my eyes. I should have called the police, but I guess I was in shock. I was so relieved when he moved away from me and stood against the wall. Slowly, I got my bearings and that's when I screwed up my courage and became the maître d. Do you think I am right about the SUV?"

"Kelly, this is an awful, unbelievable experience. Your analysis seems reasonable to me."

After psychotherapy, Kelly took a cab to the dentist for oral surgery. The surgery was to remove a tooth that had abscessed a few years earlier. Now the same tooth had abscessed again and had to be extracted. Kelly referred to it as the 'Deke tooth'. She was in earnest to yank it out.

In the dentist's office, she noticed a man in his fifties watching her. She watched him make notes of her trips to the ladies' room. After the surgery, she glared at him for a few moments until he looked away, and then she went outside and flagged a cab to go home.

Kelly had arranged for the private investigator the criminal lawyer had recommended to sweep for bugs the following day. Even though she was still swollen from surgery and on liquids and painkillers, she didn't want to cancel the appointment. To keep her company, she had invited her oldest friend, Donna, to come over. Kelly didn't want to be alone during the sweeping in case the private investigator actually found something. During the sweeping, Kelly, Donna, and Joshua went to Lawrence Park for a walk.

When they returned, the private investigator stated, "I did not find any surveillance devices in her home, in the car, or on her mobile phone."

Donna remarked, "Kelly, it is so funny Deke is going to all this trouble to have you followed. What does he expect to uncover? All you do is go to work, shop, and walk with Joshua."

Later that afternoon after Donna had gone home, Kelly and Joshua went for another walk in Lawrence Park. On the way back, she and Joshua took a shortcut along the sidewalk outside the transit station. While walking along the shortcut, Kelly spied a lowlife loitering by the station. She went up to the lowlife with Joshua beside her and took the lowlife's picture with her mobile phone.

The lowlife muttered, "Screw this. It's not worth it."

Kelly was pleased she had annoyed him and hoped he would report the incident and it would get back to Deke.

That night, Kelly and Joshua went on their usual late-evening journey. When they left the house, a cab drove by. It looked like the driver was searching for a particular address on the other side of the street. Kelly noticed the sign on the cab, 'City Cab,' was not authentic. She waited to see if anyone got out of the cab at the address the cab driver had stopped at, but no one did.

About twenty minutes later, as she and Joshua were heading home from the high school, Kelly spotted the same cab with the funny sign parked with the motor running almost in the middle of the road slightly south of the school. The car was parked so the driver could watch Joshua and her playing at the school.

On that evening walk, Kelly wrote down license plates of cars that were following or likely to be following her and Joshua. Even though doing this recording was slightly empowering, Kelly found her behavior disturbing.

In the den later that night as she patted Joshua's head and gave him gentle scratches behind his ears, she told him, "I can't take this anymore. I am getting stronger, but my actions are getting crazier. This needs to stop. I'm going to follow the lawyer's advice and e-mail Deke. What do you think, Joshua?" He blinked back at her in support.

Later that night before bed, Kelly wrote, "Deke, you are scaring me. Please stop having me followed. It is making me very uncomfortable and very fearful."

Deke quickly responded, "What are you talking about? Be serious. I'm not having you followed. I was joking when I told you I hired a private investigator to follow you. You have no reason to be frightened."

In the morning, Kelly wrote back, "Deke, it was no joke. You are scaring me. You are making me very afraid. Please stop having me followed."

Deke rapidly replied, "Stop saying I'm having you followed. I am certainly not doing that. Get a grip on yourself, Kelly."

That afternoon, Kelly and Joshua went for a long walk in Lawrence Park. She focused on the walk and pretended to ignore the lowlifes. In the evening, she and Joshua went to the high school as usual. Kelly identified two cars that took turns driving by the school as she and Joshua played. She did her best to turn a blind eye to the lowlifes they encountered as she and Joshua walked home.

The next morning, Kelly observed for the first time in a while, no one drove past her as Joshua and she walked from the house to the car. When she and Joshua drove by the transit station to go to the office, she was pleased the lowlife outside the transit station was gone.

"Joshua, I think Deke's lowlife crew is gone. Thank goodness!"

CHAPTER 24

Joshua Saves Kelly

The impending expiry at the end of April of Deke's lease for his hotel apartment created heightened tension between Kelly and Deke.

In an e-mail to Kelly, Deke wrote, "My four-month lease is expiring at the end of this month. I need to know if I can come back home. I want our life back."

"I don't see us being able to share the same household in the near future. If you want to move, you should take some action as soon as you can. I apologize if this creates a hurtful situation for you. I am doing the best I can."

In an e-mail a week later, Deke stated, "I have found an apartment with a six-month rental. I am going to need some things from the house. Here is a list of furniture, clothing, and other items I want. We can make arrangements for me to pick up the stuff."

"These are relatively small items. I can bring them to the office or to your apartment for you."

Deke had attached a song to the e-mail with the list, but she did not listen to the song until the next day. She e-mailed Deke, "When I listened to the song today, it brought back fond memories of when we first danced to it, but it also made me cry because it was about losing love."

Sending that e-mail was a mistake. Deke wanted to know, "Why did the song make you cry? What did that mean? Which keywords in the song moved you? Why are you telling me about this?"

"There is no underlying message. The song made me cry as I listened to it. I am so sad and sorry this is happening to you and to us."

"Well, you are so sad and sorry this is happening to you. Why aren't you sad and sorry this is happening to me?"

In that same e-mail, Deke had informed Kelly, "Your e-mails are encrypted. They've been encrypted for over a week. You need to sort that out. I can't read them. No one can."

How was this possible? Why did Deke wait a week to tell her about it? She was confident Deke had done the encryption. The mouse hadn't worked. Deke knew she always need his computer help.

"I don't know how to fix my e-mail problems. Please send me some instructions on what to do. Thanks."

"I sent you the instructions in the e-mail with the pop song. Didn't you see them?"

Kelly scrutinized Deke's e-mail more carefully and found the instructions. After following them, Kelly e-mailed, "I don't understand it. I didn't know it was even possible to encrypt e-mails. Are my e-mails okay now?"

"What a puzzle! Yes, your e-mails are fine now."

The next day, Deke wrote, "Dad is moving to a retirement home in Bridgetown. It's only about ten miles from where he is now. I want to visit him before he moves to his new place. Do you want to come along? Dad would be very happy to see you."

"Thanks for the invitation. I won't be able to go with you."

"I'll go with Joshua when you and Chloe go to Wichita to present the final report to Williamston Enterprises. I'll drive you to the airport and pick you up when you come back and return the car to you."

"Okay, thanks. When you take me to and from the airport, I really want Joshua to be with us in the car. I'm sure he'll enjoy his trip with you to your dad."

"Why are you making a federal case about Joshua being in the car with us? Where else would he be?"

"I'm not making a federal case. I am going to miss Joshua very much. I just want to be sure you will bring him with you to the airport."

"I'm afraid Joshua won't be with Deke when he picks me up at the airport," Kelly told Chloe on the plane on the way home from Wichita. "What if Joshua is not with him?" "Deke wouldn't dare. We'd all be on him. Try to relax."

After Kelly and Chloe picked up their luggage from the carousel, Chloe held Kelly's hand tightly as they walked to the exit and into the main part of the airport. "Be brave, Kelly," she whispered warmly.

When Kelly saw Joshua sitting patiently beside Deke, her whole body relaxed. As she approached Joshua and Deke, her tears welled up from relief and joy in seeing Joshua and knowing he would be with her. Chloe let go of her hand and as she did, Kelly sensed Chloe's relief. When Joshua was in front of her, Kelly got down on her knees and hugged him, held him for a few moments, and kissed the right side of his face gently.

While Kelly greeted Joshua, Chloe said, "Hello, Deke. Good to see you. It's late. I'm going to the parking lot to get my car and go home. Have a good night. See you at the office tomorrow. Goodnight, Kelly."

Kelly made small talk with Deke in the car on the way to Deke's apartment. They chatted about his dad, his dad's new home, and the presentation of the final report. Kelly dropped off Deke at his place and drove home with Joshua.

When she got home, she and Joshua went out for a long walk in the neighborhood before going to bed. "I am so glad to be back home with you, Joshua. Love you."

The next morning, Kelly and Joshua went to the office to spend the day. When they reached the front door of the office building, Joshua refused to enter. He stood in front of the main building door and planted his paws. "Thank you, Joshua. I know you are right. I shouldn't go in, but I have to go to work."

When she walked forward and he didn't respond, she pulled gently on his leash. "Come, Joshua. Let's go." After repeating herself again, Joshua agreed to move. They entered the building together, with Joshua walking close beside her.

Kelly and Joshua walked to the elevator, took it up to the office floor, and walked along the hallway to the family office entrance. At the front door into the office, Joshua planted his paws again. He wouldn't move when Kelly walked forward.

"Joshua, please. Let's go in." She patted his head and tugged his leash gently. Her guardian walked in, staying close beside her.

After Joshua's refusal to enter the office, Kelly took more drastic action on subsequent trips to the office to avoid Deke. She would call Chloe first thing in the morning and ask, "Is Deke going to be at the office today?"

Chloe would find out about Deke's schedule and call Kelly back. Whenever possible, Kelly and Joshua did not go in when Deke was going to be there. When they were unavoidably at the office at the same time, before leaving for the evening, Kelly would go over to Deke's office and say, "Deke, Joshua and I are leaving now. Have a good night."

On one such occasion, Kelly caught Deke by surprise. When she arrived at his desk, she briefly read a chunk of what was on his computer screen. He was scanning a website about how to secretly move money out of the country and plan an escape. She did not say anything to Deke, but she did mention it to Ella. Because she was in such disbelief about the prospect of Deke actually looking at this type of website, she simply added the sighting to her growing pile of subconscious, festering denials.

One late afternoon in early May, Kelly went to Deke's office to drop off his mail, without realizing the rest of the staff had already left. As she walked to Deke's office, she walked past Joshua who was snoozing near the front door. When she arrived at Deke's office, she stood about two feet from his desk near his office windows. He was sitting at his desk, facing his computer and screen. He was irate, ranting out loud about the bookkeeper, whom he disliked.

"I can't believe Seth didn't send out the client invoices this month. Now I won't be able to pay my disability insurance. I'll have to cancel it."

Kelly thought Deke was exaggerating at best. At worst, he could borrow a small amount of money to cover the monthly insurance cost.

Then, out of nowhere, Deke stood up, less than two feet away from her. He turned and faced her and raised both his arms straight up above his head. Being six feet four, with long, muscular arms and a middle-aged paunch, this positioning made him a striking figure. Deke leaned toward her and continued to rail in a loud voice, "Seth is such a jerk. What an incompetent! What a tool!"

Deke looked like a giant grizzly bear threatening her. She stepped slowly backward away from the bear, waving him away in a "stop, don't do that" motion, with her arms close to her body. As she backed away and turned her head slightly, she saw Joshua beside her, less than three feet away, sitting upright alertly and staring intently. When she realized Joshua was on guard, she relaxed just a little but didn't move. After about a minute of raucous ranting, the bear lowered his arms. Kelly did not move a muscle. Seeing Joshua must have been the jolt that arrested the bear.

The bear asked Kelly in a mocking manner, "Why did you step back?" imitating her arm-waving, disdainfully.

"You startled me."

"I'm angry at the bookkeeper, not you." The bear sat down. The bear had now resumed a human-like manner.

"Deke, it's time for Joshua and me to go home. Have a good night."

Over the course of the next few days, Kelly spoke to staff she trusted, saying, "Please don't let me be alone with Deke. I need to feel safe in the office. I won't feel safe if I am alone with him. Please keep watch. If you see Deke heading to my office, please come up with him. I really appreciate your help and understanding. Thanks."

After the bear incident, Joshua became more of a caretaker to Kelly. He watched over everything she did and made sure she did not harm herself. When Joshua observed Kelly had left a stove burner on inadvertently, he stood in front of the stove and barked until she came by, figured out what she had done, and turned it off.

"Thank you, Joshua, you take such good care of me."

If something began to boil over on the stove without her notice, he barked, telling her to rectify the situation.

"Thank you, Joshua, what would I do without you? You take such good care of me. Love you."

Kelly had not taught Joshua to do any of these tasks. He had figured them out for himself. Kelly was impressed and amazed by his behavior.

After the encounter with the bear, Kelly's somatic responses became more frequent and more intense. She found them harder to process out of her body. She and Joshua went on longer and more vigorous walks.

In psychotherapy, Ella said, "Kelly, you are not making eye contact. I'm here. With all you are undergoing, you are dissociated into so many pieces. Let's do some trance to help you gain back some control."

Before leaving the session, Kelly said, "Mother's Day is coming up. I'm looking forward to seeing Darcy. Happy Mother's Day, Ella. See you next week."

A few days before Mother's Day, Darcy returned from the last of four trips Kelly had paid for Darcy to take. The trips were to college campuses across the country where she had gotten accepted to do her PhD in neurobiology. The plan was for Darcy to check out each of the college towns, her department and potential colleagues, and campus life. Making sure these places were a good fit academically and could also accommodate Darcy's physical limitations and pain management needs was important to Kelly, so she had encouraged Darcy to go and had helped her organize the trips. After each trip, Kelly and Darcy had discussed Darcy's impressions and findings. Darcy had narrowed her choice to two schools.

Talking about her life and not Kelly's was acceptable to Darcy. Since January, that is what they had talked about on the bi-weekly dinners Kelly and Darcy had together or the phone calls during the week. When the family dinners stopped at the end of February, Kelly and Darcy often had dinner on Friday night. Kelly still did some grocery shopping for Darcy, but this was intermittent, and typically, she just dropped the food off inside Darcy's apartment, as arranged with Darcy, since Darcy was often out.

Kelly did not tell Darcy she was looking for a job and talking with divorce lawyers. Darcy was still in communication with her dad, she had told Kelly, so Kelly assumed she knew what Deke had wanted Darcy to know. She longed to tell Darcy what was really happening, but she felt excluded and helpless to do anything about it. Kelly did her best to make peace with her predicament, but she was failing to do so.

The Friday just before Mother's Day, Kelly got a call about the only job opportunity she had on the table. She had no other applications out there, and she had not seen anything else to apply to for weeks. Even though this position was below her skill level, it had virtually no overlap with the family business, so Kelly was enthusiastic about it.

About three weeks earlier, Kelly had received a call about the position from the woman who would be her boss, "Kelly, I am very pleased to tell you that you scored highest on the interview. I am recommending you to the CEO. We should hear soon."

Now she was told, "Kelly, I regret to say the CEO has decided not to hire externally. We are going to promote someone from within. Thank you again for participating in the interview process."

On Mother's Day, Deke sent Kelly a nice e-mail, saying, "Happy Mother's Day to a great mom."

But for the first time ever, Kelly did not receive a card from Darcy. Kelly had planned to do some grocery shopping on Mother's Day and drop off some groceries for Darcy. Holding the groceries, she knocked on Darcy's door that afternoon. She had telephoned in advance, so Kelly knew Darcy was expecting her. For the first time, Darcy did not invite Kelly in for a coffee.

"Thanks for the groceries, Mom," she said at the door. "Goodbye." Darcy closed the door.

When Kelly and Joshua returned from the drive to Darcy's, Kelly made herself an espresso and sat on the living room couch, while Joshua lay down near the window, watching her. She told Joshua, "I don't understand. Darcy and I have always been close. I am so upset. What is this rejection about?"

Joshua became deep in thought, then he blinked at her as if to say, "I understand, but I don't know. I love you."

At around five that afternoon, Darcy called Kelly and asked, "Do you want to go for dinner or something?"

"It's okay, Darcy. You sound tired. Thanks for the offer. I'll take a rain check." "Okay, Mom. See you soon."

The next afternoon, Kelly and Bea met for lunch at a favorite family spot that Kelly, Deke, and Darcy used to frequent together. As Kelly and Bea chatted over their food, Kelly spotted Deke with a woman at a table far from theirs at the back of the restaurant by the windows. Deke had his back to Kelly, but when he turned slightly, she recognized his profile. He and his lady friend looked to be on a date.

"Bea, Deke is here with another woman. I can't believe it. We haven't even agreed the marriage is over." "Do you want to leave?"

"No, I think I'll be okay. I can manage. Deke doesn't know I'm here. Excuse me, I'm going to go to the ladies' room."

As Kelly looked in the mirror by the sinks, she started to have a panic attack. When her pacing was not quelling her anxiety, she called her internist, "Dr. Mahoney, this is Kelly Delmonico. I am feeling really anxious. I'm not sleeping. My eyes won't close when I lie down. I'm concerned I'm going to get sick."

"How long have you been having trouble sleeping?"

"It's been months, but my anxiety is getting worse."

"I'll prescribe a mild nighttime sedative to help you sleep. My office will call you for an appointment to see me in two weeks to see if the sedative is helping and how you are doing."

On their wedding anniversary a week later, Deke sent Kelly an e-mail, "Happy anniversary. I love you today and always."

Kelly's financial situation was worsening. What Deke was paying her was not covering her household expenses. She was still covering Darcy's shortfall, and all the lines of credit were maxed out.

Every time she would ask Deke for help, he would say, "I have no money."

She continued her search for the right divorce lawyer. She had already met with five lawyers. One or two, she thought were great, but they didn't have the time to take on her case.

She was flabbergasted when one of the good ones told her, "I have been working for eight years with a client with three young children to secure a divorce from her husband, who has narcissism personality disorder. This is typical. I can cite other examples."

Another good one told her, "I wish I could take your case, but my caseload is full. I understand your pain. Last year, I had to dismantle my law practice and start again. My former partner turned out to be a sufferer of narcissism personality disorder. If you need a witness, I would be happy to testify to what it is like to be in a relationship with a narcissist."

Kelly was down to her last referral, the famous Peter Numehy. She drove to his office and waited in earnest in his waiting area for the late afternoon appointment. She had spent the day working at home with Joshua and then departed for the lawyer's office. As Numehy walked down the winding metal staircase out of a 1940s Hollywood movie, with his straight, black, greased-up hair tied back in a ponytail, and wearing a sleek, silk, black suit and white shirt with a thin black leather tie, Kelly became uneasy.

"Mr. Numehy, my husband Deke has narcissism personality disorder. He has assaulted me. I just can't go on with the marriage. I am seeking a divorce. Can you help me?"

Numehy retorted, "Please stop this name-calling. It is irrelevant. Of course, I can help you. When our discussion is over, I can even show you the way to the transit station."

"What?"

Kelly thought stating Deke's affliction and its seriousness was hardly name-calling. Oh my God! He is an extroverted version of Deke. I can smell that on him. I have to leave. . . now.

"Thank you, Mr. Numehy. This is not going to work out. Goodbye."

As she rushed out of Numehy's office, she could hear him yell, "I will send you my bill."

When she got home, she hugged Joshua. "I'm glad I'm home, Joshua. Love you." The butterflies were back.

After dinner and a short walk with Joshua, she sat in the sunroom with Joshua beside her, nursing a glass of sparkling water with lemon.

She told Joshua, "It is so appalling to have to earn my livelihood with Deke. I can't do it much longer. I'm trapped. I feel so hopeless. I really need some support from someone who truly loves me deeply and will miss me when I'm gone. Who should I call?" Although perplexed, Joshua blinked back at her in support.

The telephone rang. "Hello, Darcy." Kelly listened for some time to what Darcy was saying and responded with intermittent chuckling.

"Darcy, thanks for sharing those funny stories."

"Mom, is everything okay?"

"Everything's fine, Darcy. Thanks for calling. Have a good night."

Then, not more than two minutes later, Kelly called Darcy back. She got her voicemail. "Darcy, it's Mom. I am not okay. Please call me back right away."

Minutes passed. Kelly waited patiently, but Darcy did not call her back.

Feebly typing with her fingers going limp and her body shaking, Kelly sent Darcy a long, slightly incoherent text message, not rereading to check for autocorrect errors.

"I am not okay. I have reached the end of my rope. I need to feel loved? and appreciated by you and I don't feel that way. I risk you not talking to me again to punish me for talking about how I am. We are no talking really anyway.

"I feel disconnected and lost and alone and you don't really care enough about me. I feel unmoved. I imagine you won't respond. I will get that code and eventually there might be some repair.

"I would not be sending this to you if I did not feel such utter despair. I expect you won't reply back. Do you love me enough that you can actually make me feel that you do? If you can, now is the time! I need it most."

Kelly waited about half an hour for Darcy to get back to her. But Darcy did not respond at all. Still hopeful Darcy might connect, Kelly took Joshua out for his late-night constitutional. They enjoyed a walk to the high school and back.

After entering the front door on the return from the walk and removing Joshua's leash, Kelly checked her voice mail, e-mail, and text messages. There was nothing from Darcy.

Kelly lay down parallel against the inside of her front door and began weeping uncontrollably. Joshua lay down beside her. He cried in the same tone as her cries. Kelly was present just enough to notice it wasn't a dog cry. Joshua was imitating Kelly's cry incredibly well.

After about thirty seconds of Joshua's weeping like her or maybe longer, amazed and finally startled enough by his cry, Kelly woke from her heartbreak. She hugged Joshua. His warmth penetrated her anxiety and it started to melt a little. When she continued to sob, Joshua sat up beside her and barked at her rhythmically and firmly. This made her stop crying.

Strengthened by Joshua's support, Kelly stood up, looked at Joshua, who was now standing beside her, and declared, "Joshua, I am so grateful you are here by my side. I love you."

She put her arms around him and gave him a huge hug and then a big kiss on his forehead. "Come, Joshua. Bedtime."

CHAPTER 25

Calling It Quits

It took Darcy two days to respond to Kelly's voicemail. "Mom, you called me too late, dumping emotions on me at eleven at night and expecting me to drop everything and deal with you."

At Kelly's next session, she told Ella, "I just don't understand. How could Darcy respond that way? I thought we were close. We often speak later than that, even on a school night. I have always dropped everything to help her at every turn. How can she be so uncaring? She didn't say anything about what I wrote. It's all about the inconvenience I caused her. Is this my daughter?

"We have been seeing each other regularly. I helped her to go on all those trips to those campuses. I know she does not want to talk about me, but I thought this was an unusual circumstance, that her love for me would take over. I thought she really cared about me. What sort of person gets a cry of help from her mother, regardless of how good or bad their relationship is, and responds this way? What have I done wrong? Is this my fault?"

"I don't know why she responded this way. Perhaps, the next time you see her, you will get some clarity. In previous sessions with me, you did say you had concerns about your relationship with Darcy— that you may have misjudged the closeness. I think your reaching out to her was a test of that. You hoped she'd pass with flying colors, but she didn't. I'm so sorry."

At the end of the session, Kelly reiterated, "I still don't understand it. I thought Darcy and I were close. I thought she really cared about me."

At the next session with Ella, Ella asked nonchalantly, "Have you considered suicide?"

"I wouldn't give Deke the satisfaction."

"Kelly, you are strong. You are intelligent and successful. You can get through this. Let's do some trance. I think it will help you to relax and see things more clearly."

On the drive home with Joshua and all that evening, Kelly tried not to think about Darcy. But she did anyway. After her late-night constitutionals with Joshua, she got ready for bed. Joshua kept her company on the bed as she cried her eyes out until she dozed off into sleep.

In the morning, Kelly decided she was ready to tell Deke their relationship was over. She would stay home and work the rest of the week with Joshua. At home, she would pick the appropriate time to share the news with Deke. She remembered that Susan, a business colleague of some years, had invited her and Joshua to spend the coming weekend with her and her husband Zach at their farm. The couple had a two-year-old wheaten terrier, Bingley, a potential playmate for Joshua. Out of town, Joshua and she would be safe if Deke moved further along the crazy continuum.

"Joshua, how would you like to go to a farm next weekend? We can go for a swim and play ball. A few days out of town will be good for us. It'll be fun."

Not moving from his prostrate position on the floor beside her, Joshua looked back at Kelly and blinked. He had understood and wanted to go. Kelly smiled at Joshua and called Susan to accept the invitation.

As the trip to the farm approached, Kelly decided not to tell Deke about the end of the relationship before she and Joshua left. When the trip to the farm finally arrived, Kelly and Joshua were ready for the journey. Kelly had packed their clothing, some food, and amenities the night before so it was quick and easy to load the car in the morning. Joshua had plenty of room in the back seat to stretch out and sleep. Kelly sang along to some '60s music on the radio as she drove.

Upon Kelly's and Joshua's arrival at the farm, Susan and Zach each gave Kelly a hug. "Welcome!" they said in unison.

"Hi Joshua, meet Bingley. Go play!" Susan called out.

After unpacking and having lunch, Kelly sat out on the deck in the shade, with Joshua beside her, and read, while Susan and Zach gardened and Bingley looked on.

That day, Kelly spent much of her time playing with the two dogs and reading while her friends weeded and did household repairs. Kelly ran with the dogs or played fetch with them in the fallow grassy fields. Bingley loved to roll in the puddles formed by the rain from a few days before they had arrived, but Joshua was not interested. He did not really bond with Bingley but humored Kelly as she played with both of them. Kelly was in the present with the dogs and her friends, enjoying the farm fragrances, the scenery, and the company, not thinking about the situation she had left behind.

The next afternoon, they all went to a public beach nearby. The weather was too cool for the humans to take a dip but just fine for the dogs. Joshua and Bingley swam and retrieved some balls and sticks. Kelly wanted to stay all afternoon and play with the dogs.

"Come, let's go back to the farm. You boys have had a good swim. There is gardening to do and then we can all have dinner," Susan said.

Kelly responded, "Joshua, come, let's go to the car." He dutifully came and escorted Kelly to the car. They had a pleasant dinner. After dinner, the adults read and listened to music, while the dogs chewed on a rawhide Kelly had brought for each of them.

After lunch the next day, it was time to depart.

"Thanks so much, Susan. Joshua and I had a wonderful time. The barbecues were great, Zach. Hope to see you both soon. Enjoy the rest of your stay at the farm."

When Kelly arrived home, and she and Joshua walked into the house, she had a strange sensation someone had been there while she was away. After she dropped off her luggage in the bedroom, she and Joshua went into Darcy's room. It was a mess, with drawers partly open, stuff missing from her bookshelves and her bed mussed.

Before Kelly had left for the farm, she had written a short note to Darcy and left it on Darcy's pillow. The note said, "I can't believe you're you."

As Kelly scanned Darcy's bed, she realized the note was gone. Writing and leaving the note for Darcy was not a premeditated move on Kelly's part. She had not thought about writing it before she wrote it. Kelly didn't know why she sensed Darcy might come by without permission.

Before she left, Kelly had told Darcy, "Joshua and I are going to Susan's farm for the weekend to get some rest. Let's get together when we get back."

Seeing Darcy's bedroom in such a state, Kelly felt violated and angry. Again, someone had sneaked into the house and moved things about.

The next day, Kelly and Joshua went to the family business office. When Kelly's meetings were done at the end of the day, she collected her things. She had just passed by Deke's office with Joshua to say goodbye to him.

As she and Joshua were walking away from Deke's office and toward the front door to leave, Deke called out, "You have changed. Your behavior toward Darcy is reprehensible. What do you mean, 'I can't believe you're you'? What possessed you to send her that text asking her for help?"

Looking at the floor, Kelly babbled in a low voice, "Deke, this is not the right place or time."

Chloe was standing next to the front door when Kelly and Joshua got there. Kelly and Chloe chatted briefly. Seconds later, Deke arrived there, ready to leave. Chloe and Kelly peered down the hallway to the elevator. Several people were walking in the hallway, and many entered the elevator. Kelly was a bit uncomfortable, aware Chloe must think Joshua and she were safe to walk to the elevator unchaperoned, with all the people around. With Deke standing there, Kelly was too afraid to say anything to Chloe. No one accompanied Kelly, Joshua, and Deke as they departed the office.

Deke followed Kelly and Joshua from the office, down the hallway, and into the crowded elevator, out of the building, down the stairs, and across the asphalt parking lot. Once outside, Deke shouted at Kelly, even though strangers from the building were around and within earshot. Kelly didn't pick up on what he was saying. She wasn't listening. She was mortified and scared.

Joshua hadn't been out since lunchtime. Kelly intended to take him to the park across the road from the office building. Kelly wanted Deke to leave, but she was too afraid to risk anything more unpleasant. She focused on Joshua and did not make eye contact with Deke.

Deke asked, "Do you mind if I come with you and Joshua?"

Kelly said nothing. She looked around and there was no one except her and Joshua. The others had scattered and gone home. Deke was now inches from her. They crossed the street together and went to the green space. Joshua relieved himself quickly. Then they walked back toward the parking lot.

On the way back to the parking lot, Deke exclaimed, "I didn't hire a private investigator. It was a joke. I'll take a lie detector test and prove it to you!" They continued walking to the car.

After a pause, he repeated, "I didn't hire a private investigator. I'll take a lie detector test."

Kelly stopped in her tracks. With Joshua beside her, she stared straight into Deke's eyes and declared, "I don't believe you. I saw your face."

"I don't have any money to hire a private investigator. I was just joking with you. I'll prove it. I'll tell a lie detector test."

Kelly ignored his bluster. Swiftly, she walked the ten feet to the car with Joshua, opened the back door for him, watched him hop in, put on his seatbelt, closed the door, and then opened the driver's door and got into the car. She locked the doors and kept the windows closed, not wanting to listen to whatever Deke was shouting at her. She drove away, leaving Deke in the dust.

In therapy later that week, she told Ella, "I don't understand Darcy. I don't know who she is. She doesn't want to talk to me about anything, but she is sharing things between her and me with Deke, and he is attacking me for it, making me less safe.

"Darcy went into the house without my permission. I don't know why I had a premonition she might do that. It is so unlike her. She is siding with Deke. I can't believe it. Has she forgotten her entire life with me and what he has done to her? I am so hurt."

"It is hard to understand. I don't have answers for you. You need to stay strong and centered."

"I feel good about how I handled Deke in the parking lot. It was empowering, even though it was scary."

A couple of days later Allegra telephoned Kelly, "Stan and I are going to spend a long weekend at the family chalet. Why don't you and Joshua join us? It will be fun and relaxing—some free time in the woods for walking and reflection, good food, and good wine. The four of us can do a hike up to the waterfall and have a picnic on Sunday. What do you say?"

"Thanks, Allegra, it sounds lovely, but I am not up to it. Perhaps, in a month or two when I am stronger."

"Kelly, I won't take no for an answer. You haven't been to the family chalet since Mom died. We all have good memories about the chalet, and some sad ones, too, of course. Let's make some new good memories."

"Okay, Allegra, we'll go."

"Stan and I will pick up you and Joshua at ten in the morning on Friday. Then we can stay at the chalet and come back Sunday night. See you soon."

Kelly had always liked Allegra. Over the years, she had wanted to spend more time with her. However, they only met at family functions—dinners, baptisms, communions, holidays, birthdays, weddings, and funerals. That dinner with Allegra and Stan after Christmas was the first time ever Kelly had met them without Deke.

Allegra had confided to Kelly, "I consider you a sister. Wish we could be closer." "Me, too," Kelly had replied.

Deke did not support this closeness. He was not interested in seeing his sister more frequently, and as a result, Kelly and Allegra didn't spend other time together and did not become really close.

The afternoon arrived to go to the chalet. Stan and Allegra arrived a little early, but Kelly was ready, having packed the night before. She and Joshua rested in the back of Stan and Allegra's SUV as they drove together to the chalet. Joshua had his own seat and was stretched out as he lay asleep. Kelly, Stan, and Allegra chatted about small stuff on the way—the country landscapes, the traffic, and the weather.

Once at the chalet, Kelly unpacked. Then she joined Stan and Allegra outside. They all sat on lawn chairs in the shade, relaxed, and chatted. Allegra and Stan had a few beers. Kelly took Joshua for some walks on the chalet grounds and threw some sticks for him to retrieve.

When it was time to have dinner, Kelly and Allegra prepared the vegetables, while Stan made a steak barbecue with corn on the cob.

After dinner, they all sat by the bonfire Stan had made in the fire pit, while Joshua snoozed beside Kelly.

After dinner and sipping her red wine by the fire with Allegra and Stan, Kelly opened up about Deke.

"I have something I want to tell you about Deke. After Christmas, he was diagnosed with having a serious personality disorder, narcissism personality disorder. I brought you a non-technical book I read on it, in case you find that helpful."

Kelly was surprised by Allegra and Stan's non-reaction. How is it that neither Allegra nor Stan was troubled by Deke's disorder? Their faces were expressionless. What didn't she know?

Allegra revealed, "Everyone was afraid of Deke. My parents let Deke take control of them. They let him dictate what to do and when to do it because he was so smart."

Why did no one ever tell Kelly about this before? They just let her deal with him. Good luck, Kelly, he's yours now—glad we offloaded him onto you. Was it because they considered Kelly an outsider, not 100 percent Italian? No, that's ridiculous, can't be.

A minute or two of silence passed. Allegra went into the kitchen to get some drinks and returned with a bottle of beer for her and for Stan. Kelly had spent the time patting Joshua, giving him a light scratch behind the ears as he sat in front of her and looked into her eyes. Stan tended the fire, by adding more wood and moving the logs around with a big stick.

Having gained her composure after a few sips of wine, Kelly brought up what had been chewing away at her subconscious and now had muscled into her awareness.

"Allegra, why did your mother leave early when she said she would stay a month to help me with Darcy, after Darcy was born?"

"You told her to leave."

"No, I didn't. I begged her to stay. Why did your mother think I wanted her to leave?"

"Deke told my mother you wanted her to leave."

Kelly paused, feeling her feet slip from under her even though she was sitting down.

"That is just so unbelievable. I was becoming close to your mother. She was the mother I never had. Most days during her stay, we went out for a short drive for coffee and lunch with baby Darcy and chatted. Your mother's help was invaluable. I couldn't understand why your mother wanted to leave, even after I had begged her to stay. I asked Deke about it as she was leaving, but he just shrugged it off."

The mother-in-law revelation mutilated Kelly's world. It dismembered the foundations of her understanding of who she was and her relationship to the family. The ground got uneven beneath her. She got dizzy. Her heart raced. She sobbed. Then she rose from her chair and paced.

"Allegra, I am not feeling well. I'm going to take Joshua for a walk and clear my head. Come, Joshua, let's go."

When Kelly kept her mind blank and studied the night sky, the walk worked well. But she couldn't do that for more than a moment or two. Despite being with Joshua, she could not console herself. She was trembling and her breaths got shorter.

"Come, Joshua, let's go back to the chalet."

Back with Allegra and Stan, Kelly tried to gain her composure and resume the conversation with them, but she couldn't. She couldn't sit still.

"Come, Joshua, let's go for a walk."

Kelly hoped another walk would settle her, but it didn't. After four repetitions of this, Kelly took more blood pressure medication to stop her heart from pounding. It didn't help.

Allegra and Stan tried to comfort her. Their lingering hugs did not help. Kelly could not close the floodgates of her anxiety. Kelly remained in this state for a couple of hours.

"Allegra, I am so sorry. I can't settle. I need to go home right away. Please take me and Joshua home."

"Are you sure, Kelly?"

"Yes, I really need to leave. I don't feel well at all. And nothing is helping. I'll feel better back at home."

"Okay, Kelly. Let's pack up and go."

All the way home in Allegra and Stan's SUV, Kelly clung to Joshua and tried to calm down.

When they arrived at Kelly's, Allegra inquired, "It is really late. Would it be okay if we stay overnight?"

"Of course. I'll make up the hide-a-bed in the den for you. You both will be comfortable there."

When Kelly woke up the next morning, she found that her hands were still on Joshua's shoulders. She hadn't let go of him all night.

When she got out of bed to say good morning to Allegra and Stan, they were already gone.

Kelly spent the rest of the weekend in a fog, not feeling anything. At Kelly's session the next day, she discussed to Ella, "All those wasted years with my mother-in-law thinking I threw her out, and me thinking, why did she leave? After she left, our relationship was never the same. We never got close. For the first couple of weeks after she left, I called her every night to say hello and ask for advice. She criticized me. She told me I was doing everything wrong. 'Be calmer with Darcy,' she said, 'and if you are, she won't cry.' I believed her. After all, she was a nurse, and so experienced. When I learned from Darcy's pediatrician that Darcy was very colicky and that's why she was crying, I stopped asking for my mother-in-law's advice.

"Over the years, the gap in our relationship grew. I felt my mother-in-law was critical of me and whatever closeness we had disappeared. But I did encourage Darcy to become close to her.

"My mother-in-law used to tell Darcy that her behavior was bad. She was spoiled. She should eat foods she didn't like. She didn't help out enough at the chalet, and she should stop being such a snob. Despite all that, Darcy did feel somewhat close to her grandmother. Do you think there was some transference of anger toward me to Darcy?

"I still can't believe Deke did this to me and his mother. He couldn't stand the closeness. Look what his jealousy did! And almost as bad, this story probably went around Deke's entire family. For more than twenty years, Deke's family thought I threw his mother out. No one ever said a word to me—everyone's little secret about what a terrible person they thought I was. I'm sure sadistic Deke enjoyed every moment. This is just so awful!

"This makes me think Deke may be filling Darcy's head with lies. What's worse, she won't even talk to me. He is manipulating Darcy and I can't reach her. She won't let me. She has turned against me. I still can't believe it. Even if Deke is filling her head with lies, why can't she think about her past and her relationship with me, and see through what he is telling her?

"Everyone I ask about it that knows Darcy and me together can't believe it. They can't believe she is siding with Deke and turning against me. It is so painful. I am so hurt. Deke knows this, too. He is probably enjoying this as well."

"Kelly, Deke's lie to his mother is abhorrent. You like to know, at least now you know, although it is a very difficult thing to find out about. I hope Darcy will come around. Stay focused on your future and what you want to accomplish."

After the session, once at home with Joshua, Kelly concentrated on accomplishing her escape from Deke. She spent some time that evening on the internet, looking for a job, and reviewed her notes on referrals for divorce lawyers she had gotten from Susan. She hoped one of the referrals might work out. Kelly checked out her e-mails. There was one from Deke.

In it sandwiched between the complaints, criticisms, and his testaments to his love for her, he wrote, "Our marriage is over. It looks like we won't be reconciling. I am learning to live with that reality."

Does he mean it? Is he serious? Or is this another manipulation? She let his e-mail simmer at the back of her mind.

"Come, Joshua, let's go for a walk."

Joshua quickly got up from under the sunroom table near where Kelly had been seated and accompanied her to the front door to go on their walk. With the warmth of the spring air and the fragrance of the roses blooming as they walked, Kelly felt invigorated. She and Joshua walked to the school and back home. Kelly got a glass of sparkling water with lemon from the kitchen refrigerator, while she listened to Joshua's slurps from his water bowl in the sunroom. Then the twosome went up to the den to watch the late evening news.

Seated on her chair with Joshua lying down near her by the windows, Kelly mused to herself, while the television provided background noise for her thoughts. *I am so worn out from putting off Deke about our relationship. His e-mails are draining to read and to respond to. He breaches fact or stretches and pulls it. I don't have the fortitude to challenge his statements any longer. Our marriage is over. Being friends with Deke is impossible. I can't do it. I want to end my pain.*

Kelly got up from her chair and went into her office to sit at her desk and write a response to Deke. Joshua got up and followed her. He lay down under her desk and warmed her feet. Kelly started the e-mail with, "Deke, I'm so sorry to say, I agree, we won't be reconciling."

Then copying his words from his e-mail to her, she added, "I hope we can part in a calm, reasonable, fair, and compassionate manner."

Deke wrote back immediately, "Don't be so hasty. I love you. Darcy loves you. You are such a great mom. Don't throw away the last forty years together. I did not hire a private investigator. I did not have you followed. You have misinterpreted what I said. We are both better off together. I want to come home."

Despite Deke's attempt at rewriting history and her sense of loyalty and love, Kelly stood firm. She wrote back, "I think it is best that we end the marriage."

"You are wrong. You are not thinking straight. I will take a lie detector test."

"I'm sorry, Deke, it's over."

Deke did not respond. Kelly blanked the entire conversation from her mind and went to bed. She did not remember Joshua jumping off the bed to lie down by the windows.

The next morning, Kelly realized she had not used her head when she declared the end of her marriage to Deke. Her timing was terrible. The damage was done. She didn't want to change course, so she pushed those thoughts out of her mind until her therapy session with Ella a few days later.

"Ella, I was so relieved to tell Deke the marriage was over. It was a great weight off my shoulders. But what bad timing!

"I'm still totally dependent on him for money. I haven't found a job. I don't have a divorce lawyer. I haven't processed fully the frightful face, the gaslighting, being followed, being chased, the bear, Darcy's rejection, and the loss of what my family life has really been about. My immune system is shot. My allergies are terrible. My somatic responses are not improving.

"I can't bear to go into the office anymore. I don't feel safe anywhere. Oh my God! I can't believe my list.

"Thank God for Joshua! Is this my life?"

"Kelly, you have made great progress. You are getting stronger. You have undergone a terrible ordeal. And you have been exposed to very difficult revelations to process. Be kind to yourself and take good care of your health. See you next week."

Before Kelly departed, Ella hugged her. Then Kelly left to get the car and go home with Joshua. At the car, Kelly opened the back door on the driver's side, gave Joshua a prolonged hug, and said, "Love you, Joshua. Let's go home."

Kelly and Darcy Part

Despite just having declared the end of her marriage to Deke, the revelation about Deke's mom and all the other trauma she had suffered, Kelly couldn't help but focus on Darcy. She went over and over the details at home in her head and with Ella in therapy, but she did not move an inch closer to understanding. She and Darcy continued to connect but only in a superficial way.

A week before her college awards ceremony in June, Darcy telephoned.

"Mom, I am winning an award for coming first in my class and also for all the volunteer work I did for the faculty, including the mentoring. Will you come with me to the ceremony? I'd really love it if you would. I didn't invite Dad."

"Yes, of course, Darcy, I'd love to."

"But don't get your hopes up, Mom, I still don't want to go to my master's degree graduation."

"Okay, Darcy. How about we go out for dinner after the awards ceremony and celebrate the award and your graduation?"

"Sounds good, Mom. I'll see you next week."

While Kelly was pleased Darcy wanted her to attend the awards ceremony, she did think Darcy had not given any thought to the impact of her actions on Kelly, especially her uncharacteristic response to Kelly's distress call. Still, Kelly hoped Darcy might raise the matter and apologize after the awards ceremony.

At the awards ceremony sitting in the audience three rows from the front, Kelly was delighted, struggling to hold back the tears of joy and sadness. She was so proud of Darcy for her achievements.

When the event was over, Kelly took Darcy out for a celebration dinner at one of Darcy's favorite Italian restaurants. After discussing Darcy's plans for her doctorate, the move across the country, and missing Buffington, Darcy disclosed, "Mom, I am having trouble making ends meet with the money I am making from teaching and the money you are giving me. My rent and utilities have gone up and so have my physiotherapy and massage expenses. Are you able to help me out more?"

"I'll do my best. I'll see what I can do."

Kelly had given her all the money she could manage. It was time for Deke to step up and help out. If she put something in writing to Deke and copied Darcy, Deke couldn't possibly refuse to help Darcy.

As she and Joshua headed for bed, she said aloud, "Joshua, Darcy did not say a word about me. She didn't ask me anything about what is going on in my life. She didn't ask about you either. Is this the Darcy you know?"

Joshua tilted his head and opened his mouth slightly as if to say, "I don't know." Then he straightened his head, gazed into Kelly's eyes reassuringly, and Kelly felt better.

The following day, Kelly had planned to go to business meetings away from the office. Joshua was spending the day with Bailey. She had a lunch meeting with a potential new client for the family business who had contacted her with some opportunities. During lunch, the conversation was all about work. As Kelly was listening to the client, she could feel her face swelling. It was a bad allergy day. Her sinuses were worse than usual.

After lunch, Kelly went to the restaurant restroom to take a gander at her face. To her astonishment, when she looked in the mirror, she saw she had swelled up like a chipmunk. Her cheeks were huge. How could this fellow not say anything about the swelling? He had been facing her the entire time.

Kelly rushed to the pharmacy across the street from the restaurant to get an antihistamine. The antihistamine was supposed to be fast-acting. After swallowing the pill, waiting a few minutes in the pharmacy meandering through the aisles and observing nothing had happened, she called Dr. Mahoney, who directed, "Don't take another antihistamine. Go to St. Andrew's Hospital right away."

Kelly did not really want to go to the hospital, but she was a little worried. She called her client for the afternoon meeting and rescheduled it for the next day. Then, she hailed a cab and went to the emergency room. When she arrived at the triage desk, the nurse looked at her and escorted her into a room immediately. She telephoned Darcy.

"Darcy, I am at St. Andrews in the emergency room, waiting to be seen. I think I am having a terrible allergic reaction. Do you think you could come to the hospital and stay with me?"

"Okay, Mom. I'll come. I'll be there within the hour."

"Thanks, Darcy. See you soon."

By the time Darcy arrived, the nurse had already given Kelly a large needle full of antihistamine, so Kelly was a little drowsy. When Darcy approached Kelly's bed, Kelly could tell Darcy was angry.

After about a half-hour of small talk between them, Darcy said, "Mom, I don't feel well. I have a migraine." Then she slumped in the chair beside Kelly's bed.

After Kelly pleaded with Darcy a few times, saying, "Darcy, thanks again for coming. I really appreciate it. Please go home. Your migraine is really painful. I'll be okay," Darcy left.

The antihistamine knocked Kelly out. She slept for a few hours. When she woke up, she was still very swollen.

The intern who discharged her advised, "Mrs. Delmonico, when you get home, please take more antihistamine and then some again in the morning. Your swelling will subside and should be gone within 24 hours. You have had a very strong allergic reaction. In this pen is a dose of epinephrine in case you have another reaction around your mouth and a prescription for another dose. It is up to you to figure out what triggered this allergic response. Take care."

During the several hours in the emergency room, Kelly did not worry about Joshua. She knew he was well looked after. While waiting for the emergency doctor to see her, Kelly had called Liz to let her know her predicament.

Liz said, "No worries, Kelly. I will give Joshua some dinner with Bailey. Then I'll bring him home a little later than usual."

When Kelly got home, Joshua greeted her at the front door. Seeing him made her feel better. She smiled at him and gave him a hug, saying, "Love you, Joshua," and put on his leash. They went out for their late-night constitutional before going to bed.

After Kelly checked out her swelling the next morning and saw a small amount of swelling remaining in her cheeks, she decided she felt well enough to get on with her day. She resolved to take action on the financial front for Darcy. She sat down at the sunroom table with her espresso, computer, and Joshua under the table by her feet.

To Deke and copy to Darcy, she e-mailed, "The company will be receiving a small check for some strategic planning work I just finished with Organic Kitchen. This check will cover Darcy's shortfall until she leaves Buffington for school. We can afford this. Our business is doing well."

Neither Deke nor Darcy acknowledged Kelly's e-mail. Darcy did not even ask Kelly about the aftermath of her trip to the hospital. Kelly wrote again just to Deke two days later about the matter but never got a response. Kelly didn't understand why neither Deke nor Darcy had responded but hoped it was because Deke was helping out.

Money was really tight for Kelly as well. She wrote to Deke a week later, "We have no choice but to sell the house, pay off the lines of credit, and divide the remains of the house. We need some time to find a real estate agent and get the house ready for selling. Let's sell the house next spring."

Deke replied, "Agreed, sell in the spring."

With an agreement regarding the sale of the house, there was not much of the marriage that still needed to be sorted out.

Kelly wanted the opportunity to talk to Darcy about what was going on, her life, and their relationship before Darcy headed out of town to school. This longing was sawing an enormous hole in her gut.

"Darcy, I really need to speak to you about what is going on. It is important to me. Please don't put me off."

"I'm busy, Mom. Maybe on Saturday."

Saturday came and went. There was no meeting. Every time they set a date, Darcy canceled and said she was too busy organizing her trip.

Darcy was planning to take a two-week course in neuroscience in Milan in late June and then do some traveling for a couple of weeks. Kelly had agreed before Darcy's new financial issues had emerged to help her pay for her trip.

"Darcy, we really need to meet and chat about things. Please."

"Okay, Mom, I'm too busy now, but yes, let's meet when I come back from Italy."

When Darcy returned from Italy, she refused to meet with Kelly and said, "It is some kind of blackmail that I need to meet with you in order to get the rest of the money for my Italy trip."

In therapy, Kelly discussed the matter with Ella.

"I don't understand Darcy's response at all. Blackmail, what is she talking about? We had agreed to meet after her return. My financing her trip is a separate issue. I want to see her and give her the money. Does she expect me to mail it to her?

"I am so sad, so hurt and so angry. I need to do something. I can't just let her go out of town without some closure on this."

When she got home, Kelly crafted a long e-mail to Darcy. She hoped the letter would encourage Darcy to speak with her, once Darcy was more knowledgeable about the situation. She wrote,

> Dear Darcy,
>
> I write this letter because it is my only option to communicate with you. There is no person I love more or who is more important to me than you.
>
> You are in no way responsible for my wishing to sever my relationship with your dad. I was drowning in the relationship. I treaded water for you as long as I could.
>
> Right now, you are angry about the entire situation, and, in particular, you are angry at me. I have been protecting you from what is really going on and this is now working against me. My behavior toward your dad is to protect myself, both physically and emotionally.
>
> Your father was diagnosed with a serious personality disorder, narcissism personality disorder. He exhibits sadistic behavior toward me and probably has for some time. Enclosed are some details about the disorder.
>
> I have been fearful of your father for years. I did not understand the situation or what was wrong. My recent behavior toward your dad has been out of great fear and for self-preservation.
>
> Your response to me when I reached out to you in desperation was life-changing for me. It made me very sad. It made me disappointed in you for the first time in

your life and it made me angry. I'd like to think your icy response was crafted by someone else, but you sent it.

How could you chide me for "dumping emotions on you at eleven at night and expecting you to drop everything and deal with me"?

That is exactly what I expect from someone close to me when I am in jeopardy and the emotions are so serious. Especially you. I have dropped everything for you and helped you right away your entire life—for things big and small—most recently so you would get an A on your master's thesis.

When either of us is in severe emotional stress or in jeopardy or both, we need to have a strong emotional connection or nothing much is between us. We need to be able to tell each other 'I love you' and 'things will be okay'. That is all I was asking from you in the initial text of utter desperation I sent to you.

I don't want to be frozen out of your life. You can create the thaw.

I will always love you. You matter immensely to me. Love you always with all my heart,

Mom

In therapy, she and Ella discussed the letter.

"I think you wrote a good letter, Kelly. It was from the heart and clear. It is very unfortunate Darcy has chosen not to respond. I am so sorry."

"It feels like an out-of-body experience. It did not really happen. I am so devastated. Who is this person? What happened to my daughter? Who is in her body?

"The annual trip to the cottage is coming up. Should I invite Darcy? I don't think I could handle two weeks with her.

"Now I have a cottage but no family to go with it. Bea has stayed at the cottage with us before and liked it. Perhaps, she would enjoy a longer stay, just with me and Joshua. Darcy won't want to come if Bea is there. They don't get along."

Darcy e-mailed, "Mom, I will be out of town the weekend you are going up to the cottage, so I won't be able to go this year." "Okay. I will miss you. Have a good time."

Kelly, Joshua, and Bea drove to the cottage together. It was a smooth drive up. As she drove, she enjoyed the scenery and the lack of traffic. She and Bea sang the oldie pop tunes together as they listened to them on the radio.

Once at the cottage, Kelly did her best to be in the present and kept her crying bouts private. When she cried for more than a few seconds, Joshua stared into her eyes and barked one sharp bark. Kelly interpreted his actions as saying to her, "Stop crying. I'm here. You are okay." This worked. She stopped crying.

Kelly, Joshua, and Bea swam together every day at the cottage. Kelly provided Joshua with ample noodles to rescue. He dove off the dock and retrieved balls and sticks Kelly threw for him. In the evening after brushing Joshua, Kelly blew Joshua's fur dry. Then he had a good chew on one of his beef bones. After about an hour of chewing, he snoozed. Before bed, Kelly and Joshua enjoyed their quick constitutional.

Bea had planned a birthday celebration for Kelly. She knew this was Kelly's first cottage birthday without Deke and Darcy being there. Traveling from their farm to the cottage was only about twenty miles, so Bea had invited Susan and Zach for cake.

Kelly did her best to be upbeat during the festivities. Except for a few escaped tears, she muddled through and put on a happy face. She did her best to bury any sadness. Kelly was thankful Joshua picked up any pieces of portending gloom and hid them in his comforting warmth by her side.

During the cottage stay, Kelly contemplated her job prospects. She had found three different but promising positions. Two were consulting jobs and the third was to run a virtual organization. Before she left for the cottage, each company had made her an offer.

Kelly did her best thinking just before bed. Marinating on the first offer, Kelly concluded, *heading up an international virtual organization in a new area will be a good learning experience. I won't overlap with Deke and the family business. But most of my work will be on the phone and potentially at odd hours of the day or night dealing with the time differences in Europe and Asia. I think I need to be around people.*

She had high hopes for the second offer. She was looking forward to working with the head of the company, which she hadn't done since before Darcy was born. Upon reflection, she deduced, *we are both senior consultants. There is not much chance we will actually be able to work on projects together. During our lunch a couple of weeks before the cottage trip, the meeting triggered my somatic response. His knowing both Deke and me in a professional setting fired my Deke neurons.*

The third offer involved doing some work in both change management and strategic planning. Kelly knew the head of the company, Bill Chen, by reputation. Over the years, they had met a few times to explore how their firms might partner on ventures, but nothing had come of those discussions.

This will be an opportunity to focus on a different area of strategic planning. I will also be working with a colleague, whom I like, to help him launch a change-management practice. There will be minimal overlap with the family business and a new team of people to work with. I can work from home with Joshua two or three days a week.

She patted Joshua, who was lying on her bed beside her and paused. Then she decided, *working with Bill is the best offer. I'm going to take it.*

The rest of the cottage trip went swimmingly for Kelly, with walks and swims during the day with Joshua, reading and videos in the evening, and Joshua's evening constitutionals. Kelly and Bea shared the chores—housekeeping, cooking, and cleanup—and this worked out well for Kelly. Kelly actually relaxed at the cottage once she had selected which job she was going to take.

For her first day back to the family business office after the cottage trip, Kelly had planned to stay there with Joshua for only a few hours. Deke's mail had piled up during Kelly's two weeks away. Kelly dropped off Deke's mail on his desk shortly after her arrival. At the time, Deke was in a meeting with some staff in one of their small breakout rooms.

About an hour passed. Kelly was still working in her office at her computer. Joshua had been lazy, lying down by the boardroom door instead of following Kelly up to the loft. Kelly heard a noise, glanced up, and saw Deke. He was twenty feet away from her and approaching rapidly. Deke's walking around had not alarmed Joshua, and he did not follow Deke upstairs.

Deke charged into Kelly's office. He stood against the front of her desk, leaned toward her, and threw the mail she had left him at her face, without saying a word. Then he stomped out of her office. Christian, a tall, lean, twenty-something junior consultant, had seen Deke heading Kelly's way and followed him upstairs to the loft.

"Thanks, Christian, for coming up when Deke did. Did you see him throw the mail at me?"

"No, I was too far away."

"I don't feel safe at the office. This can't continue."

She was now keenly aware that staff members were not bodyguards, and their taking on this role was not fair to them or her. This would be the last time she and Joshua would go to the family business office.

As she opened the door for her and Joshua to leave the office that afternoon, Kelly turned around, scanned the office, and took a deep breath. Then she faced the opened door, and she and Joshua swiftly departed for home.

About two weeks after the mail-throwing incident, Kelly heard from Darcy. She received an e-mail from her, saying, "Mom, I love you. I miss you and want a relationship with you."

Kelly reached out, set up, and attended a dinner with Darcy, and then another. At each one, she waited for Darcy to open the discussion about the letter, or about anything of consequence, but Darcy didn't.

Before Darcy moved away to do her PhD, Kieran and Camille came to Buffington for a weekend visit to stay with Kelly and Joshua. A couple of hours after their arrival while they were on the back deck, enjoying the summer air and drinking coffee as Joshua snoozed beside Kelly, Kieran's mobile phone rang. He answered with the speaker phone on.

"Hello, Uncle Kieran. It's Darcy. Would you and Aunt Camille like to come over to my place for a visit this afternoon? I am leaving for school next week. It would be wonderful to see you both before I go. And if you could, please bring Joshua with you."

Kieran took the phone off the speaker, pressed the mute button, and asked, "Kelly, should we go? What do you think?"

"Well, it is your last chance to see Darcy before she goes. So please, go and take Joshua with you." "Alright."

Kieran, Camille, and Joshua left a few minutes later to go to Darcy's. Kelly paced up and down the sunroom, wondering how Darcy could consider it appropriate not to invite her.

Kelly decided she needed to occupy herself with more positive thoughts. She went into the backyard and did some gardening. She found the weeding therapeutic.

When Kieran, Camille, and Joshua returned from Darcy's a couple of hours later and joined Kelly on the backyard deck, Kelly asked Kieran, "Did you have a nice visit? Did Darcy say anything of consequence?"

"The visit was fine. No, she didn't say anything noteworthy."

Kelly felt shut out. She could feel her angst in her gut. She did her best to dissipate it with the sparkling water with lemon she was sipping.

The rest of the weekend with Kieran and Camille passed with walks together in Lawrence Park with Joshua, afternoon sits on the backyard deck making small talk, and barbecues Kieran made. The subject of Darcy did not come up again.

Kelly knew roughly when Darcy was leaving town but not the exact date. She had asked Kieran and Camille, but they were not sure either. She had hoped Darcy would contact her to say goodbye, but Darcy didn't.

Kelly was exhausted and decided to take some time off between jobs. Darcy's departure added to Kelly's malaise and fatigue. She did not want to risk a clash with Deke, so she asked her lawyer, whom she had retained a couple of weeks earlier—one of the referrals from Susan—to notify Deke about her plans to leave the family business.

Kelly knew she could not go back into the office without Deke confronting her. Staff would not be able to meet with her nearby without Deke finding out and perhaps making a scene. So instead of direct contact to say goodbye, Kelly sent personal e-mails to each of her staff.

Each replied, saying variants of "thank you" and "I will miss you."

After the e-mail exchanges, Kelly felt she had achieved some closure. She was finally ready for something new.

CHAPTER 27

New Revelations

Kelly started her new job in mid-September. She liked her new responsibilities and the people she worked with. It was a blessing not to be with Deke and not to feel responsible to feed every person in the company. She was developing expertise in some new change-management areas while working on more routine strategic-planning projects. She spent two or three workdays a week at home with Joshua and the rest at work, while Joshua enjoyed the company of Liz and Bailey.

Liz told Kelly, "Joshua has acclimatized to being with me and Bailey, while you are at the office. The boys have great fun playing in Lawrence Park. After the walk, we return home for a snack and some water. Then they curl up together for an afternoon nap. They look so content."

Kelly was delighted Joshua was having such a good time with Bailey. This helped her to focus on her work. On the days Joshua was with Liz and Bailey, they picked Joshua up at home in the morning and brought him home in time for dinner. In the evenings, Kelly and Joshua walked in the neighborhood and to the high school.

With work going so well for Kelly and her being able to work more normal business hours, this freed up her time on weekends to go for longer explorations with Joshua. On the weekends during the day, they went to Lawrence Park or the beach. Kelly had discovered Joshua could swim in the beach area by Grand Lake about five miles from their home. Dogs could enter the water for a swim from a long, sandy shoreline. He loved the swims and Kelly relished watching each one.

Kelly noticed Joshua would resist slightly when they started to walk on the sand after a round of swimming. But if she was careful to keep away from deep sand, Joshua did not mind the sand that much. Not wanting to upset Joshua, she was mindful to walk mostly on the wooden boardwalk when Joshua wasn't swimming in the lake.

About midway through their beach adventure, Joshua tired of the beach and wanted to go up the hill a few blocks to the main street shopping area. He pulled the leash toward the shopping area, or if he was not leashed, he headed in that direction on his own, paying attention not to get too far so that Kelly could catch up, and they could walk together.

"Joshua, wait. I'm coming. Okay, we'll go to the main street." When Kelly got close enough to him about a minute later, she put on his leash and they continued on their journey.

They walked along the main street, stopping briefly as passersby came by to pat and admire Joshua. Kelly sought out every opportunity to pat passing dogs. After about six or seven blocks, Kelly would find a restaurant where she and Joshua could sit together outside at a table to relax.

"Joshua, let's go get a drink." They would find a quiet table in the shade.

"One sparkling water with lemon for me, please, and a cold water in a bowl for Joshua. Thank you."

After they had finished their drinks and spent a few more minutes watching passersby, Kelly would say, "Joshua, let's go back to the beach."

Kelly had found a large grassy area on a plateau above the beach where she and Joshua ran together and played fetch. On one adventure at the grassy area, Joshua darted toward the beach. Kelly followed him down the hill through some tall bushes to the water. Joshua had discovered a beach area that was more soil than sand where a few people launched their windsurfers or small boats. It was also a choice spot for Joshua to go for a swim. Kelly added this location to their regular weekly travels at the beach.

Kelly soon discovered a second beach about a mile closer to home that was divided into a humans-only beach and a large, fenced-off, dog-friendly beach. The dog beach waterfront was backed by low hills with bushes and trails through them to the water as well as some sandy shoreline. She and Joshua meandered along the shore, dodging any deep, sinking sand. Joshua preferred this beach because they could avoid the sand and the beach area was less crowded. Kelly found some stony outcrops into the lake where Joshua could enter the water easily. Kelly would sit on a flat stone on one of the outcrops, throwing balls and sticks into the water for Joshua to retrieve. From this vantage point, she lingered there, watching the sailboats and windsurfers as well as the gulls, geese, and ducks.

A food truck was parked in the beach parking lot. Kelly and Joshua smelled the burgers and hot dogs cooking on the grill.

"Two burgers and a bottled water, please."

"Sure, you and your dog are going to have a picnic. He is a very handsome golden."

"Thank you, yes. We are going to enjoy these."

Kelly dressed the burgers with the usual condiments. Kelly sat on a picnic bench facing the water, and Joshua sat beside her by the bench. With her fingers, she broke up his burger into pieces and fed the pieces to him. Her burger tasted better when she and Joshua were savoring the meal together. Sometimes, they shared an order of fries with the burger.

One time, her mind wandered into unfriendly territory as she sat on the bench by the lake and enjoyed a burger with Joshua. She wondered why Deke hadn't told her about this beach. He must have known about it. Was it because he didn't want Joshua to get wet? Was Deke just being lazy? Or was it about depriving her?

On a given weekend, Kelly and Joshua often went to both beaches, one on Saturday and one on Sunday. At the beach, she was in the present, having put her predicament out of her mind. She focused on Joshua, the swims, the walks, and the lake. Trips to the beach were therapeutic for her. Joshua delighted in them as well.

Besides being with Joshua, occasionally, Kelly met a friend for dinner at a restaurant or went to a friend's home for dinner. She frequented concerts again—some jazz but mostly classical. She was content to go alone. For most of her leisure time, she just stayed close to home with Joshua. At work, she had her staff, whom she liked very much, but sometimes, there were issues.

"Ella, I had a huge somatic response at work this week. It was triggered by an encounter with Adil. He made me repeat myself a few times. It was a reminder about how Deke would not listen to me, and how I had to restate things over and over again to him. I think my neocortex knew Adil was trying to absorb what I was saying, but the rest of my brain didn't interpret his actions that way. English is not his first language. The project was a new endeavor for him. My body didn't care and protected me.

"My left eye got so heavy. It was such a struggle to keep it open. The heightened nerve sensation spread from my left eye and down my left cheek. This is one of the most intense somatic responses I have ever had. I have no idea what I can do to make sure he doesn't trigger me again."

"That was a big response. I'm glad you recognized what was happening and didn't panic. The response dissipated once you got home and spent a few minutes with Joshua. It was smart to remove yourself from the situation as soon as you could and try to eliminate the response with movement. The more you understand what is happening to you and can step back and react to it in a positive way, the sooner the response will disappear. Good work."

Kelly changed the subject after her nature break.

"Since I discovered the lie Deke had told his mother, I have been wondering what else has been hidden from me. I thought we would do some exploring here about my family. I am not looking for anything in particular. I just need to know. Talking about my dad is a big topic for me."

"Certainly, Kelly. Let's begin."

"I had always accepted responsibility for my dad's death. In my rational brain, I now know I wasn't responsible, but I have been harboring this guilt since I was twelve. When my dad told me repeatedly that his insurance would take care of us after he was gone, I got upset but I didn't make him seek medical attention. I have always regretted that, which of course is silly because I was a child and he was the parent.

"I felt I was also somehow culpable for his death because I didn't stop him from going on his fateful trip to Chicago when I could sense something was amiss.

"Butterflies were flying around in my stomach at the time, but I did nothing. With no one to talk to, these wounds stayed open, even now.

"In part, this is why I think I am so tenacious. I didn't help my dad and now I'm making up for it. I don't like to give up on anything unless I have no other choice. I think this is why I stayed with Deke too long. I am starting to forgive myself about my dad. I didn't cry on the anniversary of his death this year.

"Kieran just sent me some old movies my dad made when I was an infant and up to age nine or ten. Kieran restored them and put them on a DVD.

"As I watched the oldest movies, I recalled some of my oldest childhood memories. I am surprised at how many memories I have around the time of the birth of my brother. I have never talked about these memories to anyone before. I don't know why I remember these events and not others.

"I remember the night my brother was born. I was only three and a half years old. I was sitting alone at our kitchen table in the apartment where we lived. We had built-in benches on either side of the rectangular kitchen table. I remember looking out this small window next to me. I saw the snow coming down in big flakes and it was dark. No one else was in the kitchen with me. It's weird. I have this memory in shades of gray, no colors. I remember the stillness and quiet in the kitchen that night. I don't remember anybody else being with me. My parents told me the town had a power failure that night, but I have no memory of it.

"Was anybody else with me? Did my parents leave me alone that night?

"We lived in an apartment building. I don't know what floor we lived on. We moved away to our house in St. George soon after my brother was born.

"I remember going to the basement of the apartment building by myself. Lots of toys belonging to other children were strewn on the floor. A little two-wheeled bicycle was turned on its side on the floor—just my size. I had seen other children ride it. Riding the bike looked like fun.

"Since no one else was in the basement, I decided to try the bike out. After several trips alone to the basement to ride the bike when no one was around, I learned how to ride it. I have memories of riding in circles in the basement, dodging the other toys on the floor. No one knew I had borrowed this bike or that I had learned how to ride it. Riding the bike was my happy secret.

"When my dad bought me my first bicycle when I was six or seven, I remember being amused when he put the training wheels on it. I didn't want to tell him I already knew how to ride a bike. I waited patiently until he decided I was ready to try to ride without the training wheels.

"Not that long after we had moved to St. George, I remember my parents wanted me to give up my doll. I had carried it around everywhere and slept with it. My dad called it my booby. Oh, my Lord! Until now, I never made the connection about the name! I can't believe my parents had me walking around calling the doll my booby.

"My parents told me, 'Your doll is ratty. There's not much left of it, just some material. It's dirty.'

"I didn't want to give up my doll. My dad took me to his hall closet, just outside my parents' bedroom. I remember I looked up at him at that moment and observed he was so tall. Of course, I now know he was not a tall man.

"'Let's make a trade,' he said. 'You give me your booby, and I'll give you one of my ties.'

"I didn't want to make the exchange. My dad reached out his hands to take my doll. I refused. Then I remember giving him my doll reluctantly and picking out a tie I didn't want.

"Why didn't my parents buy me a special new doll to replace that one? After that experience, I never played with dolls, even though I eventually had a toy box full of them.

"I have never said these things out loud before. Until now, they were just childhood stories. Now they have an entirely different meaning to me."

"Kelly, this has been a stressful but revealing session. You have done great work! See you Thursday."

At her next therapy session, Kelly continued where she had left off.

"Ella, we were talking about what I had observed in the old movies my brother restored. In one of the scenes, my brother and I were walking together. My dad took the footage the morning I was going off to summer sleepover camp for the first time. I was smiling, but I was always happy to be with my brother.

"When I was eight, my parents sent me away to a month-long sleepover camp. The camp ran from the last week of June until the last week of July. No one asked me if I wanted to go. My aunt Celeste's children went to that camp.

"I remember my mother really wanted me to go. She told me I was too young to attend. You had to be nine years old by the end of June, but my birthday was in early August. I was only eight. My mother told me she was going to say my birthday was at the end of June. In order to make sure my mother remembered the fake date, my mother told me her sister Celeste was going along to help her. In telling me her intentions, I remember my mother was amused by the whole thing. She was chuckling.

"Then I didn't process the absurdity of taking my aunt with her to the camp registrar. Now I can see how ridiculous this was. My mother was certainly smart enough to remember the fake date she had selected. After all, she was a math whiz in high school and college. Why didn't she just write my fake birthdate on her cigarette box?

"Before I went to summer camp, my mother lectured me, 'Kelly, you must remember at camp your birthday is June thirtieth. You mustn't tell anyone about your real birthday. You will be in a lot of trouble if you do!'

"I never processed this until now. My parents wanted to get rid of me, didn't they? Especially my mother.

"At camp, I do remember how angry and upset I was that I had to lie about my birthday. The camp had prepared a cake for me on my first fake birthday. All my cabin mates sang 'Happy Birthday' to me. I was mortified.

"Ella, remember I had told you I spent a week in the children's hospital when I was eight? I had woken up and couldn't walk. Putting any weight on my feet was so painful. I hadn't injured myself. Even with all the testing I had in the hospital, the doctors found nothing, except my food allergies had disappeared. My body chemistry had shifted.

"Oh, my Lord! I l must have landed in the hospital after I found out about summer camp . . . that was quite the discovery. After so many years, I finally understand what happened with my feet."

After this revelation, Kelly stood up from her chair, stretched her arms straight above her head, and took a deep breath.

"Let's take a short break, Kelly. You can continue stretching. I'll make some hot tea."

After Ella poured the tea, Kelly and she sat down. After each took a sip of tea nearly in unison, Kelly continued.

"In the footage of my brother and me walking together, I was smiling but I saw I was toeing out noticeably. In older footage of me, I noticed my gait was more normal. This was pretty shocking! I believed I had always toed out in an extreme manner. I think at the time of my first trip to this summer camp, my body knew I wasn't wanted and tightened up like a corkscrew, and it still pretty much is.

"When my toeing out was extreme, my dad called me Charlie Chaplin. This teasing amused both my parents immensely. They dressed me in the ugliest black oxford shoes to correct the problem, but wearing those shoes made no improvement. They just lowered my self-esteem even further. It's funny—I'm just realizing all of this now.

"For five successive summers, my parents sent me to this camp. For five years, I swallowed fake birthdays. For five years, my cousins taunted me for the fake date. Kieran joined in when he was the right age to go to that same camp. My family made me believe the shame

I was feeling was my own doing. Somehow, my being a fraud was my fault.

"Now I understand why I have such trouble celebrating my birthday, why I feel guilty and embarrassed, getting gifts and attention. It's all about this, isn't it?

"Hmmm. Not quite. We had talked about my being a premature baby before. Even though both my parents were chain smokers, they blamed me for being in an incubator for six weeks until I grew from four to five pounds. According to my parents, it was all my fault I was born on the wrong day and in the wrong month.

"My family took away the joy of my birthday. One day, I'd like to get it back! Ella, I need to take another short break."

When Kelly returned a couple of minutes later, the session was over.

"Kelly, this has been a very difficult, but very revealing session for you. Good work today. Take some time to enjoy yourself this weekend and relax. See you next week."

The following week in therapy, Kelly continued to recall what else happened when she was eight years old. At first, nothing came to mind, then after thirty seconds of quiet, Kelly exclaimed, "Oh, my heavens! Oh, my heavens! I had that awful bike accident when I was eight or had just turned nine."

Kelly stood up, stretched her arms above her head, and touched her toes. Then she continued.

"We talked about this accident before, but I didn't know why falling off my bike was so prominent in my memory, other than the trauma and aftermath of the injury.

"I broke several teeth and had two root canals. You helped me to understand that I froze as I was bike riding. I was going up a driveway curb I had ridden up hundreds of times before. I was escaping from something that had happened at home, but I still don't know what. I was on my way to buy some fries at the local snack bar.

"Oh, now I see. The accident happened right after I returned from the first trip to that summer camp. I can't believe I didn't know all these events were connected until now. I am astounded at how compartmentalized my memories have been. I don't know why they didn't store in my brain, all together. I guess it was just too much to bear.

"I didn't realize how alone I was as a child. Growing up, I must have known subconsciously my parents didn't really want me, but I never admitted it to myself, until now. I guess I have been fending for myself for a long time.

"I don't remember anything else about what happened in my life around this time. I'll talk about something else."

"The summer after my sophomore year in high school, I had planned to work at the mall. I had a job offer at Lucinda's to sell children's clothes, but only on weekends. I don't think my mother approved of that job.

"She telephoned that same summer camp to get me a job for the whole summer. When she told me that the camp had a summer job for me, I felt her pressure to go to the camp and not stay home. I talked myself into appreciating how lucky I would be to spend the summer in the woods by the lake. I called up the camp to take the job, even though I really wanted to spend the summer in town with Deke. Deke visited me at the camp on weekends and my days off, so the summer wasn't that terrible, but I did not enjoy being at the camp.

"The next summer, I went away from home again. I had wanted to improve my Spanish. My mother did some research and found out about a private school in Ithaca where I could stay in residence for six weeks during the summer to take some courses in Spanish. I wasn't really interested in going. I wanted to spend the summer with Deke, but my mother wouldn't hear of it. Not only that, but she also made me ask her Uncle Frank for the funds to pay for the Ithaca stay. I didn't want to do that either. She insisted. I remember being embarrassed and awkward as I asked Uncle Frank in front of my grandmother, aunt, and cousins for the money, as my mother motioned me closer to Uncle Frank as I was making the request.

"My Spanish was excellent after that summer. I made some new friends at school. When I returned home from the school at the end of August, I had a bad cold. The cold turned out to be hay fever, an affliction I have endured every spring, summer, and fall, ever since. Oh my! I guess my body chemistry had shifted again.

"I can't believe it. Three times in my life, my mother went to great lengths to get rid of me. I was not aware of this each time, but I guess my body knew it. Those negative neural tracks got deeper and deeper."

"You have worked very hard in session today, Kelly. We covered a lot of ground. Please take good care of yourself. See you in a few days."

CHAPTER 28

New Therapies

With the discoveries Kelly had made in her psychotherapy session, she was feeling a renewed sense of optimism. Some things that had happened to her were starting to make sense. The pieces of the puzzle were fitting together, even though the picture they were creating of her life was not a pretty one.

She arranged to start seeing an osteopath to help quiet her nervous system. She was also going to start to see a chiropractor her trainer thought could help her with her gait. With the hope of feeling better, Kelly looked forward to beginning these new treatments.

Kelly arrived twenty minutes early for her first osteopathic appointment so she could take Joshua on a walk to explore the new neighborhood. She discovered a lovely tree-lined street, with mature oaks on both sides of the street. As she and Joshua walked along the sidewalk, she found a small, wooded area separated by two low-rise buildings, with a path leading from the sidewalk into the woods. She and Joshua followed the path. Kelly picked up a good-sized stick and threw it for Joshua to retrieve. After three retrieves and having walked the entire length of the woods, they headed back to the sidewalk and the car.

Once at the car, Kelly opened the back door for Joshua. He jumped up and sat up. She reached into the car, gave Joshua a big hug, and said, "Love you, back soon."

Joshua blinked at Kelly and she closed the car door. As Kelly walked toward her appointment, she looked back at Joshua, who was still sitting up in the back seat. He looked out the passenger's side window briefly and then laid down.

Dr. Jones welcomed Kelly into his treatment room when she arrived at his office and they went over her case history. Then he treated her.

"Dr. Jones, I feel better. A little more relaxed. How often do you think I should come in for treatment?"

"It will take regular treatment to help calm your nervous system after the trauma you experienced, but we should be able to get some good results. Every two weeks should be an effective regimen. I can book you for every second Tuesday for the next two months and then we can take stock of how things are going."

"That sounds great, thank you. See you in two weeks."

As Kelly left Dr. Jones' office and approached the car to go home with Joshua, she felt a calming from the appointment. She was also invigorated by the prospect of feeling better over time.

But once at home, she pined for Darcy. After watching a movie, she sat at her computer, trying to distract herself by working. Instead, she typed:

Hoping to receive an e-mail
For months I checked my g-mail

Sadness I could not avoid
Failing to fill the growing void

I tried not to despair
Knowing this was just not fair

Watched a biopic tonight
Music good, plot all right

Was a story about the Schumann's
And their friend, Johannes Brahms

Each night to gently pacify
I sang to her Brahms' lullaby

I cried a sea and couldn't quit
When Johannes sweetly sang it

Then Joshua gazed at me
And, with his eyes, he set me free

Kelly got ready for bed. As she did, she wondered about her appointment with her chiropractor the next day and hoped it would go well. She smiled at Joshua before getting into bed and feeling his love, she was ready for sleep.

After work the next day, Kelly and Joshua drove to see the chiropractor, Dr. Bradley. He was located north of Buffington, about an hour away at the university's suburban campus. Kelly was not sure where his office was on campus and wanted to leave in plenty of time in case she got lost. Luckily, there was not that much traffic on the way there and she found his office parking lot without much difficulty. This left almost half an hour for her and Joshua to explore the campus near Dr. Bradley's office.

Once she and Joshua were out of the car, Kelly looked around and noticed gardens at the back of the parking lot abutting the fencing. There were walking paths, some birch and maple trees along the path, as well as manicured bushes. In the distance, she could see outdoor tennis courts and a dome, which likely housed indoor courts.

She and Joshua strolled onto the main trail from the parking lot. Since no one was around, she let Joshua off-leash. He sniffed around and found a tennis ball and then another. He brought each one back to Kelly. She threw one about twenty feet or so. Joshua ran to get it and brought it back. As they continued to walk along the trail, Kelly repeated the retrieving process twice until Joshua lost interest and did not bring the ball back, preferring to sniff some trees and bushes along the way.

This was fine with Kelly. It gave her a chance to look around and admire the grounds. They continued on their adventure past the indoor courts and to six outdoor courts. On the grassy area that flanked the path, Joshua found six tennis balls, which he brought back, one at a time, for Kelly to store.

"Good boy, Joshua. I am so impressed with your hunting skills. So many tennis balls!"

He looked at her as if to say, "Glad you are pleased."

Glancing at her watch, Kelly concluded it was time to go back.

"Joshua, come."

Joshua scampered to her, being only a few feet away, and she put on his leash. Then they walked back to the car and did the usual, "Love you, Joshua, back soon," ritual.

After a couple of minutes sitting in Dr. Bradley's waiting room, Dr. Bradley came out to get her. He was very fit and friendly. Once in his office, he motioned her to sit down. He sat down on his office chair by his desk, and he turned to face her.

"Hello, Kelly, I am Dr. Bradley. How can I help you?"

"Dr. Bradley, I think you know, Kim Lee, my athletic trainer. She referred me here. She thought you might be able to help me with the chronic problems with my gait.

"The year before my daughter Darcy was born—so over twenty years ago—I broke my right ankle in two places and my right fifth metatarsal. I missed two stairs while walking down our side stairs to the laneway between our house and the neighbor's house.

"This injury never healed properly. From time to time, my right ankle seizes up, then my right knee and right hip tighten. The tightening causes pain and reduces my mobility. I spent hundreds and hundreds of hours in physiotherapy and massage. I even saw two sports medicine physicians, but nothing they had me do had worked. My gait issues would improve and then recur. Sometimes, my mobility is so constrained I have difficulty walking more than a block or two.

"Do you think you can help me?"

"Let's do a full assessment now, and then I'll let you know."

The assessment was a series of exercises Dr. Bradley had Kelly do. He also took some measurements of where her feet landed and in what position.

When he had completed the assessment, he declared, "Kelly, your feet are like cement blocks. You have almost no dorsiflexion in your feet. But if you are willing to commit to a lot of hard work, I can help you. You can get the dorsiflexion back. This will go a long way to improving your gait. Your feet will work like feet again. We should meet twice a week for a half-hour each visit and see how things go."

"Dr. Bradley, you are the first person to tell me you can help improve my gait. Everyone else talked about pain management and that it was too late to change my gait. This is so exciting! Thank you."

Kelly was quite jubilant after the appointment with Dr. Bradley. For the first time in a long time, improving her mobility was a real possibility. On the drive home, she sang the '60s songs on the radio with more verve than usual. Life was looking up.

CHAPTER 29

Christmas Season Without Darcy

Kelly continued with her treatments with Dr. Jones and Dr. Bradley all fall. She trained twice a week with Kim and saw her acupuncturist, Kala, every two weeks. As much as she could, she filled the void left by Darcy with taking care of herself.

Such a full schedule left little free time in the evenings except to go on the constitutionals with Joshua. On the weekends, she and Joshua continued their adventures at the two beaches. When it became too cold for Joshua to swim, she and Joshua spent their weekend afternoons in Lawrence Park.

Twice a week all fall, Kelly continued her psychotherapy with Ella. Kelly had not heard from Darcy since before Darcy had left town to do her PhD, and Kelly was not able to make sense of why. She continued to spend a good deal of her time with Ella trying to understand Darcy's behavior and failing.

Kelly continued to be triggered by Adil, but with the help of discussion in her psychotherapy session about the potential triggers, mastering her work life, and the passage of time, her somatic responses became less intense and less frequent.

As Christmas approached and still not having heard from Darcy, Kelly had become a cocktail of grief, anger, and sadness, but still with a small dash of hope. As a result, most of the work in therapy that fall season with Ella had involved trancework to help Kelly stay grounded.

In her last therapy session before Christmas, Kelly told Ella, "I can't believe I haven't heard from Darcy. I am so angry and so hurt. I expect she will be in town staying with Deke during her Christmas break from school.

"Maybe this is for the best. It will be hard to stay centered and calm if Darcy and I were to spend time together. I think I'll spend a quiet Christmas just with me and Joshua."

"Kelly, Let's do some trance to the end of the session."

When Kelly emerged from the trance, Ella said, "You are making progress. Focus on the positive. You are a lot stronger. You are recovering. But you are also grieving from your loss. It takes time to heal. Enjoy your time off with Joshua. Have a wonderful Christmas."

As Kelly wished Ella a merry Christmas, they embraced, and then Kelly departed. Kelly felt a little less overwhelmed, a little less foggy. She greeted Joshua in the car with a warm hug and "Love you, Joshua."

As she drove home, Kelly reminded herself that she and Deke had agreed to sell the house in the spring, but she hadn't done anything about it. She resolved to find a real estate agent after Boxing Day.

At home that night and after Joshua's late-night constitutional, she sat in the den listening to Chopin, while Joshua snoozed by the windows. Her mind wandered to thinking about what kind of real estate agent to hire. She knew she needed an agent who would be sympathetic to her, but who would not be pushed around by Deke.

She did an internet search of agents in the neighborhood and decided to make some calls in the morning to set up appointments for after Boxing Day.

Kelly had turned down invitations to spend Christmas with Kieran and his family as well as with Donna's and Bea's family but did agree to spend Christmas eve, having dinner at Bea's with Bea, Bea's brother, and nephew. Christmas eve dinner was pleasant and uneventful for Kelly, and she was happy to go home to Joshua.

Kelly and Joshua spent most of Christmas Day in Lawrence Park. It was a beautiful, crisp, winter day. There had been a light snowfall on Christmas eve. Kelly marveled at the snowflakes on the tree branches as she and Joshua ambled along the park trails. Then they promenaded down the hill to walk along the length of the now frozen creek, and back up the hill and home. There were few people in the park. Kelly savored the serenity of the park as she and Joshua walked.

Before they left the park to go home, Joshua made a snow angel at the top of Dog Hill. Kelly smiled at Joshua as he twisted from one side to the next. When he was done, he stood up and looked at Kelly for instruction. She said, "Good boy, Joshua. What a beautiful snow angel! We had a lovely long walk. Let's go home."

On Boxing Day, Kelly did some grocery shopping in the morning, with Joshua accompanying her in the back seat of the car. The twosome spent the afternoon in Lawrence Park and the evening in the den, listening to Liszt, while Kelly read the newspapers and

Joshua snoozed beside her. After reading, Kelly watched a movie. She was in the present, relaxing and enjoying the loving company of Joshua.

Even with these distractions, the pain of realizing it was her first Christmas without Darcy since Darcy was born was at her core.

She left the den and sat at her desk facing her computer. Joshua accompanied her and lay down beside her chair. She smiled at Joshua and said, "I love you, Joshua. I don't know what I would do without you."

He looked into her eyes as if to read her soul, then closed his eyes. Comforted by his gaze, Kelly began:

> No matter how I feel
> No matter how unreal
>
> No matter what I do
> I hearken back to you
>
> Thought I chose a safe domain
> Watched that space movie yet again
>
> Just when I thought I'd made it through
> My lonely brain went back to you
>
> John Glenn and his wife
> Did overcome their strife
>
> Supported each other
> No matter the weather
> One hundred percent
> A total commitment

I felt enormous rejection
When I made the connection

There was nothing I could do
My despair bounced back to you

Once her feelings were on the page, Kelly felt some solace and stood up. "Come, Joshua, bedtime."

The next morning, Kelly focused on getting on with her house move. The first real estate agent arrived at Kelly's for the interview. Kelly was impressed with her. She had sold homes in the neighborhood for over twenty years and had an excellent reputation. Kelly was leaning in her direction until she met the second agent that afternoon.

The second agent told Kelly, "I have been married twice. My first husband used to hit me, so I understand your situation regarding abuse. I eventually left my first husband, who is still in Hungary. I have been married to my second husband here in Buffington for more than twenty-five years and we have a son, who is my partner in real estate. Do you jog? I was on the Hungarian Olympic swim team, but now I just jog around the neighborhood."

"Nadia, both my husband Deke and I will have to sign the papers to retain you as our real estate agent. Here is Deke's phone number and e-mail. I will let him know you are going to contact him."

Kelly was surprised Deke signed with Nadia the next day without so much as an e-mail to her about it.

When Nadia came over the next afternoon to give Kelly a copy of the executed papers she and Deke had signed, Nadia advised, "Kelly, you should paint the house and do some kitchen renovations before putting the house on the market in the spring. I can help you choose the paint colors, the new appliances, and the materials for the renovation. I can also provide contractors."

"That sounds great, Nadia. Did you discuss this with Deke? Has he agreed? Deke and I will need to split the expenses equally. You will have to be the go-between on that. I don't want to talk to him about any of this."

"I wished to discuss this with you first. But if you agree, I can speak to Deke about it. I am experienced in such matters."

"I agree. Please discuss this with Deke and get back to me, so that we can plan the renovations."

After Nadia left, Kelly told Joshua, "Nadia is not a dog person. You didn't seem to mind, but I did. I wish she had given you a pat. We have a lot of work to do to get the house ready. It will be disruptive. Don't worry. It will be fine. We will find a better place to live. I love you, Joshua."

CHAPTER 30

Selling the House

Kelly began the process of emptying the house for sale, cleaning out years and years of clutter. One night about a month into her cleaning, as she was sitting on the living room couch rummaging through some old photo albums, she stopped to peer at a photo of herself, riding her bike with training wheels. She started to cry uncontrollably until Joshua came over to her and put his paw on her knee. She patted him behind his ears.

"Thank you, Joshua. I love you. Good boy." She tossed the bike out of her mind. She did not want to get thrown into the past. She had work to do.

About two months into the decluttering process, she had sorted enough stuff to send to Deke or Darcy, stuff they had requested she send to them or she had determined they would like. After Deke received what she had sent, she got an e-mail from him.

"I want to come to the house and look through what's left in case I want anything else. I want to come over Friday night."

Kelly telephoned Bea. "Hi Bea, Deke wants to come over Friday night to see what else he wants to take from the house. I don't want to be alone with him." "Sure, Kelly, no worries."

"Please don't leave me alone with Deke for one second. Please stay by my side. It is too risky."

"I'll bring my nephew Roger with me. With all of us there, things should go smoothly."

"I'll order some pizza with our beer. See you Friday."

Roger arrived early Friday evening.

"Hi, Kelly, great to see you. Looks like you could use some help with the leaves and winter debris on your front lawn. I'd be happy to rake them up for you."

"That would be great, thank you. Please come inside and get some pizza and beer."

"Sure thing, I'll eat outside."

While he was outside, Bea and Kelly were making small talk at the dining room table as they munched on their pizza and nursed their beer.

Kelly had left the front door unlocked for Roger as he worked, so when Deke arrived, he walked in unannounced and called out, "Kelly, I'm here. I want to look around."

Kelly looked at Bea, reminding her, "Bea, please stay close to me. Don't leave me alone with Deke."

But instead, as Kelly and Deke walked toward the basement, Bea stayed behind and did not join them. Joshua went with Kelly and stayed by her side. Deke did not greet Joshua or pat him.

In the basement, Deke rummaged through the open boxes but didn't find anything he wanted. Kelly took a small burgundy, velvet, jewelry case out of her pocket and handed it to Deke.

"Deke, when I was packing up the bedroom, I found your grandfather's watch." "Oh," he said. "Thanks."

Just at that moment, Kelly's mobile phone rang. She excused herself and took the call, but with her back to Deke. It was a call from the massage therapy clinic, confirming her appointment for the next day.

After the call, Kelly turned to Deke, but he had gone upstairs without her. As she walked up the stairs to find him, she heard him say to Bea, "How's work going? Anything exciting?"

"Things are very busy."

Then Deke exclaimed, "The watch, where is my grandfather's watch? It's not in my pocket where I put it."

"Deke that is really odd. Bea and I will look for it."

"Alright, Kelly. I'm done. I didn't find anything else I want. Good night."

After Deke had closed the front door behind him, Kelly said to Bea, "Let's look for the watch in the basement first. That's where I handed it to him. I watched him put the watch in his right pant pocket. Now he says he doesn't have the watch. How could he lose it? It's a heavy, gold watch with a gold chain. If it dropped, it would have made a thud, even on the basement carpet."

After a few minutes of their rifling through the bookshelves and the packed but open boxes in the basement, Bea cried out, "Kelly, I found the watch! What is it doing in this box? I made a mistake leaving you alone with Deke. I really did think you both needed some alone time together to deal with your personal stuff. I was wrong. I'm so sorry."

Shortly thereafter, Bea and Roger got ready to depart. Kelly thanked them both for their help and was grateful they had been there.

After their departure, Kelly e-mailed Deke. "We found the watch. I'll send it over with some other things I am sending you for Darcy."

Kelly went on an extra-long walk with Joshua, to try to walk off being with Deke. Kelly found Deke's presence in the house and being so close to him discomposing. She hoped the cool night air and the walk with Joshua would cleanse her from the experience.

Kelly called Nadia the next day to discuss plans for the sale of the house.

"I am going to go out of town on vacation to St. Thomas in April while you do the renovations and stage the house. Will that be a problem?"

"No problem. Good idea. I can supervise the work. It will go quicker with you out of the house."

Nearly every weeknight after her various therapies and on the weekends after walks with Joshua to Lawrence Park, Kelly worked on clearing out the house. As her one-week holiday in St. Thomas approached, she was somewhat confident she could finish what she needed to do before her trip.

On the day of her trip, she drove Joshua to Bailey's and spent a few minutes with Liz, Bailey, and Joshua in Liz's house. Before leaving,

Kelly gave Joshua two big hugs, a kiss on the right side of his face, and said, "Joshua, stay with Bailey and Liz. Love you! Back soon."

"Thank you, Liz, for looking after Joshua. I will miss him very much. I know he is in excellent hands and will have a great time with Bailey."

Kelly returned home, parked her car in the driveway, and called a cab to take her to the airport. On the plane, she read, watched movies, and started to unwind slightly.

Kelly's holiday was quite relaxing. She spent most of her time on the beach either swimming, reading, or snoozing. The food at the hotel was fresh and well prepared. Kelly was content. She did not think about what was going on at home. Instead, she spent her time just enjoying where she was. She was glad to have the alone time to read and de-stress.

When Kelly returned home from her holiday, she was pleasantly surprised she had some offers on the house waiting for her. Instead of taking the highest offer, which was significantly higher than the offer she accepted, she opted to sell the house to a neighbor down the street whose kids adored Joshua and whose family wanted to stay in the neighborhood.

After Nadia left with the signed papers for the house sale to the neighbor, she told Joshua, "I just sold our house to that nice family down the street with the two boys you play with, Daniel and Nicholas. I know how much you like them." I followed my heart instead of my logic. I think I was struck by the opportunity to keep a family together in the neighborhood since I couldn't keep ours intact any longer. From a financial point of view, I made a very stupid decision. I am so surprised Deke agreed to it. It was a good idea to set the house closing for the end of July. This gives us some time to find a new place to live.

"Joshua, I know you are not happy about all the changes in the house. It is stressful for both of us. We'll find a new home where we'll both be happy. I promise."

Kelly rose from the living room couch and gave Joshua a big hug and a kiss on his forehead. "I love you, Joshua. We take care of each other."

Kelly put on a Gershwin CD, sat down again, and continued her reflections. With the money from the house sale, she'd be able to pay off her debts and plan for the future. What future?

Although Kelly did not have the answer to her question, she was feeling sanguine about the choices she would make. They would be her choices. She felt lucky to have these new opportunities—to start over again and to share her life with Joshua.

The house was now virtually empty since the staging furniture was gone. She and Joshua spent most of their time in the sunroom where Kelly's work desk now was and occasionally went into the den to watch some TV. From her desk, she enjoyed looking out the window into the backyard, with the trees in full bloom, and listening to the chirping of the birds in the yard. Joshua stayed close to her as he rested under her desk.

On the day of the closing, Kelly's real estate lawyer telephoned in the early afternoon and told her, "The closing has gone through. I have deposited your share of the money into your account."

"That's good news, thank you."

That evening, Kelly had an appointment with Dr. Jones. Before the appointment, Kelly had planned to visit the ATM near Dr. Jones' office to make various transfers with the money from the house sale. She and Joshua drove to the appointment, parked the car, and then walked around the block to the ATM. When Kelly checked to see if the deposit from the house sale had gone through, the money wasn't there.

"Oh my God," she said aloud.

Trying to gain her composure, she and Joshua walked back to the car. She let Joshua into the back seat, hugged him, and said, "Love you. Back soon." Then he blinked and off she went to Dr. Jones' office.

When she sat down in the waiting area, she began to cry and couldn't stop. Dr. Jones sat at his desk and looked on as tears poured down her face. Although she tried, she couldn't stop crying.

Intermittently, Dr. Jones intervened. He explained, "Your lawyer has not run off with your money. Please calm down. Everything is fine."

Kelly knew this to be logically true but could do nothing. After about a half-hour, she stopped sobbing.

"Thank you for your patience, Dr. Jones. I apologize for this appointment. See you in a couple of weeks."

Dr. Jones looked relieved, as Kelly offered him a faint smile as she left his office to go home with Joshua.

Before she got behind the wheel, Kelly opened the back door, reached in, gave Joshua a hug, and said, "Love you, Joshua. Let's go home."

The warmth of Joshua's body on hers and his loving eyes looking into her soul helped Kelly to calm down. She was able to concentrate on the road and the drive home. As she drove, she listened to classical music and chatted with Joshua intermittently. After they got home, she and Joshua went out for their evening constitutional. When her strength and composure had fully returned that night, she called her real estate lawyer and left a strong message.

The next day, her real estate lawyer telephoned and said, "I apologize for this mishap. The bank had an issue with the transfer. You will receive the money in a day or two."

When the money finally arrived in her bank account, Kelly made the necessary transfers at her neighborhood ATM, with Joshua by her side. In her therapy session with Ella the next day, Kelly described what had happened.

"I couldn't stop crying. I was helpless. After a time, I knew I had no reason to cry, but I couldn't stop. Dr. Jones tried to help, but I had no control. What happened to me?"

"You were having a flashback to the money transfer that led to Deke's scaring you that night. Once in full flashback, it usually has to play out. There is hope for you to avert flashbacks in the future by identifying the triggers. We can work on that."

"That's helpful. I'm glad I have some clarity on what a flashback is. I guess the somatic response with Adil was also a flashback.

"It is really scary to go down that rabbit hole. There is no control. Next time, I hope I will be able to recognize that I'm having a flashback so I can climb out of it more quickly. I am glad I was not alone. I am so lucky Joshua was there with me."

"Kelly, do you know where you want to live?"

"I'd like to move downtown so I can walk to work, be closer to shopping and the downtown experience. It is uncomfortable living in a family neighborhood when my family is gone, even though I have friends in the neighborhood. I don't think it is healthy to stay in the old surroundings. I think I need something new."

"Do you want to buy another house?"

"I can't buy anything without Deke's consent until the financial separation is settled. We are almost there, so for now, I want to rent. I don't want another house. Living downtown means condo living. It will be a big adjustment, moving to a much smaller space, but it should be less to manage on my own.

"I have asked Nadia to help me find a condo to rent downtown. It is not going to be that easy to find a place that allows big dogs. Lots of places have a forty-pound restriction and Joshua is close to 100 pounds on a good day. But Nadia is persistent, so I'm hopeful."

"Good work today, Kelly. I am glad you are getting clarity on where you want to live and in what kind of space. Your fog is lifting. This is a good sign. See you next week."

CHAPTER 31

Moving to a Condo

With Nadia's help, Kelly found a lovely two-bedroom apartment by Grand Lake. With floor-to-ceiling windows in the living room, the room was bathed in natural light and with an excellent view of the lake. Although the building allowed dogs, and more than fifty lived in the building, according to the concierge when Kelly asked him, the owner of Kelly's unit was reluctant to have a dog living in her suite. Nadia negotiated a deal with the owner. She telephoned Kelly to discuss the offer.

"The owner will agree to let you rent her condo, but only if you pay a $1000 damage deposit and a ten percent higher rent."

"Oh, that is steep. But I like the location, the natural light, and the size. So okay, I'll take it. It is worth it to have a comfortable home for me and Joshua."

Three weeks later, Kelly and Joshua moved into their condo midweek. On moving day, Joshua spent the day with Liz and Bailey. The move went well. Kelly unpacked quickly. By the time Joshua returned home that night, their place looked lived in.

They went for a walk along the waterfront trail across the street from their condo building and then went to bed.

That weekend, Kelly and Joshua were off to the cottage for the annual summer holiday. They drove up to the cottage with Bea and got settled in. Once there, they all followed their usual routines. Kelly and Bea shared the cooking and cleaning. Kelly, Joshua, and Bea swam with swimming noodles that Joshua retrieved. Joshua dove off the dock and warmed in the sun. Kelly hung onto his haunches for some rides back to shore. Kelly and Joshua went on walks together along the cottage road.

Bea groomed Joshua every evening. Kelly really appreciated this, especially since she was now on high alert for any hot spots Joshua developed. He had contracted hot spots at the end of the last two cottage trips, so Kelly was now more meticulous in ensuring Joshua had completely dried off. After Joshua swam, Kelly dried him with two large bath towels. Later in the evening after Bea brushed him thoroughly and cut out his mats—activities she delighted in doing—Kelly blew his fur dry with a hairdryer.

With Joshua's recurring hot spots problem, Dr. Samuels had referred Joshua to a doggy allergist, Dr. Libbie, at the animal emergency hospital. After Joshua's bloodwork from the allergy testing had come in, Dr. Libbie had advised, "Joshua is allergic to grass, ragweed, and mosquito bites. I recommend you start to build up Joshua's immunity in April with antihistamines and continue to give him those meds every evening before bed until the first frost."

"Should I shave Joshua to avoid hot spots or opt for mosquito protection? Since mosquitoes are a more serious problem, not shaving him would be best. Do you agree?"

"Yes, Kelly. You can still thin his coat a little. We'll see how Joshua does this year with the antihistamines."

Kelly took Joshua to the groomer to trim his coat. When she picked him up from the groomer's, she told Kelly, "I spent hours brushing Joshua's coat. What a big job! He had so much loose hair trapped in his coat. I had to use a big brush. But look at him now. He looks great!"

"Yes, he does look very handsome and much more svelte in his thinned coat. Thanks so much."

Joshua seemed to swim a little faster on this trip with less baggage to carry. Kelly relaxed more. She also read more and slept in a little. The weather was perfect. She and Bea cooked gourmet meals they both enjoyed. Joshua did not get any hot spots.

Once back home, Kelly and Joshua developed a routine for condo living. Waiting for and riding in the condo building elevator and then walking half a block to relieve himself was not something Joshua enjoyed. He went as far as the big red oak tree in front of the condo building in the most urgent of situations. He preferred to go to the edge of the garden off to one side of the building to urinate.

The concierge complained to Kelly, insisting Joshua stay out of the garden and do what other dogs did—pee on the sidewalk in front of the front door of the building. Kelly considered this an unsavory alternative. She thought encouraging people to let their dogs pee on the sidewalk in front of the building was truly disgusting. She didn't really relish having to sidestep the pee puddles when she and Joshua went for a walk. Joshua could relieve himself at the oak tree or in the pocket park next door, she decided.

During the workweek, each morning and then once or twice each evening, Kelly and Joshua visited the pocket park, Bader Park, adjacent to the western end of the condo property where they lived. The park had mature trees, lawn grass, and grass-covered linear mounds about four feet high and about six feet long, some walking paths, and wooden picnic tables and benches scattered about. On the weekends, Kelly and Joshua continued their jaunts to the beaches.

Most folks Kelly and Joshua encountered in and around their condo building liked Joshua. Unfortunately, one couple thought he was stinky and complained to the property management. At first, Kelly didn't know who had made the complaint. She was just told the complaint was made by someone in the building, but she soon identified the culprit.

On a Saturday afternoon not long after the return from the cottage, she and Joshua were walking on one of the waterfront trails nearby when she overheard a woman say to her husband, "Look, there is that smelly dog."

Because of this couple's complaint, Kelly had received an official, written notice from the condo property management, threatening to have her and Joshua evicted if she didn't solve Joshua's odor problem. Kelly didn't smell anything and asked others if they did, but those she asked said they did not smell anything unusual or bad.

Befuddled, Kelly took Joshua to Dr. Samuels to find out what was causing the odor. Dr. Samuels advised, "Joshua smells like a dog. He is fine."

After Kelly received the second written warning a couple of weeks later, she knew she had a major problem. According to the letter, if there was another complaint, she would be evicted. She decided to take divertive steps before going in the elevator with other people in it. If Kelly saw that couple in the elevator, she and Joshua would wait for the next elevator. If that couple was absent but other people were in the elevator with or without dogs, Kelly would ask their permission for her and Joshua to enter.

A few days after Kelly had received the second written warning, Liz telephoned.

"I can't be Joshua's dog-walker anymore. You need to find someone to look after Joshua during the day when you are not able to be at home. The trip to your place is just too stressful for me. I can't deal with downtown traffic and the extra travel time is also a hardship. I can still look after Joshua when you travel."

"I understand, Liz. Thanks so much for all the care you have given Joshua. He is going to miss Bailey, but they will see each other when I travel."

With that revelation from Liz, Kelly began immediately that evening to shop around to find a suitable alternative—a company that would pick up Joshua in the morning, take him on several walks during the day with a group of dogs, and bring him home in time for dinner. After a few days of searching the internet, chatting with dog owners in the condo building, and doing telephone interviews of prospective service providers, Kelly was delighted to find a good dog-walking service in her neighborhood.

At first, Grace, the owner of the dog-walking service, picked up Joshua, but as she became busier, she delegated the task to others. Kelly monitored Joshua's departure and arrival with each new walker and determined that Joshua was fine. She thought she was less happy about the new dog-walkers than Joshua was. What she really wanted was for Joshua to spend the day with Bailey, his best buddy and lifelong friend.

While Kelly felt she and Joshua were adjusting reasonably well to the new dog-walking service and to condo living, she did notice she could become quite distracted. She was finding it harder to stay present. She forgot her condo keys in the car on top of the dashboard, but she didn't identify the problem until she searched for the keys at the locked door to go from the garage into the main condo building.

After two or three repetitions of this forgetful behavior, Joshua put a stop to it. When Kelly next forgot her condo keys in the car and shut the car door on the driver's side, Joshua, who was standing beside her, refused to budge even after several demands of, "Joshua, let's go," and then "Joshua, let's go now."

When Kelly pulled on his leash, he remained glued to the garage floor. The harder she tugged, the more he resisted. Once Kelly figured out what she had done and retrieved her keys, Joshua was eager to leave the garage and go home.

Kelly was amazed by Joshua's behavior regarding her keys. Like his barking when she forgot to turn off the stove, she had not trained him to do these tasks. He had learned them on his own and was making sure she was safe.

Kelly tried to take equally good care of Joshua. His arthritis bothered him from time to time and she had to give him medication, which helped, but it was not a perfect solution.

At her next appointment with Dr. Jones, he advised, "Kelly, you mentioned at our last appointment Joshua has been having trouble with arthritis in his shoulders and hips since it was diagnosed last year. I can help. You can bring Joshua to treatment with you. I will spend the first few minutes treating him. You have made some good progress in quieting your nervous system. Spending some of my time treating Joshua will not interfere with your progress."

"That's wonderful. Thank you, Dr. Jones. Let's give it a try."

Dr. Jones gave Joshua his first arthritis treatment for the first ten minutes of Kelly's next appointment. Joshua enjoyed the attention. Once his treatment was finished, Joshua laid down nearby so that he could observe Kelly.

After the appointment, Joshua did indeed have more mobility as he walked up the steep flight of stairs from Dr. Jones' office, through the door to the outside, and to their car in the parking lot. Kelly was pleased Joshua felt better.

The next day was her one-year anniversary appointment with Dr. Bradley. Kelly drove to Dr. Bradley's with Joshua, as usual.

As the trip got underway, Kelly informed Joshua with a little extra zing in her voice, "Joshua, we are going to Dr. Bradley's. Joshua and Kelly go for a walk after the appointment."

Once they arrived, she opened the door to the back seat, gave Joshua a hug, and said, "Love you, back soon," and headed to see Dr. Bradley.

For most of the appointment, Dr. Bradley tested Kelly's progress through an extensive testing protocol. Once the tests were completed about twenty minutes or so later, Kelly sat in a chair beside Dr. Bradley, watching him tally the results.

When he was done, he put down his pen, turned to Kelly, and declared, "Congratulations, Kelly. You have normal dorsiflexion in your left foot and almost normal dorsiflexion in your right foot.

"Have you noticed? You hardly toe out at all unless you are tired or not paying attention to your gait. I know this has been a painful and arduous process for you, but the results are impressive. You have shown great determination. Your hard work has paid off. Let's continue with a maintenance plan and work on the dorsiflexion in your right foot."

"Thanks, Dr. Bradley. This is wonderful news! I can't believe it. I never thought this was possible. See you next week."

When Kelly left Dr. Bradley's office, she was humming and smiling. She said to herself as she walked to the car, *breaking up the old scar tissue has been excruciating. But, look at me!*

Then she looked down and watched herself take a few steps. She could clearly see she no longer walked like Charlie Chaplin. She thought she could do even better than this with more work and practice.

When she got to the car, she opened the back door and said, "Come, Joshua. Let's celebrate. Let's go for a walk by the tennis courts and then take a new trail to the other side of the campus."

After Joshua jumped out of the car and Kelly closed the car door, she gave him a giant hug and a big kiss on his face. Then they cautiously headed along the walking path around the campus.

CHAPTER 32

Painful Separation

Kelly and Joshua continued their explorations of the new neighborhood along the waterfront as well as their daily and nightly pilgrimages to Bader Park. One early October evening after a walk along the waterfront, Kelly took Joshua to Bader Park, as usual. They did a turn on the walking paths at the front of the park near the road. While Joshua was happy to explore, he showed no interest in urinating. They took a break from the walk by visiting the sandwich and ice cream shop that fronted the southwest side of the park. The servers in the shop knew Joshua and always welcomed him with attention and pats, whenever Kelly took him into the store.

Kelly chatted with the servers and then she and Joshua departed to finish their walk.

They did their usual evening route at the front of the park again, but Joshua was not yet inspired to relieve himself. Kelly did not want to go home without Joshua having urinated. She felt it was too risky. She didn't want to have to come back in the middle of the night or early in the morning.

On a regular walk in Bader Park during the day, Kelly and Joshua would walk along the back border of the park on the grassy path, but Kelly was reticent to do that trip at night when no one else was in the park. That grassy path abutted derelict land along the back edge of the park. However, the usual park spots were not working for Joshua, so Kelly reasoned that a change of scene might be a motivator for him.

They strolled onto the grassy path that led to the back of the park. Then they walked along the back border. Kelly was careful to stay well away from protruding tree stumps that flanked the back edge of the grassy path just in front of the derelict land. Although Kelly thought Joshua welcomed these new smells, his bladder did not yield. They continued their investigations.

When they arrived at the back edge of the park near their condo building, Kelly spotted a path close to a manicured bush, which they had not explored before. She and Joshua meandered on the path to the bush. Joshua had a good sniff all around the bush and relieved himself. Kelly was delighted and smiled at Joshua. To reward him for relieving himself by the bush, they would climb the closest grassy mound and walk along the top of it—an adventure Kelly knew Joshua would love as he had enjoyed previous journeys on top of the park mounds.

The closest mound was about two feet away from where Kelly was standing. "Come, Joshua, let's go up the mound."

When Kelly looked toward the mound, she noticed the street lamp, which had been illuminated when they had walked along the back edge of the park, was now out.

She could see well enough in front of her and up the mound, so all was well. Needing momentum to reach the top of the mound because of the steep slope, she accelerated first with her left foot then her right as she climbed up with Joshua by her side, leaning forward as she went upward. Then without warning, her right foot hooked around a small wooden stump hidden in the grass as she continued her forward momentum with her left foot. She heard a snap.

She said aloud, "Mother of God! What have I done?"

Kelly landed forward, flat on her face, and torso in the grassy dirt. She didn't feel any pain from the snap. She rolled over onto her front and sat up facing the manicured bush. On her butt, she slid down the mound toward Joshua, who was now at the bottom of the mound.

After she reached the bottom, she experimented by placing a tiny amount of weight on her right foot, but this was extremely painful. Her right knee was the problem. It was very sore when she put weight on it. She tested how much weight to place on her right foot. With just the right amount, she hobbled with Joshua out of Bader Park, along the sidewalk, and into her condo building.

Once she was in the condo, her first priority was Joshua. She checked his water bowl and filled it so he could have his final evening drink before bed. He was always thirsty after a walk. Then she limped into the bedroom with bags of ice to apply to her knee. She took ibuprofen, elevated her knee, applied compression, and iced it most of the night. Joshua kept her company at his usual spot on the floor by the window where he could watch Kelly and the door.

At some point in the night, Kelly fell asleep. When she woke up in the morning and tried to walk toward the bathroom, she noticed that her right foot was very swollen, but her right knee was not that swollen, even though it really ached. When she realized she still couldn't put any weight on her right leg without causing a lot of pain, she decided to go to the hospital.

Luckily, that day, Kelly had planned to attend some client meetings and go to the office. Joshua would be spending the day with the dog-walker. She telephoned the dog-walker to make sure she was coming.

"Hello, this is Kelly Delmonico. I injured my knee. I am going to the hospital as soon as you arrive for Joshua. Please drop him off at home at the usual time."

After the dog-walker picked up Joshua, Kelly called a cab and then limped out of her building to get into it, careful to put only enough weight on her right leg to keep herself upright.

When she arrived at the emergency entrance of the hospital, she asked the cab driver, "Sir, please help me. I can't walk. Would you please go into the emergency room and bring me a wheelchair?"

"Yes, ma'am, of course," he replied and went to fetch the chair. He helped Kelly into the chair and wheeled her into the emergency room to the triage desk. He smiled at Kelly as she thanked him.

Once Kelly checked in, a nurse brought her to a bed right away. While Kelly waited to see a doctor, she called her clients to let them know her predicament and to cancel her meetings for the day.

After she had x-rays and a CT scan, the emergency intern advised Kelly, "You have a stress fracture in your right medial tibia. The break did not show up on the x-rays, but it was clear from the CT scan.

"You will be in a non-weight-bearing cast for a week. Then you will come back to the hospital to see the orthopedic surgeon to find out whether surgery on your knee will be necessary. If you don't require surgery, you will spend another seven weeks in a non-weight-bearing cast or brace. Down the road, you can expect to have a knee replacement.

"Remember, and this is very important, do not put any weight on your knee. Keep your right foot off the floor."

After the intern fitted Kelly with a cast and some crutches, ordered her a wheelchair to be delivered to her home the next day, and gave her a prescription for strong painkillers, he reminded her again about not putting any weight on her right foot and then discharged her.

Kelly called Bea, "I have some bad news. I am at St. Andrews. I broke my knee, so, unfortunately, dinner is off tonight."

"Oh no, Kelly. How awful! I'm not far away. I will be there in ten minutes to take you home."

By the time Kelly got home, the pain had set in. Bea picked up Kelly's pain prescription at the pharmacy and helped her get settled.

"Thanks, Bea, I really appreciate your help. I should be okay for the night."

"No worries. I'll call you in the morning and come by in the afternoon to see how you are doing."

After Bea left, Kelly became more aware of her pain. Her right knee was now throbbing. Her right ankle also had become very sore. Her head and neck ached.

In a non-weight-bearing cast and on crutches, how would she be able to look after Joshua? She called Liz.

"Liz, I broke my knee today. I'll be in a non-weight-bearing cast for a week until I find out about surgery. Will you be able to take Joshua until I figure out what to do?"

"Of course, Ben and I will look after Joshua. We will come by tonight and pick him up. I hope you are not in a lot of pain. Please let me know if I can do anything else to help."

"Thanks, Liz. See you soon."

After Kelly called Liz, she phoned Kieran to let him know about the injury. Kieran declared, "I'm going to take the week off and come to Buffington to look after you. I'll drive down and see you tomorrow."

Kelly's heart mangled as she heard Kieran say, "But I can't cope with both you and Joshua. Joshua will have to continue to stay with Liz and Ben."

When Liz and Ben arrived to pick up Joshua, Kelly was groggy. The painkillers had kicked in and she was exhausted from her ordeal. She was heartbroken to see Joshua go but knew he would be well looked after. She got some sleep that night.

Kelly was glad to see Kieran the next afternoon. During his week stay with her, Kelly spent most of the time lying down with her knee elevated, dozing, in pain, and occasionally watching some TV. Kieran cooked for her and did some shopping for food and supplies, including a shower seat and some storage containers so he could freeze some food he had cooked.

Having Kieran at her side was healing, but inadvertently, he triggered her somatic response. Her eyes grew very heavy. She could feel the heightened sensations on her left side from her face to her ankle. Being immobile, she could not dissipate the somatic response sensations, so she dozed through them. Kelly was in a fog and barely noticed as one day floated into the next during Kieran's stay.

After Kieran went home, Kelly reviewed her situation. Donna and Bea were planning to come by at least once a week to check on her and bring supplies. That would be a big help.

How could she manage Joshua? She didn't have any friends in the building. She and Joshua had just moved in. She hadn't had the time to make new friends. The dog-walking service could come twice during the day and once at night, but Joshua usually went out twice at night. What if there is an emergency and they had to get us out of the building? She couldn't get the wheelchair out the door if she was in it and she couldn't manage to get it out the door if she used her crutches.

The concierge was no help either. "Mrs. Delmonico, we can't store your wheelchair in the storage on the first floor," he told her. "Please be advised you cannot keep your wheelchair outside your door. This is a violation of the condo rules, which can result in an eviction."

In psychotherapy the next day, Kelly discussed her options for caring for Joshua. Her sessions were now telephone sessions since she could not conquer the steep flight of stairs to Ella's office with her crutches.

"Ella, I don't know how I'm going to manage Joshua by myself. With no place to store my wheelchair outside my unit, I can't use the chair. Using crutches with Joshua is impossible. We live on a busy street with lots of traffic. Not having Joshua on his leash is too risky. I called some home-care dog services. Having someone stay overnight on my couch is just too intrusive and too expensive."

"Have you considered diapers for Joshua?"

"I don't think that will work. Joshua will just pull the diaper off. I see the surgeon tomorrow. I hope he will bring good news." "Take care, Kelly. I hope the appointment goes well."

That evening, Kelly watched some TV and kept her mind off the surgeon's appointment. As she got ready for bed, she focused on bringing Joshua home and then went to sleep quite quickly that night.

Kelly woke up early the next morning, had an espresso while she read the newspaper, and called a cab to go to the surgeon's appointment. She tried not to worry about the prospect of surgery.

She was delighted when the surgeon advised, "Mrs. Delmonico, surgery will not be necessary. The fracture did not move anything out of place. I'll see you in seven weeks to remove your knee brace. Please make an appointment at the reception desk. Take care."

Once Kelly got home from the surgeon's, she telephoned Liz.

"Hi, Liz. I still really need your help. Although I don't need surgery, I will be in a non-weight-bearing brace for another few weeks. Will you be able to look after Joshua until I am back on my feet?"

"Of course, Kelly. Don't worry. And I'll drop Joshua off once a week on Sundays so you and he can visit while Ben and I shop downtown."

"Thanks, Liz. You're a lifesaver."

CHAPTER 33

Coping with Separation

When Joshua arrived for his first Sunday visit, Kelly greeted him at the door. "Hello, Joshua. I am so glad to see you!" She gave him a pat as best she could, while still holding her crutches. She was ecstatic to see Joshua, but she did have to hold back her tears.

"Thanks so much, Liz, for bringing Joshua."

"Ben and I will be back in about two hours. Enjoy your visit."

During Joshua's visit, Kelly lay on the living room couch and rested while Joshua lay down nearby. Kelly made sure he had water and a treat to chew on. She dozed for a bit and got herself and Joshua a snack of provolone and crackers. It was almost time for Liz and Ben to return. She called Joshua to sit by her. She hugged him and started to cry.

Because she did not want to upset him any further, she gave him a kiss on his face and said, "Joshua, you are such a good boy. Love you!"

Then she lay down on the couch, hoping Joshua would lie down nearby as well, which he did. She fought off her tears as best she could until Liz and Ben buzzed at the building door.

As she buzzed them in, she pointed out, "The door is unlocked. Come right in when you arrive."

When Liz and Ben entered her condo, Kelly called, "Joshua, come."

Sitting up on the couch, Kelly leaned over to Joshua and gave him a huge hug and many kisses. Then off he dutifully went with Liz and Ben, with Kelly scarcely having any composure at all.

This routine repeated each time Joshua had a Sunday visit with Kelly.

Three weeks into her convalescence, Kelly received an e-mail from Deke. It was about settling the spoils of the family business between them. Since Kelly had made it clear their relationship was over, and they both had secured lawyers, Deke now e-mailed Kelly infrequently and kept things more matter of fact, which provided some relief for Kelly.

Deke's e-mail said, "Attached is the questionnaire you have to fill out for the business valuation. I will respond to the same questions. Then we choose a business valuator to review the questions and look at the company's books.

"This is going to be expensive, but you didn't want to go with our accountant being our mediator. You also rejected my offer of settlement that my lawyer sent your lawyer. So here we are. Fill this out quickly, so we can get on with this."

Sitting up in bed or lying on the couch, Kelly repeatedly attempted to fill out the questionnaire but found she just didn't have the energy. She was not well enough to concentrate on the questions. Each time she attempted to answer them, she became more frustrated. The weight of the task grew heavier.

After a few days of this struggle, Kelly assessed her situation. She didn't have the fortitude or the stamina. Deke and she were not going to agree on the answers. This would get drawn out and acrimonious. This will lead to narcissistic injuries to Deke, which is just going to make matters worse. Going with the accountant was out of the question. He always sided with Deke.

The last time she saw the accountant and complained about Deke's opaqueness about their finances, the accountant said, "You know, Kelly, you can just leave him."

This was odd, she remembered thinking. It startled her. Still she couldn't trust it. Deke's lowball offer was beginning to look appealing, despite her legal counsel's advice to the contrary.

At that moment in her mind's eye, Kelly saw Joshua. He was lying on a carpet, picked his head up slightly, and looked beyond her eyes. Suddenly, her direction was clear. She had to get on her feet as quickly as she could. She wanted Joshua home with her.

Kelly's support team of healthcare professionals had been urging her, "Choose life as quickly as possible. Extricate from the marriage and start to heal."

Kelly believed Deke knew about her knee injury. He and Darcy were still communicating. Darcy must have told him about it. Kelly had called Darcy to let her know about her knee and left a voicemail.

Darcy had replied by e-mail saying, "I'm so sorry, Mom. Hope you feel better." Kelly had received radio silence from Darcy since then.

With all the strength she could muster, Kelly crafted her reply e-mail to Deke.

"I don't want to go forward with the valuation. Instead, I want to accept your original offer. I hope you will be compassionate about my situation and agree. Thanks."

Deke speedily accepted Kelly's offer, writing back, "Fine. I'll let my lawyer know."

Kelly was surprised by his quick reply. She knew she was accepting much less than she deserved, but she wanted to focus on healing and bringing Joshua home. From her experience with her broken foot and ankle, she knew she was unlikely to walk again right away after the brace was off unless she got more prepared.

She contacted Dr. Bradley. "Kelly, if you can get to my office, I can help you recover. See you soon."

At the appointment with Dr. Bradley, he reviewed her x-rays and CT scan. "Kelly, I will do mobilizations with you without your brace. I also recommend you have quadriceps treatment. While it is painful, it will really help with the extensive atrophy you have to both your legs. We can continue with your regular twice a week schedule now that you have sufficient mobility and strength."

Kelly looked at her legs. They looked like thick toothpicks, especially the right leg, which was even thinner than the left. "Okay, let's do it."

In addition to seeing Dr. Bradley, Kelly had set up home visits with Kala. Kala had told her, "I can come by once a week to do acupuncture for bone stimulation on your knee. This will help it to heal properly and faster."

Kelly had also arranged for Kim to come by twice a week to do simple leg exercises with her brace off.

About five weeks into her convalescence, Bill, Kelly's boss, paid her a visit.

"How are you doing, Kelly? I brought you some food staples. Can I help you with anything else?" he inquired as he placed the brown bags of food on the kitchen counter, put the perishables in the fridge, and left the rest of the food on the counter. Then he sat down on the black wing chair next to the couch where Kelly was seated, with her right leg outstretched on top of two pillows on the walnut coffee table, opposite the couch.

"Yes, Bill, thanks very much. Would you see if you can get my wheelchair out the door while you are sitting in it? I've tried and I just can't do it.

"If I can get the wheelchair out on my own, then I'll be able to bring my dog home and look after him myself, which I really want to do. He is staying with friends. I miss him so very much."

Kelly watched Bill as he looked about the room for the wheelchair and spotted it next to the stereo system. "I'll give it a try," he said. "I'm experienced with a wheelchair."

"Did you know about three years ago I broke my knee pretty badly and spent over a month in a wheelchair? Now I do bike marathons every year for charity."

Kelly watched Bill earnestly try to maneuver the wheelchair. But after about 30 minutes or so later, she was beginning to give up hope. Bill persevered.

After more than an hour of trying many options of innovative wheelchair gymnastics, Bill announced, "It's impossible to get the chair out if you are in it. Your doorway is too narrow. I can't hold the door open if I'm in the chair."

Then Bill sat down again on the wing chair.

"Kelly, I am going to have to let the change-management team go. I can't wait any longer for those contracts we won to come in, even though I know they'll come in eventually.

"I know when we first met to discuss where I wanted the business to go, I was keen on starting this new practice with Jordan. But now I don't think it's a winner. Your strategic-planning practice is thriving. Let's continue our work together to build on that."

Despite Kelly's best efforts to try to convince Bill to wait a little longer before terminating the change-management practice, he was not dissuaded. She would have to face those changes at the office and figure out her future.

At her psychotherapy session by phone the next afternoon, Kelly began, "I am really upset Bill fired everyone doing change management in the company. He even let Adil go, even though he worked part-time in change management and part-time with me in strategic planning. Bill had made up his mind and had fired people before he came over last night. I was the last to know.

"I don't think I'm going to like this new arrangement. I joined Bill's company, in part because I liked his team. I'll give it a try for a few weeks and see how it goes. I really loved working with Jordan. I even enjoyed working with Adil. He was so smart and worked so hard. He had made amazing progress. I'll reach out to them both and see if we can get together when I am more mobile."

"Kelly, this is a good time to take a break. Why don't you get a coffee and come back to the phone in about five minutes or so?" "Okay, I'll be back in five."

Kelly did not plan in advance what she would talk about in a session. The topics just came to her and she went with what was on her mind at the time. Lately, she had been spending the sessions talking about how much she missed Joshua and the loss of Darcy. When she returned with her coffee in her thermos which she carried in her knapsack and got comfortable on the couch, she changed the subject to her childhood. It had been a while since she had talked about that.

"Ella, when I was growing up, I never felt like I fit in. There were no girls that lived nearby. I was a tomboy, playing touch football and pitch and catch with the boys on the street, which I really loved. While these boys were my friends, they did not go to my school. They went to an all-boys Catholic school. I didn't have a best girlfriend at school and so was always a third wheel. I often got left out of the threesome when being the third person was inconvenient to the other two.

"Even my own family made me feel like an outsider. 'You don't look like a Maguire, like your father and brother,' my mother was fond of repeating to me. Then the ultimate insult: 'You look like Nana.' She hated Nana.

"My mother loved to tell this story. She would say to me, 'Before you were born and when you were very little, your nana and granddad used to have a general store in the older, poorer side of town near Cullen Street. Your dad helped out in the store. Do you know your nana chased me up and down the food aisles with a large utility knife? She was the devil incarnate. I was screaming. Your dad rushed from the back storeroom to rescue me. When Nana saw your dad, she put the knife down.'

"My dad never disputed this story, so I guess it was true.

"My mother was always criticizing me. She derided me for being left-handed. 'You do everything backward,' she would say. 'I can't teach you anything!' She never did teach me how to sew or cut with scissors, even though she sewed many of her own clothes.

"Although we were never really close to my father's family, when my dad died, his brother and family stopped seeing us. My mother told me why. With an undercurrent of blaming me, she said, 'Your uncle Max can't stand the sight of you and Kieran. To him, you both look too much like your father. It is too painful for Uncle Max to be with you.'

"I have thought about that story over the years. Each time I do, it hurts. Uncle Max's daughter confirmed her dad's sentiment when she telephoned me a few years ago after more than twenty-five years of not being in touch to tell me that Uncle Max had died, and she hoped I understood that he couldn't bear to be in the presence of me because I reminded him so much of my father. She implied the small amount of money she was telling me he left me was supposed to be recompense as if any amount of money could be.

"My dad took Kieran and me to visit his parents at their bungalow every Saturday for lunch. Sometimes, my dad would stay for lunch. Other times, he would leave us and come back just before taking us home. If he left us, he never came back empty-handed. He always brought back some of our favorite pastries to have back at home.

"Granddad and Nana were very different from each other. Grandad was a gentleman who never said much to me or my brother. He died soon after my dad did. Nana, on the other hand, was outgoing and ebullient.

"About a year after Uncle Max died, I arranged a lunch with his two children, something I had never done before. In fact, we had never gotten together either for lunch or for anything.

"I surprised myself when I decided to arrange this lunch and equally surprised when they agreed to meet me. I was trying to get information about my dad to try to help me understand things better. They told me my dad and Uncle Max thought Nana was a tyrant. I was shocked by that, as I had never seen any evidence of that growing up. But given that my dad married my mom, I can believe it now. I am beginning to see that in ignorance, I followed in my dad's footsteps in marrying Deke.

"Nana did have her good points. She was an excellent cook. Saturday lunches, Christmas Eve and Easter dinners, St. Patrick's Day celebrations, and the occasional Thanksgiving dinner with her were gourmet feasts.

"Unfortunately, like Uncle Max, she couldn't cope with the death of my dad, either. At first, after my dad's death when Kieran and I visited Nana together, she engaged with us. But after a few visits, she stopped making eye contact. She didn't converse with us. Instead, she just sobbed as if we weren't there, saying out loud but to herself, 'I miss Robbie. I miss Robbie. It's not fair. He died too young.'

"After several months of her ignoring us and repeating the same behavior, Kieran and I stopped going to visit her. You know, Nana never contacted us once we stopped visiting. Can you imagine?

"My mother's family was even worse than my dad's. My mother had one sibling, a sister, Celeste. I have mentioned her before. She is a widow with three children, a girl, and twin boys. I told you about the camp teasing. During my childhood and teen years, these cousins constantly teased, disparaged, and denigrated Kieran and me whenever we saw them, which unfortunately after Dad died was at weekly Sunday dinners and also at Christmas, Easter, and Thanksgiving when we were all at our maternal grandmother's.

"'Leftie, don't sit beside me!' my cousins would holler at me. 'Sit at this end of the table. No, the other end. We don't want your elbows bumping. You're such a spaz!' 'What are you wearing? Look at those white socks! What a twerp you are!' There were more, but I can't remember all of it. I just have the lingering damage of their insults in my bones.

"I guess out of all my relatives, my maternal grandmother was the kindest to me. For some reason, Kieran and I called her Gran, but the cousins called her Nonna. She helped me sew an apron for a home economics school project when my mother refused to help me. She let me follow her around the kitchen while I wrote down her recipes for posterity. When I learned to drive, I drove into the big city, Lincolnville, to take her to the library to borrow some books and then out for lunch to her favorite fast-food place for a burger. We both really enjoyed these outings. Although Gran was always pleasant to me and I felt a certain closeness, she never offered protection from my cousins or my mother.

"Not long after Gran died—I think it was after one of the church services regarding her death—one of my distant cousins who was also one of Gran's closest friends, came up to me and said, 'Your grandmother loved you very much. You were her favorite.' Stunned by this, I replied, 'Who? Me?' And she said, 'Yes, you were the light of her life.' I was in disbelief and still am. I don't have any evidence of this. I find it troubling. Should I believe it?"

After about thirty seconds of silence, while Kelly took some deep breaths, she continued.

"Oh, my Lord! I now understand why I was and still am so touched by Joshua's sitting on my lap at the breeders. Joshua's choosing me made me feel wanted, like I belong, like we belong together."

CHAPTER 34

Learning to Walk Again

After that last session with Ella, Kelly did not want to think about what she had uncovered about her life. Instead, as she went through her day, she concentrated on Joshua's homecoming, her rehabilitation work for her knee, and her upcoming appointment in two weeks with her surgeon to remove her brace.

When it was close to the time for Joshua's upcoming Sunday visit, Liz telephoned.

"Kelly, I'm sorry. I have to cancel Joshua's Sunday visit. We have a family emergency with Ben's mum. We'll see you next week."

"I hope Ben's mum will be okay. Please let me know. My prayers are with you. Take care."

A few days before her appointment with her surgeon to remove the brace, Kelly received a phone call.

"Hello, Mrs. Delmonico. The surgeon is away on holiday. Your appointment next week is canceled. I can reschedule the appointment for you for two weeks from your canceled appointment."

"Yes, thank you. I will see the surgeon then."

In her next psychotherapy appointment after the nurse's call which was that afternoon, Kelly began the session by expressing her heartache about the delay. Then she took a break to get a coffee and resumed her session.

"Talking about my dad has been helpful. I don't feel so guilty anymore about his death. I didn't really appreciate it before the last session that he wasn't home much.

"We rarely vacationed as a family. My dad traveled frequently on business. His trips lasted several days, occasionally more than a week. He worked late and arrived home after Kieran and I had already finished dinner.

"Sometimes, my dad drove me to school in the morning or to the few guitar lessons I took until my parents could no longer afford them. Sometimes, my dad picked me up from Sunday school. On the weekends in the summer, my dad cooked a family barbecue.

"I do remember my dad supported my tomboy predilections. 'What would you like me to bring you back from my trip?' he would ask me. 'Some baseball cards!' I would exclaim.

"My dad and I both knew my mother objected, but he bought the cards anyway, and my bicycle, my baseball mitt for playing pitch and catch, and my football for touch football. The last present he brought me was a skateboard. I remember thinking, 'The skateboard is fun, but there is no place smooth to use it. The road is so bumpy. There are so many little stones. This really isn't that much fun. I can't go fast or for long glides.'

"I just thought of another story about me and my dad. I don't know why I remember this story so clearly.

"Since I was an infant, I had trouble settling at night and sleeping. When I was seven or eight, I experienced a few days when I was particularly anxious. I don't remember why. I couldn't sleep. I went to my parent's bedroom to get some help to settle.

"Tapping my dad's shoulder gently, I said, 'Daddy, I can't sleep.' Three nights in a row, he turned over, got out of bed, and walked me back to my bedroom. He lay down beside me with his hand on my forehead. This was comforting. In less than a minute, I was asleep.

"On the fourth night, he lost his patience. He said, 'Can't you sleep on your own?' He got out of bed. He hurried me back into my room. He didn't lie down beside me. I was up for hours. I never asked him to comfort me again.

"I remember being abandoned at my dad's funeral. My mother refused to let Kieran go to the funeral, saying he was too young. He had to stay home with a babysitter. I recall getting out of the black limousine on my own. No one walked with me. I looked toward the gravesite which seemed like half a mile away. Everyone was gathered around it, but I was alone and far away. I remember feeling the ground was uneven. I saw everything in shades of grey.

"An older second cousin, who had worked for my dad one summer when the cousin was a college student, saw me standing by myself. He came over, put his arm around me, and said, 'Your father was such a wonderful person. He was the nicest person I ever knew.' Then he walked me toward the gravesite. I don't remember anything else.

"I was always closer to my dad than my mom. I loved my dad. My mother—well, she was difficult. I loved her anyway, despite how awful she was.

"My mother liked to be the victim. She told me over and over again, 'My father made me train to be a chemist during the war to help out the war effort. I hated working in the lab. I wanted to be a nutritionist. I still do.'

"'Why don't you go back to school?' I innocently asked, but she just glared back at me. Over time, as I kept getting the same response to this question, I stopped asking her. My mother preferred complaining to taking action. She seemed to imply that I was to blame.

"After my dad died, my mother spent weeks in bed, demanding Kieran and I bring her drinks and food. A babysitter came in during the day. My mother never tried to comfort me after my dad died.

"She blamed others and never took responsibility for anything. Others owed her something. Somehow, I was supposed to repair her life and make it better.

"My parents wanted their independence from the family. Instead of choosing to live near our extended family, both sides of which lived in Lincolnville, not ten blocks from each other, my parents preferred to live in a much smaller town, St. George, about thirty miles from Lincolnville, where our small home was more affordable. My dad didn't mind the long commute. When I was growing up, St. George was an intellectual wasteland. The town didn't even have a library or a municipal recreation center.

"My parents almost never went to the small community church in St. George. Instead, my mother sent me off to church alone. 'Kelly, time for church. Off you go.'

"Although I was a regular churchgoer to services and Sunday school on my own, after my dad died, I didn't feel like I was part of the church community. I stopped going to church. My mother tried to persuade me to go, but I refused.

"Kieran and I had to be bused five miles to attend the nearest high school. That's where I met Deke.

"I guess after my dad died, I was even more isolated. I had nowhere to turn. When I was living through my childhood, I wasn't consciously aware of any of this. I guess it was too painful to confront. I needed to get by somehow."

"Kelly, it must have been very difficult for you to grow up in such an isolated, non-supportive environment. You are very strong. You have overcome a lot.

"Good work today. I hope your appointment with the surgeon goes well."

Kelly was counting the remaining days to see the surgeon and remove her brace. When the big day finally arrived, the surgeon stated, "Mrs. Delmonico, you don't need to wear your brace any longer. Everything looks good. Please start physical therapy right away."

Kelly took the brace off, ready to take her first step. But she couldn't stand up. She still needed the crutches. Bearing weight on her right leg even with the crutches was too painful.

As she exited the hospital, a nurse approached her. "You are doing well for just having the brace off. Be patient. It will come."

Dejected, Kelly understood she needed to undergo another week or two of rehabilitation before she could bring Joshua home. She began her rehabilitation with the brace off right away, doing physiotherapy twice a week.

Two days after the brace removal, she went to see Dr. Bradley for her regular appointment. He advised, "Kelly, you can't keep using your crutches. Here is a cane to use. First, try with one crutch and then replace the crutch with the cane. It takes practice. When I see you next week, we can evaluate how well you are walking."

After a couple of days, Kelly walked easily with one crutch, but the cane was a different matter. She didn't use it.

When she saw Dr. Bradley the following week, she explained, "It is so painful to use the cane. My right shoulder aches from using the cane, and my right foot is so sore. I don't want to put any weight on it."

"Kelly, you must use the cane, or you will not make much progress. Stop using your crutches. I'll show you how to shift your weight and move forward with the cane. When you use the cane, your weight should be equally balanced on both legs. Begin by going a short distance, a few steps. Build to a block and then a few blocks. Slow and steady will win the race. Watch me as I use the cane and shift my weight."

"Dr. Bradley, I want to resume exercising on my recumbent bike. Is that okay?" "Yes, that should be fine. But take it slowly and build."

For the next week, Kelly practiced walking with the cane every day. Each step was an ordeal. Pressing through the intense pain, she took baby steps, grimaced at the pain, but pushed onward. After a few days of practice, she succeeded in achieving half a small block with the cane. The pain had subsided a little by this time, but it was still smarting as she put weight on her feet, in particular her right foot.

By the end of the week, having endured an insufferable amount of discomfort, her feet and legs were stronger. With the cane, she could now walk a few short blocks. But the walking was taking its toll on her right shoulder as she placed most of her weight on it as Dr. Bradley had insisted to avoid limping with the cane. Her right shoulder ached. With each progressive step, she knew she was injuring it further. She was keenly aware her shoulder would require attention once she was able to walk more normally again.

Pleased with her walking skills, Kelly tried her recumbent bike. The first five minutes were excruciating. She gritted her teeth and pushed through the punishing pain. Once she moved past that point, the pain subsided. She did another five minutes on the bike. She was on the road to recovery. She was ready for Joshua's return.

Kelly paced with the cane up and down her condo from her front door to the windows of her living room that overlooked the lake, waiting for Joshua's arrival.

When he arrived, she gave him a huge hug and some kisses, and said, "Joshua, I am so glad you are home. Love you!"

"Liz, thanks so much. Your help has been a godsend."

"Joshua and Bailey had a great time, but Joshua did miss you very much. See you soon."

Kelly and Joshua spent the evening together. He joined Kelly on the couch while she patted his head and rubbed his tummy as they watched some TV. Then she watched him chew a braided chew on the floor, slurp some water, and curl up for a snooze beside her by the couch. Before ending the evening, they went out for a very short constitutional to Bader Park. Kelly was able to move effectively with the cane and hold onto Joshua's leash with the other hand as they walked.

Writing poetry had become a compulsion for Kelly when she had strong emotions to release. She felt better after putting her emotions down on virtual paper. Before bed, on that first night together after so many weeks, Kelly wrote:

> From a long line
> Of good breeding
> He comes to me
> And helps me see
>
> With gentle loving
> His heart is bringing
>
> He watches me
> At play and in protection
> And with such total affection
>
> Great happiness today
> With our sadness well at bay
>
> We used to live in quiet misery
> Focused on the daily drudgery
>
> As full-time caregivers
> To one empty soul
> With such a heinous goal
>
> He so full of rage
> We feared to engage
>
> Yet so clever and witty
> I felt so much pity
>
> I could do no right
> The victim of his spite
>
> To another intensely needy
> In chronic pain
> With an enormous brain

But with such fragility
And so little mobility

At their beck and call
We didn't matter at all

Then that wintry night
With that terrible fright

When the rage exploded
We shook and imploded

His emptiness was asked to depart
After stomping on my broken heart

The other one
Not showing a tear
Not wanting to hear

Not even to engage
There was just too much rage

That left we two
And we knew
Just what to do

We had amusing talks
And went on wooded walks

Moved to a new place
And tried to erase
The ugliness of their disgrace

It didn't work that well
So very hard to repel
My own flesh and blood

GOLDEN LOVE

Tried to run
But was undone
Got stuck in the mud

One late night strolling
Joshua by my side

No light to warn me
Or to guide

Heard the snap of my right knee
On that grassy hill before me

No constant companion
For so many days
I missed him totally
In so many ways

Until he came along
I never fit in
I never could win
He made me belong

He is my best friend
On him I do depend
So glad he is back
To keep me on track

Two loving soul mates
We walk as one
Eager for a new start
Eager for more fun

Sleep well Joshua
Have a good night
Now that you're back
Our future is bright.

CHAPTER 35

Together Again

Now that Kelly was mobile again, she and Joshua resumed their routine of working at home together three days a week and Joshua spending two days a week with the dog-walker, while Kelly was at the office. When Kelly arrived at the office on her first day back, she noticed how quiet the office was without the change-management team members. The reality of her working alone on strategic planning and growing just her own practice began to set in.

Although Kelly was successful in bringing in two new contracts, this work required her and not more junior staff to complete. It was the type of work she used to do on her own when she ran her own consulting business years before the family business enterprise. She didn't see being able to turn this type of work into a larger practice, at least not in the short or medium term. She really enjoyed doing this type of work and didn't want to delegate it.

After three weeks of trying to make the new circumstances work, Kelly decided to leave Bill's company. She didn't see any point in waiting any longer as she felt it would take months before there might be an improvement in her situation. With that decision, Kelly e-mailed Bill and asked to meet with him the next time they would both be in the office. Two days later, Kelly met with Bill.

"Bill, I miss working with a team. I enjoy working with you, but there is little opportunity to do so. I am resigning. Here is my resignation letter. This is my two weeks' notice. I'll be leaving at the end of December."

"Kelly, I am very surprised. I thought you were happy here. Are you sure? Please reconsider."

"When I joined your firm, I did so because of its reputation, the opportunity to work with you, to build my strategic-planning practice, and to grow a change-management practice with Jordan.

"Working in a team is important to me. Now the team is gone. I am working alone. If that is going to be the case, I may as well work alone again in my own company. But I will continue to look for opportunities for us to work with each other in the future."

When Kelly got home from work that evening, she was tired but excited she would be embarking on a new adventure. She and Joshua went on a long walk. During the walk, she ruminated on her professional future. Resurrecting her own company again was a gutsy move, she began to realize.

With the two contracts she had just won and some other work she would bring with her, she would have some work for a quarter. But she would not have enough to sustain her beyond that.

Resigning was definitely not her finest hour as a planner. Her tolerance for putting up with bad situations had diminished. She was willing to take a lot more risks.

She turned to Joshua as she walked and said, "Joshua, thank you. You give me the courage to go for what I want. With you in my corner, I feel confident. I love you, Joshua. Let's go home."

Kelly departed Bill's company just before Christmas. She used the time between her departure and the holiday to shop, organize her condo, and go on long walks with Joshua.

She and Joshua spent Christmas day with Bea and her family. Darcy had e-mailed, "I am not coming home this Christmas. I need to do some research here and focus on my thesis."

Kelly and Joshua spent the rest of the holiday season with just the two of them, taking frequent, long, leisurely walks along the waterfront, in Bader Park and Lawrence Park. Kelly reorganized her home office and got ready for the new year in her own company again.

Kelly's company did well over January and early February. In mid-February, Kelly received a phone call from a former client, Maria Ferrari, the owner and CEO of a chain of retail beauty shops across the state.

"Kelly, you are a very hard person to find. I've been searching and asking around. We haven't spoken since you did some work for me two years ago. I have some change-management work to do at my head office and at each of my retail beauty shops.

"Based on your previous work for me, I changed my supply chain and manufacturing process. Now all our products are organic and developed without animal testing.

"Did you know I won a state business award for these practices last year? I want to institute some additional sustainability practices across the company. And I would like you to help me and start right away."

"Maria, it is so great to hear from you. Congratulations on your business award! I am honored and excited you would like my help to introduce more sustainability practices. Thank you so much for finding me. I know that wasn't easy."

"Wonderful, Kelly. I'll have my office set up a call with you next week to go over the details of the contract."

Kelly was delighted to hear from Maria. After the call, she took Joshua out for a celebratory walk. As they walked into the neighborhood, Kelly recalled it was great fun to work with Maria. This new work would be leading edge and would take a few months to complete. There would be some traveling away from Joshua, but mostly just day trips.

At her psychotherapy session the following afternoon, Kelly was still energized by Maria's call. The session was back in Ella's office. Now that Kelly could do stairs, she resumed the old routine of Joshua accompanying her on the drive to Ella's and then Joshua snoozing in the back seat until the session ended and Kelly returned. Since Kelly was feeling positive about the call with Maria, she briefly mentioned the good news to Ella and then her thoughts took her elsewhere.

"I am still trying to understand the broken bone to the left side of my face that happened years ago. I didn't break it when I fell off my bike. My whole face didn't land on the sidewalk. My chin hit the cement. What am I overlooking?"

Kelly paused for a few moments, stood up, stretched, and continued.

"I never really thought about this before. I am just realizing that my mother was fond of slapping my face. She was right-handed. She hit me with her right hand as she faced me.

"I have a vivid memory of the last time she hit me. I was a teenager. I had talked back to her. I had challenged one of her nonsensical conclusions. We were standing in the dining room near the kitchen door and were facing each other. She was a little taller. To my surprise, with a mighty swing, she walloped the left side of my face with her right hand, yelling, 'Don't talk back to your mother!' I was so startled. I was speechless. I just filed the incident away.

"Do you think my mother broke my facial bone?

"I asked Kieran if he remembered any injuries to my face. He recalled a bruise under one of my eyes that left me with a black eye. He thought the injury was one of my sports injuries. He was sure the bruise was not serious and did not warrant medical attention or concern.

"I have only the vaguest memory of the bruise and the black eye, once Kieran mentioned it. I am certain I never had any medical attention for a broken facial bone. I would have remembered that. This broken bone is still a mystery."

"Kelly, the left side of your face is red. Are you alright?"

"I don't know. I'm having a giant somatic response. The left side of my face feels hot. I have that weird, heightened sensation from my left elbow to my wrist, and my left knee to my left ankle—a major body migraine."

Kelly rose from her chair and swayed from side to side, raising her arms above her head and down in front of her as she reached to touch her toes. This protocol of movements, she had found, was usually successful in dissipating the response after some repetition.

After about five minutes, Ella asked, "Kelly, are you feeling better? Most of the redness is gone from your face. How are your left arm and leg?"

"I'm feeling a lot better. The response is lessening. I want to continue.

"I'm realizing how unwanted I was as a child. I remember asking my mother—I'm not sure how old I was—why my dad paid less attention to me than he used to, and my mother said, 'Your dad prefers Kieran because you don't cuddle enough. Kieran is more affectionate.'

"I remember being aghast at the time, but thinking, 'It's okay to be number two. I love my brother very much.'

"My brother and I were very close when we were young. On the weekends, I made him breakfast—some toast and hot chocolate, and the occasional instant chocolate pudding. As we ate, we watched TV or played board games, or playing cards in our basement. Our parents slept in.

"Much to my mother's chagrin, when my brother cried, he did not want my mother to comfort him. I was not in the room when this happened. My mother would come to get me. There was smoke coming out of her ears. 'Your brother is calling for you. He wants his Kelly.'

"I remember feeling it was my fault my brother wanted me. I had done something wrong, and this transgression was causing my mother grief. I love my brother and want to make him feel better. I loved to see him smile.

"I have one more strong memory of my earlier childhood. This is before my brother was born. I am not sure how old I was. I don't remember my mother being pregnant. My mother was taking me to the park near our apartment to go skating. I remember carrying my skates and walking beside my mother, but about two feet from her, as we walked across the snow-covered park to the rink. Why wasn't she holding my hand? I was only 3 years old.

"The only other thing I remember about this was the rink wasn't crowded. I skated around and around by myself. I have no idea why I remember any of this. Do you?"

"I don't know. There does not seem to be any joy in the memory. Perhaps, what you remember is the feeling of being alone. You were so young."

"With Joshua back home with you, would you like to bring him to sessions?" "Yes, that would be wonderful."

"Let's do some trance so you can get more grounded before you leave."

After the trancework, Ella said, "This has been a difficult session for you. You made some major breakthroughs. You have done great work. Please take some time to rest and process. Take good care of yourself. I will see you and Joshua next week."

The following week, Kelly brought Joshua to her psychotherapy session. Before Kelly began the session, she patted him. Touching his face and rubbing him gently behind the ears was soothing for her. Joshua steadied her. Once she stopped patting him, she watched as Joshua circled the room, in search of a choice spot to observe her and Ella. Once he found it, he lay down and relaxed. When Kelly was confident Joshua had settled, she began the session.

"Last week we talked a lot about my childhood and my mother. I'd like to move on for now and talk about Deke and my mother."

Ella nodded in agreement.

"Deke and my mother disliked each other. He knew she was often irrational. This really irked him. On occasion, he tried to have a rational argument with her. The acrimony between them heightened. The argument went nowhere. I intervened to restore peace. When we didn't live in the same town, this confrontation was more manageable. The visits with my mother were short and focused on small talk. But when she moved to Buffington after Domenic was born, the situation got worse."

Kelly noticed she was becoming agitated. "Ella, I need a nature break." Walking past Joshua, Kelly gave him a pat as she went by him to go down the hallway to the washroom.

Upon Kelly's return after having given Joshua a pat as she passed by and sat down again, Ella revealed, "Kelly, when you went to the washroom a few minutes ago, Joshua was concerned. He stood up and stared at the doorway. When I reached out to pat him, he moved away. Now that you're back, he seems more sedate and is lying down again."

"Oh, that is surprising. I guess after all that has happened, Joshua is more careful with new people and me. I'm sure he will warm up to you.

"Oh my goodness! I just had a terrible thought. I married my mother when I married Deke, didn't I?

"Up until now, I never appreciated just how similar they are. They are both so self-absorbed, hyper-critical, manipulative, never accepting responsibility for their actions. Do you think I was attracted to Deke as a mother replacement, so I could try again to secure love from someone similar to her?

"I am certain none of this was conscious. But it seems I just repeated a familiar old pattern.

"Deke's family felt comfortable to me, but now I'm realizing this familiarity was not a good thing for me, either. What a textbook stereotype I am! This is a disconcerting revelation."

Kelly recognized Joshua was picking up on her unease. He got up and sat down directly in front of her, put his right paw on her left knee, and stared into her eyes.

"Joshua, I'm okay," but he didn't move. With greater certainty, Kelly said, "It's okay, Joshua. I'm good."

He stared into her eyes again. She looked back at him and smiled. Sensing all was well, Joshua blinked at Kelly and returned to his resting spot.

"Don't be so hard on yourself, Kelly," Ella told her. "Look at the environment you lived in. You had no escape, no one to turn to. It is amazing you survived.

"You have such tenacity and inner strength. You have done so well. You have moved on from Deke. You are so much healthier now.

"See you next week, Kelly."

Ella stood up as Kelly approached and gave her a big hug. Then they said goodbye.

At the next session with Ella, Kelly went through the same routine at the beginning of the session, with her patting Joshua to get centered and calm herself before starting, and then Joshua finding a spot on the floor to lie down. This time, Joshua let Ella pat him.

Kelly began, "I received my divorce decree yesterday. But, can you believe it? The name on the divorce decree was wrong. It wasn't even close. It said, 'Kelly LaPietra.' The court gave Deke a divorce from some other woman. Apparently, only I noticed the error. I called my lawyer, who called Deke's lawyer to correct the error in the court filing she had crafted. I should receive the corrected decree in a month or so. Then I will be free, finally.

"The irony in all of this is too much. My parents destroyed any joy for my birthday. Deke ruined any celebration I might have enjoyed for our wedding anniversaries. Now Deke's lawyer is trying to eliminate my existence. I know this is an exaggeration, but this is how I feel."

Ella did some trance with Kelly for the rest of the session after that. With a spring in her step, for their evening constitutional that night, Kelly and Joshua went for a long walk along a waterfront trail. Kelly hummed a favorite pop song as they walked. She watched the white smoke from an office building rise from the chimney, spread and disappear, and then said, "I love you, Joshua, good boy," and continued their journey.

CHAPTER 36

Unexpected News

Kelly was pleased with her revitalized business venture. She had a good first quarter and the second quarter was promising. The large manufacturing consulting company with which she had been partnering on work in New York City and Buffington had offered her a senior position.

Kelly looked at Joshua as if to ask for his opinion about her job opportunity. At first, Kelly thought Joshua looked a little bewildered, but when he blinked back at her, she felt better and replied, "Let's get a snack."

Kelly went into the kitchen, grabbed some nutritious oatmeal biscuits she had baked for Joshua, made herself an espresso, sat down at her dining table, and looked out at the lake. Joshua lay down beside her. She placed the three biscuits in front of Joshua and enjoyed watching him savor each one. She heard him make a noise that sounded like smacking lips. She realized he had learned that from her. She smacked her lips on occasion as she relished one of her favorite desserts. She gave out a little laugh, beamed at Joshua, and took another sip.

She thought about her interview with the potential new employer that had taken place the day before. The senior management seemed eager for her to join and she would be working with teams. She did like the people that she had been collaborating with from this company but reminded herself it would be the first time in her career she would be an employee of a publicly traded company. She liked that there was a small office in Buffington and wondered how often she would travel to the head office in Atlanta.

As Kelly nursed her espresso, it was becoming increasingly apparent to her she did not have a safety net in her company of one. The draw of the offer increased as she took another sip and gave Joshua a pat. Still not sure what she wanted to do, she opted to call her potential boss and ask for another meeting.

A week later at this meeting, she negotiated to be able to work from home three days a week, and more if she could make that effective. She pushed for a higher base salary and also negotiated another week of vacation. All in all, she was satisfied with the results and looked forward to receiving and signing the employment letter.

Her new job was to start in early May, a couple of weeks before Joshua's eleventh birthday. For the remainder of April, Kelly planned to take Joshua for his annual checkup and get him and herself ready for the transition to a new job.

At Joshua's annual checkup, the vet technician remarked, "Joshua is such a good dog. He is so gentle and affectionate. We are all amazed at how he raises his paw before we ask him to for his shots or to draw blood. He is such a good-natured soul."

Other than reinforcing his current treatments for his chronic ailments, Dr. Samuels gave Joshua his heartworm package and a clean bill of health.

Before the checkup, Kelly had noticed a few instances where Joshua had rubbed his butt against the grass in Bader Park on their morning trips. Since this scooting had stopped, she didn't mention it at the exam. When Joshua rubbed his butt again a few days after the checkup, Kelly became concerned. Within the week, she and Joshua were back to see Dr. Samuels.

"Dr. Samuels, Joshua rubbed his butt a few times before we saw you last week. I didn't mention it because he had stopped doing it, but he did it again a few times. That's why we came back for you to take a look. Perhaps Joshua ate something that isn't passing. My neighbor's pit bull at our old house had a blocked anal gland and it was painful. As far as I can tell, Joshua isn't in any pain."

Dr. Samuels did a thorough exam and said, "I can feel a tiny growth or scar tissue the size of a pea in Joshua's soft anal tissue. It could be cancer. The only way to know for sure is to do a biopsy. Do you want to wait and see how this develops or see a specialist right away?"

"I don't want to wait. How quickly can Joshua have the biopsy?"

"I'll make the arrangements and take the first available spot. Joshua will receive a local anesthetic, so he shouldn't be groggy or in any pain after the procedure. You should be able to bring him home once the procedure is finished."

"Okay, I'll wait for your call. Thanks."

Kelly was shell-shocked by the news about a potential cancer. She went on automatic pilot following her routines until she received the call from Dr. Samuels regarding the time of Joshua's biopsy.

During the waiting period, she started her new job. She struggled to cope with their IT systems and was finding that incredibly stressful. She was both apprehensive and excited about working on one of their key change-management files, while she also continued to work on what she brought with her to the new company, in particular, her work with Maria.

Three days after the visit with Dr. Samuels, Joshua had an appointment for the biopsy. Kelly and Joshua drove to the appointment and sat in the waiting room. A few minutes later, the nurse came to take Joshua into the treatment area. While Kelly waited for Joshua to return, she concentrated on reading her newspaper, as she drank a coffee. She was agitated but hopeful.

When the nurse brought Joshua back to the waiting area, Kelly gave Joshua a hug and said, "Love you, Joshua, let's go for a walk."

They went on a short jaunt for Joshua to relieve himself. After the walk as he jumped up onto the back seat of the car, Kelly said, "Good boy, Joshua. I love you."

Once back home, Kelly put her personal troubles out of mind and focused on her work that afternoon. Her IT stress grew as she discovered that her computer had not been properly configured and it would take days to sort out the problem. That night, she tried to relax with Joshua, as they went for a couple of short constitutionals. She spent the rest of the evening reading and listening to Chopin.

The next day, the surgeon called Kelly with the news about the biopsy. He advised, "Joshua has aggressive anal cancer. Fortunately, his cancer is in the very early stages. The tumor is tiny. Surgery will remove it."

"How soon can you do the surgery?" Kelly replied, noticing a large lump in her throat and the butterflies were back.

"When I took the biopsy, I discovered Joshua has an irregular heartbeat. Before I can do the surgery, Joshua will need to pass an exam with a cardiologist before I can remove his anal sac. The cardiologist will not be able to do the test for a few days. Please bring Joshua back here next Tuesday at one p.m. for the test."

With the news about Joshua, Kelly felt more on edge. Her sleep that night was interrupted with short waking periods. A heart problem? What is that about, she wondered, as she tossed and turned in her bed.

She managed through the next few days trying not to think about anything but work, even during her trip to the cardiologist with Joshua for his test before surgery. Kelly continued to muddle through her IT and computer issues at work, all of which were adding to her already distressed state.

Two days after the cardiology test, the cardiologist telephoned. "Mrs. Delmonico, this is Dr. Goode, Joshua's cardiologist. Joshua passed the test, but he does have a heart problem. He has a leaky auricle that leaks blood into his ventricle. He does not need medication at this time.

"You can bring Joshua in for surgery on Monday at 8:30 am. There is no preparation necessary for the surgery."

"Thank you, Dr. Goode, we'll be there."

After she got off the phone with Dr. Goode, Kelly e-mailed Darcy to let her know about Joshua.

"I hope the surgery goes well," Darcy replied in an e-mail the next day. "Please give Joshua a big hug for me."

During the days before the surgery, Kelly made sure Joshua had a wonderful time. On Saturday and Sunday, Kelly and Joshua spent the afternoon at Joshua's favorite beach, where Joshua retrieved tennis balls and sticks from the lake. They enjoyed their burgers together, sitting by the water. They went for three or four walks every day near the condo and delighted in the drives and play in the vicinity of Kelly's various therapies.

The night before Joshua's surgery, Kelly wrote:

> Tomorrow is
>
> A very big day
> The lord wouldn't have it
> Any other way
>
> I dreaded this
> All weekend long
> For you Joshua
> I must be strong
>
> Noticed your rubbing
> In a certain place
> I really didn't know
> What I'd have to face
>
> Got you checked right away
> No time to think or delay
>
> Found a growth deep inside
> That you couldn't really hide
>
> All weekend pretending nothing wrong
> Am certain you know I'm acting strong
>
> Between bouts of weeping
> I'm hardly sleeping
>
> We play and you swim
> Am trying desperately not to be grim

Don't leave me Joshua
Not now

I'm not ready
I'm not very steady

Can't manage not tethered
Can't cope being severed

I love you dearly
You are my family

Your eleventh birthday
Is next Friday
Let's celebrate
Let's recalibrate

Let's play
Please stay

Tonight, before bed
I whispered in your head

I love you Joshua

Fight, Joshua, Fight!

CHAPTER 37

The Recovery

Kelly did her best to hide her terror from Joshua. Before she dropped him off at the surgeon's, they went for a longish walk in the neighborhood of the hospital. Kelly window-shopped and chatted with Joshua.

"Joshua, what do you think about that side table? Would it look good in the living room by the couch? Let's get a coffee."

Once in the hospital, Kelly and Joshua waited in the waiting room. She patted Joshua's head and gave him gentle scratches behind the ears as he sat beside her for a few minutes, before lying down nearby and closing his eyes.

About ten minutes later, the vet technician approached Kelly. "Mrs. Delmonico. It's time. Joshua will be fine. He is a strong fellow. We'll call you when the surgery is over."

"Thanks very much."

Kelly gave Joshua a hug, a little scratch behind the ears, and said, "Joshua, love you. Back soon," and smiled at him. Once he was out of sight and earshot, Kelly cried.

After gaining her composure, she headed back to the car and drove home. She spent the rest of the day at home distracting herself by working, while she waited for news about Joshua.

Mid-afternoon, the surgeon called. "Mrs. Delmonico. The surgery went very well. The tumor was very tiny. I am certain I removed all of it. Joshua is resting comfortably. You can come by tomorrow after dinner and take him home.

"He will need to rest for a few days and will be on mild painkillers, but he should recover nicely. I have referred him to an oncologist, who will call you for an appointment to discuss follow-up treatment."

"That's wonderful news! Thank you."

Kelly was relieved but still traumatized. She immersed herself in her work and did not pay attention to much else until it was time to bring Joshua home from the hospital.

When Kelly picked up Joshua, she could see that he was not one hundred percent present. She did her best not to cry when she saw him, and said, "Joshua, good boy. I love you. Let's go home."

When he heard, "Let's go home," he perked up, and off they went to the car to go home, but a little more slowly than usual.

Kelly stayed home with Joshua and nursed him for the rest of the week. By the end of the week, he was fully himself again. They went for long walks in the neighborhood, but he did not play ball or go swimming.

A week after the surgery, Joshua and Kelly met Joshua's oncologist, Dr. Hart, who advised, "Joshua needs multiple rounds of chemotherapy. His first dose will be in two weeks and then at three-week intervals until November."

"Dr. Hart, will Joshua have bad side effects from the chemotherapy? Is there any preparation for him that I need to do?"

"Any side effects should be mild. Chemotherapy is more tolerated in dogs than in humans. Joshua should do well on the treatment. If he does have issues, then we can treat them."

When the morning arrived for Joshua to have his first chemotherapy treatment, Kelly did her best not to draw any attention to it. Kelly and Joshua sat in Dr. Hart's waiting room, waiting patiently for Joshua's treatment. There were other dogs with their owners also waiting for their turn for chemotherapy, but Joshua ignored them. After a few minutes, he laid down beside Kelly. Kelly smiled as best she could at the other owners and their dogs.

"Joshua, it's your turn. Let's go," the nurse said as she took Joshua's leash from Kelly.

"Good boy, Joshua, see you soon," Kelly said as she watched Joshua and the nurse walk to the treatment area.

Sitting with the other dogs and owners was both reassuring and nerve-wracking to Kelly. As she waited, she tried to dwell on more pleasant things. But she had trouble sitting still and headed out to the street to window shop and get a coffee. On her walk, she tried not to think about her mother's cancer. She did her best to be in the present and enjoy her surroundings, before returning to Dr. Hart's office to resume her wait for Joshua.

After his treatment, the nurse brought Joshua back to Kelly who had returned about ten minutes earlier.

The nurse advised, "Joshua was the perfect patient. He did not resist when the needle was put in his paw for the drip. Then he sat calmly for the twenty minutes, while the drip was administered."

"I'm glad it went well," Kelly said. "Are there any restrictions on what he can do now that he has had the first dose?"

"No, he should be fine. You have diarrhea and nausea medicine in case Joshua has any side effects. Please call us over the next couple of days to let us know how Joshua is doing."

"Thanks. Come, Joshua. Let's go home."

Joshua did well on the first round of his chemotherapy. He was tired but did not have diarrhea or nausea. After the first week and a half, he was back to his old self. Kelly and he resumed their walks, trips to the beach, and burgers by the shore.

Although Kelly didn't let him swim, he didn't seem to mind. After a subsequent round of chemotherapy and with Dr. Hart's okay, Joshua resumed his swims at the beach.

At her next acupuncture appointment, Kelly discussed Joshua's cancer. Her acupuncturist, Kala, advised, "I know of a trained vet, Dr. Abrams, who also does animal acupuncture. If you are interested, I will connect you with this vet. In Florida, she studied animal acupuncture as well as traditional veterinary medicine. She may have a different perspective on preventing Joshua's cancer from recurring."

"I'm willing to try anything to help Joshua. Thanks."

Joshua had his first acupuncture treatment a week later. Kelly told Dr. Abrams, "Joshua doesn't seem to mind the needles. He likes the attention. Is it okay for him to walk around like he is with the needles in him?"

"Yes, that's fine. Most dogs do that."

Dr. Abrams recommended, "You can put Joshua on a special diet that will put a ring around his cancer and contain it."

"Okay, we'll give it a try. Does it taste good?"

"Here are the cooking instructions and a list of things to buy. You cook them together in a steam cooker over a period of hours. This diet will keep up Joshua's energy."

"Okay. I hope Joshua will like the stew."

After the treatment, Kelly and Joshua went for a walk in the neighborhood around Dr. Abram's office. Kelly found a new burger spot for her and Joshua to try out. She tied Joshua's leash to a restaurant table outside, went into the restaurant, and ordered a burger for each of them with all the trimmings as well as some water to drink. Kelly did not really like the taste of this burger.

"Here, Joshua, you are a lucky fellow. Here is the rest of my burger." Kelly watched as Joshua wolfed down the rest of her burger in one gulp. She gave Joshua a pat and remarked, "Glad you liked it, Joshua. Let's go home."

On the drive home, Kelly wondered whether the acupuncture treatment was yielding results. Although she was uncertain that they were, she decided to continue with Joshua's treatment. Driving to see Dr. Abrams once a week would give her and Joshua another outing together, and another burger for Joshua.

The next day, Kelly bought all the ingredients for Joshua's stew and cooked it. It smelled bad. She mixed small quantities of the stew in with his regular dog food. Kelly watched as Joshua dutifully ate the food, but he did not savor it.

For dinner the next evening, Kelly mixed in a little more stew, but she added some gravy on top of the stew to mask its taste. As Joshua ate, Kelly sat at the dining table with her espresso and read her mail.

After a few moments, she exclaimed, "Oh, look, Joshua, here is my divorce decree. Freedom at last! Now I can buy a condo and we can have our own home."

Kelly got up and went to the pantry to get Joshua a treat. "Here are two dog biscuits to celebrate. Let's go for a walk."

That evening after the walk, as Kelly was getting ready for bed, she was still feeling buzzed by the divorce decree. She said to Joshua, "We go to the cottage this weekend. Things are looking up for us. Bedtime."

Joshua hopped up onto the foot of the bed and laid down. "Good night, Joshua. Love you."

Kelly was looking forward to going to the cottage. For the last two summers, Kelly, Joshua, and Bea had gone to the cottage together. This time, only Kelly and Joshua were going. Bea had moved to Dublin just before Joshua was diagnosed with cancer. The move to Dublin was a wonderful opportunity for Bea. She would head up a business think tank there. Kelly was glad the timing of the cottage stay was between Joshua's chemotherapy treatments.

Rather than being upset about Bea's departure, Kelly was relieved. She had received an e-mail from Darcy before Bea moved to Dublin, complaining Bea had been sending her nasty e-mails for months and wishing she would stop.

Kelly had written back, asking, "May I please see the e-mails? What is Bea saying? I had no idea Bea was writing to you. I had nothing to do with it, I promise. Bea never mentioned it. Why didn't you tell me before?"

Darcy, replied, "I thought you knew. The e-mails are private and not nice."

"Bea, please stop e-mailing Darcy," Kelly wrote. "I appreciate you are trying to help, but it is not working. Why didn't you tell me you were in touch with Darcy and have been ever since you stayed over that night? What are you saying to Darcy? She is finding the e-mails upsetting."

"The e-mails are private, just between me and Darcy. I won't share them with you, but I will stop e-mailing."

Kelly initially thought Bea was communicating with Darcy to help Kelly. But the more she thought about it, the more she began to perceive it was sneaky and interfering. It was worsening the relationship between her and Darcy.

She wondered what kind of friend would do that. Perhaps, Bea's e-mailing explains Darcy's inexplicable behavior toward her. But with Darcy not sharing, how would she ever know?

With Bea not in the picture, the upcoming visit to the cottage would be the first time she and Joshua would be alone together at the cottage. This would also be the first time just the two of them would swim together. She had a few misgivings about that, not knowing how they would adapt.

Their drive up the cottage went well. Joshua slept through it stretched out on the back seat. Kelly sang along with the '60s songs on the radio. There wasn't much traffic, so Kelly arrived relaxed and a few minutes early.

Once at the cottage, Kelly unpacked and made a savory, veggie barbecue for her and Joshua. She integrated the vegetables into some of the medicinal stew she had brought for him. After dinner, they relaxed and listened to classical music before going to bed. Kelly got immersed in a good book on strategic planning.

The next morning, Kelly and Joshua went for a longer than usual walk along the road. When they returned, Joshua took a dip in the lake, followed by doing some surveillance of the shoreline, before he and Kelly rested by the water, Kelly in her Adirondack chair, and Joshua in the shade sleeping beside her.

After lunch and some additional reading by the lake, it was time for Kelly and Joshua to go swimming together. Although a little reticent at first, Kelly welcomed the challenge.

She was thrilled Joshua did not rescue her or bring her back to shore. Instead, he stayed a few feet away from her, dog-paddling in synchrony with her swimming strokes. After twenty minutes or so of swimming together, Kelly gently held onto Joshua's haunches, and he brought her back to shore. Once out of the water, Joshua lay beside Kelly in the shade as she sat on her chair, read, and listened to jazz.

After a while, Joshua decided he wanted to go for another walk. He got up and signaled his desire to Kelly, with his hips turning in the direction of the road. Picking up on the signal, Kelly responded, "Let's go for a walk, Joshua," and off they went.

After the walk, they returned to relax by the water. When Joshua wanted to go back into the water, he just dove off the dock or waded in from shore. Often, Kelly joined him in the water. When she didn't, she watched him from the dock or the shore, throwing in balls or sticks for him to retrieve until he tired of the fetch. Toward the end of the afternoon, she decided to sit by the dock with her fishing rod in the lake and had some success. She caught a decent-sized lake trout and put it in her pail for dinner.

At dinnertime, Kelly called, "Come, Joshua. Time to make dinner."

They went up the hill to the cottage and into the kitchen to get to work. Under Joshua's watchful eye, Kelly prepared their food. They had a fish barbecue with baked potatoes, broccoli, and Caesar salad. Before giving Joshua his share, Kelly mixed into his stew some gravy she had made especially for him. Then she gave Joshua his portion of the fish dinner, placing it on top of the stew, rather than mixing it in.

After dinner, Kelly sat on the couch and read as Joshua snoozed by her side on the floor. She brushed out his fur, dried him with the hairdryer, and gave him his evening meds. They went out briefly for the late-evening constitutional and got ready for bed.

"Joshua, bedtime," Kelly said as she gave him a big hug and a kiss on the right side of his face before getting into bed. "Good night, Joshua. Love you."

Kelly and Joshua repeated most of this routine for the remainder of their stay at the cottage. The only significant deviation from the routine was Kelly did not fish every day. On those days, she barbecued either beef burgers, veggie burgers, or chicken breasts.

Joshua and she had a good rest during their cottage trip. She didn't totally relax, knowing they were going home to more chemotherapy. Kelly did her best to be in the present and to enjoy their cottage days together. She cherished every moment with Joshua.

CHAPTER 38

New Beginnings

Joshua's chemotherapy treatment after the cottage trip didn't go well. He experienced fatigue, nausea, and diarrhea. Kelly gave him the meds she had for nausea and diarrhea. Although these meds worked, they caused Joshua to be a little more tired.

Kelly called Dr. Hart to discuss the situation.

Dr. Hart advised, "I'm glad the meds helped, but Joshua did suffer for a few days. I think I can lower his chemotherapy dose a little, without increasing his cancer risk. The reduction should really help with the side effects. As an additional precaution, please give him the meds for these in advance of his next chemotherapy treatment."

Kelly followed Dr. Hart's instructions. Chemotherapy went well. This time, Joshua did not suffer any side effects. To celebrate, Kelly took Joshua for a swim at his favorite beach on both Saturday and Sunday. Each day, they enjoyed a burger by the shore.

Kelly's annual testing with Dr. Bradley was coming up a few days later. She looked forward to the walk with Joshua around the campus and to the results of the testing.

At the appointment, Dr. Bradley explained, "Kelly, you have recovered well from your knee issues. You now have normal dorsiflexion in both your feet. Congratulations! Let's continue with a maintenance program that includes strength and flexibility training."

"Dr. Bradley, I would like to be more active, even play a sport. I know tennis and other sports with a lot of running are out of the question. I will stick to your 'Don't run for more than five minutes' rule. What do you suggest?"

"I think slow-pitch softball in an entertainment league might work."

"That sounds great. I have wanted to play baseball since I was a little kid with a baseball glove. I played a lot of pitch and catch, but there wasn't an organized girls league where I grew up."

"I will e-mail you some information about a league that might be a good fit for you." Thanks, Dr. Bradley, I am excited about this."

Kelly brought Joshua to her first softball game. It was a cool Saturday afternoon in September and there were lots of people and dogs enjoying the fall air. Before the game, Kelly took Joshua to the off-leash fenced-in area right beside the diamond. Joshua did not like being there. He wasn't interested in playing with the other dogs and stood beside her until they walked the perimeter of the off-leash area together. With the game about to start, Kelly tied Joshua behind the fence at home plate. He enjoyed the pats from other players as he looked around or chewed the braided chew Kelly had brought for him.

When Kelly went up to bat, Joshua barked and barked. She didn't know why he barked. She considered this unusual behavior on Joshua's part as he did not bark very often. Did he sense Kelly was a little scared at the plate? Or was he reacting to her swinging the bat at the ball?

With Joshua there, Kelly didn't feel so out of place. Most of her team members were experienced, and at least twenty years younger. She wanted to play. She needed to figure out how to keep up and fit in.

When Kelly got home, she turned her mind to more practical matters. She had not made any progress in finding a condo to purchase. Although she had contacted her real estate agent shortly after her return from the cottage trip, she had not begun her search. She had been too preoccupied with work and managing Joshua's illness. She committed to calling the real estate agent in the morning and to begin looking as soon as the real estate agent could set up appointments.

Joshua didn't go with Kelly when she ventured out with the real estate agent to look at prospective condos to buy. Instead, he stayed home with a good bone and enjoyed a walk with Kelly when she returned.

Towards the end of October, Kelly found their new home. When she got home after signing the papers for the condo, she told Joshua the news, "Joshua, come. I found us a much nicer place to live and not far from here. Let's go for a walk to the new neighborhood tonight so you can see where it is."

During the walk, Kelly showed Joshua some of the highlights. "Look, Joshua, there is our new home. I want to show you the backyard."

They walked to the side driveway and looked around. On one side of the driveway was a courtyard and a square gravel park especially for dogs to do their business. As Kelly and Joshua walked in the courtyard by the gravel park, Kelly noticed the plastic bags for dog droppings, placed strategically near the entrance of the gravel park on the cement wall. When Kelly took Joshua into the gravel park, other than sniffing, he did not perform.

"Joshua, let's go to Laurel Park."

She and Joshua walked back to the street, crossed it, and walked less than a block to a good-sized park.

"Joshua, this is Laurel Park. Let's go play." Kelly noted how well-lit the park was and was pleased.

After the play in Laurel Park which amounted to two retrieves of a stick, meeting and greeting some dogs, a walk along the park perimeter, and a quick urination, Kelly asked, "Joshua, how do you like the neighborhood?"

Joshua blinked at Kelly, signaling he liked it. "I think we are both going to enjoy living here. Love you, Joshua. Let's go home."

The closing for her new condo was the same week in November as Joshua's last chemotherapy treatment. As with the sale of the house, Kelly went with Joshua to use an ATM to move money around related to the purchase, but this time, it was at the ATM at her local bank, about five blocks from Bader Park.

When Kelly and Joshua reached the ATM, she looked in front of her to get her bearings before pressing the ATM keys and noticed that the buildings, sidewalk, and bank machine were slanted and in shades of gray. For a few seconds, her head was empty. She hugged Joshua. This helped her get back to the present.

"Joshua, I love you," she said.

After this, Kelly carried out her transactions without issue, but the shades of grey persisted. Slowly as she walked with Joshua away from the ATM and toward home, concentrating on the walk and Joshua, the colors of Kelly's surroundings returned. Kelly walked on even ground.

In psychotherapy, the next day, Kelly recounted the incident to Ella.

"My rabbit hole experience was in shades of grey, like the greys of my childhood memories. I wasn't expecting to go down the rabbit hole. I think because the neural pathway of the purchase was so near the previous two traumatic neural pathways related to banking, I had a flashback. I'm so glad Joshua was with me again.

"Ella, do you think I will experience flashbacks from now on every time I use an ATM?"

"It's possible but I don't think you will. This flashback was shorter and less intense. There were no tears. I think you recognized you were having a problem and pulled out of it more rapidly. And remember you didn't have a flashback when you did your banking after your house sale closed and the lawyer sorted things out."

"Joshua and I are moving into the condo tomorrow. He is spending the day with the dog-walker. I don't have much stuff to unpack or organize. I haven't had a flashback with any of my moves, so things should go well."

By the time Joshua got home on moving day, Kelly had unpacked and was ready to give him his dinner. She put some '60s rock music on and sang along with the DVD. As she got their dinners ready, she danced around the kitchen, retrieving food from the fridge, filling and cooking in pots on the stove, and setting the table. Kelly noticed her unexpected exuberance and realized she was finally experiencing a truly happy moment.

The week after her move, Kelly commenced her first multimillion-dollar project with her new employer. Her boss had been building up to this project, having her lead other smaller projects.

As the project manager handed over this big project to Kelly, he explained, "I'm off on a leave of absence for six months. My wife and I plan on doing some skiing in Italy and then some hiking through the mountains, followed by sunning along the Mediterranean. Good luck with this project! I'm sure it will go well."

Although the handover seemed relatively straightforward to Kelly, the following week, her stress levels soared as the real situation became more apparent. She discovered the project had a very tight timeline, unforgiving contract terms, and a difficult, demanding client. When she also discovered this project was already well over budget before the handoff, she got a massive somatic response. It felt like rubber bands were around her forehead. Her eyes were heavy and pounding.

Over the next few weeks, as she continued to manage this project, she experienced the same response in meetings with the client on the phone as well as face to face. In her mind, she began to refer to this project as 'the project from hell.'

In therapy, Kelly discussed the situation with Ella. Each time she started to talk about it, she became very anxious and had a giant somatic response. She spent the rest of the session doing trancework with Ella.

At home to mitigate these responses, Kelly spent more time on her recumbent bike. Spending twenty or thirty minutes on the bike sandwiched between walks with Joshua to Laurel Park loosened the rubber bands and eventually, they disappeared. Her eyes opened fully, and the pounding dissipated.

Her first business trip for her new employer, which was to present some interim findings related to the project from hell, was set for mid-December to Anchorage. Kelly was concerned about finding proper care for Joshua during her trip. Liz had told her, "I can't look after Joshua. Our new black lab, Rosie, is a rescue. She does not tolerate other dogs in her space other than Bailey. I'm sorry."

She called Grace, Joshua's dog-walker. "Yes, Kelly, I take dogs overnight. I'd be delighted to look after Joshua while you are in Anchorage. He is such a good dog. I'm already familiar with his drug regimen."

"Thanks, Grace. I am so relieved. Joshua will enjoy being with you."

Kelly's business trip to Anchorage was a success. She negotiated a budget increment which put the project just barely in the black and she strengthened the relationship with the client.

When Grace brought Joshua home, Kelly ran to the door and gave him a big hug. "Joshua, I love you. Let's eat and go for a long walk to check out all the beautiful Christmas lights."

The following week at her therapy session, Kelly briefly talked about the trip to Anchorage. Then she disclosed, "I got an e-mail from Darcy yesterday. I haven't heard from her in months, not since she told me about Bea and the e-mails. Darcy wants to see Joshua. She's coming to town for her Christmas break and staying with her dad. I was so surprised to hear from her, but I didn't get the impression she wants to see me.

"She asked, 'Mom, I'd like to take Joshua for a walk. It's okay if you are not around. I'll come over and take him on my own.'"

Ella called out, "Kelly? Kelly, where are you? You froze just now, telling me the story. I'm bringing you back to the present. Let's start again. Tell me what sensations you feel in your body as you tell me the story. When you feel angry toward Darcy, where do you feel that in your body? As you feel the sadness, where do you feel that?"

"Okay, I'll start again. Darcy called me to say she is coming to town. She is staying with her dad and wants to see Joshua, but she doesn't care if I'm not around when she sees him.

"Now that I'm thinking about it, I feel pain in my chest from the sadness and the start of a low-grade headache, which I can tell will get worse if I allow my anger to grow. I never paid attention to any of these feelings in my body before. Now I will.

"I replied to Darcy, 'I'll meet you at Dante's Diner. The three of us can go for a walk before dinner and then we can eat. I'll take you back to your dad's after dinner. We can set the date and time when you are in town.'

"I'm very apprehensive about seeing Darcy. I want to see her, yet she is so angry with me. I can feel the rage and I don't know what it is about."

"Kelly, you need to protect yourself when you see Darcy, so you don't get emotionally injured. Try to visualize that you are wearing a suit of armor, so you are safe. Or another image that works for you. Try not to let her rage penetrate you. If you get triggered with somatic responses when you are with her, disengage and move as you need to so the responses will dissipate. If you have to leave, leave. Your health is what is most important.

"Good work, today. Merry Christmas to you and Joshua. Please try to get some rest. See you in the new year."

Ella gave Joshua a festive pat, Kelly and she embraced, and then Kelly and Joshua left for a walk before going home.

Over the next few days, Kelly readied herself for the holiday season. She had refused an invitation to spend the season with Kieran and his family and with Donna's. Kelly still wanted to spend most of her time alone with just her and Joshua. She had the distinct impression Darcy was not interested in spending any part of the season with her.

As the time to see Darcy approached, Kelly grew anxious about the impending meeting, although there was a little earnest amid her anxiety. When it was time for the dinner date, Kelly met Darcy at Dante's. They greeted each other with an embrace.

Just before Darcy sat down at the table, she said, "Mom, I love you very much." Kelly hugged her a little tighter and sat down at the table. During dinner, Kelly followed Darcy's efforts to keep the conversation light.

"I have such excellent recipes, Mom. You may find these meals novel and tasty. I'll send you the recipes." "Thanks, Darcy."

Then Darcy led what Kelly perceived was an aggressive discussion on details of cooking techniques and interesting marinades they could also use. Kelly got the feeling Darcy felt she knew more about cooking and how Kelly should cook than Kelly did.

Darcy soon changed the subject to pots. "Mom, I found the most fantastic pots. You should really get new pots. I can send you details on what I bought."

Why was Darcy's tone so superior? It wasn't what she said, but how she said it. Kelly began to shift in her chair as she listened to Darcy.

Although Kelly was becoming tired of the conversation, she did her best to be enthusiastic. "That's great, Darcy. Easy cleaning pots sound like a real-time saver."

When Darcy switched the conversation to running shoes, Kelly was enlivened. She needed a new pair that would provide more support. But she was disheartened by Darcy's haughty, dismissive tone toward her. It was disrespectful. Kelly did not understand where it was coming from. When they were finished with the meal and Kelly had paid, they left the restaurant to go to the car to get Joshua. As they got close to the car, Darcy asked, "Mom, is that your car?"

"Yes. I really like it. It's the first car I ever bought myself. It has a great fuel economy and an excellent environmental rating. It's also fun to drive."

"Mom, you know, there are so many cars exactly like this on the road where I live. They are everywhere. It's no big deal for me to see one."

Kelly swallowed her disappointment and Darcy's disrespect and opened the back door of the car and removed Joshua's seat belt. Joshua jumped out. Darcy took his leash, and they left the parking lot to go for a walk on a quiet street nearby. Darcy and Joshua walked together in front of Kelly.

Joshua walked slowly on leash with Darcy. He kept looking back at Kelly as Darcy walked him. It was clear to Kelly he was uncomfortable walking with Darcy and with Kelly behind him. Kelly walked briskly to catch up to Darcy and took the leash from her. The three of them walked side by side for a quarter of a mile and then returned to the car for the drive home.

Before Darcy got out of the car to enter her dad's condo building, Darcy reached over to the driver's seat to give Kelly a hug. Darcy had parted without making any plans to see Kelly again before Darcy left town for school.

As she drove home with Joshua, Kelly held back her tears and tried not to think about how superficial the time with Darcy had been.

Darcy had enjoyed telling her what to do and her tone had been patronizing. And she wouldn't even give an inch about the car. Kelly could feel the pain in her chest as she reflected. For the remainder of the drive, she turned up the volume on the radio and drowned out her sadness by singing along with the '60s songs.

When she and Joshua were back at home in the condo, she gave Joshua a big bear hug, saying, "I love you, Joshua. I don't know what I'd do without you. Let's go for a walk."

When they returned from the walk, Joshua had a slurp from his water bowl. Kelly and he went upstairs to Kelly's office. She sat down at her computer and typed:

> Didn't occur to me to question
> Your surprising declaration
>
> Said you love me very much
> Can you be so out of touch?
>
> No thank you for my birthday wishes
> No virtual hugs or belated kisses
>
> E-mail silence for so many days
> Pierced my heart and made me craze
>
> When I was in a brace all alone
> You didn't even pick up the phone
>
> When I was at the end of my rope
> You chided me and I lost all hope
>
> You fretted about the time and hour
> Flexed your muscles and your power

Didn't pull me off the ledge
Ignored that I was on the edge

You stay with him the abuser
Listening to him my accuser

Nothing I said about his disorder
Resonated with you and created a border

As I am writing and relating
My frustration is abating

Although this is but a partial list
I have enough to get the gist

I now see so very clearly
Just how much you love me dearly

CHAPTER 39

The Collapse

Kelly and Joshua enjoyed their January together. The project from hell was still stressful to manage, but Kelly was coping better, with fewer and milder somatic responses. She had developed strategies to manage the project more effectively and to keep it within the remaining budget. She was still able to stick to her routine of working at home most days and spending as much time with Joshua as she could.

She and Joshua went on walks along the waterfront and in Laurel Park and explored their new neighborhood.

One evening in early February, they were in Laurel Park. The sky was clear. The air was still. Kelly and Joshua had just finished their trip along the perimeter of the park. They walked to the large, open, snowy field to join other dogs retrieving and chasing each other.

Kelly had a green tennis ball with her and threw it a few feet for Joshua. He casually trotted the short distance to retrieve it, sat down, held the ball in his mouth, and stared at her. She wondered why Joshua was just sitting there with the ball in his mouth and not moving. That struck her as strange behavior on his part, but perhaps, it was just because he did not want to retrieve it again. So instead, she and Joshua trekked across the field toward home.

The field was in a trough about four feet below the main park area. Halfway up the hill, Joshua seemed to fall down onto the snow. Kelly sat down in the snow beside him and talked to him so he would move.

"Joshua, get up. Let's go." She paused and repeated, "Joshua, please get up. Let's go."

Nothing happened. She tugged a little on his leash, but he did not move.

Then beginning to panic, Kelly said quietly aloud, "Oh my God! Joshua is unconscious."

Kelly tried to rouse him, calling out more loudly, "Joshua! Joshua!" Nothing. She put her arms around him, rocked him gently, and continued to call his name.

When he didn't respond, she held him tighter and spoke louder. "Joshua don't leave me! Joshua, don't leave me!"

Louder and louder, she yelled as her cheeks got a little wet, "Joshua! Joshua, don't leave me!"

After about two minutes, he was conscious again. Kelly tried to get him up to sit, but he was like jelly and couldn't hold the position. After a few tries, she raised him into a sitting position, but he still couldn't move.

They sat in the snow together. Kelly gazed into his eyes and patted him gently, saying repeatedly in a soothing voice, "I love you, Joshua. I love you, Joshua."

A few more minutes passed. Kelly tried again to get Joshua to move. By this time, Kelly had attracted a small crowd. Two women with their dogs, one with a boxer and one with a standard poodle, came by.

"Is there anything we can do?" they said in unison.

"Please call the animal emergency hospital to see if the hospital has an ambulance service," Kelly replied.

A moment or two later, the woman with the boxer called out, "I just called. The hospital doesn't have that service. What about a cab?"

"I don't think a cab driver will carry Joshua to the cab. We are too far from the road. The Zev Zola Pub is across the street next to my condo building. Perhaps you can round up some strong young men to carry Joshua into my car."

As the woman with the poodle headed for the pub, Joshua moved his head. Kelly stood up and tugged gently at his leash.

Kelly called out to the woman with the poodle, "Joshua is moving. I think he will be able to get home on his own steam."

Joshua continued to move slowly. Kelly stopped to let him rest between short intervals of crawling a few more feet, until eventually, Joshua was able to walk on his own into their condo building, the elevator, and into Kelly's condo where she retrieved her car keys. The two women and their dogs had accompanied Kelly and Joshua from the park to the condo and continued to walk with them until Kelly and Joshua escorted them to the exit out of the condo garage.

"Thanks so much for helping me. I really appreciate it. Hope to see you again soon," Kelly said to both women.

"Be well, Joshua. See you soon, Kelly," replied the woman with the poodle as both women gave Joshua a little pat.

Kelly gave their dogs a quick pat on the head. She waved to them as she watched them exit the garage.

By the time Kelly and Joshua arrived at the hospital twenty minutes later, Joshua acted like he was fine and jumped out of the car. Kelly told the emergency doctor who greeted them at the emergency door what had happened.

The doctor whisked Joshua into the treatment area, came out a few minutes later, and advised, "I am Dr. Angel, the emergency doctor on call. We need to stabilize Joshua's heart. He should stay in ICU overnight and until he is stable. Here are the papers for you to sign. I will take you to see Joshua."

Kelly dealt with the paperwork and handed the papers back to Dr. Angel, who showed Kelly into Joshua's ICU unit. It was an area with cement walls, some blankets on the floor, and some pillows. Joshua was hooked up to a heart monitor. Kelly lay beside him for as long as she could, until after one in the morning. She ignored the butterflies in her stomach and pushed away thoughts about her dad and Domenic.

Joshua spent four days in ICU. Kelly spent each day with him after work from late afternoon until well after midnight. He wasn't eating the food the hospital staff were giving him, so Kelly brought his favorite foods and some treats. She left some food for him for the next day. He heartily ate everything she fed him. She passed the time patting him, lying down beside him, adjusting his pillows, giving him water, making sure he was comfortable, and talking to him.

Since Joshua was attached to the heart monitor, he wasn't able to move much. When the technician arrived to take him out, Kelly tagged along and took the leash. She and Joshua walked together for the short jaunts.

When Joshua was strong enough to leave ICU and go into a regular treatment area, he went for an assessment with Dr. Goode, the cardiologist who had seen him before his anal sac surgery. After the assessment, Dr. Goode called Kelly to explain the situation.

"Joshua has a mild to moderate heart disease. He needs daily medication to stabilize his heart rhythm. He does not have congestive heart failure. This is good news. He may not get that for two to three years. Signs of that are coughing, increased respiratory rate, decreased exercise tolerance, collapse, restlessness at night, and decreased appetite.

"Joshua's heart issues may be a result of his cancer. Please get in touch with Dr. Hart to set up an appointment. I have already spoken to him. He will do an abdominal ultrasound to rule out cancer as the cause of Joshua's unusual heart behavior.

"Be careful with Joshua's level of activity. Avoid long walks, great stress, excitement, or extreme activities. Let Joshua determine his own exercise level. He may suffer mini-collapses. This is expected. Please do not worry about them.

"Set an appointment for Joshua to see me in three weeks to have a heart monitor test. This is to make sure the medication and dosage of his heart meds are working.

"Joshua will be discharged tonight. You can take him home after dinner."

All Kelly could say was, "Thank you, Dr. Goode. We'll see you in three weeks."

Four days later, Joshua had his abdominal ultrasound with Dr. Hart who told Kelly, "Everything looks fine. I didn't find any sign of cancer. The cause of Joshua's heart problems is not from his cancer."

Even when Kelly arranged for Dr. Goode and Dr. Hart to talk to each other over the phone about Joshua's heart issues, they both advised her after the call that they couldn't figure out why Joshua's heart was failing.

At the next appointment with Dr. Goode, she fitted Joshua for a mobile heart monitor to record his heart rate over a three-day period. The heart monitor was a box harnessed to Joshua's chest, which was shaved to the skin in the shape of a rectangle. This left Joshua with an unsightly haircut, Kelly thought, and it was making her sad.

Based on the results from the heart monitor test, Dr. Goode added a heart medication to Joshua's daily regimen. Two weeks later, Joshua had a heart monitor recheck and a follow-up appointment with Dr. Goode to see if the medications were working. The results correlated with a bad experience Kelly and Joshua had suffered in the snow.

Kelly and Joshua had continued to make the pilgrimages together to the college campus to see Dr. Bradley and to go for now shorter walks before her appointment. Earlier in the week, when Joshua was wearing the heart monitor, they were on such an adventure.

Several feet of snow covered the ground, but paths were cleared for walking. Kelly expected they would stay on the paths. As usual, she let Joshua off his leash. He took a turn off the path to sniff a tree and ended up stuck in a large snowbank. When Kelly rushed through the snow to rescue him, she sunk into the snow, which was almost waist-high. After pulling Joshua out of the snow, they followed the path Kelly had made with her boots out of the snowbank back to the car.

Dr. Goode asked, "Did anything unusual happen on Monday? Joshua's heart rate went through the roof. It is amazing he did not have a major collapse."

"Yes, unfortunately, he got stuck in the snow and I had to pull him out. It was very stressful for both of us. I will be more careful in the future."

The following week, Kelly had to make a day trip to Maria's head office. She arranged for Joshua to spend the day with one of Grace's dog-walkers. The day before the trip, Kelly telephoned Grace.

"I will be gone for the day. Because of Joshua's serious heart condition, he needs to take it easy, no long walks, nothing strenuous. I'll be home before dinner. You can bring him home at the usual time. I will write out the instructions for his dog-walker and leave them at my front door on the table as usual. Please make sure she understands Joshua's situation. I will be gone before she picks him up." "Sure, Kelly, no problem."

Kelly was pleased the business trip to Maria's was a success. Maria had some new work for Kelly to do, which would build on the work Kelly had already done for her. The new work would be innovative and exciting. Kelly had a relaxing train ride back home and looked forward to spending the evening with Joshua.

While Kelly was walking home from the train station, the dog-walker telephoned. "Hello, Kelly. Joshua has collapsed on the sidewalk. He's been lying on the ground for ten minutes."

"Oh, my Lord! You must get Joshua to stand up. Please get him to stand. Make sure he is conscious. Where are you?"

"We are about ten blocks from the train station at the corner of Fitz and Forrest." "I'll be there in about ten minutes or so. Please get Joshua to move."

Kelly flagged down a couple of cab drivers, but when she told each she wanted to make two stops, one to pick up her large, docile, old dog and the other to take him home with her, they refused to transport a large dog. Kelly realized she needed to go home and get her car, so she telephoned the dog-walker to let her know.

"I can't get a cab. I'll get my car and see you in about 15 minutes. How is Joshua?" "Joshua is conscious, but he doesn't want to get up."

"Please, keep trying. He needs to get up. See you soon."

When Kelly arrived to pick up Joshua, she saw that he was lying down, but his head was up, and he was fully conscious. The dog-walker helped Kelly to move Joshua into the back seat of the car. He did this mostly on his own, but he needed help with his back legs.

After the dog-walker joined Kelly in the front seat, Kelly asked her, "What happened? What are you and Joshua doing so far from home?"

"Joshua and I went for a walk downtown. I could see he was getting tired, so I tried to take transit, but he collapsed and was unable to climb the steps of the bus."

Kelly hit her left hand against her left hamstring, but she said nothing. She dropped the dog-walker off where she wanted to go, and took Joshua home, making sure Joshua was okay. Kelly called Grace.

"You and I spoke about Joshua's condition. I gave you instructions and left written instructions for the dog-walker. Did she not understand the instructions? Did you not reinforce them? She took him on a long walk, and he collapsed. She can't be Joshua's dog-walker anymore. Can you take over?"

"I did go over Joshua's needs with her. I don't know what happened. But I can no longer be Joshua's dog-walker. I look after a group of small, young dogs. That will not be good for Joshua. I don't have a suitable service to offer you."

Kelly was now on the hunt to find appropriate care for Joshua. She investigated dog-sitting services where the person would come into their home and spend the day or night with Joshua. At first, Kelly thought this dog-sitting service could be a good solution. Joshua would be at home and in his own space. But then she recognized it would not be the same dog-sitter each time.

Next, Kelly inquired at the animal emergency hospital and with Dr. Samuels. Initially, no one had any ideas. Then as Kelly pressed Dr. Samuels' staff, one of the technicians mentioned to Kelly, "I know a couple of technicians who might be able to look after Joshua. I can give you their phone numbers and let them know you will be calling."

"Thanks very much. That will be wonderful. I will call tomorrow."

The first technician lived too far away and didn't have the time, so Kelly called the second one.

Claire said, "I work at a veterinary clinic down by the waterfront right near your condo. I don't live far away either. I can pick up Joshua and take him home with me when I am not working at the clinic or take him with me to the clinic when I am working."

"This could be a great solution. Let's meet tomorrow after your workday. We can meet on a bench in Laurel Park."

"Sure, that will be good. I look forward to meeting you and Joshua."

When Joshua and Claire met, she took to Joshua right away, and he took to her. They went for a short walk in the park together, while Kelly looked on from the bench.

Claire advised, "I work for Dr. Golding. He uses laser treatment for arthritis. I think this will really help with Joshua's mobility. It will make him feel better. To start, the treatments would be twice a week and then after one month, they would be once a month. I think you will see great results. I can set up an appointment for Joshua for this weekend."

"Yes, please," Kelly replied.

After Claire gave Joshua a nice scratch behind the ears, they parted.

Kelly took Joshua to Dr. Golding's for a morning appointment that weekend. Dr. Golding owned a small but welcoming clinic with an office cat and pooch, an old Pekinese belonging to Dr. Golding and his wife, who was the nurse at the clinic.

Dr. Golding explained the procedure. As he did, he handed Kelly a pair of plastic glasses and said, "Please put on these glasses. They will protect your eyes from the laser. The treatment will take ten minutes and won't hurt Joshua. I will do a laser treatment on his shoulders and hips. It will make him feel a lot better."

While he performed the laser treatment, Dr. Golding continued, "I understand Joshua had anal sac surgery last May. I work at the hospital part-time where Joshua had the surgery. Do you know why Joshua has his heart problems?"

"This remains a mystery. I am hoping Dr. Hart and Dr. Goode will figure it out."

"If you like, Joshua is most welcome to stay at the clinic even when Claire is not available to look after him. He will get along fine with my Pekinese, and I can monitor Joshua closely. He can have free rein of the office."

"That would be fantastic. Thanks so much."

Two days later, Joshua's mobility was much better. He walked more rapidly and with ease. The laser treatments were helping. Kelly was delighted with the results.

CHAPTER 40

Heartbreak

Kelly and Joshua enjoyed a few weeks without drama. They took shorter but frequent daily walks and had quiet, restful evenings.

One evening in mid-April, Joshua vomited. Kelly took Joshua to the animal emergency hospital right away.

Dr. Angel advised, "It's not clear why Joshua was vomiting. The vomiting has stopped now. I have arranged for him to see Dr. Goode in the morning. Keep a close eye on Joshua, but there's nothing to do for now."

In the morning, Kelly took Joshua to see Dr. Goode. "Let's do another heart monitor check. I'll see you early next week to discuss the results." Before Kelly and Joshua left, Dr. Goode gave Joshua a big smile, a prolonged pat, and some healthy dog treats.

At his next appointment with Dr. Goode, she declared, "I need to adjust Joshua's meds again to make them a little stronger. I am adding another medication for you to give him at the same time as his bedtime meds."

Joshua's new heart medications reduced his appetite. He needed more encouragement from Kelly as well as treats to flavor his food. Kelly stopped trying to force-feed his cancer diet to him. Instead, she hunted for edibles she would cook for him that he would fancy—chicken, salmon, pasta, some of his dry dog food, whatever she was eating, and a braided dog bone for dessert every few days.

Despite his eating the new foods Kelly was preparing and the stronger medication, Joshua had another collapse. Kelly and he were on their way back from a relaxing stroll in Laurel Park. Joshua was fine until he wasn't.

He lay unconscious on the sidewalk in front of their condo. Kelly sat on the ground beside him and put her arms around him firmly, while gently calling, "Joshua, Joshua, I love you. Please get up."

After about a minute or so of repeating her refrain, Joshua was conscious again. When he sat up, Kelly hugged and kissed him. "Come, Joshua, let's go home."

Kelly remembered that Dr. Goode had warned her Joshua might have a mini-collapse and not to worry about it. He would recover from it. Although Kelly was certain this was a mini-collapse, it's very disquieting and worrisome, nevertheless. That evening, she and Joshua rested and went on very short constitutionals. Kelly listened to Mozart while immersing herself in reviewing some work reports.

In the weeks that followed, Joshua continued to have mini-collapses on a regular basis. With each mini-collapse, Joshua appeared a little weaker to Kelly. She needed more time on her recumbent bike to help her cope with her anxiety over Joshua and the stress of her work situation.

The project from hell was ongoing. There were new stresses related to managing difficult staff and resource shortages, making it very challenging to meet deadlines without Kelly putting in very long hours. Even though Joshua's health was deteriorating, he continued to stay by her side and watch over her if she became too distracted, bringing her back to the present with his paw on her knee or a warning bark at the stove.

She thought to herself as she cooked, *I have a strange feeling about what is happening to Joshua and me. The harder I try to repair his heart, the more this opposite force I feel is fighting to take him away from me. I feel like I am in combat to save Joshua's heart. But he has given so much of his heart to me, I think I may be losing the battle.*

The pain of watching Joshua's health worsen was excruciating. Daily, she cried secretly, she thought, so as not to alarm Joshua. She wondered why even though she and Joshua had beaten his cancer, now for no apparent reason, he was having serious heart issues. Why couldn't she mend Joshua's broken heart with love and care?

By mid-May, Kelly was bone-tired, overstretched with her work situation, and dealing with Joshua's disease. The project from hell had finally finished, but now she was in a period of rebuilding and finding her place in the firm. She was still working on an exciting project with Maria but having trouble leveraging resources to get the work completed.

Joshua's appetite worsened. Finding food he was willing to eat was becoming harder and harder. Kelly was running out of ideas to flavor his dog food. The foods he was willing to eat were not ideal, but his eating them was better than his not eating. He needed food with his medications to keep them down.

Kelly went to the supermarket every day, trying to find some new flavor Joshua might enjoy. Cheese strings and cold cuts worked for a few days. By this time, he had already rejected steak, hamburger, sausage, bacon, pasta, poultry, and fish. The week before Mother's Day, all he wanted was wieners. He ate a whole package of eight large wieners at one meal.

Since the breakup of Kelly's marriage, Mother's Day had not been a day Kelly looked upon favorably with anticipation. This Mother's Day, she was planning to spend the day with Joshua. As she opened her mail the Friday before Mother's Day, her tears dripped onto the card she opened from Darcy. It was the first communication from her since Kelly and Joshua had seen her last Christmas.

The card was an embossed picture of a small wood carving of a mother and baby elephant, with the baby's trunk holding onto the mother's tail. A note on the back of the card said, "I love you, Mom. Glad you are back in my life."

Kelly sent her a thank you note shortly thereafter, but she did not hear back from Darcy.

Kelly and Joshua spent Mother's Day at his favorite beach. He retrieved sticks she threw in the water only a couple of feet, and they meandered along the shoreline. They enjoyed their burgers by the water.

That evening, Joshua suffered a bout of diarrhea and vomiting. He was groaning. Kelly couldn't tolerate Joshua being in any pain. His suffering was contagious. Kelly rushed him to the animal emergency hospital.

Dr. Angel advised, "Joshua's vital signs are good. His poor appetite is most likely due to the cardiac medications, or it could be because of some other underlying disease. None of the medical tests we did are revealing anything new.

"Here is some medication for Joshua's diarrhea and vomiting. He likely won't need this for more than a day or two."

Kelly was relieved the medications Dr. Angel had prescribed were working. Joshua's diarrhea and vomiting disappeared within 24 hours.

A few days later, Kelly took Joshua back to the emergency hospital because he was coughing.

Dr. Angel examined Joshua and advised, "Dr. Goode should take a look at Joshua. I will set up an appointment for him to see her tomorrow. You can bring him back then."

Kelly took Joshua home and tried not to worry. The next morning, she and Joshua went to see Dr. Goode.

"Hello, Joshua. Here are some dog biscuits," Dr. Goode said as she gave Joshua a loving pat on his head and a scratch behind his ears.

"Kelly, here is a dose of an antidepressant for Joshua. It will calm down Joshua's cough. He won't need more than one dose."

Kelly told herself, *Perhaps, Dr. Goode should have given me a dose as well.*

The cough medicine worked. Joshua's cough cleared up quickly. After that, Kelly had a few uneventful days with Joshua until his regular checkup with Dr. Hart.

Dr. Hart said, "Joshua's liver needs a boost. Here is a medication for him to take. He will just need a few doses. Nothing to be alarmed about, just to monitor. There is no sign of cancer."

"I am grateful, Dr. Hart," Kelly responded. "Thank you."

By this time, Joshua's mobility had become restricted even with the regular laser treatments. He was toiling to get in and out of the car. The walk up the slight incline to the condo garage parking spot had become too much for him.

Kelly responded to his reduced mobility by taking him on shorter walks in Laurel Park and stopping more often for rests. She looked on as Joshua munched on the young grass shoots. Kelly admired the new flowers blooming. Joshua looked at Kelly with frustration, each time they paused.

Kelly smiled and said, "Let's go over by that bush. The grass looks tasty there. I love you, Joshua."

The frequency of Joshua's mini-collapses was increasing. Almost every evening, Kelly looked on helplessly as he had a mini-collapse in the living room. When he knew one was coming, he would look at her sheepishly as if he were doing something wrong. Then he would hide by lying down behind the black leather wing chair closest to the window where Kelly couldn't see him very well and then collapse.

Kelly was too worn out and foggy to do anything except watch Joshua try to deceive her and respect his privacy. Regardless of Dr. Goode's reassurance about the short-duration collapses, Kelly despaired and did her best to mask her tears from Joshua.

By early June, each subsequent dose of Joshua's medication became harder and harder for Kelly to support with a well-lined stomach. Kelly had tried all the different dog foods, canned and dried, organic and not, as well as all the different dog treats at the pet store. These had worked for a short while, but then Joshua lost interest. She had cooked roast meat he liked and some pureed root vegetables, but he was eating less and less of these, too. Kelly experimented with different kinds of homemade pizza—pepperoni, green pepper, and fresh tomatoes were his favorite. At first, he ate the whole pizza, but then slowly, his pleasure in that diminished as well.

Kelly asked all the dog owners she knew as well as all of Joshua's medical team members for suggestions for foods. As his appetite continued to shrink, Joshua's energy level dropped. He no longer chewed his braided compressed beef bones or his doggy biscuits.

Kelly took him on even shorter walks and less often. On a given walk, if Joshua was interested in doing more, Kelly followed his lead. She knew in her head the situation was unsustainable, but her heart refused to accept it.

On a Friday morning in mid-June, Kelly had an important meeting with Maria and her board of directors at her head office. Kelly's plan was to take an early morning train. Claire was coming to look after Joshua for the day.

After dinner the night before the meeting with Maria, Kelly took Joshua out for a walk to Laurel Park. They walked slowly along the park perimeter. Joshua munched on some grass and then they went home. At home, Joshua lay down and snoozed, while Kelly sat on the couch and reviewed her papers for the meeting.

Around ten-thirty that night, Kelly was ready to take Joshua out for his late-evening constitutional before bed. Engrossed in her work, she had not been paying attention to Joshua. As she got up from the couch to get ready to go out for their walk, she noticed Joshua was lying in the hall by the entrance to the kitchen. This was not his usual spot. He usually lay against the wall in the hall or by the windows in the living room.

As she walked toward him, his head was up, and he just looked at her.

"Let's go for a walk, Joshua," but he didn't move. He continued to stare. "Come, Joshua, let's go for a walk."

After the second command and no movement, Kelly got on her knees, looked Joshua in the eyes, and repeated gently, "Joshua, let's go for a walk."

When nothing happened, she became discomposed, but still with a quieting exterior said, "Joshua, let's go. Please get up. Time to go for a walk."

When Joshua remained immobile, Kelly realized he couldn't get up. She tried to get him up by lifting him but couldn't make him budge. The jelly had returned. She tried a few more times, but he just stared at her.

She thought to herself, *Maybe I should just wait. This may just be another mini-collapse. No, this feels different. I don't know why. I want to take him to see Dr. Angel, to get some help. But I can't move him.*

With all the composure she could muster, she said, "Joshua, I'm going to the concierge to get help. You are okay. I love you. Back soon." She kissed him on his cheek, left the condo, and took the elevator downstairs to the concierge.

She explained to the concierge, "My dog Joshua is ill. It is an emergency. I need to borrow the luggage trolley. He is too big and heavy for me to carry him to my car."

"Do you need some assistance?"

"Yes, please."

The concierge accompanied Kelly to her condo. When she got back home, Joshua was in the exact same position, unable to move.

"Joshua, I'm going to lift you onto the trolley. We'll go for a drive to see Dr. Angel. It's okay. I love you."

She lifted Joshua onto the trolley as gingerly as she could, pushed the trolley through her front door, down the hall, into the elevator, and then from the elevator to her car. The concierge followed them to the car. To get Joshua into the car, Kelly needed help from the concierge. She opened the back door on the driver's side and went into the back seat.

"Please go to the passenger's side back door and lift Joshua into the back seat. I'll go to the other side and help."

As the concierge lifted Joshua into the back seat, Kelly did not take her eyes off Joshua. She swallowed her panic and tried to look as reassuring as she could.

When Joshua was lying on the back seat, Kelly put his seat belt on and hugged him, saying, "Everything is okay, Joshua. We'll go for a drive to see Dr. Angel. I love you."

"Thanks so much," Kelly said to the concierge. "Please return the trolley."

The concierge nodded and left.

On the drive to the emergency hospital, Kelly comforted Joshua. "Joshua, everything is okay. Joshua and Kelly go to the hospital. We're going to see Dr. Angel. She will take care of you. You are okay. I love you."

As Kelly spoke to Joshua, she could feel the tears welling up and the butterflies in her stomach flapping their wings. Twenty minutes later, they were at the front door of the hospital.

As Kelly got out of the car, she said, "I'm going to get Dr. Angel. Back soon. I love you." Two minutes later, she returned to Joshua with a gurney, a technician, and Dr. Angel. "Let's see if Joshua can get out of the car on his own," remarked Dr. Angel.

Kelly opened the back door, removed Joshua's seat belt, and said, "Joshua, come," and he jumped out of the back seat onto the ground to greet Dr. Angel, like everything was fine.

Dr. Angel took his leash and walked him back to the treatment area. Kelly went into the hospital and registered Joshua at the front desk.

When she finished the paperwork, a nurse came for her and took her to where Joshua was in the treatment area, waiting to be seen. Joshua was tied to a post. Dr. Angel and the others were preoccupied with a medical emergency, so Kelly and Joshua waited.

Kelly spoke to him repeatedly, saying, "Joshua, everything is okay. I love you," as she hugged and patted him, swallowing her panic.

Near midnight, she said to one of the technicians, "Joshua needs to go out. It's been hours since he has relieved himself."

"Certainly. Let's go."

Kelly untied Joshua's leash, and the three of them went out for the constitutional. They walked a couple of short blocks. As they walked, Kelly observed Joshua's mobility was better than it had been earlier in the day. The laser treatment Joshua had received two days before had kicked in. Joshua had a bounce in his step.

The technician said, "Joshua is okay. Can you manage without me? I have another patient to attend to."

"Yes, we'll be fine."

Shortly after the technician departed, Joshua urinated. Kelly and he headed back to the hospital. When they entered the waiting area, Kelly wanted to walk straight back to the treatment area, but Joshua wanted to go elsewhere. Kelly followed his lead. He took her directly to the clients' bathroom, and they walked in.

She stood in the middle of the room in a daze. "Joshua, why are we here?"

A few seconds later, it clicked. Joshua was taking Kelly to the bathroom! She hadn't relieved herself for a long time either. She and Joshua had been to this bathroom together many times over the years. But on those occasions, Joshua was accompanying her. Now he was taking her. How did he know?

Kelly gave Joshua a huge hug and said, "I love you, Joshua. Good boy, you take such good care of me!"

When they got back to the treatment area, the nurse took Joshua into ICU. Dr. Angel came by and told Kelly, "I would like to keep Joshua overnight to make sure his heart is stable. I spoke with Dr. Goode. She will see Joshua in the morning. Then you can bring him home after he is discharged at dinnertime."

"Okay, Dr. Angel. I'd like to stay with Joshua for a few minutes."

"Of course, Kelly."

Kelly stayed for about an hour until one-thirty in the morning. She made sure Joshua was comfortable, his pillows were organized, and he was hydrated.

She told him, "I'm going to see Maria tomorrow. Then I'm going shopping for food for Joshua. You are such a good boy. I love you. Back soon."

Kelly gave Joshua another big hug and a few kisses and said reassuringly, "I love you. Back soon."

Under ordinary circumstances after that refrain, when Kelly started to get ready to leave, Joshua would blink his eyes to let her know her departure was okay with him. When he didn't blink back at her, she sensed something was wrong. "Joshua, are you okay? I love you. Back soon."

Joshua gazed at her, and with the heartening blink of his eyes, let her know he had understood, and it was okay for her to go. She kissed and hugged him again. "I love you. Back soon."

Early the next morning, Kelly got a call from Dr. Angel. "Dr. Goode just saw Joshua. She recommends he take stronger heart medication. This medication has an excellent chance of working, but one of the very unlikely side effects is sudden death. How do you want us to proceed?"

Kelly heard but did not process the part about the sudden death. "Okay, Dr. Angel, please give Joshua the new medication."

"He will get the medication later this morning at the usual time for his morning meds. Have a good trip."

At seven in the morning, Kelly was on the train and on her way to the meeting with Maria. She was doing some last-minute preparations as well as eating some breakfast. She was expecting to arrive at her destination at around ten-thirty. Just before ten, her mobile phone rang.

"Hello, Kelly. This is Dr. Angel. Joshua has just died. The new medication was administered around nine-thirty this morning. Shortly thereafter, Joshua's heart stopped. We tried everything to resuscitate him, but nothing worked. His heart failed. I am so sorry. Joshua was such a wonderful dog."

Kelly screamed out a loud cry. She couldn't stop crying for a minute or two. She tried desperately to gain her composure to continue the conversation with Dr. Angel. She asked, "Did Joshua suffer?"

"No, he didn't suffer. Both Dr. Goode and I were very surprised by the outcome. It was very unexpected. The prognosis for Joshua had been good. Joshua loved you very much. You took such excellent care of him. I would have made the same decision as you did about the new medication."

"Thank you for all the exceptional care you gave to Joshua."

"Kelly, you can come to view Joshua's body later today. Will you be able to make it?"

"Yes, I'll be there after dinner."

"Would you mind if I spend some time with you and Joshua when you arrive?"

"That would be fine. See you tonight."

Kelly tried to keep her composure on the train but failed. She cried loudly and inconsolably in her train seat. She was sitting by herself, but the train was quite full. She couldn't stop crying, lying on the seat, and flailing about. After about twenty minutes, someone came over and gave her a small packet of tissues. She stopped crying for a moment to say, "Thank you."

When the train arrived at her destination, she was able to move from inconsolable weeping to sporadic tears. In the cab to Maria's office, she tried hard to stop sobbing as she sat in the back seat. When she reached Maria's main office building and entered, she turned off the waterfall and tried to focus on something else. When she saw Maria, they exchanged a warm greeting, with Kelly exhibiting full restraint. But after a few minutes, she felt she was about to lose control.

"Maria, my dog has just died. I found out about it on the train here. I am extremely upset."

"I am so sorry, Kelly." Maria gave her a sincere hug.

When Kelly realized the board of directors meeting was about to begin, she shifted to the tasks at hand and blocked out her pain. As a result, the meeting was a success. Returning home on the train, she was numb. Her head was empty.

When she got home from the meeting with Maria, she called Darcy but got her voice mail and left a message.

"Darcy, I am so sorry. I am so sorry to tell you Joshua died today. His heart failed. I am so terribly upset. Please call me. Please come home."

CHAPTER 41

Mending a Broken Heart

After dinner, Kelly drove to the animal emergency hospital to see Joshua. When she arrived, they were expecting her and sent her to one of the medical rooms. A few minutes later, Dr. Angel wheeled in Joshua on a gurney. She had placed a blanket on him to keep his body warm, but his handsome face was uncovered. He didn't look exactly like himself, but it was still him.

Dr. Angel patted his head and said, "I'll give you some time alone with Joshua now. Would it be okay if I come back?"

"Yes, that will be fine." Kelly patted Joshua's head gently and cried.

When she returned, Dr. Angel told Kelly, "Joshua was a very special dog, the sort of dog that movies are made about. You took such wonderful care of him. No one could have done better. You loved Joshua very much and he knew that. I am going to miss him. I don't often form such a bond with my patients. Joshua was very special."

Kelly thought to herself, *This is comforting. I really need to feel I did everything I could for Joshua. He deserved nothing less.*

"Kelly, do you know what you want to do with Joshua's remains?"
"Yes, I would like to have him cremated."

"We have a catalog of beautiful urns. I'll bring it to you in a few minutes after I see some patients."

Kelly continued to pat Joshua and cry. When Dr. Angel returned, she showed her the catalog. Kelly picked a beautiful gray stone urn. They both patted Joshua.

"I need to go now, Kelly. I have work to do. Please stay as long as you like." Kelly did not keep track of the time. She did not know how long she stayed with Joshua. When she could muster enough strength and began to be aware Joshua was gone, she gave him a final pat and went home. She cried all the way home to her condo.

When she got home from the hospital, the phone rang. "Mom, I am so sorry about Joshua. I am in New York City, visiting Hannah. I am here for the weekend but can be home with you on Monday."

Kelly was very disappointed Darcy did not want to come home right away.

"That's okay, Darcy. I'll be alright. You don't have to come home."

After Kelly spoke to Darcy, she called Kieran and told him the terrible news. He was consoling and said, "You and Joshua had such a special bond. Joshua treasured and loved you very much. We all loved Joshua. We will miss him."

After the call with Kieran, Kelly felt a little better, but she cried for hours. In between bouts of weeping, she wondered how she was ever going to cope without Joshua.

The next morning, Kelly woke up and glanced at where Joshua would normally be lying on the floor in her bedroom. He wasn't there. The reality of what had happened the day before was beginning to sink in. She felt a deep sadness weigh heavily over her entire body.

She got out of bed, looked around her condo, and all she saw were aspects of her life with Joshua. After a lonely breakfast reading the newspaper and nursing her espresso, Kelly began to organize Joshua's belongings. She gathered up his water and food bowls and his leash and collar and put them away in her bedroom closet. She cried as she transported them there. She decided to give away Joshua's treats and most of his toys to the other dogs in the building and brought them to the concierge for distribution. She kept a couple of prize tennis balls, a couple of rubber balls, and a partially chewed braided bone.

After the initial clean-up, Kelly scanned her condo and spotted some markings on the wall. They were Joshua's grease marks from where he liked to lie down in the hall. Kelly was so grateful for those grease marks.

Kelly tried to get a grip on herself. That afternoon between her crying and her desolation, she watched some old Hollywood musicals to try to cheer herself up. The distraction worked a little, but she didn't dare go for a walk in the neighborhood for fear of totally breaking down. She was glad she had food and could stay in and just be with herself.

Her Saturday sadness and grief dragged into Sunday. Kelly tried not to think about burgers at the beach or her evening constitutionals with Joshua. She was acutely aware that so much of her life had unfolded with just her and Joshua. She zoned out on bad TV most of Sunday and read the newspapers.

Sunday evening after dinner, her fog lifted just enough for her to realize she was overdue for some medical testing. Over the last few months, she had been entirely focused on Joshua and work. As a result, she had put off some routine medical testing, specifically an EKG. She decided to go first thing on Monday morning to get it done.

A few days after the testing, she got a call from Dr. Mahoney. "Kelly, please go to the hospital right away. Your pulse is only forty. This is dangerously low."

"I'm feeling fine. I was just about to go for a walk along the waterfront with some friends."

"Kelly, this is serious. Please go now to the emergency at St. Andrews. I'll alert the emergency department you are on your way."

Kelly called Donna to cancel the walk. She took transit to the hospital.

After the testing was done, the emergency doctor brought Kelly the results. "Mrs. Delmonico, your pulse is sixty. That is fine. But you have a potassium deficiency. Consider eating more bananas to get your levels up. You can go home now."

"Thank you, doctor." *So*, Kelly thought to herself, *When I am totally devastated, my pulse drops dangerously low and I should eat more bananas.*

After the return home from the hospital, Kelly diverted her attention away from Joshua by diving into her work. She tried that for the next couple of days, but working was painful at home without Joshua. The emptiness gnawed at her gut.

Kelly decided to take a few days off to grieve. She told her boss, "Dan, I am very upset about the death of my dog, Joshua. I can't concentrate. I need to take some time off and grieve."

"Sure, Kelly. I understand. You lost a close family member. Take as long as you need."

"Thanks, Dan. I'll see how I am at the start of next week."

During her time off, Kelly tried to embrace a new routine of going to her medical appointments and working out. Although her routine was starting to take shape, Kelly's grief was not subsiding. However, she did experience a welcome moment as she was touched when she received a thoughtful card signed by her staff and others expressing their condolences.

Kelly went back to work the following week. A couple of weeks passed, with one day bleeding into the next. When Kelly thought about it, she couldn't recall much of what she had been doing to pass the time except working, working out, going to medical appointments, and following the routine of living.

In mid-July, Kelly got a call from Tony, Deke's former prodigy. Tony was now a photographer in Seattle, but he had told Kelly he visited his family in Buffington from time to time.

"Kelly, I'm back in town. On Saturday, I can deliver the pictures of Joshua I took last year. The pictures I framed came out quite well. I think you will like them. The two photo albums with all of the photos of you and Joshua also look great."

"That's wonderful, Tony. I'll be home. Send me an e-mail when you are on your way. See you then."

The same day Tony delivered the photos to Kelly, she hung them up. In her front hall not far from the grease marks, Kelly placed the three photos of Joshua that Tony had taken and framed. She centered them on the wall above a glass table, on which she had placed Joshua's urn. She had also asked Tony to frame one of the photos Bea had taken of Joshua and Kelly the last summer they were all at the cottage together. Kelly put it on the opposite wall facing the urn. She placed one photo album on her coffee table in front of the couch in her living room and the other one on her office bookshelf for safekeeping for Darcy.

Once the photos were hanging up, they gave Joshua a palpable presence in Kelly's condo. The photos filled a tiny part of the hole in her heart. She printed a photo of Joshua at age seven at the family business office, sitting and intently watching, which to her meant that Joshua was still watching over her. Kelly taped it to the wall overlooking her home office desk. When she gazed at these photos of Joshua, to her surprise, they gave her some inner strength. She had never felt this way about photographs before.

Although the photos made her feel better and she was feeling a little stronger, she decided she just couldn't face going to the cottage alone. So that evening, she telephoned the cottage owner, told her about Joshua, and was able to cancel her reservation without penalty. She went online and found a resort where she could rent a cottage, but where there was a resort dining room as well. She felt lucky there was an opening at the resort for a cottage during her usual two-week holiday. She hoped a new location would help her create new, positive memories of cottage life.

When it came time to go to the resort, Kelly was energized but a little nervous about being at a family resort alone. She packed the car trunk, but she left the back seat of the car empty. With good driving instructions and light traffic, Kelly arrived in time to unpack and have dinner at the resort dining room at a table by herself. After dinner, she explored the resort grounds, then returned to her cottage to read and listen to jazz before bed.

That night, Kelly had an unusual dream. She was riding on a skateboard up and down hills and steering in and out of traffic with ease. She felt a warm breeze blowing across her back. She moved her left arm up and down to keep her balance. She held onto a rope in her right hand, which was attached to something she couldn't see. She was concentrating on the road and enjoying the ride. The ride went on for some time. Then she woke up.

The next morning as she ate breakfast and sipped her espresso seated at her cottage dining table overlooking the lake, she thought about her dream. She had no idea what it meant.

Kelly went about her day at the resort, spending time on her balcony reading and then swimming in the lake in the afternoon before having dinner in the resort dining room. After dinner, she went for a walk around the resort and then read and listened to music before bed.

The next morning, she woke up and realized she had experienced the same dream. She noted it and went on with her day, without trying to make sense of it.

When she awoke the third morning having had the same dream, she decided to analyze it as best she could. She thought there must be some reason why she kept having the same dream.

As she sat on her balcony overlooking the lake, sipping her espresso, and eating her toast, she wondered, who is at the end of the rope?

After a pause and another bite of toast, she said aloud, "Oh my goodness! Joshua is on the other end of the rope."

Being on a skateboard is so strange. She hadn't ridden one since she was twelve or thirteen. The skateboard was the last gift her father had given her. She hadn't asked for it and was always disappointed she couldn't go very fast with it because she couldn't find a smooth enough surface. The road on her street was bumpy, with small potholes, little pebbles, and dirt. Riding on a skateboard, what does that have to do with anything?

Then it dawned on her. The skateboard was her foundation, what her father had imparted to her—his guidance, his caring, such as it was. Then came Joshua, who truly looked after her.

She thought the dream meant Joshua and her dad were still with her, with Joshua at her side. Joshua's kind and gentle spirit were within her, guiding her. With Joshua's love in her heart, she was ready to soar.

That evening, feeling a little more optimistic about herself and her life, Kelly wrote:

> No one really loved me
>
> No one really cared
> No one really saw me
> No one really dared
>
> You changed all that
> You came and sat
>
> Upon my lap
> And never left me
>
> A happy consort
> A constant comfort

GOLDEN LOVE

With a wiggle
And a swish
Escape and fun
And a little run

The source of joy
In my life

So busy being the mother
And the wife

Through all the anguish
And the strife

You never let me down
You never let me down

You made me smile
Instead of frown

Such a brave soul
You protected me
From that evil troll

You made it clear
Do not draw near
Be torn apart
If he dared to start

Lonely and in pain
Our two months apart
For you and me
Such a terrible strain

Immobile
Leg in a brace
So much grief
To embrace

I counted the minutes
To our Sunday visits
I'd fall apart
Before you'd depart

Such an empathic soul
You kept me focused
You kept me whole

You watched my keys
You watched the stove
Kept me company
When I drove

You witnessed me
Watched over me

Protected me from danger
And the stalking stranger

You helped me see through the fog
I thought you were the perfect dog

My dearest friend
I wish I'd held you
At the end

I think of you every day
I miss you in every way

Light of my life
The joy of my soul
To honor you
Is my goal.

The rest of Kelly's cottage stay went well. She relaxed and recharged a little. She kept to herself, swam, read, cooked a few barbecues, and had most dinners in the resort dining room.

Once back home, Kelly resumed her normal routine. She worked and saw friends on occasion and tried to stay upbeat. She knew Joshua did not want her to have a heavy heart.

In a flash of inspiration one fall morning, while eating breakfast at her dining table, she decided to write the story of her life with Joshua. But from time to time other than think about what she might write, she did not put pen to paper. She continued with her usual routine.

A week before Christmas, Darcy telephoned.

"Mom, I'm coming to town and staying with Diane this time, not Dad and his wife. How about we spend Christmas eve and Christmas day, together? I'd love to see you again before and after New Year's before I head back to Boston."

"Darcy, that sounds wonderful. Please call me when you get to town, so we can make more definitive plans."

When Kelly hung up the phone, she cried. She was very surprised about the call from Darcy and what she had to say.

That night, Kelly still felt heartened by Darcy's phone call. As Kelly sat in front of her computer reviewing her e-mails, she decided to begin to write the story of her and Joshua. Still sitting but not typing, she hearkened back to the day she brought Joshua home from Kate Munsey's, the dog breeder.

Kelly remembered her puppy sitting on her lap and gazing into her eyes as Kate exclaimed to her, "Joshua will be the love of your life."

That statement had niggled away at Kelly all these years, with Kelly wondering what Kate had meant.

Now Kelly finally understood. She said quietly aloud, "Joshua is the love of my life. And he always will be." Then Kelly smiled and began to type.

www.ingramcontent.com/pod-product-compliance
Lightning Source LLC
Chambersburg PA
CBHW050847210726
48290CB00004B/1118